High Meadows Series:

The Hope of Wind River

Grace
I hope You enjoy
my story.
God Bless You
Connie Seibert
Live to serve Christ
Read to serve better

High Meadows Series:

The Hope of Wind River

Book 1

Connie Scibert
with
Sandy Maxwell

TATE PUBLISHING
AND ENTERPRISES, LLC

Published by Tate Publishing & Enterprises, LLC
127 E. Trade Center Terrace | Mustang, Oklahoma 73064 USA
1.888.361.9473 | www.tatepublishing.com

Tate Publishing is committed to excellence in the publishing industry. The company reflects the philosophy established by the founders, based on Psalm 68:11,
"The Lord gave the word and great was the company of those who published it."

Cover design by Arjay Grecia
Interior design by Jimmy Sevilleno

Published in the United States of America

ISBN: 978-1-62854-905-8
1. Fiction / Christian / Western
2. Fiction / Westerns
13.12.03

ACKNOWLEDGMENTS

I TRUTHFULLY HAD NO idea what I was doing when I started this journey of writing a book. There have been many who made the trip unforgettable. The first to inspire me didn't even know they were part of the trip. Melissa and Jessica Liner along with Hannah and Mary Bennett were with me in our small church library one Sunday after church. We were all looking for something good to read. Like me, these four young teenagers have a love of the west. The thought popped in my head that there just isn't enough good, clean, western fiction books. I should write one.

That flash of a thought drove me to write my story down. I can't tell you how much I enjoyed creating my story. My husband of fifty years would stand over me, asking if I was through with the next chapter yet. Thanks, Ron, for the encouragement. I love you.

My sister, Sandy Maxwell, was the one reading the road map, telling me where to go, and informed me when I made a wrong turn. Her whole family has been wonderful encouragers, cheering me all the way. I know this is my story, but it is *our* book, Sandy. I can't thank you enough for all the time, work, encouragement you've put into our adventure. If you hadn't been along for the ride, I probably would have turned around, gone home, and parked the car.

The wonderful Christian writers who wrote the book, *A Novel Idea*, created one of the detours I made. Reading that book helped me to realize I really didn't know what I was doing. My sister and I started all over. Thank you, Christian writers, for the detour that took me to the next town.

Next was my first professional critique. I don't remember where I heard about it, but somewhere I got the name of a service called the Writers Edge. They were professional and honest in their assessment of my work. They were complimentary at first, then told me what I needed to do to make it presentable. They were so honest I wondered if it would be worth going on, but I did what they said I needed to do: a line by line rewrite. Ugh! I had just learned the easy part was creating the story.

When I had done the best I could, it seemed like a dead end. I've lived long enough to wait on the Lord and be still and know he is God, but he does use people to deliver the swift kicks we need to get us moving. Yes, my sister insisted I send my story to Tate Publishing. It scared me to death. It was another swift kick, and I started the motor again and went to the next town of Mustang, Oklahoma.

Tate Publishing, as I write this, I know I've got a ways to go before I reach my destination, but thank you from the bottom of my heart for taking the wheel. So far, the drivers you have given me have been very nice and helpful. I'm looking forward to us arriving at our final destination.

When I look back over this four-year trip, I can see the hand of my Heavenly Father working out the details. Thank you, Father, my heart overflows with gratitude.

CHAPTER 1

May of 1859—Southeast corner of the Colorado Territory

"RISE AND SHINE, partner! It's time to hit the trail."

Maxi slowly sat up and squinted at the campfire. A strong aroma of coffee covered the memory of her dream. She rubbed her eyes and peered into the darkness beyond the firelight. Shivering, she pulled her blanket tighter around her shoulders.

Richard grinned at his seventeen-year-old daughter. "We have a long way to go. You better toughen up, young lady. Look at the horizon; the sun's fixing to show its face. See that pink glow along the tops of the mountains?"

Maxi looked but couldn't appreciate the pink glow. It was too early, and she was too cold.

"Sorry you're so cold, Baby. Guess we are a little high in the mountains for this time of year." He took a long pull on his coffee. "Why don't you fix breakfast this morning? That'll warm you up. I'll tend the horses, get them packed and ready."

"If you're going to wake me before the sun comes up, the least you can do is bring me some of that coffee," she grumbled good-naturedly. The dream that was troubling her came into focus again as she watched her father pour the steaming liquid into a cup. He then bore it ceremoniously to his pampered daughter, bowed low, and offered her the cup.

Maxi giggled, eagerly accepting the coffee. "Oh, Pa, you can always make me laugh. Is this the way I'm supposed to get toughened up? If it is, then I like it." The steam rose and clung to her face. She breathed in deeply, finally putting the cup to her lips. "Hmm…the first sip is always the best."

Again, the dream pushed to the forefront of her thoughts. She'd had this same dream at least twice this last week and didn't know what to make of it. "Pa, do you think dreams mean anything?"

"Well, now, that's something to think on." He gazed toward the coming sunrise, gathering his thoughts. "What have you been dreaming that's bothering your pretty, little head?"

"I guess it's kind of silly, but it's about Michael. In my dream, I can see he's in danger. The path he's walking on is bordered by tall grass, and a mountain lion is in the grass, crouching and ready to spring as he walks by. It's so clear that I can see the cougar's ears laid flat, and his amber eyes watching Michael's every move. I can even see the MM you had engraved on the stock of his rifle. You know, the one you gave him for his sixteenth birthday. Anyway, what's so disturbing is he doesn't even know he's in danger. I try to warn him. I scream his name over and over, but he doesn't hear me. That's when I wake up." She put the cup to her lips again as she waited for her father's response.

He was quiet for a few more moments. "You know, I think you're excited and anxious about finding your brother. That's probably the way your mind works out the worry. I wouldn't pay too much attention to it, Baby."

She smiled at his use of the name Baby. She'd asked him a long time ago not to call her Baby anymore, but it was obviously a hard habit for him to break. Secretly, she thought he said it on purpose to get her all riled up. She fussed at him once in a while but mostly let it go.

After a simple breakfast, Maxi busied herself with the cleanup. From the corner of her eye, she saw her father watching her. She knew that when he looked at her with that faraway look in his eyes, he was thinking of her mother. They both had long, straight, black hair and sky blue eyes. Many times he'd told her, "If you want to remember what your ma looked like, just look in the mirror."

Richard kicked dirt on the last glowing ember of the campfire as Maxi finished the cleanup. "You ready to ride, Baby?"

"I'm always ready to ride. You should know that by now." Mounting her horse, Ginger, she headed up the trail, taking the lead.

The morning sun began to warm her into contentment as they made their way over the mountain trail, and she settled in for the long ride ahead. She leaned forward and patted her horse, her reddish-brown coat gleaming in the sun. "What would I do without you, ole girl? You would tell me if that silly, old dream meant anything, huh?"

Richard Mayfield was astride his big gelding, Jake, just a ways behind Maxi. She could hear him singing, quite off-key, about some yellow rose in Texas. Another off-key strain of her father's song came wafting over the mountain air, bringing a smile to her lips and heart. She loved her father more than anything. They had been constant companions since the death of her mother some years ago.

Minutes passed. Then abruptly, her pa's singing stopped, and she heard a strange commotion behind her. She turned in her saddle and peered through the sunlight. Pulling down her hat to shield her eyes, she was quite startled to see only Sweet, the pack horse, standing on the trail. "Where's Pa and Jake?" Her heart skipped a beat, and she bailed off Ginger and ran back to where Sweet was standing. Stunned, she stood staring down the embankment that had given way to a veritable landslide. At the bottom, Jake was on his side, thrashing, heaving, trying to get up.

"Easy, Jake! Easy, boy, lay still!" She picked her way down the loosened dirt searching frantically for her father. He was lying motionless, partly covered with the soft earth when she spotted him. "Pa! I'm coming, Pa! Oh, please be okay...please be okay." Anxiously brushing the dirt from his face, she cried out, "Pa, can you hear me?"

Richard was struggling to breathe, his mouth working to make words that didn't come. Maxi's heart thumped wildly as she watched his face and waited. An *eternity* seemed to pass when finally he said, "Jake...rolled on me...can't breathe..." His voice was barely more than a whisper.

"I know, Pa, I know. Don't talk if you don't want to." But she wanted him to talk. She needed him to tell her what to do. She felt helpless as Richard struggled to breathe, his breath coming in short gasps.

"Go, find your brother...remember the money...Oh, God... send angels to watch...my Maxi."

Dread gripped her heart like an iron fist. She held her father's hand, willing him to breathe normally. "Pa, you're going to be all right. Do you hear me? We'll get through this together. I'm right here, and I'm not leaving. Do you hear me..." Her brave voice trailed off, and she thought she felt the slightest squeeze from her father's hand as he labored to hold on to life.

Suddenly, Jake started thrashing again while still trying to get up. She glanced down at the injured horse and was appalled to see a jagged bone sticking out of the gash in his leg. "Jake's hurt pretty bad." The words blurted out, and immediately, she wished that she could rein them back in. Her father didn't need any more stress. He turned his head ever so slightly to look at his daughter, his mouth twisting in pain as he tried to tell her something. Maxi leaned closer to his mouth. "Put him down…please."

The enormity of this request slammed her. She stole another glance at the suffering animal and knew that was exactly what she had to do. She hurried up the embankment to her horse and pulled her rifle from the scabbard, then made her way down to Jake. The horse's suffering was so heartrending that she ended it quickly. Choking on a sob, she rushed back to her pa, kneeling at his side. "It's over, Pa, I'm back now. I wish you could tell me what to do. I know you're hurting real bad." As an eerie silence permeated the mountainside, she realized with a start that her father wasn't breathing.

"Pa?" She shook him gently and found his hand. "Pa?" There was no response. Placing her cheek close to his mouth, she listened for the ragged breath that had claimed his last moments. She stared into his unseeing eyes, all the while denying the awful truth. "No! This just can't be!" Her wonderful father was gone. "Oh, no. What am I going to do? Oh, Pa." She sat in stunned disbelief, her head on her father's chest, still hoping to hear his heart beat or feel the rise and fall of his chest. "Don't go, Pa, please, don't leave me!" Slowly, as acceptance of the truth came, so did her tears. Her sobs nearly tore her apart, burning her heart and choking the breath from her. "How could this be happening?" she cried over and over.

Eventually, she began to realize the seriousness of her situation. *I've got to pull myself together. Think. I've got to think. What would Pa tell me to do? Go back the way we came? No, he said to find Michael. That's what I have to do. Find Michael.* Among all her jumbled thoughts and emotions, an awareness began to prick at her senses.

She was not alone.

Tentatively, she raised her head and looked around. There was nothing. Then her gaze drifted upward. Right on the edge of the embankment was the form of a person, bathed in a glow of mysterious light.

It's an angel! Or is it a girl? Could be the angel Pa asked God to send. She isn't a very big angel. Maxi sat mesmerized, gazing up at the angel as the angel stared down at her. Neither moved nor spoke a word for several long moments. Maxi's curiosity made her break the silence. Her throat was dry, and her voice cracked a little, but she uttered the only word that was on her mind.

"Angel?"

The angel's eyes grew large, and she nodded. The two continued to stare at each other. With a slight quiver in her voice, Maxi asked hopefully, "Did you come to help me?"

Again, the angel nodded and began to make her way down the embankment. Maxi didn't look directly at the angel, thinking it might be impolite. Keeping her eyes averted, she asked, "Will you help me bury my father?"

"Of course I'll help you," said a soft, melodious voice. "Do you have a shovel?"

Captivated by the voice, Maxi almost looked right into the angel's face. She caught herself in time. "I have a small one on my pack horse. I'll go get it."

As Maxi got to her feet, the angel said, "If you have an extra blanket, bring that to wrap around your father. I'll look for a place to bury him."

Maxi nodded, grateful the angel was there to offer direction. She felt strange about what they were going to do. It just didn't seem right to bury her pa. Maxi started the climb up the embankment while the angel turned her attention to the surrounding area. Several yards further from where Richard lay, the slope was less steep and actually began to level out. The angel stood assessing the area when Maxi came back. "Is this the place you picked?"

"If you like it, I think it's a fine place. The ground doesn't seem too hard, and there are plenty of rocks to put on top." Making a wide sweep with her arm, the angel spoke of the beautiful view of the valley. "It's even facing east!"

"East?" Maxi quickly thought of her mother's grave, trying to remember what direction it faced. "Is that important?"

"I don't guess it's all that important, but Christ is supposed to return in the east. It's just a tradition with some people to bury their loved ones facing that direction."

"Oh. I think this place will be okay." Maxi didn't really understand, but she wasn't about to question the angel.

"I'll dig first," the angel offered, taking the shovel.

Maxi nodded forlornly and found a rock to sit on. Her mind churned with the painful memories of the morning. *Why? Why did it have to happen? What else could I have done? Why did Pa have to die? Why? Why? Why?* Grief was strangling her, smothering every bit of emotion from her, except the grief itself. She wept quietly, not wanting to disturb anyone or anything, for this grief was her own. Finally, her tears were spent, and she sat staring into space but not really seeing. Gradually though, the angel came into focus, and she realized anew why she was here.

She studied the angel with acute awareness now, almost with a critical eye. The angel's pale, yellow dress was worn and loose fitting, and her brown shoes were scuffed. Realization hit her with a jolt. *That's no angel! She's just a girl like me!*

Maxi stared at the petite girl whose mature curves were obvious beneath her thin dress. *No wonder I thought she was an angel with all that white hair. And curls! What a glorious sight. With those dark brown eyes, pretty face, and white curls falling to her shoulders, why anyone would think …*

Impulsively, Maxi blurted out, "You're no angel! You're just a little girl!" The outburst seemed like an accusation, and the surprised girl looked up. Feeling emboldened, Maxi railed, "What are you doing up here in these mountains? And just why did you say you were an angel? That wasn't very nice of you to lead me on like that!" Her words had tumbled out like a dozen puppies scampering off the front porch and no way to stop them. She waited, defiantly. "Well…?"

The smaller girl stopped digging, a shocked expression on her face. She didn't move for a few moments. Then brushing back some curls, a slight smile played at the corners of her mouth.

"No, I'm not an angel, you can be sure of that." Her pleasant voice was firm but very kind. "My *name* is Angel, given to me by my mother who said I was her mountain angel when I was born." Her gaze was steady, looking straight into Maxi's eyes. "As to why I'm in these mountains, I'm not sure that's any of your business. I have the right to be here just as much as you do."

Maxi was taken aback, not expecting retaliation. Before she could respond, Angel gathered herself up to her full height and announced, "And I am *not* a little girl. I turned seventeen on the fifth of May. So, as you can see, I am a *woman*." She held the shovel out to Maxi. "If you want me to leave, I will. I need to be moving on anyway."

Maxi jumped to her feet, startling the other girl. "No! Don't go. Please don't go. I'm sorry I sounded so cross. I didn't mean it. I'm just overwhelmed." She sat down again and covered her face with her hands. "All of this has just been too much."

Almost immediately, a soft hand was on her shoulder. She looked up into Angel's kind, brown eyes and felt a warm blush spreading across her face. "It's…well, it's just that I felt so foolish when I thought you were a real angel, and you're just a lit—a *woman* like me." She shrugged, realizing there wasn't a reasonable explanation. "I don't suppose there are real angels anyway. I was just so confused after all that's happened this morning."

"That's okay. I've known grief myself. My ma and pa are both dead, and it was one of the hardest things I've ever been through. I miss them terribly." She looked over at the unfinished grave. "I'll stay until we get your pa buried. Then we can both be on our way."

Relief flooded through Maxi. "Next time you shovel, you can use my gloves. It looks like you're starting to get blisters." Without another word, she took the shovel and began digging with all the energy she could muster.

They worked in silence, one digging while the other rested. It was exhausting work, but they kept at it. Finally, Angel straightened up from her turn. "I think this should do it. Let's get your father." She hesitated and looked at Maxi. "If you're ready."

Maxi nodded solemnly, and they walked to where her father lay.

"Someone needs to get the personal belongings from your father's pockets. I'll do that if you don't feel like you can."

Maxi thought about it for a moment. "Thanks, but I guess I should be the one to do it."

"What's your name? I don't know what I should call you."

"My name's Maxine, but everyone calls me Maxi. You can call me that."

Angel pulled a handkerchief from her pocket and asked Maxi to get it wet, then gently closed the man's eyes. When Maxi came back, Angel cleaned the trickle of blood from the corner of his mouth. "I'll go get my things across the creek and give you time with your father."

Maxi reluctantly started pulling things out of her father's pockets. She expected him to sit up any minute and ask just what did she think she was doing. Her mind wandered to the other girl, wondering where she had come from and where she was going. *I like her kind face, and yes, all those curls. Most of all, I love the tender way she touched my pa.* She looked across the creek and saw that Angel was on her way back. She was carrying a long, brown coat and had something strapped to her back. *What in tarnation is that contraption?*

Angel stopped a few feet away and dropped her coat, then pulled her arms out from the straps of the contraption. She very carefully put it down beside her coat. "Shall we move him now? I don't mean to rush you, but I really need to be on my way."

She realized that Maxi didn't know what to do next, so she gently began giving her instructions. "Just hook your arm under his shoulder, like this, then we can pull him over to the grave." When they reached the grave, they rolled him onto a blanket. Reverently, Angel pulled the blanket tightly around him. Lastly, they each took an end of the blanket, and with all their strength, they lowered the body into the shallow grave. "I can do this next part. Why don't you tend your horses, and I'll call you when I'm done."

"Thanks, but that's not practical. It goes faster with both of us working."

"Okay, if you're sure."

Maxi was sure. She was beginning to feel in control of herself again and wanted to get the job finished. Not that she didn't feel grief, she certainly did, but it just wasn't so numbing. Instead, the weight of responsibility was settling on her shoulders.

They were exhausted after filling in the grave, and they took a break at the creek to quench their thirst and wash. Afterward, they rolled, shoved, and carried all the rocks they needed for the top of the grave, then stood looking at their finished work.

"Was your pa a believer?"

Maxi didn't have to think twice about that. She knew her father believed in Jesus. He even made a point of sharing his faith with others. "Yes, we can be sure of that."

"That's wonderful! That'll be a comfort to you. Do you want to say anything now? A prayer, maybe?"

Maxi nodded and took a deep breath. She clasped her hands in front of her, then hesitated for just a minute. *What can I say about you, Pa, except that I love you very, very much, and I miss you so badly. I'm so glad you were my father, and you taught me so much.* "Pa..." Her voice cracked, and that's all she could get out past the knot in her throat. There was a long pause. "I just can't do it."

"That's okay, you don't have to say anything. Can I say a prayer?"

"Yes, go ahead."

Angel bowed her head but quickly looked up again. "What's your pa's name?"

"Richard Mayfield." And for the first time, Maxi smiled at Angel.

Encouraged, Angel bowed her head again. "Father in heaven, I didn't know Richard Mayfield, but from what his daughter said, he knew you, and because of that, I know he's in heaven with you right now. I don't understand why things like this happen, but my ma always said we have to trust you on these things. So, Heavenly Father, help Maxi to trust in you. Comfort her heart and send your angels to watch over her. Amen."

A comforting peace came to Maxi's heart. At the same time, a strange thought went through her mind. *Angels? I may have to start believing in them.*

Angel went to get her things. She seemed anxious to leave, saying the day was more than half over. Maxi watched as she slipped her arms through the straps of the contraption and could now see that it was a wicker case. Then, Angel bent to pick up her coat, and a bit of panic clutched Maxi. "You're leaving now?"

"Yes, I need to go."

"But why? I don't understand why you have to go. Can't we travel together? I don't know what I would've done without you today. Let me pay you back for what you've done."

"You don't pay people back for helping you in a time like this. Just accept it as God's gift to you. I'm sure you would've gotten your pa buried just fine, but I'm glad I was able to help a little."

"Not a little, you helped a lot! Where are you headed?" Maxi was hoping to detain her a little longer.

"I was told there's a town over that mountain. I'll be headed that way."

Excitement was all over Maxi now. "That's the direction my pa and I were going. Can't we go together?"

Angel walked several paces, then stopped and slowly turned to face Maxi. "I don't want to bring trouble down on you. There's a couple of men out there who are looking for me. I couldn't live with myself knowing that if they found me, they'd find you too. They are mean, horrible, and dangerous men. So help me, I'll throw myself off a cliff before I'd let either one of them touch me!" She searched Maxi's face, looking for understanding. "So you see, it's best for me to go on alone. I'll try to reach that town over these mountains, find some kind of work to support myself, and, hopefully, be okay."

Maxi looked at her pleadingly. "But listen to me. If they are around here, they might run into me anyway. If we're together, we could protect each other. Pa's rifle was busted when Jake rolled on it, but I have my rifle and Pa's pistol. My pa always told me that if a man came at me to do me harm, to shoot and not feel bad about it." She looked carefully at Angel, hoping she was getting through to her. "Let's go together. Two will be better than one. I have supplies and two horses, and we can help each other out, you know, like sisters. Well, we might be friends, anyway. Please ride with me."

Angel stood quietly, gazing at the distant mountain, her lips moving ever so slightly. *Is she praying or talking to herself? Is she ever going to give me an answer?* Finally, a little smile worked its way onto Angel's face, and Maxi knew she had won.

"I hope you won't be sorry for talking me into this, but what you say makes sense. I figure we're pretty close to the same age, so we can't be sisters but maybe friends. By the time we get over that mountain, you may not want me for a friend."

"We're closer in age than you might imagine. I turned seventeen on the first day of May, so that makes me four days older. I'm your elder, so you'll have to show me respect."

Angel grinned at Maxi's humor, saying she would take that into consideration.

"So it's settled. We go together. Can you ride or shoot a pistol?"

"I can ride, but guns are another matter."

They started toward the horses. "I'll rearrange the supplies on Sweet so you can ride her. She's a gentle horse and won't cause you any trouble. I'll fix the halter for control, but she'll just follow Ginger anyway. *Oh, Pa, if only you were here, I wouldn't have to do all this. It breaks my heart to leave your saddle, but there's no way for me to take it.*

A loud growl emitted from Angel's insides, and she grabbed her stomach, smiling sheepishly. "Guess I need to eat something, haven't had anything yet."

"Well, girl, why didn't you say something? I feel embarrassed all over again, you working so hard this morning helping me, and here I've let you starve. I know I have some dried beef and a couple of biscuits in my saddlebags. Will that be enough for now? You can eat while I get the horses ready."

"Thank you so much, Maxi." She took the food and sat on a rock, bowing her head for a moment before taking a bite.

Maxi couldn't help but glance at Angel occasionally while she repacked the supplies. There was something definitely intriguing about this young stranger who had come out of nowhere, right at the time she was needed the most. *Well, I'll have to take good care of her. She seems so…so fragile. Guess I did beg her to come with me, so yes, I'll take really good care of her.*

Maxi looked one last time at her father's grave. Loneliness squeezed her heart, and she wondered how she could stand to live without her pa. But the words of Angel's prayer came to her, bringing a new thought. *You're not really there, are you, Pa? You're in heaven with Ma. Oh, how I wish I could be there with you both.* Sighing softly, she determined to carry that thought in her heart. It would give her courage to leave this place: a place she would never forget.

CHAPTER 2

THE SOUND OF Angel's footsteps tugged Maxi back from her thoughts. She forced a smile and nodded toward Sweet. "Ready?"

"Yes. Thanks for the food. I sure needed it." Angel led the horse to a big rock, stepped up on it, then hoisted herself up on Sweet's back.

Maxi mounted and took the lead. She studied the brush and path ahead while Angel kept watch on their back trail. They rode steadily for a couple of hours until they reached the ridge of the mountain. Maxi reined in Ginger and dismounted. Angel slid off Sweet and rubbed her backside. "My feet are grateful for the ride, but my backside is of a different opinion." She stood in front of the horse, patting and speaking softly, so Sweet would get to know her better. "You're named right. I can tell you're one of God's sweet creatures."

"I'm going to walk a little and stretch my legs," Maxi said. "I won't go far."

Angel nodded and watched Maxi disappear into the brush. She lifted her face to the sun as a cool breeze pulled at her curls. She closed her eyes, and her lips moved silently in prayer. She thanked God for watching over her and for giving her a traveling companion, perhaps even a companion who would become a true friend. A rustling noise caused her eyes to open. She saw Maxi coming toward her with flushed cheeks and a bit of excitement in her voice.

"Angel, I found some tracks! Two horses came this way, maybe last evening. They were traveling on the other side of the creek. They crossed over and hit the trail we're on. If it's the two men who are looking for you, I think they're well ahead of us."

Angel was silent a moment, looking worried. "Do you think it's safe to stay on this trail? Maybe we should find a game trail through the timber and go down that way."

Sensing Angel's anxiety, Maxi's sharp eyes swept the area again as she stood with hands on hips contemplating their position. "I know I'm just guessing, but I think those men are far enough ahead of us that we'll be safe on this trail. Besides, we don't know this country and could run into worse problems if we leave this trail. I think we should keep going like we are."

"Okay, I'll trust your judgment. But I dread the thought of running into them. No telling what those evil men might do."

"You'll have to tell me more about them, maybe at camp tonight. I want to know what to expect if that does happen." Maxi went to her saddlebags and pulled out her father's pistol. "I've been thinking about this. I want you to carry Pa's pistol."

Angel flinched and started to protest when Maxi held it out to her. "I don't know…"

"Look at the deep pockets in your coat. It's perfect for keeping the pistol close to you. I'll show you how to use it, and you can practice until it feels familiar enough."

Angel wasn't convinced. "Do you really think I need to carry a gun?"

Maxi was adamant about it. “Yes, I do! Let’s say a man or large animal, like a bear, came into our camp tonight and tried to attack us. It might take both of us to fight it off or kill it. You having that pistol could save our lives.”

Reluctantly, Angel conceded. “Well, I could shoot either one of those worthless men, but I might have a hard time shooting a bear.” She took the pistol and put it in her coat pocket.

“Are you serious, you wouldn’t shoot a bear?”

“Well, not unless I had to.”

“I certainly hope if we run into one you’ll make up your mind real quick.” Maxi shook her head in disbelief. “We better go. We need to get off this mountain and find a place to camp.” She pulled herself into the saddle and turned to watch Angel climb on a rock and hoist herself up on Sweet’s back. *I need to do something about that as soon as I can. I sure wish I could have brought Pa’s saddle.*

The descent was slow. The trail was littered with rocks and dead brush that had rolled down the mountain during the winter and spring weather. The girls walked when the horses had a hard time keeping their footing. Finally, just as the sun sat low in the west, Maxi pulled up and surveyed an open area. “Over there by those rocks, it looks like there might be some shelter. If that’s a stream by that grassy place, we should be set.”

Checking the area out, they decided they liked the place and immediately began setting up camp. The horses were drawn to the grass and began grazing while the girls scoured the area for firewood. They found plenty, and Maxi was quick to get a fire going.

Angel offered to cook and sorted through the supplies. She filled a small pot with water and boiled a couple of potatoes that she cut into pieces. Unwrapping a good sized chunk of ham, she cut off a few pieces and tossed them into the pot, then carefully rewrapped the ham and tucked in back into the sack.

Maxi had been getting their bedrolls sorted and had brought over water from the creek, then found the tin plates and cups.

The food was beginning to smell good, and she realized she hadn't eaten since breakfast—the last breakfast she would ever share with her pa. His bedroll, plate, and cup that he would never use again reminded her of the awful accident. The young, white haired girl stirring over the fire in place of her pa was the strangest of all. Not that she didn't like the girl, she did—a lot, in fact. Angel had been an immeasurable amount of help. She had been comforting, and now she was cooking and tending to chores like she had been doing it all her life. Maxi was liking her more and more. She just missed her father so much.

"Hungry?" The question broke into Maxi's thoughts. "It should be ready in a few more minutes."

Maxi nodded and found a place to sit close to the fire. "I was just thinking that I haven't eaten since this morning. Sure smells good."

"Well, I hope it tastes good too. Are you ready to hear about those two men out there looking for me? I can talk and stir at the same time."

"You know I do. I've just been so curious about them. I'd like to know more about your family too, where you're from and why you're out in the mountains all by yourself."

"Goodness, I'll have to tell you my whole life story."

"Guess you better get started, then. Just be sure to dip me some of that food when it's done."

Angel took a deep breath. "Here goes. I was born in the mountains of Arkansas. My ma and pa were the most wonderful parents anyone could ever want. Pa's family was what everyone called those mountain people. We were considered poor and uneducated, and I suppose the way some people think, that would be true. But I never felt that way. The men in my pa's family worked with wood, and my pa could make the most beautiful rockers and chests you could ever imagine. That's what he did in his spare time. Mostly, though, he was considered the preacher for the mountain people. They said he had a gift to preach the

Word. That's why he went down to the city to a Bible school for a year. He wanted to be educated about the Bible so he could help people understand it correctly."

Angel smiled, and her eyes danced as she told the next part. "That's where Pa first laid eyes on Ma. They went to the same church. The way she told it, they took one look at each other, and that was it! But there was a problem. Ma's family was well-to-do, and they didn't think Pa was good enough for their youngest daughter."

She paused reflectively, like the thought had just come to her. "It must have been hard for them, trying to stay away from each other, and yet their love pulling them together. When Pa finished his year at school, Ma had to make a choice. Grandfather told her that if she ran off and married that mountain boy, she would be disowned and could never come back. My ma's name was Marie, and she was a beautiful woman inside and out. She loved my pa so much that she packed her things, loaded them on his wagon, and left with him. Said she was never sorry."

Angel stirred the food, then tested a potato for doneness. She gazed into the coming twilight before continuing. "Pa was the first to die. He was coming back from a trip to the city where he would go once or twice a year to sell his wood furniture. No one knew what went wrong but figured something spooked the mule, and the wagon went over a cliff. Looked like his head hit a rock, and he died on the spot. I was about twelve at the time. Ma and I usually went with him, but she had just had a miscarriage and wasn't able to make the trip, so I'd stayed to take care of her. Ma was so lost for a long time. The grief of losing the love of her life and the little baby boy was almost too much for her. I thought maybe I was going to lose her too. It was such a sad time in our lives.

"Ma was more educated than any of the other mountain people, so she taught me and most of the other children. She also loved music. She could play the violin and sing so beautifully, it just made you think you had died and gone to heaven. I miss her so much, at times it makes me ache inside." She paused to dab at her eyes. Then, she dipped some of the food onto a plate and handed it to Maxi.

"Ma took sick the winter I was fifteen. Our neighbor, old Granny Anderson, was like our doctor up there in the mountains. She tried to nurse Ma back to health, but she just grew weaker every day. I guess Ma figured she wasn't going to make it, because she arranged for friends to see that I got to her sister when the time came. Ma had an older sister who had married a man that was headed to the Colorado Territory to set up a ranch. Her sister sent only a couple of letters in all the years we lived in the mountains. My aunt said her husband was a big, rich rancher with lots of cattle and other animals. They had two wonderful boys, and she couldn't be happier. That's how I ended up here in these mountains. With the help of some friends going west on a wagon train, I made it to Aunt Justeen's place. Oh, yes, I'd also spent two days with an old prospector. Now that was an experience! He was a kind old man, but he talked constantly. He had more stories to tell than I've heard or will ever hear in my lifetime." Angel chuckled at the memory of the old man. "Riding in that bumpy old wagon of his made it a very…long…two…days." She dipped some food onto the other plate and set it aside to cool while she continued, her expression changing dramatically.

"Maxi, you have never seen anything more pathetic than Aunt Justeen's place. Her husband had died two years before, and her wonderful boys? Those boys were mean, ugly, and worthless. They hunted and trapped when they felt like it, but other than that, they were lazy. I can't think of words bad enough to describe them. They would steal from anyone and often did worse. There were two or three other men who would hang around for Aunt Justeen and me to wait on. One of them, named Clint, kept trying to get his hands on me. My cousin Stewart and that Clint are the two who are trying to find me. Clint makes me sick! It wasn't just his foul mouth that was disgusting, but also, he never bathed. You could smell him before you saw him. I was afraid to go anywhere by myself for fear he'd catch me. Since Aunt Justeen didn't have a husband, I slept with her. So I was safe at night. I was there for only a couple of months, but I hated every minute of it."

Angel took a bite and shook her head while she chewed. After several more bites, Maxi urged her to go on. "Keep going, Angel, I want to hear all of it."

"Well, Aunt Justeen was nice to me, but I think she knew I would never be safe there. She said I would be safer with God's creatures. So we planned my escape. She told me how to get to the town down in the valley. Said she would keep it a secret as long as she could that I had left the place. Then early one morning, I gave her a hug and left, taking what food she could spare. The first day was good. I didn't think I was being followed. On the second day, I heard them but was able to stay hidden. I slept in a tree the second night and about killed myself after I went to sleep and almost fell out of the tree. I won't do that again unless I tie myself in place."

Angel paused and let out a big sigh. "I ran into you this morning, so you know the rest. I have nowhere to go except that town in the valley. Maybe I can find some kind of work to support myself."

Maxi leaned toward Angel and said, "I reckon you're about the bravest girl I know."

Angel blushed and shook her head. "I just did what I needed to do, that's all."

The sun had disappeared long before the story ended, leaving a half moon among millions of twinkling stars. The dark and quiet of the evening lulled the girls into a sleepy silence.

"Think I'll go to bed, Maxi. It's been a long day." Wrapping tightly in her coat, Angel lay down on the other side of the fire in Mr. Mayfield's bedroll.

Maxi banked the fire and spread out her bedroll. It felt different making camp with someone other than her pa. She had always felt safe and secure with him around. Now, she would have to take care of herself and, also, the young woman across the fire from her. Angel seemed so gentle and kind, yet there was strength in her. *We'll be all right,* she told herself while brushing at the tears that came no matter how hard she tried not to cry.

It seemed Angel had read her thoughts. "Maxi, are you afraid?"

"No," came her immediate reply. A few seconds later, she added, "Well, yes, I guess I am. I'd be crazy not to be afraid since there's so many dangers out here. We have no choice, though, but to do the best we can and go on. If we stay alert and keep our wits about us, we should be okay."

"The first day I was out by myself, I did okay, but when night came, I was terrified. This country is a lot different than the mountains back home. Halfway through the night, I realized that God's in these mountains just like he's in the mountains where I grew up. Actually, he's everywhere I go. I remembered a Bible verse that says, 'I will never leave you nor forsake you.' So I kept saying that verse until I went to sleep. I'm a little afraid now, but it's comforting to be with you."

"Yeah, I know what you mean. I can't tell you how glad I am that you decided to come with me."

The girls fell silent again, and Maxi's thoughts returned to her pa. She lay on her back, looking up at the stars, feeling a huge hole in her heart where her pa had been. She vowed to herself to be brave, knowing that's what he would want her to do.

The noises of the night had Maxi reaching for her rifle more than once. A pair of amber eyes watched intently from the top of a high rock ledge before slinking back into obscurity. Adding wood to the fire helped drive away some of the dark fears. But the emotions of the day couldn't be driven away. They gathered into a tight, heavy ball that wedged itself against her heart.

Finally…she slept.

CHAPTER 3

THE FOLLOWING DAY when the warm spring sun was straight overhead, Maxi and Angel found themselves on an open, grass-covered knoll overlooking a valley. "Angel, are there any of those finger cakes left that you made this morning?"

"Yes, there's enough for us to have two apiece. Shall we take a break and finish them off?"

"Yeah, I'd like to get closer to the edge and see if I can find a way down from here."

"Okay, I'll get the cakes. You go ahead and look. Be over in a minute."

Angel dug out the finger cakes, found a canteen, and joined Maxi by a rock ledge that had a marvelous view of the valley. "Wow, that's beautiful! Do you see a trail that leads down?"

"I see several that might work. See that stand of trees?" Maxi pointed to the north. "Look right beyond that."

"A farm! It looks like a farm. Is that a pond behind the barn?"

"Looks like it. I think we should check it out. Maybe we can bathe in the pond. That gust of wind off that hillside this morning put a layer of dust on both of us." Maxi was thoughtful while she chewed the last of her finger cake. "When we get to those trees behind the place, we need to stop and look it over carefully before we ride into the yard. Could be a bunch of no-good men down there. We don't need that."

The trek down the mountain was slow and tedious, but they finally found themselves in a sheltered stand of trees looking at the backyard of a neat but small farmhouse.

"What do you think, Maxi?"

"I'm for going in. There's a little boy playing in the dirt by the house, so I figure a family lives there. The place looks cared for, and there's not a man alive who could hang clothes on the line that neatly. There just has to be a woman of the house."

"Okay, then let's do it."

Chickens scattered as they rode slowly into the yard. A dog spotted them and began a barking tirade that sent the young boy bolting up from the dirt and running to the back door, slamming it on the way in. A ladder lay on the ground by the barn, a corral held a couple of horses, a large neatly groomed vegetable garden was all staked out, and, yes, there was a pond beyond the barn. Maxi's attention came back to the house when a woman, with the boy in tow, came out the back door. She looked surprised to see them but smiled hugely.

"Well, land's sakes, what've we got here? Two young ladies come to visit." The woman stepped off the porch and came toward the girls. "Get down off them horses, and tell me what y'all are doing out here in the middle of nowhere." She had a pleasant, motherly face with light-brown hair pulled back into a bun. Her pale blue dress was covered by a clean but faded yellow apron sporting large pockets on the front.

Maxi liked her immediately. She swung off Ginger and held out her hand to the woman. "My name is Maxine Mayfield, ma'am, and this is Angel…" Stopping short, she realized she didn't know Angel's last name. They shook hands while Angel slid off Sweet and came around to face the woman. "Pleased to meet you, ma'am."

"Well, the pleasure's all mine. I'm Martha Carter, and this here is my boy, Jefferson. The one peekin' out the door is Cynthia." Martha turned to the door. "Cynthia, come on out here and say hello to these here ladies." The door opened wider, and a girl of about eleven or twelve stepped out on the porch.

"I was hoping, ma'am—" she didn't get to finish her sentence.

"Now, Maxine, you jes' call me Martha. That's all right by me."

"Okay, Martha, and you can call me Maxi. I was hoping we might use your pond for a bath and, if you don't mind, sleep in your barn tonight. We had a gust of wind this morning that coated us with dirt."

"My, my. Y'all come on over t' the barn and bring them horses." She led the way down the worn path. "Jes' unload your belongins in the barn and put them horses in the corral. As for a bath in the pond, y'all are welcome to use it, but I've got a couple of washtubs ya might like instead." She gestured to the tubs hanging inside on the wall. "Course, you'll have to heat up the water, but I'll let y'all decide that, an' you can sleep up there in the hay loft. Now, where y'all heading to?"

Maxi answered, "Well, we're going to the Wind River area up in the northern territories. My brother has a cattle ranch there, and I'm going to live with him."

"Oh my. Such a long ways t' go, huh? And you ladies all by yerselves?"

"My father was with me up until yesterday. He met with a terrible accident." Maxi looked away, closing the subject.

"I *am* sorry, Maxi, didn't mean to pry none." Martha then turned to her children. "Jefferson, come help me put the ladder up. Cynthia, go see 'bout your pa."

The girls traded a puzzled look. Angel shook her head and shrugged. Whatever it was with their pa, Martha had given no indication. They had only to wait a few minutes, and Martha was back in the barn. "I need t' tell y'all 'bout my husband, Jack. He's most usually a good-natured man, but he's had a couple of problems lately that has him as irritable as a cornered polecat. Jest a couple days ago, he cut his leg accidental like. It's healing up pretty good now. At least he's up and starting to do chores again. I know it still hurts him, but he's not limpin' as bad. Now today he woke up with a bad toothache. Seems it's drivin' him crazy, already he's talking 'bout having me pull it out. Never done anything like that before. Hope I don't have to figger out how to do it."

Angel looked at her with sympathy. "Maybe I can help, Martha. Can I meet your husband?"

"Shore, y'all can meet him. Jest don't take it personal if he's a mite cranky." She turned toward the door, motioning for the girls to follow. "We'll have a cool drink in the kitchen." Martha held the back door open, and they entered into a very neat and clean kitchen.

Oh, that smells good, Maxi thought. *Bet it's beans cooking. She must have made a cake or maybe cookies. I just got a whiff of cinnamon, or maybe that's nutmeg…*

"Jack, this here is Miss Maxi and Miss Angel."

They had entered a cozy living room from a short hallway off the kitchen. A brawny looking man with tousled blond hair sat in a rocking chair by a window that looked out on his garden. One side of his face was noticeably swollen.

"Ladies, this here's my husband, Jack Carter."

Mr. Carter seemed taken aback by suddenly having two young ladies standing in front of him. He didn't stand or move out of his chair but nodded at the girls. "Pleased to meet ya'll."

"Mr. Carter, your wife has told us about your bad tooth. Would you show me which one it is? I may be able to help." Angel could tell he was trying to suppress his pain, but she saw right through his facade.

Everyone stared questioningly at Angel and waited for Mr. Carter's response. Maxi sidled closer to her and whispered urgently, "What are you going to do? Angel, you shouldn't—"

But Angel appeared not to hear. She intently watched Mr. Carter, waiting for his answer. His eyes darted from Angel to his wife, then back to Angel. Finally, he nodded. "Don't know what ya can do 'bout it, but guess it won't hurt none to look. It's this one right here." He pulled on the corner of his mouth and pointed to the offending tooth.

Without hesitation, Angel stepped up to Mr. Carter and gazed into his gaping mouth. She straightened up and looked at him with a sympathetic smile. "I know a treatment that will help with the pain and maybe save your tooth."

Jack Carter rubbed his swollen jaw and looked skeptically at Angel. "Now, what would a young lady like you know about doctorin'?"

"Where I grew up, our neighbor lady was the doctor for all the mountain people. They came every day asking for advice about treatment and herbs. I helped her a lot and learned many things about healing. No one knew for sure just how old Granny was, but Ma and I figured she had to be ninety, at least. She had a lot of experience with bad teeth. What I want to do isn't going to be real pleasant, but I've seen it work many times."

Finally, he shrugged his shoulders. "Guess I'd try about anything now. Crazy tooth kept me up most of the night, an' right now it's throbbin' pretty bad. This bad leg kept me laid up so's I got behind on the work around here. Can't afford to be feelin' poorly now, so if you think you can help me, young lady, let's get on with it."

"Let's go to the kitchen since everything I'm going to need will probably be in there."

"What is it you'll be needin', Miss Angel?" Martha questioned.

"I need some liquor, like brandy or whiskey. Also, garlic or onions. Garlic would be best. Then rock salt."

"Sure, I've got all that. I keep a bottle of whiskey for doctorin'. Use it to make syrup when the young'uns get a cough. I'll round up everything." Martha scurried out of the room while the rest made their way to the kitchen.

"Just sit down at the table, Mr. Carter. We need to use the whiskey first as soon as your wife gets back with it."

Maxi thought she saw the corners of Mr. Carter's mouth twitch as she stood by watching the proceedings. She was sure of it when he made his next comment.

"I might decide I like the way ya' doctor, Miss Angel."

Mrs. Carter came back just in time to hear his comment. They all heard her conspiratorial whisper to Angel, "Now ya know why I hide it in a safe place."

Jack Carter grinned. "Oh, Martha, I know every hidin' place you have, and I ain't bothered it yet," he protested smugly.

Angel poured a small amount of whiskey into a cup and handed it to Mr. Carter. "I don't want you to swallow this, just hold it in your mouth around your bad tooth. While you do that, I'll fix the garlic." She turned to the counter with Mrs. Carter looking on.

Jack took a drink from the cup and let it slide right on down his throat. He looked up at Maxi and winked. Then he took another drink and held it in his mouth until Angel turned to see how her patient was doing. As soon as she went back to the garlic preparations, he swallowed the liquor in his mouth. Quickly, he swigged the last bit, holding it innocently in his mouth against the throbbing tooth. Maxi had a hard time not giving him away. She could hardly hold back the giggle that was threatening to escape.

The pained expression on Jack's face concerned Angel. "Isn't it starting to help?"

He swallowed in order to answer. "I think maybe it's startin' to work some. If ya' would pour jest a lil' more in the cup, I'll try it one more time. That should do it."

Angel reached for the cup, but Martha beat her to it. "Let me pour it this time, Miss Angel." She handed it back to her husband with a sly grin. "You're a sneak, Jack Carter, and you're not foolin' me one bit. But never mind this time. If it helps your tooth and your grouchy ways, it'll be worth it."

The love between the two was evident, in spite of the tender reprimand. Martha explained, "My husband was right fond of whiskey before we were wed. He promised me if I'd marry him, he'd not touch another drink. As far as I know, he's kept that promise—until today, that is."

Jack swallowed the liquor in his mouth. "I most shorely have kept my promise, and I ain't one bit sorry I made it either." He smiled warmly at his wife. "T'day is different. I'm bein' doctored, and now I'm ready for what's next."

Angel turned to him. "Okay, I've cut this piece of garlic in half and hollowed it out. It will fit over your tooth like a cap. There are a few pieces of salt embedded in the garlic. You need to hold it on the tooth as long as you can. It shouldn't be painful, but you'll just smell like garlic. So will the house for a few days, but that's a small price to pay if it heals." Mr. Carter worked the piece of garlic into place. "That looks good. Now carefully bite down and hold it there as long as you can. You'll probably need to do this for a few days."

"Thank ya' so much, Miss Angel." Martha then turned to Jack. "Go on in to your rocker, Jack. Ya' might as well rest a bit fer now. We'll be workin' in the kitchen what with supper fixins and all. The young'uns are outside, and I'll make shore they leave ya alone."

Jack nodded and limped in to his rocker.

"I married one fine man, girls. He's a hard worker, and it bothers him somethin' fierce to be alayin' around. How can I ever repay ya', Miss Angel?"

"Like I told a friend once, you don't repay people for things like this." She flashed a knowing smile at Maxi. "Just accept it as God's gift to you. I'm glad I was able to help, and I sure hope it works."

Martha hugged Angel. "I truly believe y'all were sent here by the good Lord himself. We shorely did need ya. Now, let's get that drink I promised." She bustled around getting glasses from the top shelf of a cupboard and set them on the table. The children suddenly appeared at the back door, like they knew it was time for a treat. Cynthia carried in a jug of cold tea from the springhouse. "Cynthia, bring that tea, and fetch them cookies over there. These ladies might need a bite, seein' as how supper's off a ways."

Angel was delighted with the cookies. "Hmm, these are delicious, Martha. I've never eaten cookies like these.

"Well, actually, these here are biscuit cookies. My ma used t' make 'em for us kids all the time, and now, I make 'em for my young'uns. They shore took a likin' to 'em."

When they finished the tea and cookies, Maxi and Angel offered to help with chores. "Well, I thank ya kindly. Guess there's nothin' so pressin' it can't wait a mite longer. Figger the young'uns here can handle most of what needs doing, what with me out there givin' a hand. Y'all are hankerin' for a bath anyways. When ya' finish with your drink, you can go on an' get that done an' whatever else you need to do. Jefferson can show ya where to heat the water. I'll work on supper for tonight."

After bathing and washing out their clothes, Maxi went into the house to see if she could help Martha. Angel went to find the children to see if she could help them do chores.

Later, wonderful aromas filled the kitchen as Mrs. Carter, the two children, Maxi, and Angel gathered at the table. They had decided to let Mr. Carter rest. When encouraged to share their story Maxi started by telling of her fathers accident. Angel then told what had happened in her life to bring her and Maxi together on the mountain. The Carters sat spellbound, especially the children. Mrs. Carter shook her head when they finished their story. "Now, more 'n ever, I'd like t' keep ya here with us."

Jefferson spoke up, "Ma, do ya' think them two men that come by yesterday was them bad ones lookin' for Miss Angel?"

An anxious look passed between Angel and Maxi.

Mrs. Carter answered, "Course, it mite not a been them two what's lookin' for ya, but jes' the same, there's danger out there."

"We know! Oh, how we know," Maxi said. "My father's dying wish was for me to find my brother. No disrespect meant, Martha, but that's what I intend to do. I'll not let my father down."

"You're a mighty brave one, ya are, Miss Maxi. I hope the best for ya. Jest wish there was more I could do for ya."

"I appreciate that, Martha. You all have been more than kind to us."

"Well, land's sakes, I do believe there's some pie here that needs eatin'. Cynthia, fetch some coffee cups whilst I cut this here pie."

They lingered over the dessert, not so much for the goodness of the pie but for the companionable conversation and the sweetness of fellowship.

When Angel finished her pie, she asked a surprising question. "Martha, I noticed a violin in your living room. Do you play?"

"No, no. My pa played, an' I kept his fiddle hopin' one of the young un's here would take a likin' t' it. Why heavens, Miss Angel, are ya interested in the fiddle?"

"As a matter of fact, I am. My ma taught me to play."

Maxi's eyebrows drew up into high arches. "Oh?"

"Well, land's sake, child, let's hear it. We all can sit in the livin' room and give a listen."

They all trooped into the living room where Mr. Carter was waking from a nap. Jefferson was so excited that he ran to his father. "Pa! Miss Angel's goin' to play the fiddle for us."

Angel picked up the instrument. "Only if it won't bother you, Mr. Carter."

Almost spitting garlic out of his mouth, Mr. Carter managed a garbled, "No bother. Go ahead."

"Martha, there's a string missing."

"By george, you're right. Plumb forgot 'bout that."

"Aw…," the children protested, disappointed.

Angel smiled at them. "Don't worry. I'll be right back."

Maxi felt all their questioning eyes upon her as the back door opened and shut. She shrugged her shoulders. "Really, I don't know what she's up to. Could be she knows where to buy a violin string."

CHAPTER 4

ANGEL WAS GREETED with enthusiasm when she returned to the living room carrying her own violin. The children seemed especially interested. They cheered and clapped, then watched with curiosity as she tuned the instrument. Maxi was just as curious, but she couldn't quit thinking about Angel's wicker case and how she always handled it with care. Now she knew why.

"This was my mother's violin, and one of my greatest treasures."

She held it gently and reverently, then placed it under her chin and drew the bow over the strings. The most beautiful sounds filled the room. For close to an hour, that room was like the stage of a theater. The audience, captivated by Angel's skill, was plunged into a whirlwind of emotions as she played happy toe-tapping songs, a classical piece, and hymns that stirred their hearts.

What else can this girl do? Maxi thought. *I wonder how many more surprises my new friend has in that wicker case.*

When the last strains of "Amazing Grace" faded, Martha voiced what they all felt. "That shorely was beautiful, Miss Angel. I hate for ya t' quit. Why, I think I could listen t' you all day long. God has blessed ya with a special talent. He shorely did."

While Angel let the children examine her violin, she stole a look at Mr. Carter. She was pleased to see that he seemed more relaxed and not as tense with pain. Cynthia gave her a hug, which Angel warmly returned. Mr. Carter removed the piece of garlic from his mouth. "Truly did enjoy it, Miss Angel." He then worked the garlic back on the infected tooth with a pleased look on his face.

"Thank you. I'm glad you all enjoyed my music." She looked at Maxi.

"We better help Martha clean the kitchen."

As women will do, the three shared their sorrows and encouraged each other as they tackled the kitchen chores. "The pain of losing a loved one never goes away completely. It eases some as time goes by," Martha told them. "As time goes by, dearies," she repeated.

When the kitchen was in order, the tired girls followed Mrs. Carter out to the barn. She held the lantern while they got into their bedrolls. "We're in bed now, Martha. Good night," Angel called out.

The barn door squeaked, and soft footsteps padded away into the dark. The smell of hay was somehow relaxing, and the girls knew they were safe for the night. "This family is wonderful. Do you ever think of having a nice home with a husband and children, Maxi?"

"I guess so. It seems like such a long way off though."

"I suppose God has someone for us. Like Martha says, 'As time goes by, dearies.'" She chuckled softly. "I just love that woman. It's going to be hard to leave tomorrow."

"Yeah, it will be." Long moments later, a sleepy voice came out of the darkness. "Angel?"

"Huh?"

"What *is* your last name?"

Angel smiled inwardly. "My name is Angel Marie Hawkins. Good night, Maxi."

They slept like sacks of sand, unmoving, unaware, until the squeak of the barn door roused them into semi consciousness. Maxi lay staring up at the barn roof. Shafts of sunlight were streaming in like shooting spotlights on unsuspecting actors. A calico cat sat in the beam of one shaft, contentedly licking its paws, then rubbing its face with the paw. It jerked its head in the direction of every little snap and creak; staring intently at an unseen intruder, then relaxing, it resumed its face cleaning. Maxi watched it for several long moments, but the overwhelming need to stretch made her yawn and push her arms up out of her blankets. The startled cat leapt out of sight. She looked over at Angel who was curled on her side, eyes shut.

"Angel? You awake? I think we slept the morning away."

"Hmm, and it felt good."

The barn door squeaked again, then footsteps on the ladder brought a grinning Cynthia into view. "You awake? Ma said for me to bring your clothes up t' ya." She laid them on the hay, then plopped down and waited for a response.

"Thanks, Cynthia. I'm awake, but I don't know about that sleepyhead Angel."

"Ma said to come eat. Food's 'bout ready."

"Your ma sure is a good cook. You ought to feel real fortunate to eat such good food all the time." Maxi stood and brushed off her clothes. She then rolled up her bedding. "Come on, sleepyhead, let's get going. I'm going to go wash up."

Angel was reluctant to roll out, but she knew Cynthia was waiting on her. She slipped on her yellow dress and tried to tame her curls. "Well, little miss, shall we go to breakfast, or is it noon meal already?" She gestured toward the ladder, and Cynthia started down.

The smell of fried bacon greeted them at the back door. "Jest in time, ya two, find your chairs now." Martha nodded once at her husband, then bowed her head while the others followed suit. Mr. Carter said grace, and the food was passed around. A satisfied lull ensued as plates were filled, and each one settled down to eat.

Angel noticed Mr. Carter was chewing very cautiously. It appeared the swelling had gone down quite a bit. "How's the tooth this morning, Mr. Carter?"

"Your docterin' must be workin'. It feels some better this mornin'."

"I'm glad. You know you need to do that treatment several more times to make sure the tooth is healed."

"I shore do thank ya'. Martha will know what to do now, thanks to you."

Their conversation was light and cheerful until the end of the meal when Mr. Carter cleared his throat, rather loudly. "We'd like t' talk t' ya 'bout that town you're headed to. It ain't a good place, not good at all for two young ladies like yerselves. Why, all that's there is a tradin' post, a bar, and a few rundown houses. Miners come down from the mountains, an' them an' a bunch of rowdy no gooders go t' the bar t' drink and play cards. Y'all can imagine all the trouble they cause. Now, if ya have t' go t' the tradin' post, be sure an' go in the daylight. Don't ever go in the dark."

Mrs. Carter explained further. "There's no law or no church either. We jes' want t' warn ya so's y'all kin be aware of the situation. Ya need t' be very watchful, ya do."

Angel looked stricken. "So, there's no job possibilities?"

Jack shook his head. "Colorado City or Denver, them's the bigger towns what would have the jobs." He pushed away from the table and stood looking down at the girls but saying nothing. Then he turned toward the back door.

"I appreciate you telling us about the trading post, Mr. Carter. Thanks for the advice."

Mr. Carter nodded at Maxi before he stepped out the door.

Maxi and Angel started to clear the table, but Martha stopped them. "Now, Cynthia, here, she kin help with cleanup. Y'all need t' pack up and git them horses ready t' ride. We'll be out directly."

Jefferson tagged along behind the girls, full of chatter. He said he aimed to help them load up the horses and could probably lift really heavy things. Angel directed him to the ladder of the hay loft. "Do you think you could climb up there and toss our bed rolls down? That would be a big help."

"I shore can," the little guy who looked like his father, gushed with eagerness. He quickly scampered up the ladder and tossed the bed rolls over the side.

Angel looked up just in time to see her wicker case in Jefferson's hands. "Wait! Don't throw that! I'll come get it!"

The young Mr. Carter looked two inches taller when he stood before Angel, looking hopeful. "Anythin' else?"

"Um…yes. You can help me get Sweet from the corral." She turned to go, with Jefferson right on her heels.

Maxi was saddling Ginger in front of the barn and grinned at the pair as they passed her. Jefferson rushed ahead to open the gate of the corral. She thought of the black mare and remembered how feisty the horse had been yesterday, kicking up her heels and showing off. An idea gelled in her mind. *I have to find Jack Carter! Oh, I hope he's agreeable to this.* Maxi saw him at the edge of the garden, hoe in hand.

He looked up as she approached. "What kin I do fer ya, Miss Maxi? Ya needin' any help?"

"I just thought of a way you can help us out, if you still want to."

"Well, you jes' say it, an' if I kin do it, I will."

Maxi took a deep breath. "Would you be willing to sell me your black mare?"

Jack looked surprised but said nothing. He gazed toward the corral where he could see Angel and Jefferson with the horses. He rubbed his chin, as though that would help him make a decision. Then he looked back at Maxi, still silent.

"I would trade my pack horse plus some money for her. I don't know if mine is as valuable as yours, but whatever you think is fair, I'll go along with." She paused and let him think on it some more. "I've been thinking about Colorado City and Denver and how far they are. We need to travel a lot faster than what Sweet can go. She's not very old, and she's been trained only to be a pack horse. Just a little work with a saddle, she would be a good horse for Martha or your children." Maxi paused again, wondering what Mr. Carter was thinking. She wished she could read his mind; he still hadn't said anything. She went on, "I think we'd be safer if Angel had a horse that could give a good run if needed. That horse of yours looks like she has a lot of run in her. They sure seem to like each other, don't they?"

At long last, Mr. Carter made an offer. "I'd be askin' fifty dollars fer her, an' that's with a saddle t' boot. Saddle's old, but in good shape. Kin ya pay that much, Miss Maxi?"

"Yes, I can. Oh, thank you, Mr. Carter! This means so much to me." Maxi had the urge to throw her arms around him but held back. "Do you think Angel can handle her?"

"Reckon so. I been workin' t' gentle her fer Cynthia. I'll saddler her up if ya want."

"That would be great. Thanks. Angel can try her out. Please don't tell her you sold the horse to me. I know that sounds strange, but I don't want her to know just yet."

"Whatever ya say, Miss Maxi, fine by me."

Angel watched with interest as Mr. Carter saddled the horse and held the reins out to her. "Ya want t' see how she rides?"

She looked confused, glancing at Maxi. "I'm not…I don't know…if we have time."

Maxi nodded. "Go ahead. We have time."

Angel rode around the barnyard a few times, then pulled up to the fence that Mr. Carter was leaning on. "She's a good one, all right, a real beauty."

"I think she needs a run, Angel. Take her down to that yellow bush and back."

"Okay, I will." Leaning forward, she spoke softly to the horse. "So you think you want to run, huh? Well, let's fly like the wind!" The sight of her yellow dress and white gold curls flying out behind her was just plain fun to watch. Maxi had to laugh.

"Why, that girl handles her jes' fine, Miss Maxi. She won't have no trouble a'tall with that horse."

"Let's shake on it, Mr. Carter, and thank you so much!" She turned to her saddle bags to get the money, but Jack seemed anxious about something. "Is everything okay? You can change your mind if you want to."

"Nah, it's not that…it's jes, well, me and the missus is already worried 'bout ya going off by yerselves. Any way we kin talk ya out of it?"

"No, but thanks for your concern. Like I told you before, I'm going to find my brother. He's all I have left in the world." She handed him the money.

"Wish I could see ya safely t' yer destination. Yer headin' into Ute country, so ya need t' be ready for anythin'. The cholera killed off most o' the Comanche, doubt they'll give ya any trouble this far north." He eyed Maxi's horse and her rifle. "Kin ya use that there rifle yer carryin'?"

"I can, and I will, if needed."

"Good. There's a road of sorts goin' to that tradin' post, jes travel a steady pace most of t' day. Ya should make it before dark."

"Angel plans to find work somewhere up the road. I know she can make up her own mind, but I'm hoping to convince her to go with me."

Martha, Cynthia, and Jefferson came to stand by Jack while they all watched Angel ride back to the yard. Her cheeks were flushed, but she sported a happy smile. Maxi told her they were going to take the mare and leave Sweet with the Carters. She half-expected a protest on Angel's part, but Angel only nodded and said okay. Her eyes misted when she hugged Sweet one last time and said good-bye to the horse.

They arranged their gear and packs, hugged the Carters, and thanked them profusely for their fine hospitality and friendship. Only when they reached the yellow bush did they stop waving, then turned and faced the trail in earnest.

They rode in silence for a long time, each immersed in her own private thoughts and memories. Finally, Angel spoke up, "Are you worried, Maxi?"

Maxi glanced at her but didn't say anything right away, mulling the question over in her head. "Yeah, I guess maybe I am. I'm realizing more and more how much I had depended on Pa to take care of me, you know, work out all the details of everything. Now, I've got to take care of everything myself."

"You mean like this black horse I'm riding?"

"Oh, I just traded Sweet for her, that's all."

"Maxi, I was not born yesterday. You bought this horse, and I know it. I was okay with Sweet. I was getting rather attached to her. Besides, I can't have you buying things because of me. It just isn't right."

"Now, don't get all excited about it, and listen a minute. Last night, before I fell asleep, I thought of quite a few situations we might find ourselves in. It's a wild, dangerous country out here, and we need to move a lot faster than Sweet can go. We're in Ute country, but there's also Comanche that raids through here. Mr. Carter said it's hard to tell if the Ute will be friendly. Then, there's wild animals, four-legged and two-legged, if you know what I mean. We're going to go into that trading post, and I'm going to outfit us a lot better. I want to travel faster."

Maxi looked at Angel trying to read her mood. "Do you understand what I'm saying? We'll leave the trading post as soon as we possibly can and head out of town. Then, we'll need to find a good hideout to spend the night. We don't want to get caught by any of those dreadful men the Carters were talking about."

Maxi knew that Angel was not going to like having money spent on her, so she quickly added, "Besides, I'm going to hire you."

Angel's head whipped around, and she pinned Maxi with an intense glare. "You're going to *what*?"

"Hire you. You're going to work for me. You've been wanting a job. Well, now you've got one."

Angel started to protest, but Maxi held her hand up, cutting her off. "Listen, just hear me out, okay? I won't leave you at that trading post, Angel. You can do our cooking and wash my clothes. That will be your job. If I remember correctly, we'll be going through Colorado City, Denver, then Fort Laramie. After that, I don't know. I think Denver is the biggest town and probably the best place to find a job. So no matter where you find work and decide to stay, I'll let you know how much you owe me for the mare. If you work for me till I reach my destination, then you won't owe me a cent. The black will be yours." She paused for several minutes, letting Angel absorb all the information. "By the way, Mr. Carter called her Raven. You can change it if you want, but that's what she's been called."

Finally, Angel was able to put her thoughts into words. "You're not fooling me one bit, Maxi. You just want to be the boss. You want to sound all business like and in charge…but…you're a softy!"

"Are you mad at me?"

Angel laughed. "Oh, no. I'm not mad." She flashed a genuine smile at her friend. "I want you to know, though, I appreciate you taking care of me. I'll do my job the best that I can, and I'll pay you back as soon as I can. As usual, what you say makes sense."

"So we have a deal?"

"Yes, we have a deal. Besides, I feel about you like I did about Sweet. I'm getting rather attached to you." After a bit of silence, Angel announced decisively, "Her name will be Sweet Raven."

The mid-afternoon sun shone like a vengeance on the two riders. After a couple of hours, they stopped under a large cedar to quench their thirst from their canteens. Neither girl voiced her thoughts, but both were thinking, *I hope we don't run into those two vile men anywhere around that trading post.*

CHAPTER 5

"IT SURE TURNED hot today." Drops of tepid water ran down Angel's arm and onto the ground. She was pouring water into her hand, trying to splash it onto her reddened face.

"Yeah, looks like we're in for summer weather from here on out. We'll get you a hat at the trading post, don't want you to burn up."

They rode steadily until they crested a hill and spied a few buildings in the distance. Maxi sighed with relief. "I can't believe it. That has to be the trading post. The way Mr. Carter talked, it would be almost dark before we reached it. But I'm glad we have so much daylight left. Let's make use of it." Maxi prodded Ginger, and they wound their way down to the outskirts of the village.

Angel scanned the few buildings ahead. "I'll have to admit, I'm a little nervous about going into this place. It doesn't look like much."

"Let's ride in like we know what we're doing. My pa always told me to hold my head up and act confident. Most of the time, people will treat you with respect. When we get to the post, look for a split riding skirt, like mine, or a pair of pants. We both need riding gloves. Mine are worn out. You're getting sunburned, so find a hat that suits you. Can you think of anything else?"

"Not right now."

Maxi stopped in front of the trading post. "Let's be quick. Ready?"

"Ready as I'm going to be."

Maxi noticed stares from a few men across the road, who were hanging around the bar. She ignored their rude comments as she dismounted but made sure they saw her pull her rifle from the scabbard. She stood by Sweet Raven, acting as a shield for Angel, as she dismounted.

"Thanks. Will you stand there like that when I have to mount again?"

"Sure, let's go find you some better clothes."

The girls climbed the three steps onto the boardwalk that ran the full width of the log building. A mixture of smells lured them into the large rectangular structure.

The clanging cowbell on the door had summoned a short, stout man who appeared from a side room. A dingy white apron hung around his neck with long ties circling his hefty middle. His eyes widened at the sight of the girls. He reached up and plucked a pencil from behind his ear, then put it back in place. "Hello, ladies. Doing a little shopping this afternoon?"

"Yes, sir, we are." Maxi glanced at Angel who was already browsing the shelves. "We'd like to look around a bit, if that's all right."

"Perfectly all right. Look all you want." He took the pencil off his ear again and put it right back where it had been. "If you need any help, just let me know."

Angel found a pair of boy's dark-brown pants, a tan shirt, and a wide brimmed straw hat that she felt would meet her needs. She took the items to the front counter. The strange, fidgety proprietor was doing his best to look busy as he occasionally glanced toward the girls.

"Is it okay if I lay these here while we finish shopping?" Angel asked.

"Sure, go ahead," the man answered.

Maxi's ears perked up at the next bit of conversation. She heard the man ask, "What are you ladies doing out here all alone in this country?"

"Oh, we're not alone. My father is somewhere around. He watches over us like a hawk. I'd feel sorry for anyone who tried to harm us." She quickly turned and walked back to where Maxi was.

"You surprise me, Angel. You told a lie."

"I didn't lie. My Heavenly Father does watch over me, and I do feel sorry for anyone who tries to harm me."

"You really do believe that, don't you?" Maxi handed her a pair of gloves to try on.

"I believe it beyond any shadow of doubt. He's proven it many times. Don't you believe it?" Angel paused to admire the gloves. "I've never had riding gloves. These are perfect. I love them."

Maxi struggled with an answer to the question. "I believe in God but don't know how I feel about him watching out for me. I know I need to settle it in my mind. I want to believe."

"Not in your mind, Maxi, in your heart. God does love you, and he wants you to give your life to him. The Bible says to seek him, and you will find him. I'll pray that he will help you find your way."

"Thanks, that's nice of you," was the half-hearted reply. "Let's finish our shopping and get out of here. The day is going fast." That one little question caused turmoil inside Maxi that she didn't want to deal with. Still, she couldn't keep the next thought from creeping into her mind. *If God loves me so much, why did he let my pa die?*

After finding the food items they needed, Maxi paid the owner. Before reaching the door, she turned to the man again. "I almost forgot, sir, I was to ask how far it is to Colorado City."

"About thirty some miles. Tell your family to be careful out there. This is Ute country. Keep your eyes open and your rifle ready."

"We will. Thank you, sir, and have a good evening."

The girls stepped out on the boardwalk, and immediately, Maxi realized they had an audience. "Looks like we've caused a stir. Put the hat and gloves on now. Can you hold the pants and shirt in front of you till we get out of town?"

"Yes, I can do that."

"While I load these things in our food sack, you climb on up. That will shield you from the men across the street. As soon as you're in the saddle get Raven moving. I'll be right behind you."

"I won't leave you, Maxi!"

"Okay, we'll stay together, but stay in front of me." Maxi put her foot in the stirrup and glanced over the saddle. Several men were chuckling as one of them started walking her way. She hit the saddle and calmly turned her horse at an angle so that her rifle was aimed at the man's chest. The man halted in his tracks, while the others stood quietly watching. A fly buzzed the man's whiskered face as she made eye contact with him.

A voice from the group called out, "I think she means business with that rifle, Jeremiah. I don't think I'd mess with her."

Maxi never took her eyes off the man who had stopped in the middle of the road. She could tell he was trying to make up his mind whether or not she meant business.

Then another voice from the group called out, "There are some of us who don't take kindly to men molesting young ladies. If she don't shoot you, I will."

The audacious man didn't hesitate for long. A sheepish grin crept onto his face, and with a tip of his hat, he apologized. "Sorry, miss. Guess I forgot my manners. Didn't mean to scare you." With that, he turned and went back to his buddies.

Maxi turned her horse and headed toward Angel as several voices drifted her way.

"I think she would've shot a hole clear through you, Jer."

"Did you see that pretty, little white-headed gal had her pistol out?"

"You might have had several holes in you, cowboy!"

Raucous laughter followed Maxi down the dusty road. Sure enough, Angel was putting the pistol back into her pocket. Maxi smiled her approval. "Let's get out of here before they forget their manners again."

Several miles out of town, Maxi brought Ginger to a stop. "Would you have shot that man, Angel?"

"Don't be silly. You know I couldn't hit anything. I've never even shot this pistol. I thought maybe I could scare him, if nothing else."

"That was smart thinking, thanks. Let's head to those cottonwood trees. "Hopefully, there will be water and grass."

"Okay, lead on. I'll follow."

They meandered around the brush and rock until they found a secluded spot that harbored a small stream. Grass grew in abundance, and a smattering of white daisies gave the place a peaceful feeling. "What a pretty spot! What do you think, Angel?"

"I love it. Do you want to do the same as we did the other night? You take care of the horses while I start collecting firewood?"

"Sure, sounds good to me." Maxi dismounted and looked around for the best place to stake the horses.

Angel had gotten off Raven and had taken only a few steps when suddenly, she froze. "Maxi!" she hissed. "Come here quick! Over by that big rock. Someone's lying there on the ground."

They stared for a few moments, then inched their way closer, straining to see if it was truly a person. "It's a boy. An Indian boy!" Maxi whispered nervously. "He's not moving. I think he must be asleep." She grabbed Angel's arm. "Let's go!"

"Wait! I think he's hurt. I'm going to see if I can help him."

"No! We need to get out of here before someone else comes." Maxi glanced around. I'm sure there must be someone with him. They might come back any time."

"I have to go see."

"No, Angel, don't go over there. What if it's a trap? He may be just a boy, but he's big enough to be dangerous."

"I have to go help him. I won't leave someone who's hurt and might need my help. And I don't care if he is an Indian."

Maxi looked at her sternly. "I thought I was the boss."

"You can be boss about some things, but not about this. I think God wants me to help whenever I can. I'll have to tell you the story of the good Samaritan."

"I remember the story." Maxi was miffed by this time, realizing she had lost this argument. "Okay, but walk slowly over to him, and don't get in front of my rifle. He might be playing possum."

Angel walked over to the boy. She gently brushed some hair away from his face and knelt beside him. "Come here, Maxi. He's unconscious."

Maxi moved closer to get a better look at the boy. He was probably around thirteen years old, and it was obvious he had been severely beaten. One eye was badly swollen, and blood was caked on his face. "Do you think you can do anything for him?"

"I'm going to try. You stand guard, and I'll see what I can do." Angel quickly collected the things she needed. She dipped water from the stream and retrieved her wicker case, then knelt beside the boy. "There's a deep cut on the side of his head that needs stitches. I'll sew it up while he's still out."

Maxi was, again, amazed at Angel's abilities. Clearly, she knew what she was doing. She cleaned the wound and stitched it closed. Then, took a tin of salve and applied some to the wound. Gently, she washed blood from his battered face.

"Poor boy, he looks bruised all over. I wonder if any bones are broken." She looked over his muscular frame. "This forearm has a slight sway. It's probably broken. Must have used it to protect himself from the blows when they were hitting or kicking him. I better splint it. I need to find some smooth sticks."

Angel prepared the sticks that she'd found, then tore a few strips from the cotton fabric that was wrapped around her violin. The boy moaned softly as she aligned his arm. "I hope he doesn't wake up before I can get this arm wrapped." Moving quickly and skillfully, she finished wrapping the arm, then sat back on her heels inspecting her work.

"His breathing seems smooth and regular, but it wouldn't surprise me if he had some cracked ribs. The thing that worries me is he's still unconscious."

Angel felt a light tap on her shoulder and looked up to see Maxi with a finger to her lips, signaling her to be quiet. Alarmed, she tensed, waiting and listening. After a moment, she whispered, "What is it?"

Maxi didn't have time to answer. A man's voice boomed out of the brush. "Here they are, Clint! Told you I saw them coming out of the trading post. Didn't I tell you I'd find them for you?" Eyeing Angel, he sneered, "Well, hello, cousin. You sure are a hard one to find."

The sight of the man repulsed Maxi as she watched him dismount his horse. A quick look, and she knew why Angel had run from her Aunt Justeen's. Neither girl had time to say anything before Clint came bursting through the brush leading his horse.

"Howdy, Angel. Mighty fine to see you again." His eyes roamed over Angel, and he added another, "*Mighty* fine." Then his eyes drifted to Maxi. "Looks like you found yourself a right, purty friend. A might prickly, though, with that rifle pointed at me." He leered at Maxi. "Why don't you put that thing down, little lady. I won't hurt you."

Maxi was unmoving, so he tried another tack. "Hey, Clint, ain't that the little Injun brat that wouldn't share his rifle?"

"Looks like him all right. The dirty little Injun picked a fight with us. We shoulda killed him!"

Angel came to her feet. "*You're* the ones who beat this boy near to death? I wouldn't claim you as kin for anything in the world, Stewart. Now get out of here and leave us alone!"

Stewart leered, his lustful eyes dancing over Angel. "It don't really matter whether you claim me or not, cousin. Clint, here, has put his claim in on you. He's going to take you back home to be his woman. Said he'd even marry you. That's an offer you can hardly refuse. You'll probably grow to like him, if you give him half a chance." Both the ruffians laughed wretchedly.

Angel clinched her fists. "Clint isn't taking me anywhere, now git!"

"Like I said, you don't have a choice." Smirking, Stewart started toward Angel. But he had misjudged the prickly, young lady with the rifle, and it cost him. A shot rang out. He grabbed his arm and howled, "Put that thing down, you stupid little idiot! You might shoot better next time and kill me!"

In the blink of an eye, Maxi worked the lever of her Winchester rifle. She never took her eyes off the man. "I hit exactly where I aim. If you don't get on your horse and get out of here, I promise to put the next one between your eyes or straight through your heart. The choice is yours."

In the next instant, Clint lunged at her. A whooshing sound and a scream rent the air as he dropped to his knees right in front of Maxi. She stared at the man, his eyes wild, like he couldn't quite figure out what had happened. Blood oozed from around an arrow in his left shoulder.

As awareness came to his eyes, he frantically searched for the source of the arrow.

Maxi never lost her focus or wavered but kept her rifle on the men. "If you will do as you're told, you might live. If you don't, you're going to bleed to death right here!"

Clint knew they were in serious trouble and made a quick decision. "Let's get out of here, Stewart." He glared at Maxi as he threatened, "If I ever see you again…I'll kill you!"

Stewart's arm was bleeding profusely, and he was beginning to look pale and sick. He looked at Angel and pleaded, "Angel, help us out here. Stop the bleeding and bandage us up first. Come on, please?"

In a voice that brooked no argument, Maxi ordered, "Angel, don't you dare go near either one of them. They're on their own. If they get out of here now, they can probably make it back to the trading post."

"My…rifle…"

Maxi realized the voice behind her came from the injured boy. She leveled her voice at the men. "Leave the rifle on the ground, and leave, now!"

A lot of groaning and loud cursing assaulted the air as the men struggled to get on their horses. They roughly jerked them in the direction of the trading post, leaving as noisily as they had come. Maxi didn't relax her guard, even then.

Angel picked up the rifle and took it to the boy, laying it by his side. "You speak English?"

"Speak good English."

"What's your name?"

"Little Crow."

"I'm Angel, and my friend is Maxi. How do you feel, Little Crow?"

"Head hurts." As he reached for his head, he realized for the first time that something was on his arm. He looked at Angel with questioning eyes. "You fix?"

"Yes, and I think the bone is broken. You need to be careful for a while so it will heal. I also stitched the cut on your head. Do you hurt anywhere else?"

"Hurt plenty."

"I'm sure you do. It was a bad beating they gave you. I have something that might help the pain."

"Pain no matter. Need water."

"I'll get you some." He drank thirstily as Angel filled the cup two times.

Little Crow saw Maxi anxiously looking around the area. He understood what she was looking for. "Grandfather shoot arrow. He follow men, make sure they not come back."

Maxi relaxed and found a place to sit before her rubbery knees buckled. She was determined not to show how badly the incident had shaken her. *Why did you leave me, Pa? Why? I've always counted on you to protect me. Now I have no one.*

Suddenly, an Indian man was standing beside Little Crow. The powerfully built man, dressed in simple buckskins, looked to be in his fifties. His dignified bearing prompted Maxi to jump to her feet. They gazed at each other for a moment, each trying to read the other's thoughts. Satisfied with his appraisal, the man squatted next to Little Crow and spoke to him in their own tongue. The girls watched warily and waited.

Finally, the man stood. Little Crow spoke proudly, "This is Grandfather, Red Fox, chief of Ute tribe. Grandfather say, stay here, rest all night. Grandfather keep watch, no one bother."

"Wait!" Angel hurried to one of the sacks behind her saddle. It was the one Mrs. Carter had sent with them. Taking out some bread and a slice of ham, she walked to Red Fox. "Here's some food we want to share with you." She smiled shyly. He took it, nodded once, and was gone as quickly and quietly as he had come. "What are we going to do, Maxi?"

"It's getting too late to do much of anything now. We barely have enough light to gather wood for a fire. We're probably safer here with Little Crow than out in the dark by ourselves. We'll just have to trust Red Fox."

"I don't think he'll harm us. Besides, my father is still around. He did a good job of protecting us today. I do feel sorry for those men who tried to harm us. They won't feel like coming after us for a few days—that is, if they made it back to the trading post."

"I suppose you're right. We'll be long gone by then. Let's get settled for the night. Are you okay, Angel?"

"Yeah, I'm okay. I'm going to go over by the horses and change into those pants. Then I'll be ready to ride in the morning." Angel changed, then quickly gathered wood, and started a fire. They ate, then started settling down for the night. While they were laying out their beds, Little Crow started moving around.

"He's trying to get up, Angel. Should we help him?"

"No, let him do it himself. He's a proud, young man and probably has had all the attention he wants for tonight. I think he'll be fine."

From the corner of her eye, Maxi watched the boy get up and slowly walk toward some brush. Suddenly, he went out of sight. "Where did he go, Angel? Do you think he's up to something?"

"The only thing he's up to is getting rid of all the water he's been drinking."

"Oh."

"You've been on the alert all day, Maxi. You're just a little jumpy. You told me the other night how brave you thought I was. Well, let me tell you, nothing I've done compares with what you've done today. You're something else. I don't think you're afraid of anything."

"If you only knew! I was sure that man in front of the trading post could hear my heart pounding."

By this time, Little Crow had come back to his blanket. Carefully lying down, he turned his back to the girls and seemed to go to sleep. As they lay on their beds on the other side of the fire, Maxi contemplated Angel's remark about her father watching over her. *It's a comforting thing to have a father to protect you. God, are you watching over me too? I miss my pa.* A tear trickled down her cheek as she closed her eyes trying to get lost in sleep. Slowly, her body relaxed as slumber engulfed her.

It wasn't the hushed sounds of daybreak that roused Maxi from sleep but the loud growl of her own stomach. *Food.* Why was she smelling food? Her sleepy thoughts tried to sort it out. *Pa must be fixing breakfast. When did he catch fish? I don't remember...* Her eyes flew open. The fire had been built up, and Red Fox sat with his grandson. The source of the aroma became evident when her eyes wandered to the fire. Four sticks were stuck in the ground. Each held a fish angled over the fire. Maxi sat up and nudged Angel. "We need to get up and cover some ground today."

A sleepy voice answered, "Do I smell fish or am I dreaming?"

"Yes, you smell fish. It looks like they're about ready to eat. I need coffee though. That's your job, so roll out and get with it." Maxi headed for the creek but not before she heard a low grumble from her new employee.

"Yes, boss."

As soon as the last bite of fish was eaten, Little Crow and his grandfather stood to their feet. Little Crow went to Angel. A turquoise stone, about the size of a nickel, stared up at her from the palm of his hand. A thin leather strip was laced through holes that had been drilled into the stone, making a beautiful necklace.

"Oh, how pretty!" She looked at him, waiting for an explanation.

"Little Crow give White Cloud, medicine woman, gift. Good medicine."

"White Cloud?"

"Grandfather give name." He reached out and took one of her curls and rubbed it between his fingers. "Soft like clouds. Grandfather like small curl to keep. People believe story better if he can show hair, big medicine."

"Why not?" Angel said with surprise. "I have plenty of curls to spare. Thank you, Little Crow, for the gift. I will treasure it. Tell your grandfather I am honored to have the name White Cloud. Now, give me your knife." Pulling at one of her curls, she cut off a piece and handed it to Little Crow, who in turn handed it to his grandfather. Red Fox looked pleased as he carefully tucked the lock of hair in a small pouch that was on his belt.

Red Fox then approached Maxi. She stood tall with her shoulders back, tamping down a feeling of apprehension. He took her hat and put one of his own feathers in the band of the hat. He handed it back to her as Little Crow interpreted. "Red Fox, Chief of Ute, say brave warriors wear feather of eagle to show brave in battle. He gives Princess Warrior feather to show she brave in battle." Smiling, he added, "Grandfather have two wives already. Would take Princess Warrior for third wife, but two wives enough trouble!"

Stunned, Maxi's eyes grew large, and she blushed a deep pink but recovered quickly. "Tell Red Fox I thank him for the feather of the eagle. He honors me. I don't want to add more trouble to his life. I'll go find my own husband."

Little Crow translated what Maxi said. Red Fox, Chief of the Ute, burst into laughter, which was a rare sight. Little Crow seemed surprised as he watched his grandfather. His smile showed love and respect for this man, who at the moment was showing great pleasure in his interaction with the two white women.

"We go now. Grandfather say you follow trail this way, cross big waters careful. Ute watch, no one bother White Cloud, Princess Warrior." The two turned and walked away, disappearing into the timber.

For no reason whatsoever, Maxi and Angel erupted into giggles that threatened to take their breath away. "As I live and breathe, Maxi, I can't believe what just happened. Do you realize what an enormous compliment Red Fox paid you? There's no doubt you impressed him."

"I don't understand why. He scared me, but I wouldn't want him to know it."

The need to cover ground got them both scrambling.

CHAPTER 6

BY THE TIME they were ready to go, it was evident the weather would be windy and overcast. "We'll be lucky if we don't get rained on today, Angel."

"If rain is the worst thing that happens, I'll be a happy woman."

It never rained, but water was, however, one of the problems of the day. The first small creek they had to cross, Angel found out that Sweet Raven didn't like fast-moving water. The next stream was deeper and wider, so Maxi had Angel cross with Raven close to Ginger. It worked and calmed the younger horse. Even though the girls felt they were being watched, they never saw a soul—that is, until in the distance, they spied a wide, rushing river. Maxi stopped and exhaled a low whistle through her teeth. She scanned the banks, then focused on something down the river.

"What is it, Maxi?" Angel followed her gaze.

"Looks like…is that Red Fox?"

"Well, I would say it's him." Angel chuckled. "Just look at him, Maxi. What a magnificent picture he makes sitting on his Indian pony. Are you sure you don't want to be his third wife?"

"Stop it, Angel! You're going to tease me forever about that, aren't you?"

"Why not? It's probably the only time I'll ever see you blush. And I have a feeling you don't blush very easily."

"I'm going to ride straight to the river. If he's still in that spot, we'll ride over to him. He's got some reason for being there."

"I agree. He's probably there to help us cross." Angel couldn't help but snicker. "Lead on, oh, Princess Warrior!"

As they got closer to the chief, Angel sucked in her breath. "It's wider here, Maxi. I'm getting nervous."

"Yeah, but it's probably not as deep. The water seems to be flowing slower."

Red Fox didn't waste time trying to communicate. He nodded a greeting and pointed at Angel, motioning for her to come to him. Then he reached out and took the reins from her.

"Hang on, Angel, he's going to lead Raven across!"

Alarmed, Angel glanced back at Maxi. "Will you be okay?"

"Don't worry about me. Ginger likes water. You just hang on!"

Red Fox led Raven into the water, then stopped and looked back to make sure Maxi followed. She urged Ginger into the river, gaining a slight nod of approval from the chief.

Raven panicked when the bottom dropped off, but Red Fox stayed in control, keeping the frightened mare close to his horse. He eased off the back of his horse, hanging onto the mane until the strong pony found solid footing. Never letting go of Raven, he quickly slid back onto his horse. A few moments later, they climbed out onto the far bank.

Angel let out a big sigh. The chief handed her the reins, gazed admiringly at Maxi, let out a whoop, and then went racing off to a distant hill where three other Indians waited.

They watched the Indians ride out of sight. "Well, mice in the pantry!" Angel blurted. "That Indian chief has more surprises than there are flowers on the prairie. By the way he was looking at you I thought maybe he'd changed his mind and was going to take you for his third wife."

"Well, I haven't changed *my* mind. I still want to find my own Prince Charming."

Before Maxi and Angel left the river bank, they checked their packs. Angel was relieved that her violin made it without getting wet. She had forgotten about it in the excitement of the crossing.

Maxi said they needed to cover more ground but would stop early to make camp. That way, they could lay their bedding and clothes in the sun to dry out. When they finally found an adequate place, they laid the wet things on the willows that grew beside a creek.

The gauzy, gray skies of evening were settling on the campsite when the girls finished their meal. Angel took the last drink from her canteen. A quick glance at Maxi showed her deep in thought. "What are you thinking about? You look so serious."

"I'm thinking about some things I need to tell you."

"What things?"

"First, let me tell you this. You were right to help that Indian boy. You have a kind heart, and I'm glad you helped him."

"Thank you. I think that's what God wants me to do, help people. What else is on your mind?"

"My family. I want to tell you about them. Just a few things for now, then more later. This is the important part." Maxi paused and looked up. Twinkling stars studded the canopy of the early night sky and a fresh breeze brushed her face. She gathered her thoughts, then started her story.

"You already know my mother and father are dead. I only have one person left who is family, and that's my brother, Michael. He's five years older than me. I didn't know it at the time, but the idea of farming was Ma's. Pa would do about anything for her. When she died, it became evident that Pa and Michael hated farming. After a few years, things started to go down hill.

Michael and Pa were at each other's throats all the time. When Michael turned seventeen, he told Pa he was leaving with a close friend of his. Their intentions were to hook up with a cattle drive and head north. When they got out there, they would use their money from the drive and find a place of their own to raise cattle. It hurt Pa, but I could tell he didn't blame Michael. Pa was stuck with me then. He kept trying to make a go of the farm, but after a few years, he hired out to different ranches around our area, always dragging me with him."

"Did you ever hear from Michael?"

"We didn't hear from him for at least two years. Then we got a letter saying he'd found a place in the Wind River area in the Dakota Territory. They had big plans. He carried on about the beauty of the west and the wide-open spaces. When he invited Pa and me to join him and his friend, Pa's life seemed to take on new meaning. I've never seen him so eager and happy about anything. I naturally got excited when he said we were going. It was quite an adventure for us. Pa sold the farm, but I don't know what he got for it. Probably not much since it was in such bad shape. I do know he saved money from his work on the ranches, and that's what I need to talk to you about."

"About the ranches or about the money?"

"About the money we have with us. Ma inherited a sum of money from her parents when they died in an accident. That money was left in the bank for a rainy day. Pa drew that money out when he sold the farm and everything else we owned."

Maxi paused, chewing on her bottom lip. "He hid the money in different places. Most of the bank notes are hidden in the hem of the two rain slickers we're carrying on our horses."

Angel's eyebrows arched, and her eyes wandered to the saddle bags and other supplies. "I had no idea…"

"I know, but I'm telling you this for a reason. There's money in the pack on Sweet Raven and more in my pack. Pa had a sum in his money belt too. I can't wear the money belt, so I've hidden it in my things. We need to take really good care of those rain slickers. Earlier today, I was thinking about Pa's accident and realized if something happened to me, you wouldn't be aware of all the money we have with us. This is a lot to put on you, Angel, but I need help, and you're the only one I've got right now. Here's my request. If anything happens to me, I want you to take the money and use as much as you need to find my brother. Give him the money, and he'll help you get to wherever you want to go. He's a good brother. I love him, and I've missed him more than I can ever say. Anyway, that's what I'd like you to do, if you will."

"It scares me to think about going on a search like that, but I could never say no to helping you. You've been so good to me. I'll do the best I can to find him. Just don't let *anything* happen to you."

"Thanks, Angel."

After a moment of reflection, Angel smiled. "As for me, I have no one, anyway, no one who would care if I lived or died. If something happens to me, don't fret about it. Do what needs to be done, and know I'm with my ma and pa in heaven. I've never had a brother or sister, and I envy you for having a brother to go to. You're being like a sister to me now, and you'll never know how much it means to me."

Maxi looked pleased and nodded. "Let's try to get some sleep now."

"Yes, princess. Is there anything else I can do for you before you retire?"

"Smarty!" A dirt clod smacked Angel's thigh.

Angel couldn't figure out why she woke so early, but the horizon told her dawn wasn't far off. In the cool, quiet morning, a muffled noise drifted her way. Blinking and straining to see what was out there, she froze. *Oh, no! I've got to warn Maxi!* She slowly reached out and touched Maxi's head. Much to her relief, Maxi didn't move. As quietly as she could, she whispered, "Don't move, Maxi."

"I hear it. What is it?"

"Be quiet and just…don't…move."

CHAPTER 7

IT MUST BE *a snake! Out here, probably a rattlesnake. Please, God, not a snake. I hate snakes. I must trust Angel. Don't move, don't move.* Suddenly, something grazed her feet. She was gripped by a strong urge to jerk them away. *Don't move, don't move.* Moments passed. Three more featherlike brushes touched her feet. Holding her breath, she waited another minute, then raised her head. About eight feet away, a mother skunk with three babies waddled their way toward the creek in a perfect line. The little black and white procession, with their own kind of danger, disappeared in the shadows of brush along the creek.

"Are they gone, Maxi?"

"Yeah. We're safe now. I'm glad they didn't get close to the horses. What a mess that would have been. I'm absolutely relieved we didn't get sprayed."

"For sure the town of Colorado City wouldn't want us."

"Well, I'm awake now. Might as well get a fire going, if these embers will cooperate. I need coffee. Oh, wait. That's your job now."

"Okay. I'm on it." Angel reached for her shoes. "I wonder how far we are from town. How far do you think we traveled yesterday?"

"I'd guess close to twenty miles. It looks like the trail goes higher in the foothills. We'll be able to see more when we get up there."

"Shall I make finger cakes? The flour and baking powder tin stayed dry, so we're in business, if that sounds good."

"I won't ever argue about you making finger cakes."

About an hour later, the girls had ridden to a higher elevation and got a surprise. They could see Colorado City in the distance. A mile outside of town they ran into the main road. "I think we're losing our Indian guard," Maxi said, looking at the mountain side. An Indian waited until he was sure they saw him, then quickly turned and rode south into the trees.

"We still have my father protecting us," Angel answered. She fell in beside Maxi, and they headed to town.

Main street was noisy and busy, but they couldn't help but notice all the attention they were attracting. "I know we look kind of rough, but why is everyone staring at us? You'd think they had never seen two women on horses before."

"Beats me, Angel. Look, people are even coming out of the stores to stand and stare. Wonder why they're so interested in us."

They rode past a hardware store where two old men sat on a bench out front. Obviously, both were hard of hearing. "Suppose that's them?" one shouted to the other.

"Yep, guess so!" the second man shouted back. "Sure a lot younger than I thought. Hard to believe!"

The girls traded puzzled looks just as Maxi spotted the sheriff's office. "Let's stop here. The sheriff might tell us where to find a place to stay the night." They tied their horses at the rail, then walked up the steps and into the building.

Sitting behind a desk, a man was sorting through papers. He glanced up, giving them a quick once-over. About middle aged, the man wore a sagging mustache under his nose that made him look grouchy. But he smiled at them, and they saw eyes that twinkled like a mischievous boy playing a prank. His voice was warm and pleasant but laced with surprise. "Well, I'll be! I didn't know whether to believe it or not!" He gave the impression of someone who loved a good joke.

Maxi was quick to respond. "I don't understand what you're talking about, Sheriff. And why has everyone been staring at us?"

Still grinning, he jumped enthusiastically into an explanation. He said he had a friend who was a scout with the army and who had dropped in yesterday to pay him a visit. The friend told how he had run into a Ute brave who had been friendly to him once. When his friend asked the Ute why he was in the area, the Ute said he was guarding two white women for Chief Red Fox. Seems the chief told his tribe about the two white women who had helped his grandson after he had been beaten by evil men. The white women had given him medicine and tended his wounds, then protected him again when the bad men came back. The chief gave orders that those two white women were not to be harmed. They were to be protected from all danger.

The sheriff looked at them in amazement and shook his head. "The Indian called you White Cloud and Princess Warrior." He looked directly at Angel. "I reckon I can tell which one of you is White Cloud!" He made her blush, saying she was the prettiest little cloud he ever did see. Turning to Maxi, he declared, "And you, young lady, are as beautiful as any princess I've ever dreamed of."

"I don't feel much like a princess right now. What we did wasn't that much, but it was nice of Red Fox to watch out for us."

"Well, you surely must have made an impression on that chief. He's known as a vicious warrior. You don't hear about Indians protecting white women. Just baffles me." Shaking his head in wonder, he seemed to tuck the story away for later thought. He looked up at the girls again. "Now, what can I do for you two?"

Maxi answered, "We need a place to stay tonight, maybe two nights, and a livery stable, if there's one around. Thought you could point us in the right direction."

"You bet I can! Come on out front with me." He led them to the boardwalk, then pointed down the street. "Last place on the right is Mrs. Frazier's boarding house. She's a fine woman. You'll be safe and taken good care of at her place. Now, just past the boarding house, we have a livery stable. It's on the left side of the road. I have to warn you, your story spread like wild fire, and folks are mighty curious about you two. They're good people, though, and shouldn't bother you none. The troublemakers come into town on weekends. Mostly, they're a bunch of miners or cowboys coming in to buy supplies and let off steam. If you have any trouble send someone to get me." He paused, thinking hard on something. "I guess I might as well tell you. There's some who may look down their noses at you. They hate Indians and won't understand why you helped one. Just pay 'em no mind."

"Thanks, Sheriff, for the advice and the help. Let's go, Angel."

They rode slowly down the dusty road, aware of the public scrutiny. Angel shook her head in bewilderment. "This is all kind of crazy, Maxi. It's almost funny in a way. Maybe God has more of a sense of humor than I ever imagined."

The horses were left at the stable, and the girls walked a short distance to the boarding house. They found Mrs. Frazier, a warm, friendly woman. She made every effort to make the girls comfortable in a cozy room where they would share a bed. After a bath and fresh clothes, the girls fixed their hair and walked to the stores down the street. Maxi bought ribbons for their hair; then, they stopped at a small café to get something to eat. The young woman who waited on them said there really were no good jobs for a decent woman. Maybe starting a business of doing laundry or sewing might bring in some money. She told them in no uncertain terms that she wouldn't want to do laundry for a living.

After leaving the café they took their time walking back to the boarding house. Mrs. Frazier was in the kitchen preparing supper. She refused to let the girls help right then, telling them to relax in the parlor where it was cool and quiet. She told them where to find books and a checkerboard, and she would call them if she needed help. They played a few games of checkers; then, Maxi piped up with a request. "You know what I'd really like, Angel?"

"What's that?"

"I would love to hear you play your violin. Would you do that for me?"

Angel smiled in agreement. "I would be happy to play for you. Wait here."

She returned with her treasured instrument and began to play.

The noise and bustle in the kitchen quieted as the sweet, lovely strains found their way into each room of the house. *I wonder if you know the effect your music has on your listeners,* Maxi thought. *People are compelled to stop and listen.*

"Sing the ones you know, Maxi!"

"If I sing, I'll mess it all up."

"Oh, come on!"

They were caught up in singing and playing until suddenly, Mrs. Frazier was at the parlor door. "I do hate to interrupt that beautiful music. Don't think I've ever heard such wondrous sounds from a violin. And what a lovely voice you have, Maxi. I could use some help about now though. Will you two set the table for me? The others will be coming in soon. You'll find the dishes in that cupboard there. There will be six of us tonight. Mr. Clark is bringing a guest, Alex Phelps, our blacksmith. It wouldn't surprise me if he just wanted to meet my young lady boarders." She grinned. "Can't blame him at all. That Jim Clark is a fine, young man, runs the freight wagons from Denver, stays here when he's in town." She turned back to the kitchen, then stopped. "Oh, Angel, will you leave your violin in the sitting room and play for us this evening? I sure wish you would come to church with me in the morning and play for us there."

"I guess I've lost track of time and didn't realize tomorrow is Sunday. Maxi and I will talk about it. Thank you for inviting us."

They finished setting the table just as Mrs. Carol Conrad, the other boarder, came in. She appeared to be in her late twenties and was pleasant-looking with a nice smile. Mrs. Frazier had already told them that Mr. Conrad had died a year ago, and the young widow had moved into town to work at one of the stores. They introduced themselves.

"It's so nice to meet you, Angel, and did you say, Maxine?"

"Yes, but you can call me Maxi, if you like."

"All right, but I do think Maxine is a beautiful name. I'll look forward to visiting with you later. The town is in quite a stir about the two of you. I was hoping I'd get to meet you. Right now, though, I need to go freshen up before supper." She excused herself and went to her room.

"That's a good idea, Angel. Let's go freshen up too."

"What are we going to do to freshen up?"

"We can put the new ribbons in our hair."

"Oh, I forgot about them. That would be nice."

A short time later, they heard men's voices, and Mrs. Frazier called everyone to come to supper. She introduced each one, then motioned for them to sit. Jim was asked to say grace, then the tantalizing dishes were passed around.

"This was simply delicious, Mrs. Frazier. I haven't had pot roast with all the trimmings in a long time."

"Well, thank you, Angel. I'm pleased you enjoyed it. Would anyone like a second piece of cake?"

Both men decided they needed another piece of the delicious chocolate cake. The ladies declined but enjoyed watching the men polish off their bounty. Mr. Phelps, the blacksmith, patted his stomach and groaned. "That's about the best cake I've ever eaten, Mrs. Frazier. Thank you for having me sit at your table."

"It's a pleasure to have you. We'll have to get you to come again sometime soon."

"That would make me mighty happy. I don't do too bad cooking for myself, but it gets mighty lonely."

Maxi remembered all of a sudden that she was supposed to check in with the stable owner. "Mrs. Frazier, do you think it's too late to walk down to the stable?"

Jim answered first. "I would be glad to walk with you, Miss Mayfield. I need to let all this fine food settle. A walk just might help."

Maxi looked to Mrs. Frazier for approval, and seeing her smile and nod, she felt comfortable accepting his offer. "That would be very nice of you, Mr. Clark."

"Please just call me Jim."

"Okay, Jim. Would you like to walk with us, Angel?"

"I think I'll stay and help Mrs. Frazier with clean up. You go ahead, Maxi."

Looking at the others, she extended the invitation. "Anyone else care to walk with us?"

Carol Conrad opened her mouth to speak, but Alex Phelps jumped in before she could get a word out. "If it's all right, Mrs. Conrad, I would like to stay and visit with you for a while." It was evident that he had drawn up all his courage to declare his desire to spend time with the lady. He shyly fixed his eyes on her, waiting for an answer. He was rewarded for his courage with a brilliant smile.

"I would enjoy that immensely, Mr. Phelps. But only if you'll call me Carol, and may I call you Alex?"

"I would like that, Carol."

Mrs. Frazier looked pleased with the arrangements. "Well, now that's settled. Jim, you and Maxi go on, but take my shawl on the peg by the front door. Carol, you take Alex to the parlor. Angel and I will get the kitchen in order. Don't dilly-dally, now. I think I've talked Angel into playing her violin for us tonight. I'm really looking forward to it."

Maxi plucked the shawl off its peg as Jim opened the door. Stepping out onto the porch, she felt somewhat uneasy but couldn't identify the source. "It's a little cool this evening but feels good to be out in the fresh air." She fumbled with the shawl, trying to wrap it around her shoulders.

"Here, Maxi, let me help." Jim took the shawl from her and gently laid it around her shoulders.

"Thank you." She felt a flutter in her stomach. *What's wrong with me? I'm so jittery. You'd think I'd never gone for a walk with a man before.* As soon as the thought went through her head, she had to stifle a giggle. *I'm so silly. I have* never *gone for a walk with a man before! Mrs. Frazier seemed to think it was okay. Is it okay, Pa?*

Jim glanced at her. "I'd sure like to know what you're thinking. Seems you were about to laugh one second, then turned awfully serious the next."

"I was thinking about my pa. Just wondered what he would think about me taking a walk with a man. He was always very protective of me. My mother died when I was young, so he took me to work with him since there was no one else to watch me. He hired out to the ranches in our area, and there was always a bunch of cowboys hanging around. He must have threatened every one of them 'cause they always treated me politely and respectfully."

"You speak as if he's no longer living."

"He isn't. He died about a week ago, had an accident up in the mountains. I feel so empty not having him here to look after me. I miss him a lot."

"I'm sorry, Maxi. I had no idea. Are you okay?"

"Sure, I'm okay." Abruptly, she changed the subject. "Mr. Phelps seems to be interested in Carol Conrad."

"I hope to shout he is! Poor guy has been trying to work up the courage to talk to her for quite awhile now. He pert near begged me to bring him tonight. I told him if he didn't speak up and let her know he was interested, I was going to box his ears. I was proud of him and glad Mrs. Conrad was agreeable."

"You like playing cupid?"

"Not me. Just seems bashful guys need a little push in the right direction. Not every man is as outgoing and friendly as I am." Maxi glanced at him and caught his mischievous grin. "She's a fine lady, and he's a fine man, so why not! Besides, it's up to them now."

They had arrived at the stables, and Maxi quickly checked in with the owner. In a few minutes, they were on their way back to the boarding house. "I didn't need to worry about the horses. They have been pampered, as well they deserve. Let's hurry, though, and get back. I wouldn't want to miss anything."

The rest of the evening was lively and fun. Angel played a variety of music. The songs with quick tempos required clapping and a lot of toe-tapping from the audience. She played favorite hymns, then a classical piece that touched her emotionally and brought tears to her eyes. "Sorry," she murmured quietly, dabbing at the trickling tears. "That one reminds me of my ma. We used to play it together."

Mrs. Frazier stood. "That's okay, Angel, we understand. You look tired, though, and it's been a long day for all of us. You don't need to play anymore tonight." She addressed the others. "By the way, tomorrow is Sunday, and you are all invited to dinner after church services." She tempted them even more by mentioning fried chicken, all the trimmings, and apple pie for dessert.

Jim spoke first. "I'm sure sorry to decline the offer, but I have to leave bright and early. I might lose my job if I don't stay on schedule. There's plenty of men who would be glad to take it if I got fired." He looked at Maxi. "When you and Angel get to Denver, look me up. If I'm free, I'll show you around town."

"That sounds great! Thanks, Jim."

He said good night to everyone and went to his room.

"Guess I better get on home." Alex Phelps turned to Mrs. Frazier. "I'd be glad to accept your invitation." He then smiled at Carol, showing a deep dimple at the corner of his mouth. "I truly enjoyed visiting with you, Carol. If you don't object, I'd like to call on you again."

"Please come as often as you can, Alex. After dinner tomorrow, maybe we can go for a buggy ride or a walk."

"A splendid idea! If you will allow me, I'll bring the buggy and pick you up for church in the morning."

"That will be fine. Come a little before ten, and I'll be ready."

Alex bid everyone a good night, and Mrs. Frazier saw him to the door. Then she turned and declared to Carol, "Well, that was a pleasant surprise! A little romance is just what this house needs."

They laughed as Carol blushed. "He's a fine man. I'll have to admit he surprised me by showing interest in me for the first time. I've caught him watching me but couldn't tell what he was thinking."

The ladies bid good night to each other and went to their rooms as Mrs. Frazier locked up for the night.

Maxi and Angel couldn't settle down right away. They blew out the lamp, quickly undressed, then snuggled down into the soft quilts. "Phooey, Angel! I should have looked for nightgowns in the General Store but just didn't think about it then."

"Could be there wasn't any if all the women do their own sewing. I don't remember seeing any gowns. I had to leave mine at Aunt Justeen's 'cause there wasn't room in my case for it." She was silent for several moments. "Seems like a long time ago." Changing the subject, she asked, "What do you think about staying here another day, then leaving on Monday? I really do want to go to church in the morning. I haven't been in months."

"That's fine with me, Angel. How do you like Colorado City? Do you think you might stay here?"

"I don't know yet. I need to pray and ask God where he wants me. Maybe tomorrow I can find some quiet time and pray. It's an important decision for me. Will you pray with me about it, Maxi?"

"I'll try, but I haven't been praying much lately. Seems God doesn't hear my prayers. But I'll try." A few moments later, she said, "If it matters, Angel, I want you to go with me."

Angel was touched and softly replied, "It matters, Maxi. Thank you."

They lay in the darkness, each with their own thoughts, until finally, they drifted into a deep sleep.

CHAPTER 8

SUNDAY DAWNED BRIGHT and clear. Jim Clark left early, taking his breakfast to eat on the way. A light breakfast awaited everyone else. Alex Phelps picked up Carol Conrad, as promised, and Mrs. Frazier, Maxi, and Angel walked to church, Angel's prized violin wrapped securely and held protectively in her arms.

"We're blessed to have a fine, young pastor, Reverend Daniel Scoggins, whom we all love. He doesn't have a wife, so that keeps the ladies of the church busy taking care of him. I thought he might show an interest in Carol, but can't say that he has. A couple of other ladies in town have their eye on him. Can't tell that he's interested in them either. Maybe he's just not ready for a wife. The church building burned down last year. We finally finished rebuilding and got it ready for services a couple of weeks ago. We're rather proud of it."

As they arrived at the church, the girls voiced their approval of the new and clean-looking building. Window dressings and other furnishings were arranged tastefully and showed a caring congregation worshiped there. The people themselves were warm and welcoming and very eager to meet Maxi and Angel. There were a lot of introductions before the service began. Alex and Carol sat together, smiling, engrossed in quiet conversation.

Mrs. Frazier ushered the girls toward the front to find a seat, then glanced around, locating her pastor. Maxi watched with interest as Mrs. Frazier quickly made her way over to the man. He stopped politely when Mrs. Frazier detained him between the piano and pulpit, giving her his full attention. The two conversed a moment; then, the pastor looked in Angel and Maxi's direction. He acknowledged them with a courteous smile and nodded. Mrs. Frazier then seated herself, her face like that of a proud mother whose child had accomplished something stupendous.

The pastor sat down in a chair behind the pulpit, a cue to a young man who appeared at the front. He rallied the congregation's attention and started the service with a prayer. Then lively, upbeat singing followed, led by another somewhat older man. After the offering plates were passed around, Reverend Scoggins walked to the pulpit, looking out at the people expectantly.

"Before I begin my sermon, we have a special treat this morning. A young lady, whom I'm sure you have all heard about by now and most of you have met, is going to play her violin for us. Miss Angel Hawkins, will you come up now?" He stepped back to his chair as people stirred and shuffled, straining to see the guest musician. By the time Angel stood at the front, the small congregation was still and attentive, with all eyes on her.

Maxi felt a little nervous for her friend. She watched Angel smile shyly at the people she faced. Then she placed her violin under her chin and drew the bow across the strings, and all nervousness dissolved. The congregation fell so quiet you could hear a pin drop. It was beautiful violin music at its best. Her white curls were tied back with the new pink ribbon, and she had on her pink church dress with the multicolored flowers. God's presence was evident, a sense of peace and love filling the room. The listeners were so mesmerized that no one noticed the pastor slip to the front row to watch Angel play—that is, no one except Maxi!

No wonder you love her so much, God. She's so special. Maxi just happened to glance at the pastor while he sat spellbound and was not taking his eyes off the lovely young lady who looked the perfect picture of a young pastor's wife. A tiny scowl worked its way between Maxi's eyebrows. *I wonder what he's thinking! Could be he just likes the music…right? Well, jangle my spurs! I'm not stupid and neither is he. I wouldn't blame him one bit if he fell on his knees right here and begged her to marry him! Maybe we shouldn't have stayed another day to go to church.* Maxi felt a little guilty about her thoughts and determined to bring them back into good graces. She forced herself to pay attention to Angel rather than look at the pastor.

The medley was finished, and more than a few were dabbing at their eyes. "For this last song, I'd like for everyone to sing along. I'm sure you know it, so stand and sing with me." Obviously, they all knew the song, for their singing raised the roof with "When We All Get to Heaven."

Reverend Scoggins preached with passion about the resurrection of Christ. He said because of Christ's victory over death and the grave, all can have the hope of heaven. One only has to do what Romans chapter ten says: confess Jesus as Lord and believe God raised Him from the dead, and you will be saved. For it's with your heart you believe, and with your mouth you confess, resulting in salvation. Maxi was so absorbed in the sermon, she couldn't know that Angel was praying earnestly for her.

The service finally ended with the pastor's prayer.

They walked back to the boarding house in excellent mood, especially Angel. "It was so good to be in church again. I loved it! Everyone was friendly and thanked me for playing. I really enjoyed the pastor's sermon. I thought it was very inspiring. You have a wonderful pastor, Mrs. Frazier."

"I'm glad you both came with me this morning. We did have a good service, especially with you playing for us, Angel. Well, look! Alex's buggy is in front of the house. Guess I better get our meal on the table."

Mrs. Frazier opened the door to the house and called out, "Anyone hungry?" Grinning broadly, she took her hat off, hanging it on a peg beside the door. She was a woman on an important mission, feeding a group of hungry people! Quickly, she disappeared into the kitchen.

"Let's set the table for her, Angel."

"Sure! You get started while I put my violin away."

They were almost finished with the task when they heard knocking on the door. Mrs. Frazier called from the kitchen. "Will one of you girls get the door for me?"

Maxi opened the door to see the pastor standing on the porch. "Hello, Reverend Scoggins. Won't you come in? I'll go get Mrs. Frazier."

Right then, Mrs. Frazier appeared, bearing a large platter of fried chicken. "Oh, hello, Pastor. You came just in time. We're ready to sit down and eat."

"Thanks, but I didn't really come to eat, Mrs. Frazier. I would like to speak to Miss Hawkins, if I may."

"Of course, you can speak to Angel. And you can eat too. You know you have an open invitation to eat here any time. Do you have any other invitations?"

"Well, no," he admitted.

"Then you just hang your hat by the door. I'll not hear another word about it. Where is Angel?"

"Right here, Mrs. Frazier."

"Daniel is going to eat with us. Then he wants to speak to you."

"Oh, okay." Angel set down a large bowl of potato salad. "Hello, Pastor Scoggins."

Carol and Alex had entered the room by that time. and all eyes were on Angel, making her feel uncomfortable. Mrs. Frazier, the perfect hostess, kept things moving. "Okay, now, everyone find a place to sit, and let's eat. Pastor, will you say grace, please, when everyone is seated?"

Polite and friendly conversation flowed along with the food, but Maxi's thoughts were troubling her. *What could the preacher want to talk to Angel about? You'd think if he wanted to thank her for playing her violin, he would just say so.*

By the time they'd finished their apple pie, she knew the pastor was interested in Angel. It was the way he tried to draw her out in conversation, the way he looked at her with that charming smile. *A person would have to be blind or stupid not to see what's happening. I wish we'd left yesterday!* She inwardly scolded herself, but it didn't help. *Oh, fiddlesticks! Who could blame him? She would make a perfect preacher's wife. I wonder what she's thinking.*

Alex stood and reached for Carol's hand. "If everyone will excuse us, Carol and I are going for a buggy ride. Thank you, Mrs. Frazier, for the wonderful meal."

"We enjoyed having you, Alex. You two have a nice ride. Now, the rest of you go and relax. Daniel, you know where that bench is out back under the big cottonwood tree. You and Angel can go out there to have your little chat. Maxi, you're welcome to the parlor. When I finish in the kitchen, I'm going to lie down and read for a while."

Maxi stood and grabbed the empty pie pan. "I'd rather help you, Mrs. Frazier. It's about time I made myself useful."

"Well, I won't turn down any help, but please don't feel like you have to."

"I don't, really. I want to help."

Mrs. Frazier soon became aware of Maxi's sullen behavior. She scrapped the plates a little too aggressively, wiped the table a little too roughly, conversation was limited to one or two words, and she was clearly wrapped up in a bad mood. Finally, Mrs. Frazier asked pointedly, "You worried about Angel?"

Maxi tensed, her eyes downcast, her hands soaking in the hot, soapy water. "No, I'm not worried about Angel. I'm worried about me. I haven't known her very long, but I've come to care for her a lot, like I would if she was my own sister. Every day I find out how special she is, and I honestly don't want to go on without her!" She lifted a glass from the dishpan, jammed the dishrag into it, and scrubbed furiously.

Mrs. Frazier thought the conversation had ended, but then Maxi started in again.

"But I have to. The last thing my pa asked of me was to find my brother. So that's what I'm going to do. It just makes me sad to think about leaving her." Another glass suffered a brutal scrubbing. Then she half-turned toward Mrs. Frazier, voicing her true fears. "Do you think Reverend Scoggins is interested in her?"

Ah, so that's where the rub is. Mrs. Frazier knew she had to answer carefully. "Well…I'd have to be blind not to see that he's attracted to her. I've never seen him show any woman in town special attention, other than what a pastor normally would." She paused a few moments before going on. "He's a fine man. Any woman would be lucky to capture his heart."

"I'm sure you're right. And any man would be blessed to capture hers. She's smart and old enough to make up her own mind. I guess I shouldn't worry about her."

"Angel is not the only one who's smart. Just pray for her, Maxi. That's the best thing to do. Then let God speak to her heart."

"Of course, you're right, but I'm not very good at praying."

"Then, I'll just pray for the both of you."

"Thank you, Mrs. Frazier."

"You're welcome, dear. Now you go rest awhile. I'll dump the dishwater."

Daniel Scoggins waited for Angel to seat herself on the bench, then sat a polite distance from her. They were out back of the house, under the old cottonwood tree. "Mrs. Frazier and I sit out here often, to talk and pray together. She's an incredible person."

"I agree. She's been wonderful." Angel sat quietly, waiting for the pastor to continue. She felt like the bench was getting smaller. Her proximity to this man of God was causing her anxiety, and she wasn't quite sure she knew what to do with it. *I feel like a little girl waiting to be scolded. How silly of me. He's just a man, a very nice-looking man, I'll have to admit. Why does he want to speak to me? Maybe I did something wrong this morning…get a grip, Angel Hawkins, and just ask him.*

"Is there something—"

"I just wanted to—"

They looked at each other and laughed.

"I'm sorry," he said. "You go first. What were you going to say?"

"I was just going to ask if something was wrong."

"Oh, no, nothing's wrong. I just didn't get a chance to talk to you this morning after church."

"You were so busy with your congregation that I didn't get a chance to talk to you either. I wanted to tell you how much I enjoyed your sermon. It was so timely too. Maxi is struggling with her relationship with Christ, and you made the scripture so clear. I'm sure God will use it to help her understand. I don't know if you've been told or not, but she lost her father about a week ago. I think she's questioning God's love for her."

"That's a hard one when you lose a loved one. I'll pray for her to understand and receive Christ into her heart. What about you, Miss Hawkins? You talk about Christ like you know him in a personal way."

"Yes, I do. My pa was a preacher for the mountain people in Arkansas where I grew up." Angel liked talking about her old home and began to relax. "I grew up knowing the consequences of sin and the gift of salvation that Jesus provided for us by his death. I gave my life to him when I was ten years old." She looked down where her hands lay folded in her lap. "Since my pa and ma died, I don't know what I would have done without God's love and presence with me."

Daniel didn't respond for a long time. Angel timidly looked up into the pastor's face. His pale blue eyes looked back, glistening with unshed tears. Her stomach flip-flopped, causing her to look quickly back down at her hands.

Daniel cleared his throat. "Miss Hawkins—"

"Please call me Angel."

"Okay, Angel. I want to tell you that you've touched my life today. When you played your violin this morning, it blessed me more than I can say. I could feel the presence of God, and somehow, it drew me closer to him. That's what I really came to tell you. But since visiting with you, I would like to ask if I may call on you this next week. Would you mind?"

Angel's head came up with a jerk. She looked into his eyes again and realized he was serious, very serious. Slowly, a pink blush bloomed on her cheeks.

"I'm sorry, Angel, I've embarrassed you. Please forgive me for being so bold. It wasn't very thoughtful of me to blurt it out so quickly. Now I'm embarrassed."

Angel laughed. "Please don't be. You just really surprised me. I've never had anyone want to come calling on me. I feel so…I don't know…honored. If I stay in Colorado City, there's nothing I would enjoy more than to have you call on me." Her face quickly clouded to doubt as she gazed up into the heavens. "But I don't know if I'll be staying here. Maxi is leaving in the morning. I told her I would pray this afternoon about my decision to go with her or stay here. I want to be in God's will, so I need to spend time alone to pray about it."

"I see. I was told you would probably stay here. Perhaps I misunderstood. I'll have to admit I'm a little selfish. I'd like for you to stay. Just know that I'll be praying with you about your decision." He rose from the bench. "I should go now. I want to visit one of the members who's been sick. Are you going in?"

"No, I think I'll stay out here. It's so nice." She stood and offered her hand. "Thank you, Pastor Scoggins. I've enjoyed visiting with you."

"It's Daniel. And I've enjoyed visiting with you too. No matter which way God is leading you, I've been blessed to know you. I'll just get my hat and be on my way. Good-bye, Angel."

"Good-bye, Daniel."

He held her hand for a moment longer, then let it slip from his. He turned and walked to the door without looking back.

What a wonderful man! God, please help me know what to do.

She sat on the bench for a while longer, then went in. Finding Maxi asleep on the parlor couch, she studied her for a bit, taking in her resolute features, her sturdy shoulders and strong but feminine frame. This girl would climb the edge of the earth to find her brother. Nothing would hold her back, and Angel knew it. She took a deep breath. "Hey, sleepyhead. You still want to go for a walk?"

Maxi's eyes fluttered open. "Sure. Is he gone?"

"Yes, he left an hour ago. I've been out back, praying."

"What did he want to talk to you about?"

"You'll never guess."

Maxi stretched and yawned. A smirk appeared on her pretty features as she reached for her boots. "Ha! You'd have to be dimwitted not to see the man is smitten with you. And it's only been one day." She jammed her foot into a boot. "What are you going to do, Angel?"

"I'm going to put on my old dress. Then I'll tell you as we go for our walk."

In a few moments they were out the back door, Maxi leading the way. "Mrs. Frazier said there's a pond back here a ways, to just follow the path, said she walks out here all the time."

A beautiful afternoon awaited the girls. Wild flowers dressed up the scrub brush that grew along the pathway. They walked leisurely, watching a squirrel scamper across the path and disappear into the brush. "I hope the snakes around here keep to themselves." Angel said.

"Me too. I *hate* snakes!" Maxi halted abruptly. She turned to face Angel. "Okay, out with it! Here I am, dying to know what you've decided, and we're talking about snakes! What did you think of Pastor Scoggins? What did he have to say to you?"

Angel grinned mischievously. "If I was mean, I'd keep you in suspense awhile longer. But since I'm such a nice person, I'll go ahead and tell you." She turned back to the path, motioning for Maxi to come along. "Daniel is so wonderful, Maxi."

"Daniel, is it?" Maxi's sarcasm was evident in her voice.

"Yes, he asked me to call him Daniel. He's the kind of man I could only dream of finding. He's a Godly man, one I could marry and serve God with. I will never understand it, but he's not the man for me. I tried hard to hear God tell me to stay and get to know him." With a big sigh, she continued, "It doesn't make sense right now, but I don't feel this is where I belong. So…I'm going with you. If you'll have me."

Maxi felt the urge to jump up and down; she was so excited. Instead, she calmly put her arm around Angel's shoulder. "I could tell this was a hard decision for you, Angel. I wouldn't blame you one bit if you did stay here. I think you'd make a wonderful pastor's wife. But I'm so glad you're going on with me!"

Angel's smile shined. "Thanks, Maxi. Daniel didn't propose to me. He only asked if he could call on me this next week. I'm sure God has a wife in store for him. It just isn't me."

They walked in silence for a ways before Angel asked, "How did you feel about the church service this morning?"

"It was good. I really enjoyed it. It's been a long time since I was in a service like that. The sermon really made me think. I'm not sure I'm going to heaven, and that bothers me. Pa knew he was going to heaven and looked forward to it. He wanted to be with Ma again. I want to be with them too. Do you think God wants me? How can I know? How can I know for sure, Angel?"

"Let's talk about that." They had reached the pond and searched for a place to sit. "Mrs. Frazier probably sits on this log. The grass is all beaten down right here."

"Who could blame her. It's so pretty and peaceful."

"Yes, it is." Angel waited a few moments before she spoke again. She quickly sent a prayer heaven-ward. *Thank you, Father for what you are doing right now and help me to say the right words.* "Maxi, God does want you, don't ever doubt that. But because of your sins, you are not worthy to go to heaven to be with him. No one is. We all deserve death because of our sin. The good news is, he loves us so much that he provided a way for us to be in heaven with him. God's son, Jesus, died in our place as a sacrifice for our sins. But you have to acknowledge that. You have to talk to God, tell him you know you've sinned. Do you understand what sin means?"

"Sure, I do know that."

"Okay, when you talk to God, tell him you know you've sinned, that you're sorry, and you want to give your life to him. Tell him that you accept the gift that Jesus gave to you by dying on the cross."

"That's all?"

"Simply put, yes. But Jesus dying was no small thing. Can you imagine what it must be like to watch your only son die for a bunch of people who don't deserve it?"

"I'd never thought about that, Angel."

"It has to be a decision you make from your heart. Then you can know and trust that God will do his part. The Bible states, 'Whosoever shall call upon the name of the Lord shall be saved.' Would you like to do that now? If you want me to leave for a while so you can pray, I will. Or I'll stay right here with you."

"Stay with me, Angel." Maxi closed her eyes, and shortly, she started to pray. "God, thank you for loving me. I'm sorry I haven't done what I should. I know I've sinned, so please forgive me. I want to give my life to you. Please accept me. Take care of my ma and pa. I look forward to seeing them again some day." A long pause was followed by amen.

"Amen," echoed Angel. A sweet spirit filled their hearts and bound the girls together. Angel saw tears in Maxi's eyes that mirrored her own. "Maxi, you are really my sister now, in a special, spiritual way." For the first time since they met, the girls hugged each other.

The sun had dipped low by the time they started back to the house. "The mosquitoes are coming out. Let's hurry!" Angel urged as she slapped a big one that landed on her arm.

A note from Mrs. Frazier told them she was visiting friends and to help themselves to whatever snack they wanted. A piece of cold chicken and a couple of rolls and butter with a glass of lemonade made them happy. They decided to turn in as soon as possible and get an early start in the morning. They sorted and packed their belongings, said good night, and fell asleep in a very short time.

Early the next morning, Mrs. Frazier greeted them cheerfully at breakfast. "My goodness, I'm sure going to miss you two around here. It's only been two days, but I'm awishin' you could stay."

"Sorry, but we do have to go." Maxi sipped her hot coffee. "I wish we could take you with us. We're sure going to miss this good cooking!"

"I agree with that," Angel nodded. "We'll never forget you, Mrs. Frazier. You've been so good to us. Will you do something for me?"

"If I can, Angel. What is it?"

"Give Daniel a message for me. Tell him thank you for his prayers. Maxi gave her life to Christ yesterday, and I know what I need to do to be in God's will. He'll understand."

Mrs. Frazier brightened. "Is that true, Maxi?"

"Yes, it's true."

"Well, no wonder you look so happy this morning. I'm truly glad for you. I'll be sure and give that good news to Daniel."

"Thank you. We really need to get going, Angel. Let's get our things now before we change our minds and stay."

They excused themselves from the table and went to gather their belongings. Minutes later, as they stepped from their room, they were surprised to see an army officer in the front doorway talking to Mrs. Frazier. She directed her gaze toward the girls and informed them, "Your escort is here."

The girls stopped and stared. Maxi stepped forward then. "What are you talking about, Mrs. Frazier?"

"Lieutenant Wade Castor here says he is to escort the two of you to Denver." Her shoulders rose in a shrug as she stood there looking perplexed.

Maxi swiftly pulled her thoughts together. "Lieutenant Castor, I don't understand. We didn't ask for an escort, and it's really not necessary for you to see us to Denver."

"Begging your pardon, ma'am, but it truly is necessary. I have my orders. The commander of the fort said I was to see that you get to Denver without a scratch, or he would skin us all alive. He said we would be sorry we ever joined the army if any harm came to either one of you. Furthermore, he said he would not have any

Indian chief taking better care of our women than the US army. So you see, we don't have a choice in the matter."

Mrs. Frazier grinned. "I quite agree with you, Lieutenant Castor."

Maxi and Angel looked at each other in bewilderment, then shrugged. "I guess we don't have a choice. We need to get our horses and stop at the general store for a few supplies," Maxi told the lieutenant.

"Miss, you don't need a thing but your personal belongings, of course. We were ordered to take good care of you, so you don't need to buy a thing."

As they stepped out onto the porch, all three women stopped dead in their tracks. There, in the dusty street, were two orderly rows of mounted military men, about twenty in all.

"I do declare! I've never seen anything quite so magnificent! What an escort you two are getting. Almost makes me want to go with you," Mrs. Frasier said.

Two soldiers rushed up the steps and took the saddlebags from the girls. One of the men reached for Angel's wicker case, but she held on firmly. "Thank you, but I'll carry this case."

The soldier looked at the lieutenant who motioned for him to leave the case alone. He smiled down at Angel, though, as he backed away.

They made quite a show, the young ladies walking down the road with the army following them. Maxi nudged Angel as they made their way to the stable. "Our father must think I'm going to be a lot of trouble."

"What do you mean, Maxi?"

"You get an Indian chief to watch over you. It takes a whole army to watch over me!"

CHAPTER 9

THE FIRST DAY on the way to Denver was pleasant. The soldiers were eager to take care of the girl's every need, from setting up a small tent for them to sleep in, taking care of their horses, cooking the evening meal, to giving Angel instructions on how to use her pistol. When the girls talked together about how pampered they had been, both were surprised to find they were uncomfortable with all the attention. They had both been raised to do their share of the work. The most enjoyable thing that happened was listening to one of the men play his harmonica around the fire that night.

The next morning was a different scene from the previous day, as wind rattled the tent walls, waking the girls early. "I wonder what today is going to be like. The air smells like dust and rain," Maxi mumbled.

"Well, the wind will make us miserable no matter what. If it's cold, it makes us colder. If it's hot, it makes us hotter." Groaning,

Angel pulled her blanket over her head. "Do I have to get up now? It's still dark."

"Go ahead and stay there awhile, grumpy, there's not much going on out there." A gust of wind shook the tent sending Maxi under her blanket again. "Maybe I'll stay here awhile longer too."

They didn't get to linger, for sounds of activity in the camp grew louder as the soldiers began their day. "I guess we might as well get up, Angel. We wouldn't want to keep the army waiting. Besides, I think I smell coffee." Pulling on her boots, Maxi said, "I'm going to slip out to the bushes at the side of the tent before it gets light."

Throwing back her blanket, Angel sat up and grabbed her shoes. "That's a good idea. It's hard to have any privacy with twenty men hanging around."

The soldiers made quick work of breaking camp. Breakfast consisted of whatever they could carry with them. A short time later, they were all in their saddles, headed north. A smattering of rain fell every now and then, but it was the wind that made their ride miserable. Dust swirled everywhere, coating everything it touched, especially their noses and mouths. But as luck would have it, the relentless wind had chased the clouds away, and by noon, ole Sol was making a welcome appearance.

"I'm sure glad that wind died down."

"So am I. That sun feels good."

"You were right, Angel, the wind makes everything worse. Guess I shouldn't complain. It could have poured rain all morning along with the wind."

The military patrol and their two charges were encountering more and more traffic on the road as they got closer to Denver. Mostly, it was men on horseback. A few were farm wagons with women and children. They passed a small wagon train headed in Denver's direction. Making good time was difficult because everyone wanted to know the latest news.

"We sure are getting some funny looks from people, Maxi. I wonder if they think we're criminals arrested by the army, or maybe they think we're very important women who need protecting."

"I suppose people would be curious. It's sure hard to make any time when they all want to stop and talk. I guess the army is the natural source of information about Indians or outlaws."

"I'm glad we have an escort. Some of the men we've passed were really creepy looking," Angel shuddered. "Especially the one on that big, black horse."

"Yeah, I saw him. Are you forgetting our father who is around somewhere?"

"Maybe for a minute. Thanks for the reminder." Angel couldn't help but smile even if she felt scolded for her lapse of faith.

The weather turned quite warm by mid afternoon. Corporal Jamison, who had been riding beside the lieutenant, slowed his mount until he was riding next to Maxi.

"One of our men knows about a small lake out here. It's west of the road about a mile on. Lieutenant Castor says we'll find it and make camp there for the night. He's going to send a few of our best hunters out to find some fresh meat, so with a little luck, we should have a good meal tonight. We'll be taking you into Denver tomorrow. It's not too far away now."

"Thanks, Jamison," Maxi said. I'll have to admit a hot meal sounds really good."

"Guess I better go tell the others what the plan is, and get Cooper up front to lead the way."

A couple of hours later, they were setting up camp by the lake. The girl's tent was being assembled, and their horses were taken care of. "Here we are again, Angel, with everything being done for us. Why don't we check out the lake? Maybe we can find a good place to wash off some of the dust."

After washing, they went back to the tent to stretch out for a while. They savored the quiet, restful time. The door flap was pulled open to let in fresh air, and they listened as a bird in the bushes sang its heart out. Maxi finally spoke. "I've been thinking about something, Angel. I noticed you have a Bible, and since I have my pa's, well, I was wondering..."

Angel rolled to her side and propped herself up on an elbow so she could see Maxi. "What? What are you wondering?"

"Well, if we could read the Bible together and say a prayer before we go to sleep—that is, if you want to. What do you think?"

"What do I think? Maxi, I would dearly love it! I'm so glad you want to. It will be good for both of us."

Maxi was so encouraged by her enthusiasm that she asked something else. "Another thing. Will you play your violin tonight? I think the men will really enjoy it. But more than that, I would love it. You're so blessed to have had a mother who taught you to play so well. I guess that's one thing I missed in my life, not having my mother around to teach me things. My pa did the best he could. He loved me and gave me a good life, but sometimes I wonder about all the things I've missed."

Angel's thoughts turned to her own experience. "I know what you mean. I feel the same way about not having my pa around. I guess we'll never know what all we've missed. I've found I'm better off not to dwell on it. I just try to remember the good times we had together."

They were quiet for a while longer, each with her own thoughts. Then Angel said, "By the way, I'll play tonight if it works out. Let's wait and see."

They lay in the silence of the tent but could easily hear the men out at the lake. Very solemnly, Angel said, "I hope a person can't die from too much attention because if it were possible, we will surely die before this night is over."

"Angel, if you get me to giggling, I'll throw you out of this tent!"

It was a good thing the girls rested and a very good thing a person couldn't die from too much attention. They got just that, a lot of attention. The hunters came in with a deer, so fresh venison was their evening meal. As they were finishing supper, the lieutenant was approached by one of the soldiers. "Sir, there are two wagons coming into this area. Looks like families in them, sir."

"Private, when they get closer have one of the men from the wagons come and talk with me."

The wagons did indeed turn out to be two families, with children too numerous to count. They were from Missouri looking for land to farm. The man in charge, a Mr. Croy, told the lieutenant that they would like to camp on the other side of the lake. "We won't be any trouble, Lieutenant. Someone in Denver told us about this area and the lake. We're going to check it out tomorrow."

"That should be quite all right, Mr. Croy. One thing I will ask of you though. When everyone heads to their beds, I'd ask that you all stay close to your wagons. I'll have men patrolling the area. Wouldn't want anyone to get hurt if one of my men mistook them for a troublemaker."

"Sounds reasonable. Thank you, Lieutenant."

When all the chores of the evening were finished, the soldiers began to settle in for the night. Soon, the sounds of a harmonica came wafting through the still air. After a couple of songs, Angel approached the private who was playing. "Private, would you mind if I played along with you on my violin?"

He looked surprised to see her standing there with her violin in hand. "As one musician to another, Miss Angel, I would be proud to have you play with me. I'm Private Downs." Angel found a place to sit next to the private. "What would you like to play, Miss Angel?"

"It doesn't matter, you just take off, and I'll catch up."

When the two musicians joined their instruments, they soon had everyone's attention. A few of the men eventually began to sing along.

> Oh, don't you remember sweet Betsy from Pike
> Who crossed the big mountains with her lover Ike.
> With two yoke of oxen, a large yellow dog

And a tall Shang-hai rooster an' one spotted hog
Sayin' Good-by Pike county, farewell for a while.
We'll come back again when we pan out our pile.

Sounds of dogs barking, roosters crowing, and Private Tucker giving a perfect squeal of a pig, were inserted in all the right places. Even Lieutenant Castor couldn't help but laugh at the silly additions to the song. Before they could start another song, one of the night patrol came into the firelight. He approached Lieutenant Castor. "Sir, the family from the wagons are coming. They'll be here shortly."

"Okay, Private, thank you for the notice. You can return to patrol."

"Yes, sir."

Everyone had heard the report and were looking into the darkness. Finally, a group of people came into view. "Don't mean to interrupt, Lieutenant."

"That's all right, Mr. Croy. Is there something wrong?"

"No, sir, we just heard the music, and there's nothing we like better than a good old singing. My daughter, Sarah, plays the accordion, and my brother, Zeb, over there, picks a guitar better than most. We was wonderin' if we might join you for a spell. If it's not to your liken, we'll go on back and have our own camp fire singin'."

"We don't mind at all, Mr. Croy. Tell your people to come on in and find a spot to sit."

"Thank you, Lieutenant." He turned to his family. "Come on in, Zeb, an' bring Sarah with you. Let's hear what you all can wring out of those instruments."

The musicians settled close to Angel and Private Downs. "Is there anything you would like to start with, Miss Sarah?" Private Downs asked.

"I can play 'Camp-Town Race Track.'" Sarah was shy but eager.

"Start it off then. We'll be right behind you."

Sarah was good on her small accordion. She started the song, and the others joined in. On the second time through, one of the men started singing.

> Camp-town ladies sing this song, doo-dah, doo-dah,
> Camp-town race track five miles long, oh doo-dah day.

When that verse was finished, someone else added a new verse. By the time they got to the fifth verse, everyone was laughing and having a good time. Sarah had by then lost some of her shyness. "Pa, why don't you call a square dance?"

"Well, we'll have to ask the lieutenant." He looked at Lieutenant Castor for approval.

The evening was going smoothly, so Lieutenant Castor agreed.

Mr. Croy's voice boomed, "Okay, everyone, find a partner! We're going to stir up the dust on this here prairie with a little square dance!"

No one had to be told twice. A scramble ensued as soldiers and the Croy Clan searched for partners and space for several groups of four. Maxi had about ten men head for her at the same time. But they gave way for Corporal Jamison as he outranked most of them. "Okay, Jamison, you get the first dance, but don't think you'll get any more," one of the men teased.

An odd mixture of soldiers, women, and children danced under the stars that night. Maxi didn't get to rest once. She danced with all of the soldiers who weren't on patrol. Angel and Sarah were coaxed into leaving their instruments and dancing with some of the soldiers. Sarah was a pretty girl, which didn't go unnoticed by any of the young men. During a pause, she approached Maxi and whispered, "For this next dance, do you think you could get one of the men to ask my sister to dance? She's shy and won't come close, but she's back in the dark by the tent. She loves to dance, but is terribly shy."

Maxi turned to locate the shy girl that no one had noticed. "That shouldn't be a problem. I'll see what I can do."

Just then Private Tucker walked up to Maxi. "It's my turn, Miss Maxi, if you don't mind dancing with a big ox."

"Tucker, I wouldn't mind at all dancing with you, but I have a favor to ask. There's a girl over by our tent. She's shy and won't come over, so would you mind asking her to dance this one with you?"

Disappointment was all over Tucker's face, but he couldn't say no to Maxi. "Just for you, Miss Maxi, but I get the next one."

"I promise, Tucker, if I can still stand, you get the next one." She watched Tucker fade into the shadows and, when she turned back, was surprised to find Lieutenant Castor standing before her.

"Maxi," he said, "this next dance will be a waltz. Would you mind at all dancing this one with me?"

"I will be happy to."

Lieutenant Castor took her hand as the music began. She spotted Private Tucker and smiled. "Will you look at that, Lieutenant." There on Private Tucker's arm was a young woman about eighteen or nineteen. She was a bit taller than Maxi and had long, wavy, dark-brown hair. She had a figure most women would die for. "I don't think Tucker is going to mind not dancing with me now. Look at your men, Lieutenant," Maxi laughed. "They can't figure out where she came from."

Lieutenant Castor looked around at his men and Private Tucker as the waltz continued. "For the safety of the young women, I may have to call it a night soon."

"The only danger here is that I might not be able to walk tomorrow. When you do decide to call it a night, would you ask Angel to play her medley of hymns? I think you'll be surprised and glad you asked her. I've never heard anyone play like she does."

"Of course. That sounds like a perfect ending to a very enjoyable evening."

After a couple of more songs, Lieutenant Castor got everyone's attention. "We need to call it a night now, but before we go, Angel, would you favor us with your medley of hymns?"

Everyone found a place to sit. Maxi noticed most of the soldiers had a child on his lap. She watched the listeners around her, firelight dancing on their faces as they sat entranced. *Oh, Angel, I'm so blessed to have you for a friend and sister.*

As Angel finished playing and lowered her violin, she told the gathering, "I have enjoyed tonight more than I can say. I feel like I have made some very special friends. Thank you, everyone. I'll say good night now."

People were reluctant to move until Private Downs, who played the harmonica, spoke into the silence, "Gosh, Miss Angel, I'm not a musician at all, compared to you."

"You're a fine musician, Private Downs. I was blessed to have played with you." The group slowly began to disperse. Angel found Sarah and Zeb and thanked them for participating.

Mr. Croy spoke to Lieutenant Castor, "Thanks, Lieutenant, for letting us join you all tonight. It's a night we'll not be forgettin'."

"I won't be forgetting it either, Mr. Croy. You have a fine family, and I wish you luck in finding your farm. This seems like good country. Maybe your search for the right place will soon be over." The men shook hands, and the Croy clan bunched and headed out into the night toward their wagons.

Sarah turned and ran back to Maxi. "Thanks, Maxi, my sister had a nice time." Her eyes twinkled as she added in a whisper, "I think she's quite smitten with the redheaded Private Tucker. He asked her if he could find her and pay a visit if he ever got over this way again." Sarah giggled as she headed off toward her family, disappearing into the darkness.

The girls finally made it to their tent and collapsed on their beds. "I'm exhausted, Angel, but I had a wonderful time. What nice people."

"They sure are. I'm going to miss all these men. I haven't enjoyed myself like that in a long time. By the way, let's make our Bible reading and prayer a short one tonight. I'm so tired I can hardly move."

"Ha! You don't know what tired is. You only had to wrestle with a violin, but I had to wrestle with a bunch of lonely, love-starved soldiers."

One look at Maxi, and Angel burst into a gale of giggles. Between bursts, she managed to say, "I'm sorry...I'm just tired... can't help it."

The giggles were contagious, and Maxi joined in. "Stop it, Angel!" she finally ordered, breathless.

"I can't..." She had a hiccup.

What they couldn't hear was the conversation across the campground. "Think they're laughing at us?"

"Who cares."

"If I could hear that sound every night for the rest of my life, I would die a happy man."

Echoes of amen were heard around the flickering campfires. For just a split second, the lieutenant wondered if his men had been praying, but he quickly dismissed the thought. "Not a chance," he murmured softly. He fell asleep with a smile on his face.

The next morning, noises of horses moving around were the first sounds that penetrated Maxi's dreamless sleep. "Ooh! I haven't even stepped on them yet, but I can tell you I won't be walking anymore than necessary today. My feet hurt!"

"Poor little Princess Warrior. She can shoot men down, shoot the head off a snake, but can't take a little dancing."

"Doesn't the Bible say something about compassion?"

"Oh, all right. Scoot over here, and I'll give you one of my famous foot rubs."

"You will? Really?"

"Yes, now scoot. I've never heard you whine before. It's not very becoming, you know."

"How famous are your foot rubs?"

"Very."

Maxi stuck her feet in Angel's face. "Then show me."

Angel pulled her wicker case over and began searching for something in it. "Here it is, my foot potion." She quickly began kneading the bottoms of Maxi's feet, applying deep pressure to the heels, then working up to the toes. She then applied some salve from the tin she had pulled out of her case and began massaging again.

"Angel, you can never leave me. You and that case will have to stay with me forever…and give me foot rubs."

"I charge a lot for a foot rub. You couldn't afford me. This foot rub is going to cost you a flannel nightgown."

"You've got it! And I'm going to throw in some scented soap. I like a rose scent, how about you?"

"Lilac-scented soap would be wonderful. Now, let's get out there so we can get to Denver, or you might have to dance tonight too."

A man called from the outside the tent, "Breakfast and coffee are ready."

"Let's hurry, Angel! Denver's waiting."

CHAPTER 10

THE LIEUTENANT RODE right to the sheriff's office when they arrived in Denver. He instructed half the men to enjoy leave for five hours and the other half to set up camp outside of town. After five hours, they were to trade places. Whoops and hollers sounded from the men as they scattered but not before waving good-bye to the girls.

"Let's go meet the sheriff," the lieutenant said. "He should be able to tell you the best place to stay."

Entering a small nondescript building, they found the sheriff sitting behind a cluttered desk. He looked up and smiled in greeting. "Howdy, I'm Sheriff Crawford. What can I do for you?"

The lieutenant stepped forward offering his hand to the sheriff. "I'm Lieutenant Castor, Sheriff. This is Maxine Mayfield and Angel Hawkins. My men and I have escorted them here to Denver."

"What's the army doing escorting civilians these days?"

"It was orders, Sheriff. You'll enjoy the ladies' story, but I think they should tell it."

Maxi looked at the lieutenant. "We won't ever forget our time with you and your men. You can certainly report to your commander that your mission has been accomplished with our complete satisfaction. Thank you, again, Lieutenant."

"It's been my pleasure. I wish the west had more ladies like you two." He shook hands with both of them. "Take care, and if you're ever in our area again, look us up."

Sheriff Crawford proved to be a perfect audience. He sat behind his desk, leaning forward in anticipation, as the girls relayed their story. Sorrow etched his face when Maxi told of her father's accident. When Angel told of her flight from her Aunt Justeen's ranch, he looked like he might explode. "I'd like to get my hands on those two!" His fist pounded the desk top.

He offered words of admiration for how they tended the Indian boy, and pride shown in his eyes at the part where Maxi shot the good-for-nothing cousin. "You did the right thing, girl. Your pa would've been proud of you."

Disbelief was the only word to describe the sheriff's expression when he heard the next part of the story. "He gave you *gifts* and *Indian names?*" He sat shaking his head. "Then declared his Indian scouts would protect you? If you say it's true, it must be. But it's hard to believe. Never heard anything like it before. Leave it to Red Fox to do the unusual. No doubt you made a big impression on him."

Chuckling out loud, he continued, "I know the major at Bent's Fort, and I can see him huffing and puffing over Red Fox protecting two white girls. If I remember right, I think he has a daughter about the same age as you two. Anyway, I'm glad he sent his men with you. What are your plans while you're here? How can I help you?"

"I'm not going to stay long, Sheriff. I need to find a way to get to the Wind River territory up north. My brother left two years ago to start a cattle ranch up there. We got a letter from him asking my pa and me to come help him with the ranch. It was my pa's dying wish that I go find my brother. I know it may seem unwise to you, Sheriff, but I'm determined to go on. I may have to go alone, but I will, if I have to. God has seen me this far. I trust he'll see me the rest of the way."

"There's no doubt he's been watching over you. Does that mean you'll be staying in Denver, Miss Hawkins?"

"I haven't decided yet, Sheriff. I'll need to find a job if I stay. Maxi wants me to go on with her. I have to pray about it and make my decision. If you know of any jobs available, I would appreciate you letting me know."

"I'll do that, Miss Hawkins. I'll talk to my wife tonight. She'll probably know more about that than I do. I suppose you need a place to stay. Do you have funds for a boarding house?"

"Yes, that's not a problem," Maxi answered.

"Well, I know of a good one. It's a family establishment by the name of Jordan. They're fine Christian people, run a clean place, don't sell liquor, and the food's good. All that's hard to find in one place. Mrs. Jordan can make the best pie anywhere around the territory. A lot of decent folks are moving to this area, a lot of riffraff too. Denver is going to be a good quality town some day, but right now, it's a little on the rough side. Well, do you want me to take you over, or do you think you can find it?"

"I'm sure we can find it if you point the way. Is there a place to stable our horses?"

"There's a stable right close to the Jordan's. They can point it out to you. Larry Spriggs takes excellent care of the animals left with him."

"Thank you, Sheriff. We appreciate all your help."

"My pleasure. If I have any information for you, I'll leave word at the Jordan's front desk. Now, let me point you in the right direction."

A short time later, fifteen-year-old Lucinda Jordan greeted the girls in the front lobby. After finding out the sheriff had sent them, she led them down a hallway on the first floor. "This is one of our nicest rooms." She opened the door and stepped back so the girls could enter first. Lucinda was pretty with straight, brown hair, slim figure, and eyes that shone with curiosity. "Are you ladies traveling alone?"

Angel and Maxi stared at Lucinda for a moment, then looked at each other and started laughing. Angel explained, "It's a long story, but we did start out alone. God has sent some of the most extraordinary people to escort and protect us."

Lucinda looked confused. "I'd like to hear about it sometime, but we're awfully busy right now. You'll be safe here though. This hall is where my family sleeps. It's the only room on the first floor that we rent out, and that's only to special people. The rest of the guests stay on the second and third floors. Will this room be okay?"

"It's a wonderful room. Perfect for us, don't you think, Maxi?"

"Yes, lovely. I like the two beds. I won't have to put up with you hogging the covers."

Before Lucinda left, she pointed out the livery stable. "The best way to get there is to take your horses back to the main road and go around the field."

When they unloaded what they needed off their horses, they rode to Mr. Spriggs's stable. He was a tall, thin man in overalls who kept his grounds and buildings in excellent condition. Pleased, Maxi made arrangements to leave the horses in his care.

"Shall we go back through the field, Maxi?"

Before she could answer, Mr. Spriggs offered his advice. "Probably be okay, but Ugly stays out there. Just watch out for him"

"Ugly?" they chorused and stared up at the tall man.

"Yeah, that's what I call him. Ugliest creature I ever seen. I recon' it's a dog but never seen one quite like this one. Won't let anyone come near him or touch him. He's so skinny, I feel sorry for him, I throw a bone his way once in a while. There's a path worn through the field, so I figure Mrs. Jordan feeds him too."

"I think we'll take the road then," Maxi decided. "I'm not sure I want to meet Ugly right now." As they walked, they made plans for the day. "Let's hurry and clean up, then go see the town."

"Yeah, definitely clean up first. I'd like to get out of these boy's pants and look decent in case I get a chance to talk to someone about a job."

"I don't mind cleaning up first. It's you talking to someone about a job that I don't like."

"I know you feel that way. But I need to be ready in case God opens a door of opportunity. I can't deny I'm nervous and more than a little anxious about all this."

"I don't blame you. I'm feeling on edge, myself, wondering how I'm going to continue on. I hope Sheriff Crawford comes up with something. Maybe there will be a wagon train going up north, and they'll let me go along, at least to Fort Laramie."

CHAPTER 11

AS ANGEL FINISHED bathing and was trying to tame her wild curls, she was bombarded with anxious thoughts. Her usually strong faith seemed to disappear. *Why am I feeling so panicky? God, help me to lean on you. Show me your will for my life.* She was praying as Maxi came into the room.

"Mrs. Jordan told me about a general store not far from the sheriff's office." Both girls were excited to go shopping in Denver. Maxi, especially animated, was bubbling over as she told what she had learned. "The owner's wife has a room in the back of the store where she fits and sews for women. I want to go there first, if you don't mind."

"No, I don't mind. It should be fun. Maybe I'll get some ideas about a job or even find work there."

Mrs. Buttsman, the owner of the store, welcomed the girls when they entered. She helped them find what they needed.

Maxi put Angel in an embarrassing situation when she told Mrs. Buttsman that Angel was looking for work. The lady told

Angel that she had more help than she needed. Maxi paid for their purchases, and they stepped out on the boardwalk. She knew she was in trouble. "You mad at me?"

"Yes…no. At least I know there's not a job available at the store. I'd never have known if you hadn't said something. Besides, I can't stay mad at you for very long." She paused a few moments. "That was a sneaky thing to do though, putting me on the spot like that."

"I'm sorry. I'll try not to interfere in your business from now on."

"Is that a promise?"

"No. I'll try though." Maxi quickly changed the subject. "I'm hungry. There's a café across the street. Shall we try it out?"

"I'm willing if you are. Just a cold drink of water sounds good."

"I need more than water. Let's cross after these two wagons get by."

There was a help wanted sign in the window of the café they entered. Angel asked about the job and the rotund, sober-looking proprietor apologized. "Sorry, I hired a kid this morning. Just haven't taken the sign down yet."

While eating, Maxi heard two men across the room talking about a wagon train that had left for Fort Laramie two days ago. With a big sigh, she admitted that it was too risky to try and catch up with them. "They probably wouldn't let a single woman join them anyway," she conceded.

Two discouraged young women left the café.

As they walked down the boardwalk, they saw several of the soldiers who had escorted them into Denver. Corporal Jamison waved and yelled for them to wait. Then he ran across the street, dodging a couple of horses. "Nice to see you again. You both look mighty pretty. Did you get all settled in a room?"

"Yes, the sheriff told us of a wonderful place to stay," Maxi answered.

"Good, I'm glad." Then he hesitated. "I hope you won't think I'm butting into your business, but I feel I should tell you that it might not be safe to walk any further down this way. There are a few saloons and other businesses that are starting to get busy about now. A bunch of rough characters down the street act like they're looking for trouble."

"I'm glad you told us, Corporal. We weren't aware of the situation and sure don't want any of that kind of trouble. Thank you. We'll just turn around and head back to the boarding house," Maxi said.

"It was truly good to see you again. I've got to gather up my men and head back to camp. Do you want me to walk you back to your place first?"

Maxi was touched by his kindness but responded, "No, that won't be necessary. I'm sure we'll be safe walking back the way we came. Thanks, anyway."

"Okay then, take care. Good to see you again."

"And you too. Good-bye, Corporal," Maxi said.

"He's such a nice, young man and rather handsome too," Angel remarked.

"Yes, he is. But I don't think he's our type."

"Now just what do you think is our type?" Angel questioned.

"I really don't know. But if he ever comes along, I hope I'll recognize him."

"Maybe we'll just be two old spinsters and this old spinster is going back to her room and take a nap."

And that's just what Angel did. At least she lay down and closed her eyes but couldn't sleep. She tried to read her Bible but couldn't concentrate. Feeling like she was being watched, she looked up.

"I thought you were going to nap," Maxi commented.

"I thought so too. But there's too much to think about. You know, I've always had decisions made for me. I did what my ma and pa told me to do. Before my mother died, she had made all the plans for me to go to Aunt Justeen's. Then, Aunt Justeen planned my escape from her place. And now, you've made most of the decisions for us."

"You made up your own mind about Reverend Scoggins," Maxi couldn't help but remind her.

"That's true. I still wonder, though, if I made the right decision about him and leaving Colorado City."

Angel's forlorn, little face looked so sad. Maxi wanted to encourage her but wasn't sure how. Trying a distraction tactic, she suggested, "Why don't you play your violin? Maybe that'll cheer you up."

"I'm not much in the mood to play. Besides, it might bother someone."

"Not at this time of day. I can't imagine anyone being bothered by your playing. Go ahead and play. We have some time before we go to supper."

"I guess I could play softly. That's hard for me to do though. I get lost in the music and forget about my surroundings."

"Well, I'll tell you if you get too loud."

Just as she said she would, Angel lost herself in her music. Time slipped by, and before she knew it, Maxi said it was time to get ready for supper. "I hate to stop you, but we need to get our shoes on and freshen up."

"I'm glad you suggested that I play. It really did calm me down."

CHAPTER 12

LATER, LUCINDA GREETED them in the dining room. "Good evening. I've been saving you a table by the window. There's a beautiful view of the mountains, and we have such glorious sunsets. I thought you might like that."

"I'm sure we will. Thank you, Lucinda," Angel said.

Once seated, Lucinda told them what was available for the evening meal. "The special is chicken and dumplings with vegetables and fresh bread just out of the oven. Ma will fix steak or eggs if you don't want the special. I can tell you, though, her chicken and dumplings are the best in the area."

"That sounds great. I'll have the special."

"Might as well make that two," Angel agreed.

Lucinda was on her way back with their drinks when she paused, addressing someone in the doorway. "I'll be with you gentleman in a moment," she said, flashing a brilliant smile.

As she put the drinks on the table, Angel glanced up at her. "Are you all right, Lucinda? Your face is really flushed."

"Yes, I'm fine, thank you." She straightened up and took a deep breath.

Still concerned, Angel quietly suggested, "Maybe you could take a moment and get some fresh air. That might help."

"I don't think fresh air will help me right now." She turned back toward the kitchen.

"I wonder what's wrong with her," Angel whispered. "She really did look flustered."

Maxi nodded knowingly. "I'm afraid I'm going to have the same problem."

"What are you talking about, Maxi?"

"Two of the most handsome cowboys I've ever seen just walked through the door! I think my heart might stop beating. When you take a look be prepared for a heart-stopping experience."

Angel rolled her eyes. "Don't be silly." She picked up her glass of water.

Suddenly, the light outside changed, pulling their attention to the sunset. "Oh, Maxi, look at that! That is so beautiful!" The sun had dropped behind the stately mountains, coloring the clouds that hovered over the snow-capped peaks. The sky glowed in vivid hues of magenta, and streaks of deep orange shimmered at the edges, melting into shades of lavender. Light filtered through the clouds sending pillars of dancing radiance along the mountains. Most stunning of all was a brilliant gold light edging the clouds. "It takes my breath away!"

"I know! I've never seen anything to match it!"

They watched the changing skyline until Lucinda brought their food. "Here you are. Nice and hot. What do you think of the sunset?"

"It's spectacular!"

"Magnificent! I'm glad you saved this table for us." Angel's eyes were still on the fading light.

"The view isn't so bad across the room either," Lucinda whispered boldly. She sashayed to another table as Maxi stifled a giggle.

Confused, Angel finally glanced across the room. "Ooh!"

"Angel, you're staring. If you don't look at me right now, you're going to start drooling."

Angel quickly looked down at her food. "I don't drool, Maxi." She took a deep breath while a slightly crooked grin formed on her lips. "I'll have to agree with you, though, they are two of God's finer works. Too bad you're not staying in Denver, Miss Mayfield. Who knows what might happen."

Maxi stole another glance across the room, then dreamily looked back at her friend. "I've made a decision. I really don't want to be a spinster, and I'm going to do everything I can not to be one." Angel clapped her hand over her mouth stifling a giggle.

They were finishing their meal when Sheriff Crawford walked through the dining room door. "Look who just came in," Maxi whispered across the table.

The sheriff paused, tipped his hat to them, then walked to the table where the two cowboys were seated. As the men talked, they kept glancing over at the girls' table.

"Do you get the impression they're talking about us, Angel?"

"I can't imagine why they would be, but yes, I'm getting the same feeling."

Moments later, the two cowboys, along with the sheriff, got up from their table and came toward the girls. The tallest one had dark-brown hair, blue eyes, and broad, well-muscled shoulders. His friend, half a head shorter, had sandy blonde hair that swept his forehead. His keen, hazel eyes immediately locked on Angel's. She admired their clean-shaven faces and nice clothes, and couldn't help but notice how wonderful they smelled.

"Hello, Miss Mayfield, Miss Hawkins. I have a couple of young men here I want you to meet. I asked them to come here tonight so I could introduce the four of you." Nodding toward Mr. Dark-Brown Hair, he said, "This here is Marty Swanson. And this other young man is Justin Myers. Would you mind if we join you for a few minutes?"

"Of course, Sheriff," said Maxi. The girls scooted their chairs over to make room while the men pulled up other chairs and sat down. The blond cowboy seemed to make sure his chair was very close to Angel's. She was nearly afraid to breathe.

Quickly, the sheriff became the center of attention as he told them his plan. "Since I talked with you ladies this morning, I've had an idea rolling around in my mind. I'm not trying to butt into your business or tell you what to do. It's just that you ladies are in need of someone to get you up north, and these men are heading that way. They're taking a herd of cattle back to their ranches. I've known Marty's father for a long time. We did some exploring and trapping years ago. You can't find a better man anywhere. I would trust his son here with getting my own daughter across the country."

Marty started to say something, but the sheriff stopped him. "Now hear me out, son. I know it's asking a lot to be responsible for two young ladies while you're going across country with a bunch of cattle. Truth is, we all need a little help at times, and these ladies do need help. If I understand from what they've told me earlier, they'll go alone if they have to. That's just a hard pill for me to swallow.

"Now, I'm going to leave and let the four of you talk it over. Maybe you can come to some agreement. If you can't, no hard feelings. Miss Mayfield, you let me know what you decide. If it doesn't work out, I'll try to help find another way. Just couldn't think of a better man than Marty here to help you out. Don't sell these ladies short, boys. After hearing their story, I think they have what it takes to make it." He stood and scooted his chair back. "I'll be going now. The pie and coffee are on me."

Both men stood, and Marty offered his hand to the sheriff. "Thanks for the vote of confidence, Sheriff. I'm not sure about all of this, but we can talk it out."

"That's all I ask." Shaking hands with Justin, he said, "Good night, all of you. Have a safe trip back home, Marty, Justin. I'm going to go home and get my supper now."

The men took their seats again, and an uncomfortable silence surrounded the table. Finally, Marty broke in, "Now don't that beat all! I don't know about the rest of you, but I feel like someone just threw me a hornet's nest, and I'm not sure what to do with it."

Nervous chuckles went around the little circle, but as usual, Maxi came to the rescue. "I think we need to know a little more about each other before we can discuss anything important. Would you tell us about your ranches and your families?"

Lucinda brought everyone a piece of pie and more coffee. She seemed to linger longer than necessary as she filled their cups. Then she cleared the supper plates from the table and disappeared into the kitchen.

Maxi and Marty seemed to be comfortable doing the talking, so the other two just sat and listened. Even though she said nothing, Angel was very much aware of the man who smelled so good and sat close to her.

What's that he smells like? I can't quite place it. Whatever it is, I love it. Maybe a fresh pine forest or some kind of spice. She smiled inwardly. *Snap out of it, silly girl. Pay attention to what's being said…why is this cowboy making me feel so weird and wonderful? Silly me. Act normal, breathe! Oh, mice in the pantry! I know he can read my mind and knows exactly what he's doing to me.* As if to prove her point, Justin glanced at her and smiled. Her heart flip-flopped. *I knew it! I knew it! He does know. What am I going to do? Well, I can't run and hide, so I'll just try to calm down and enjoy the scenery. Oh, good one, Angel Hawkins.*

Marty was in the middle of telling about his family's ranch when Angel managed to drag her attention back to the conversation. "The Myers's ranch is only a few miles away from ours. Our fathers had known each other for a long time. They were the first ones to start cattle ranches in that area. My father brought us out first. Then Justin's father went back south and brought his family out."

"Then it's just you and your parents on the ranch?" Maxi asked.

"Well, that's what we started with. Both ranches have grown, and believe me, it's taken a lot of work. That's what this trip is all about. We're buying more cattle to build up our herds. The foreman of my ranch, which is the Double S, is buying cattle from a man out north of Denver. We'll be leaving tomorrow morning to meet up with the foreman. We've bought all our supplies today and have them already loaded in the wagon. We'll be ready to pull out first thing in the morning."

Maxi shifted in her seat. "Oh, you're leaving in the morning? First thing?"

"Yes, we need to be at our rendezvous point to meet Travis, the foreman."

"If you decide that we can travel with you, I can be ready. Angel is still deciding what she's going to do. I want her to go on with me, be part of my family." Maxi smiled mischievously. "My friend here has an independent streak."

Angel could feel the cowboy's eyes on her. Her cheeks began to warm into a blush under the scrutiny.

Marty looked from Angel to Maxi. "What about you two? Have you known each other long? Where are your families?"

"The only family I have left is my brother, Michael. He and his friend left our home in Texas a few years ago to start a cattle ranch in what he called the Wind River area. Have you ever heard of it, or Michael Mayfield?"

"Sure, I've heard of the Wind River, but I've never heard of Michael Mayfield, sorry." He noticed the anxious look on Maxi's face, then quickly added, "When you put the word out at different posts, it'll get around. He'll know you're looking for him soon enough."

"I don't think tomorrow would be soon enough." Sadness flickered across Maxi's face as she took a sip of her coffee. "I wish I didn't have to tell him our pa died."

"What happened to your pa? I'll understand if you don't want to talk about it, but I'd like to know."

Maxi told the story of her pa's accident. She went on to tell of how Angel had fled her aunt's ranch and briefly gave a sketch of how they'd gotten to Denver. "So you see, I have to go on and find Michael. It was the last thing my pa asked me to do. I just have to go on."

Marty looked at Angel. "Don't you have some relatives you could go to, Miss Hawkins?"

"Please, call me Angel. And no, I don't have any relatives who would take me in. I'm praying God will show me what to do. I would like to be able to support myself but haven't found a way yet. My life is a bit of a mess right now, but I'll make a decision by morning. I won't hold you up."

"Well, I think we've heard all we need to for now." Marty set his cup down. "I'm going to be up front with you. The foreman from my ranch is in charge of this trip. I don't think he's going to like it one bit if we bring a couple of ladies to travel with us. It's a dangerous trip but looks like you already have faced some of the dangers out in this wild country. I'm sure you can understand our concerns. Why don't we sleep on it and meet back here for breakfast. I'll know what should be done by then. Does that sound okay with everyone?"

"Yes, it does. Thank you, Marty. I appreciate you being willing to even think about taking us with you. If the sheriff trusts you, I will too. If you decide you can't take us with you, I'll understand. We'll accept what you decide. Oh, by the way, my name is Maxine, but everyone has always called me Maxi."

"Okay then, Maxi it is. We'll say good night and meet you here in the morning. Is that okay with you, Justin?"

Justin jerked his head up. "Uh, sure, sounds fine to me."

All four stood at the same time. Angel brushed against Justin's arm as he reached over to help move her chair back. She quickly looked up at him. "Oh, excuse me. I didn't mean to be so clumsy."

She felt a warm sensation where he had touched her, and her heart skipped a beat. Looking up into those pleasant eyes, she felt drawn into their depths.

He smiled down at her, a crooked little smile. "That's all right. I didn't mind one little bit."

His deep, masculine voice caused her to look at his mouth. She couldn't help herself; it was such a nice mouth. Then her eyes traveled back up to his hazel ones that were dancing with merriment. *He's teasing me! Oh, he's saying something. Pay attention, breathe, talk.*

"I'm pleased to have met you, Angel. We'll see you in the morning."

She managed to offer her hand. "Pleased to meet you too, Mr. Myers."

"Just call me Justin."

"All right, Justin." She heard the others say good night, but she couldn't shake the feeling it was all a dream. *What's the matter with me? If he'd held my hand a moment longer, I'd melted like butter on a hot day…right at his feet!*

"Angel?"

I think I understand the word swoon a little better. Oh, good grief! I don't even know anything about him.

"Angel."

Probably has a wife and a bunch of kids. I'll probably never see him again after breakfast. How can one man make me feel so—"

"Angel!"

"What!"

"Are you all right? You're awfully distracted. Lucinda is trying to tell you good night."

Angel could feel her cheeks redden. "I'm sorry, Lucinda. I didn't mean to be rude."

"That's okay. I think I understand. They are handsome, and I'm more than a little jealous you got to visit with them. See you two in the morning."

Back in their room, the mood was a mixture of Maxi bubbling with excitement to Angel being pensive and subdued.

Maxi babbled with enthusiasm. "Let's put on our new nightgowns and talk awhile. I can't believe what just happened! I might have a way to get to my brother after all. It just happened so fast." She was suddenly struck with a sobering thought. "Of course, those cowboys may decide not to take us. Maybe his foreman will say no." After a few moments she went on. "They were so nice. Don't you think they were nice, Angel? I hope they let us travel with them."

"Yes, they were very nice. But it's hard to tell in such a short time what they might decide. Don't get your hopes up too much, Maxi."

"You're right, but I just can't help it. I don't think I'm going to be able to sleep. I'm so excited."

"Well, you better try. It may be a long day tomorrow. Whose turn is it to read scripture tonight?"

"It's your turn. I read the sixth chapter of John last night. I guess you could read the seventh chapter."

"No, I think I'll read the ninety-first chapter of Psalms instead. It's about God's protection, also one of my favorites. It will be good for me to hear it again."

"Are you afraid, Angel?"

"No, afraid isn't the right word. I think maybe, confused…oh, I don't know. I'm just in a turmoil!"

"Would a certain cowboy have anything to do with your turmoil?"

A slow smile made its way onto Angel's face as she contemplated the question. "I'll admit a certain cowboy didn't help any. I was so shocked when the sheriff brought them over to our table. I could hardly eat my pie. I was so nervous. You seemed to be comfortable with them though."

Maxi considered that. "Yes, I guess I was. Probably 'cause I have a brother about their age. It made me miss him more than ever. I've been around cowboys a lot, but I think these two are special."

"I agree, but we shouldn't think about them too much. We may never see them again after breakfast."

"Let's pray really hard that they'll take us with them."

"Why don't we just pray that God will do what's best for us?"

"Same thing, isn't it?" Maxi grinned playfully.

"You know it isn't. But I'm pleased that you're seeing the need to pray. I've found the chapter now. Are you ready to listen?"

"Sure, go ahead."

Angel read the chapter, then looked up to see Maxi staring into space. "Did you hear anything I read?"

"Yes, I heard. I like that chapter too. Will you help me find it in Pa's Bible so I can read it again sometime?" Sitting on the side of Maxi's bed, Angel showed her how to find the book of Psalms, then let her find the chapter herself. "Here it is. Look, Pa underlined this part, 'He will give his angels charge over thee.' I guess he did believe in angels."

"It looks like he did, Maxi." Angel let her reflect on what she'd found and went back to her own bed. She pulled back the covers and sat on the side, waiting for Maxi to get ready for prayer.

Maxi looked up. "You read tonight, so it's my turn to pray."

"Please pray that God will show me what to do."

"Can I pray that he'll make you go with me?"

Angel saw the mischievous gleam in Maxi's eyes. "I'll leave that up to you, but I wouldn't want to tell God what to do. Well, let's pray now and turn out the lamp. I need to meditate and wait for God's direction. I probably won't talk anymore tonight. I hope you'll understand."

"I do, but will you open the window? It's really stuffy in here. Guess I'm too used to sleeping out in the open."

Angel pushed the window up and propped it open with a stick that was on the windowsill. A soft breeze whispered its way into the room.

Maxi said a prayer, then settled down for the night.

Angel lay on her bed looking out the window at the night sky. A few stars twinkled, and she silently spoke to God. *Heavenly*

Father, I know your word says you're watching over me. Thank you for that. You know I need some guidance right now. I feel so confused about what to do. Please show me whether I should continue on with Maxi or stay here in Denver. I want more than anything else to do your will.

She lay quietly for a while, waiting for what…she wasn't sure—maybe for a scripture to come to mind, one that might give her an answer. But there was only silence. Silently, she sang a song of praise. But there was only silence. *Father, where are you? I feel so alone.* A tear trickled down the side of her face, followed by another, then another. Feeling the dampness on her pillow, she sat up and quietly swung her legs over the side of the bed.

The calm that had been in her heart was slowly slipping away. In its place was self-rebuke. *Oh, stop it! It's silly to cry.* She swiped at the tears that persisted and took a deep breath. *I need to think of this logically. What prospects do I have for a job? There's not one for me at the general store. I don't even have money to rent a room until I work and get paid. Maybe Maxi would give me enough to get started. She would do it, but it's just not right for me to ask.*

She listened to Maxi's soft, regular breathing and knew sleep had found her friend. She began to quietly pace the floor. With every step, the room seemed to close in on her. Misery and wretchedness found fertile soil within her heart. *That just isn't fair! Is that what you want for me, God? Why did you take my ma and pa from me? I have no one who cares about me! What am I suppose to do, mooch off Maxi all my life? It's not right. I was taught to take care of myself. I don't want to live off someone's charity!*

A still, small voice had been trying to get her attention and let her know she was headed in the wrong direction with that kind of thinking. But by then, despair had taken root. Self-pity was quick to find a place to send down its own roots. *Why? Why, God? Why do I have to go through this?* Self-pity invited anger, and anger pulled in depression. Angel had very little experience dealing with these strong feelings. She was overwhelmed. *I can't think! I have to get out of here! I just can't breathe!*

As quietly as possible, she took off her gown and slipped into her pants and shirt. She put her shoes on, then made a quick decision. Taking her coat, she tossed it out the window, then climbed out after it, landing with a soft thud on the ground below.

CHAPTER 13

GOOD, I MADE *it.* Angel picked up her coat. *Oh, mice in the pantry! I should have left a note for Maxi. Guess I'll have to be back before she knows I'm gone.* At the edge of the field behind the boarding house, Angel found a path. More than halfway across the field, she stopped. Taking a deep breath, she lifted her face to the heavens. Out loud, she addressed the Almighty. "Okay, this is just you and me, God. I need answers because I'm going to have to tell everyone what I've decided in just a few hours…so I need answers now. Why are you being silent? Why won't you answer me? Where are you, God?" She realized her hands were fisted tightly. In her mind, she screamed, but it was actually a strangled, anguished groan. "Where are you, God?"

She stood in defiance waiting, knowing God could strike her down for demanding answers when she had such a faithless heart. Then she heard his voice.

"I am right here."

Those four words were her undoing. Shook to the very core, Angel fell to her knees, knowing that God had just spoken to her. She bowed her head to the ground. "I'm so ashamed, Father, please forgive me. I'm so full of arrogant pride." As she confessed her sins, tears flowed unbidden down her cheeks. She sobbed her confessions until there was nothing more she could think of to confess. The weariness in her bones began to dissipate, and her heart felt lighter than it had in a long time. "Oh, God, thank you for forgiving me. I'll trust you to give me the words I need when I need them. I've acted like a foolish child who just had a temper tantrum. I'm so sorry."

Still on her knees, she began to fumble in her pockets for a handkerchief. Suddenly, she froze. There, right in front of her, was an animal sitting just a few feet away, and she was looking straight into its eyes. Neither animal nor girl moved a muscle or blinked an eye. As seconds passed, realization washed over her. Timidly, she asked, "Ugly? Is that you?"

The animal cocked its head and took that as an invitation. He came at her with tail wagging vigorously and gave her a slobbery kiss with his tongue. She smiled in surprise. The second wet kiss started a giggle bubbling up inside of her. The third one took her down, laughing uncontrollably. Ugly slathered on the affection until Angel sat up begging him to stop. "Ugly, *please*, that's enough!" She gently pushed him back.

The dog's tail wagged so furiously that his whole back half was dancing. He turned and dashed into the brush. Angel thought he had run off, but in a minute, she heard him coming back. He stopped in front of her and dropped something, almost in her lap. "What's this? You've brought me a present?" On closer inspection, Angel shuddered. "You've brought me a dead…rat? Oh, how I hope it's dead."

Trying to ignore the rat, she stood and thanked the dog as she scratched him behind his ears. "I don't want to call you Ugly. That just sounds so disrespectful." She thought a moment, then put her hand on the big dog's head. "This is what we're going to do. From this moment on, you shall be called, Sir Ugly, my friend and protector, my knight in furry armor." He responded by engaging his tail again and answered with a soft woof.

"Come, walk with me, Sir Ugly. Let's go sit against the tree by Mr. Spriggs's place." They had taken just a few steps when the dog stopped and looked back. "What is it? Oh, my gift. How careless of me. Go on. Go get it!" He dashed back, grabbed the rat, and then caught up to Angel. They came to the tree, and Angel sat down leaning back against the trunk. After dropping the rat close by, the strange dog laid his head in her lap. Angel lifted her eyes to heaven in silent prayer. *God, you're so good. What a special way to cheer me up. Thank you for sending Sir Ugly and… the rat.* The strange companions sat for a while, she petting the shaggy head, he soaking up the attention.

"I wonder what time it is," Angel finally murmured. "It'll probably be light before too long. Sir Ugly, would you like to go with me to see Sweet Raven before I go back to my room?" She shifted, and the dog got to his feet watching her with anticipation. "Okay, let's go. We have to be very quiet. I don't want to wake Mr. Spriggs."

They stepped through the barn door and stopped just inside so she could get her bearings. In moments, she was able to make out shadowy details. Feeling her way along, she located the stall where Sweet Raven was. She spoke a soft greeting to her horse. "It's just me, Raven. I came to say hi." He nickered at the sound of her voice. *Maybe this is good-bye instead.* It was hard to think about, but she knew if she didn't go with Maxi, she wouldn't keep the horse. "You've been a good friend, Raven. Thank you for carrying me all the way to Denver. I'll never forget you."

Hot tears began to course down her face as she wrapped her arms around the horse's neck. "I didn't think I had any more tears, but here they come again. You understand, don't you, girl?" It wasn't really a question, and she didn't try to hold back her tears as she cried into Raven's neck. Finally, totally drained, she leaned back onto the boards of the stall and let herself slide down to the straw at her feet. Raven nuzzled her neck as she laid her head back and closed her eyes.

Maxi slowly roused from a deep sleep. Stretching and letting her feet slide over the edge of the bed, she sat up. The last evening's events replayed in her mind and brought a small ray of hope. She smiled. *I'll soon know if I have a way to continue on to find Michael!* That thought spurred her to action. She hurried to the washstand and poured water into the bowl. Hanging over the stand was a mirror that she spoke into as she washed her face. "You awake, Angel? We need to be getting up. I don't want to be late for our meeting with Justin and Marty."

There was no response, so she turned to the bed by the window. "Angel, wake up." She squinted into the light gray of morning. Angel's tousled bed came into focus. *Where did she go? Oh, probably the chamber pot, of course.* She relaxed. But a glance at the door told her something wasn't right. *The door is locked on the inside. She didn't go out the door.* With that thought, she turned toward the window that was still propped open. *That's the only other way out of this room. Why would she go out the window? Did she run away?*

She searched the room for clues but then spied the wicker case. *No, she hasn't run away. She would never leave her mother's violin. I would have heard if someone had come in the window and dragged her out. It just can't be that.* Perturbed, she concluded that for some strange reason, Angel had climbed out the window and would soon be back. Trying to convince herself of that, she got ready for breakfast, then hurried to the dining room for that all-important meeting.

She made her way to the same table they had occupied at supper. One of Lucinda's brothers came in with a pot of coffee. "Want some coffee, ma'am?"

"Yes, please."

"You want to order your breakfast now?"

"No, I'm expecting some others. I'll wait for them before I order." With a cup of coffee in her hands, she sat nervously looking out the window then back to the door.

Angel didn't appear. But ten minutes later, Justin and Marty arrived. They headed right to the table where Maxi sat alone. "Good morning, Maxi," they both greeted her.

Justin quickly looked around the room. "Where's Angel?"

"Well, I'm not really sure." Maxi seemed a little embarrassed. "She left our room sometime during the night. Her things are still there, so I'm certain she'll be back. It's just not like her to do something like this. She has always been so dependable and considerate. Actually, I don't know what to think."

Marty spoke up. "Well, let me make a suggestion. We'll order a cup of coffee and wait a few more minutes. If she doesn't show up…we'll go find her."

Justin's concern spilled over as he tried to reassure Maxi. "I know you're worried, but try not to make too much of it. There's probably a good reason why she's late."

"I know. You're probably right. She was rather quiet last night struggling with the decision of what to do. Things happened kind of fast for her."

The men finished their coffee in a short time. Justin was anxious to get out there and find the young lady who seemed to monopolize his thoughts late into the night. "How are we going to do this, Marty?"

"Since you've got to go check on the mules, you head toward the stables. I'll go the other way and stop in at the sheriff's office. I'll tell him what we've decided. Maxi, you stay here in case she comes back. We'll meet back here in about thirty or forty minutes. Does that sound okay?"

They agreed, except Maxi was wishing she could be out doing something. Waiting was not her favorite thing to do. More than anything, she wanted Marty to tell her what they had decided. But the men seemed anxious to find Angel. It was going to be a long thirty minutes.

Justin rode into the yard of the stable and was met by Mr. Spriggs. "Hello there, young man. You out for those mules already?"

"Not just yet, Mr. Spriggs." Justin dismounted. "I wanted to let you know I'll be back for them in a little while. Right now, though, I'm looking for a young lady. She's slightly built with white curly hair. Her name is Angel Hawkins. You seen anyone around here like that?"

"Well, maybe I have…and maybe I haven't." He regarded Justin soberly. "If I have, what was it you were wanting her for?"

"I'm helping a friend find her. We want to make sure she's okay."

The strange man pulled out a handkerchief and wiped his nose. He folded it several times before stuffing it back into his overalls pocket. "Guess I'll tell you then," the older man said decisively. "I know exactly where she's at. In my stable, curled up and sound asleep, in the corner of the stall with that black horse of hers. I seen her first thing this morning sitting out under that old cottonwood tree with Ugly."

Justin blanched. "Ugly?"

"Yep. That's the name I give him 'cause he's the ugliest cur I ever did see. He was all snuggled up with his head in her lap. And that there was real strange 'cause that old hound don't like anyone. He hangs around here 'cause I feed him once in a while. But he sure don't let anyone touch him. When he's here, he'll bark once to let me know someone's come around."

"He must not be here now." Justin looked around, a little antsy. "I never heard him bark. Where is he? Did you see him leave?"

"Now, hold your horses. Don't rush me. I don't get to talk this much very often, and this is kinda important to me." He rubbed a callused hand over his scruffy chin and squinted up at the sky. "Now, let me see. I decided to let her just sit under that tree with Ugly and I'd go tend to some chores out back. From the side pasture, I seen her go into the barn. Then when I came back, I stepped in to check on her. I never seen anything so heartbreaking in my whole life, like the sight of that little lady with her arms around that black horse's neck. She was crying her heart out too. It wasn't just a few tears either. No, sirree, she was sobbing and shaking all over. I can't think what would cause her such pain. I've never known what to do with a woman's tears…or a woman, for that matter. But I won't let you or anyone else hurt her no more."

His voice was stern, and Justin knew he meant every word. "Mr. Spriggs, I assure you…"

The older man held his hand up to stop him. "I ain't finished yet." He slowly turned, spat on the ground, then dragged out the old handkerchief and wiped his mouth. After the ritual of folding and stuffing, he finally continued, "I went in a little while later to check on her again and couldn't believe it. There she was in that stall, sound asleep with Ugly lying right there beside her. He gave me the *evil eye*." Mr. Spriggs stared hard with his eyebrows knit and his eyes bugged out. "I looked at that black horse, and he gave me the evil eye too. I know animals, young man, and I wasn't about to bother her. I would've had to go through both that horse and that dog, so I just let them be." He paused and scratched under his hat. "I'm sure she has the gift," he said in a conspiratorial whisper.

"Gift? What do you mean?"

"Well, the gift of love for animals, you know, the kind of thing that the animal knows she won't hurt them and they love her back."

"You might be right, Mr. Spriggs. I've known a few people kind of like that." Justin had been outwardly patient with the older man's lengthy narrative, but inwardly, he was very anxious to get to Angel. "Anyway, I promise I won't hurt her for anything. It's important that I talk to her and find out if she's okay. There are people waiting for us."

"I believe you, boy. You go ahead. And if her body guards let you in, you take care and be gentle, you understand?"

Justin nodded and headed for the barn. Before he got there, he was confronted by Ugly who had squeezed out through the door. Dog and man sized each other up. Ugly bared his teeth, growled a threat, and then trotted across the yard to the cottonwood tree.

Mr. Spriggs chuckled. "You've had fair warning, young man. Take care how you handle things in there."

Justin stepped through the doorway, pausing to let his eyes adjust. He heard her voice before he saw her. She was standing in front of the black horse, talking softly. He strained to hear what she was saying.

"Oh, Raven, I love you. I've been so confused, but I think I'm going to be okay now."

"That's the way I feel about my horse," Justin said brightly. "He's been so faithful to me, I just can't help but love him. He never complains and always listens to everything I say."

Angel froze. She didn't immediately turn around, but she knew that voice. It was a nice voice, one she thought she might like to hear more often. She took a deep breath and slowly turned. Yep, there he was. She stepped out of the stall and walked over to stand in front of him. "Hi, Justin. What are you doing here?"

"Looking for you. Maxi's a bit upset."

"Oh, Maxi! I'm so embarrassed! I hope she'll forgive me."

"I'm sure she will. But we need to get back and let them know you're okay." He stepped toward her and gently took hold of her shoulders. She looked up at him, and he simply fell into her big, brown eyes. "Angel, I need to know if you're all right. We've decided to take you and Maxi with us, that is, if you're going on. I need to know if you're up to it. Can you handle it? There might be some pretty rough times."

She tried to focus on what he was saying, instead of the warmth of his hands on her shoulders, instead of the shape of his chin, instead of his beautiful, hazel eyes, instead of being utterly blown away by…*him*! It took several long moments for her to finally find her voice. "Yes, Justin, I'm ready. And with God's help, I can handle anything."

They stood looking at each other for a few moments longer. Then reluctantly, he released her shoulders to reach up and pull a piece of hay from her hair. "You know, even though you're dressed in boy's pants with tear streaks on your face and hay in your hair, you're still the prettiest thing I've ever seen."

She darted past him before he could see her blush, then ran her fingers through her hair to shake the hay loose. "I'll wash in the water trough out front before we go."

Justin grinned. "I'll go tell Mr. Spriggs you're okay and that we're leaving."

They met out front by Justin's horse. He helped her up behind him, and they rode silently for a short ways. Angel felt the need to explain herself but struggled for the right words. Finally, she broached the subject. "Justin, I want to thank you for not pushing or questioning me about what I did. Someday, I'd like to explain it to you, but right now, I just can't. And thank you for coming to find me."

"I'd like to hear it, Angel, and you're welcome. I'm just glad I found you safe and sound. Right now, I'm looking forward to getting some breakfast. My stomach's getting acquainted with my backbone."

A few minutes later, Justin and Angel walked through the door of the dining room. The relief on Maxi's face made Angel feel terrible for putting her friend through such a trying ordeal. She immediately went to Maxi and gave her a big hug while whispering in her ear. "I'm so sorry, Maxi. Please forgive me. I'll explain it all to you later. Okay?"

Maxi nodded, then studied Angel's face. "As long as you're all right, I guess I can wait to hear what happened. Although, I can't imagine what." She brightened then. "They're going to take us with them, Angel! Have you decided what you're going to do?"

"Yes, I'm going with you."

Maxi joyously threw her arms around Angel again, leaving no doubt about what she thought of the decision. "Good! Then I forgive you."

Angel apologized to Marty for all the trouble she'd caused.

"Don't worry about it. Everything worked out fine. So let's eat! I'm hungry."

They enjoyed a hearty breakfast as they made plans for the day. "How long will it take for you two to be ready to go?" Marty questioned.

"Not long at all," Maxi answered. "When do you want to leave?"

"Well, we're packed now, but we have to get the mules and hitch the wagon up. We can leave as soon as that's done. The sheriff wasn't in his office awhile ago, and I'd like to go back, tell him what's going on. But that shouldn't take very long."

"We don't have a lot. We can probably be ready in thirty minutes or less. Can you be ready by then, Angel?"

"I should be able to get my ten trunks packed by then. Will you come by and pick them up, Marty?"

They laughed at Marty's face when he heard that. His eyes widened at the "ten trunks" part. "I hope you're teasing. Really, how many trunks do you have?"

Maxi was still grinning. "We don't have any trunks. Everything we have can fit on our horses. And we can be ready in thirty minutes. Oh, and just so you'll know, we'll pay our way. When you decide how much we need to contribute let me know."

"We're okay for now. I need to talk to Travis first, so we'll discuss it later." He pushed his chair back and stood up. "Okay then, in thirty minutes, we head out. I'm on my way to see the sheriff now. We'll all meet at Spriggs's stables."

As soon as the girls stepped into their room and shut the door, Maxi turned to Angel, ready for an explanation. Her voice was full of hurt. "Angel, I was so worried about you! Why on earth did you leave without telling me?"

Angel hung her head. "I know. I'm ashamed I worried you. I honestly intended to be back before you woke up. Can we just sit a few minutes while I tell you what happened?"

They sat on the sides of their beds facing each other. Angel took a deep breath, gathered her thoughts, then began. "I couldn't get to sleep last night. I tried praying but felt my prayers were going nowhere. I was so confused about what to do. I've wanted to be independent and felt guilty that you're having to buy things for me and feed me. I feel like a leech, and that hurt my pride. I tried to work things out in my mind, but nothing made sense. Even working seven days a week, like dishwashing, I wouldn't make enough to pay rent and live on. I don't even have the money to start out with. Everything overwhelmed me. I felt so alone. It was like God had deserted me. Of course, I knew he hadn't, but at the time, that's how I felt. I was pacing around this room, afraid I'd wake you up. I just had to get out in the fresh air…so…I climbed out the window. And…I walked through the field."

She paused, and a smile lit her face. "I found peace out in that field, Maxi. I didn't know what I was going to do yet, but I knew when the time came that I'd know what to tell you. And—"

"And what?"

"And I met Ugly out in the field."

"That's awful! Did he threaten you?"

"No, he didn't threaten me. He brought me a gift. He's so sweet. I think he must be lonely."

"A gift! Angel, you're not making any sense. How can a dog bring you a gift?"

Angel couldn't help but laugh. "Well, to him it was a gift. He brought me a dead rat and dropped it right in front of me. I sure was glad it was dead."

"No, I can't believe it! I've never heard anything like that before."

"We had a cat once who would bring us dead mice and leave them by the front door. Anyway, they were dead most of the time."

"Angel, come on!" Maxi was losing patience. "What did you do then?"

Angel shrugged. "I went and sat under a cottonwood tree with Sir Ugly and the dead rat." She answered as if it was the most perfectly logical thing a person would do.

Maxi stared at her for a few moments, not knowing whether to laugh or cry. "You're kidding, right?"

"No. I thought maybe God would speak to me then, but there was nothing. I finally slipped into the barn to see Sweet Raven. That's when the tears came again. I didn't know a body could hold so many tears. I just couldn't stop crying. It seemed like there was a river of tears in me, and they were going to come out, even if I drowned in them. I found myself in the corner of that stall, exhausted. I just meant to rest a moment, but I fell asleep."

"How did God tell you what to do?"

"Well, not like I thought he would. I had a dream that I feel was from God. That's how he helped me."

"What was the dream, Angel? Tell me."

"Well, at first, I was in a small back room washing dishes. I could picture myself working from sunrise to sunset. As I worked, I got smaller and smaller, just started shrinking. It got harder and harder to lift the dishes or reach the sinks. I realized I was dying. I knew then that living inside a town like this, or any other town, was not for me. It would kill me, mostly in spirit.

"Then all of a sudden, a wind came and blew me into the air. I was riding on the wind with a fresh breeze blowing in my face. It was glorious! The wind carried me high, then would dip down, and let me see the trees, mountains, lakes, and all of God's creatures. I would go high, then dip down again. Then, I was floating over what seemed like a sea of grass, dipping up and down with the flow of the land. I felt so free and alive.

"It came to me then that I should live on the land, not in towns. I don't know what God has planned for me, but I'm going to step out on faith, and go with you. I'm trusting God that he will show me the way."

Maxi nodded. "Wow, I just didn't realize the depths of what you were going through, Angel. While listening to you, I tried to put myself in your shoes. I think I can understand how you feel. I'm so happy you're going on with me. No matter what happens, you'll always have a place with me. We are sisters, after all. We have to stick together and be there for each other.

"I'm just not sure how to ease your mind about feeling like a leech. I don't want you to feel that way. That's certainly not how I feel. You're giving me so much just by being with me. Without you, I would be alone in this world. Let's just take one day at a time for now and see what happens. I'm new at faith, you know, but I'm learning. Now, let's get our things together and go show that foreman what we're made of. He won't dare send us back here to Denver."

CHAPTER 14

THE GIRLS HAD been anxious all day about meeting the foreman, Travis Buchannon. The day had gone well enough, and Angel surprised them all by showing what she could do with the team of mules who were named Samson, Delilah, Mary, and Martha. She was quite delighted with the names and the mules. She explained to Justin that she had learned to handle mules while on the wagon train going to her aunt's ranch.

That evening at the rendezvous spot, the girls helped set up camp, then went to work preparing a meal that would hopefully impress the boss; they made sure there was a big pot of coffee ready.

Travis finally came in to eat and to meet the girls. He let them know that he didn't like the idea of having them on the trip, but since they had come this far, he'd let them stay on. "You'll have to work like the rest of us," he said. "I'd hope to hire a couple more men by now but haven't found anyone willing to make the trip. Do either one of you know anything about horses?"

Maxi volunteered to help with the horses, and Angel said she would do the cooking and help drive the wagon.

"Okay, we'll see how it works out," Travis said. "Anything you do will be appreciated. Maybe with Angel cooking, we won't starve to death." He tipped his hat and went back to the herd.

Both girls decided they liked Travis and would work hard to prove themselves. They felt sure they had been accepted when all the men bragged on the food. They met two other men from the group, Bill Gray and Paul Miles. Bill was an older man, a horse wrangler, who would show Maxi how to do her new job. He was friendly and full of gab, and the girls liked him a lot. Paul was a young man, close to the same age as Marty and Justin who worked on the Double S Ranch. He was the quiet type who said only one word, "Thanks," after he finished eating.

The girls were finally left to themselves to do the cleanup. Afterward, Angel said she was going to go say good night to the mules. "I won't be long."

Maxi built up the fire, then decided to get ready for bed. She was involved in getting her bed ready when Justin rode in. He pulled his bedroll off his horse, looked around, and asked, "Where's Angel?"

"Listen, you can hear her."

He walked to the edge of the firelight and stood still for a moment. A soft lilting giggle rode in on the night air. "Delilah, quit pushing. I'll say good night to you in a minute. Samson, you did a good job today. Now all of you go to sleep. We have a lot of work to do tomorrow."

Justin was still looking out into the darkness. "She's quite a lady…and full of surprises."

"Yes, she is. Wait till you hear her play her violin." *I wonder if you know it, cowboy, but looks to me like you're falling for her.*

Justin turned his attention back to making his bed on the opposite side of the fire. "I'll be anxious for that surprise. Good night, Maxi."

"Night, Justin."

A short time later, Angel came in quietly and began rolling out her bed. Suddenly, she stopped and walked to the end of the wagon, peering out into the darkness toward the deep woods.

"What's wrong?" Maxi whispered.

Angel seemed perplexed but came back to her bedroll. "Probably nothing. I keep thinking I hear something out there."

"Could be an animal, maybe a rabbit or something."

"Yeah, you're probably right. Let's try to get some sleep."

The next morning, Angel woke before the sun sent its first rays into the morning sky. She hadn't slept very well but made herself get up early to make biscuits for breakfast. Maxi left to learn her new job, leaving Angel alone with all the cleanup and loading the wagon. An overwhelming feeling burdened her as she looked around at the big mess. Before she came undone, however, help came along in the form of a good-looking cowboy. He got the mules harnessed in short time, and with both of them packing the wagon, they finished quickly. "Thanks, Justin, that helped a lot."

"It's the least I can do after you made such good biscuits this morning. I'll have to add cooking to your list of talents. You ready?"

"All ready."

"I'll ride a ways with you and stay close in case you have any trouble. You look tired today. You okay?"

"I'm tired from missing sleep for two nights in a row, but I'll be fine. Probably sleep like a baby tonight."

A couple of hours later, Angel stopped to give the mules a rest. She set the brake, stood up, and stretched. Justin rode up beside the wagon. "I think I better take a turn. There's a steep drop ahead that might be a little tricky."

She tried to look brave. "I could probably make it, Justin."

"I don't doubt you could make it, but I think you're getting tired. No sense in pushing yourself too much the first day. You're doing a good job, and it's sure helpful. Travis doesn't say much, but I think he's impressed with you and Maxi, especially after those biscuits you made this morning."

She looked pleased. "I hope we can keep it that way."

"If those mules are rested, why don't you ride Butch down and wait for me on the other side of the draw. Think you can handle him?"

"I don't see why not, unless he's hard to get along with."

"No, he won't give you any trouble. When we get over the next rise, the ground is pretty even. It should be easy going for you then."

Angel could feel Justin's eyes on her as she rode his horse to the edge of the draw. The first few feet were the worst part of the downward slope. She felt Butch hesitate on the edge of the drop. "Okay, Butch, it's going to be all right. Justin trusts you and so do I. Let's go on over." She kicked firmly in his sides, and the big gelding took a couple of steps over the edge. She gave him plenty of rein so he could find the best footing. At the bottom, she reined him in, then watched as Justin took the wagon and team down the slope and up the other side. She met him at the top. "Thanks, Justin. I'm glad you came along."

"You're welcome. Do you want to ride Butch awhile longer, or are you ready to take over the wagon again?"

"I'm ready for the wagon. You're right. It looks pretty easy up ahead. I saw a few cows straying, so I think you're needed more with the herd than with me."

Justin jumped to the ground before Angel could dismount. She was surprised to find his hands firmly on her waist lifting her to the ground. "Oh! I didn't know you were going to do that."

"Sorry, I didn't mean to startle you." He smiled down at her. "I should have thought to help you up on Butch. He's so tall. How did you get up on him?"

"I cheated!" she said. Standing very still, her breath caught. She could still feel the warmth from his hands on her waist, the closeness of him. "I stepped up on a big rock to get in the saddle. When you're short, you learn to take advantage of things like that."

His expression turned serious. "Angel, can you shoot a rifle?"

"I guess so. Maxi gave me her pa's pistol when we started traveling together. I've practiced with it, and she told me to carry it in my coat pocket. I keep the coat there on the wagon seat close to me."

"That's a good idea." He took a red neck scarf from his back pocket and handed it to her. "If you need help with something, take this scarf and tie it on the nail on the top corner of the wagon. That's the signal that you need something. Don't fire your pistol, or the whole bunch will come riding in thinking there's danger. If you do need that kind of help, don't hesitate to fire a shot"

"Okay, I can do that."

"Good girl!"

He mounted and rode toward the stray cows.

Angel climbed on the wagon seat and began to fuss to herself. *Girl! Is that what he thinks of me? Just because I'm small, everyone thinks I'm a little girl.* She started the mules forward, then smiled. *He doesn't look at me like I'm a little girl.*

The rest of the day went smoothly though the weather turned blustery. Dark clouds whipped overhead but didn't drop any rain. As the sun started its descent behind the mountains, the wind finally died down. Justin rode up to the wagon. "There's a place up ahead where we'll spend the night. Go on past the Aspens and you'll see an open area where there's water. I'll be right along to unhitch the mules. See you soon."

Angel drove the wagon past the Aspens and toward some willows. She saw there was already a fire pit with rocks stacked around it. "Looks like someone else thought this was a good spot." She set the brake and climbed down. "The men spent the night here on their way to Denver. That's why Justin knew about this spot. It's a real pretty place too, don't you think so, Samson?"

She walked around the mules talking to each one. "I know you're anxious for a rest and want to munch on this wonderful grass. Justin will be here in no time. Be patient now while I go find some dead limbs to start a fire."

Angel wandered around the area looking for anything that would help start a fire.

"I see you found our spot," Justin called to her as he dismounted.

"Yes, and it's just beautiful here."

He pointed toward a large pine tree and told her she would find some firewood there. "When we were here before, I cut down a dead tree right on the other side of that pine. There's a lot of little stuff you can use for kindling. When I finish unhitching the mules, I'll help you get the bigger pieces." He watched her for a minute. "Do you want me to stay and help you with the cooking, or do you want me to go relieve Maxi and send her in to help you?"

She stopped in her tracks and looked back at him. He had a silly little grin on his face. *I think you're testing me, you handsome cowboy. I wouldn't want you to get too sure of yourself and get the big head.* Calmly, she answered, "It's not that I don't enjoy your company, but it would be nice to have Maxi help me. I haven't seen her all day."

Justin shrugged, trying to look dejected. "Okay…if you prefer her company to mine." He headed toward the wagon to unhitch the mules.

She noticed the grin still on his face and was wishing she had asked him to stay. *He probably knows more about cooking than Maxi does. Still, it'll be nice to see her and hear about her day.* She consoled herself with that thought as she traipsed off to find the dead tree.

Later, Maxi came in with four fat rabbits. "Bill went back to that steep draw and shot these for supper. Think we can figure out something to do with them?"

"Rabbit stew sounds good, but we don't have any vegetables except potatoes. There wouldn't be time to simmer them anyway.

Let me see. I know! I'll use the bacon grease from this morning and fry them. I found two loaves of bread stored in a tin, so we need to use them before they dry out. I'll toss in some ham in case the rabbits aren't enough. Then, I'll make a big pan of gravy. I think men like any kind of gravy, as long as they can sop their bread in it. Well, how does that sound?"

"Great, as usual! Bill said he was so hungry he could eat them raw."

"Okay, then. If you'll skin the rabbits, we'll get started. I guess the worst thing that can happen is they'll fire me as cook."

"Ha! There's no chance of that."

A little later, Maxi came back with the rabbits, ready to be cooked. While Angel cut them into pieces, they shared their day with each other. "I liked working with Bill and the horses."

"Did you see Paul or Marty today?"

"Saw Paul for just a moment. He stayed to himself most of the time. Bill told me his mother is a pretty Mexican lady. She cleans and cooks at the Swanson ranch. His dad worked there too but died a year ago in a horse accident. I love his smile. He isn't as tall as Marty, but wow, what a build! They're both strong and work hard, from what I could see. Marty comes around when he has a chance. He's so fun and nice, always trying to make me laugh." Maxi looked at Angel. "Well, enough about that. How did your day go?"

"It went just fine. I'm tired, but it's a good tired. In another day or two, I'll be used to handling the wagon. I've used muscles I didn't even know I had. There's really not anything new to tell you. I drove the wagon…end of story. That's probably how every day is going to be."

The men took turns coming in for their supper. Maxi cornered Angel by the side of the wagon. "Don't even think about getting out of the cooking," she whispered. "Look at them put that food away!" As each one ate and got ready to go back to work, they complimented and thanked the girls for the food.

Travis came in last and headed straight for the coffee pot. "Did those yahoos leave me anything to eat?"

"We made sure they did. We put some back for you."

"Thanks, that was nice. Gotta keep the boss happy. Just keep that in mind." He grinned, then took a sip of coffee. "Seriously, though, it's a real treat to have someone cook for us. Usually, we just scramble for whatever we can find. Or whatever we can roast over a fire on a stick." He started to fill his plate but stopped and stared down into the big skillet. "What's this, gravy?"

"Yes, just water gravy, but it tastes pretty good," Angel answered. "You can sop your bread in it."

He broke off a piece of the thickly sliced bread and ran it through the gravy, then popped it into his mouth. "Hmm, hmm, that's good! I don't care what kind of gravy it is…it's good!" He sat on the ground, leaned against a log, and went at his food like a starved man. Finally, he raked the last piece of bread through the remaining gravy on his plate. Looking hopefully at the gravy pan, he asked, "Have you girls eaten yet?"

They grinned at each other knowing what he was really asking. "Yes, we ate with the other men. Go ahead and finish it off."

He didn't need to be coaxed. He got up and finished off the last bit of gravy and a piece of ham. Sitting quietly, with a satisfied look on his face, he swallowed the last of his coffee. "You girls did real well today. Bill said you did a good job with the horses, Maxi. He was impressed with that horse of yours too. Ginger, right? Has she worked cattle before?"

"Yes, my pa trained her. I've helped with cattle roundups before. Everyone was protective of me, but I did quite a bit, actually."

"I saw you go after those cows that lagged behind. There was a real possibility that we could've lost them if you hadn't acted. I thought then that maybe you'd had some experience." He studied her for a minute. "Keep up the good work, but don't put yourself in any danger."

"Okay, I'll be careful."

He started toward his horse. "You doing okay, Angel?"

"Yes, I'm fine, thank you."

"Okay, then. You two turn in as soon as you can. Gotta grab sleep whenever there's an opportunity." He mounted and rode into the darkness.

After cleanup, Angel did as much as she could to be ready for the next day. She started a big mess of beans cooking; then made a fresh pot of coffee for the men during the night. "I'm going to say good night to the mules, then take Travis's advice and get some sleep."

"Okay, but don't stay long, Angel, or I'll worry."

"I won't be gone long. Don't want you to worry."

CHAPTER 15

ANGEL WAS UP before Maxi. She was glad to see that those who came in for coffee had added wood to the fire. The beans were nice and tender. *Good. I'll put the bacon grease in them, add a little salt, and that'll be tonight's meal.* She quickly made up a batch of biscuits, put them in the large skillet, and placed them on the coals that the beans had been on. *Where's that lid? I know I saw it somewhere…there it is.*

"What can I do to help?" whispered a man's voice that was so close to her ear she jumped.

"Justin Myers! It's not nice to sneak up on someone like that. I almost swung and hit you with this lid."

"It might've been worth it if you'd kiss it and make it feel better."

She couldn't see his hazel eyes in the dim morning light, but her big brown ones immediately sought out his mouth. She could see it well enough to make out that teasing, crooked little grin. Quickly, she looked away. "And why would I do that when there's so much work to be done? And yes, you can help. Get out that slab of bacon and slice some of it for me."

"All right, but I like my idea better."

Angel's thoughts went back to that nice mouth. *I wonder what it would feel like to kiss that teasing, silly grin off his face? Mice in the pantry! I've never had thoughts like that before. Angel, you're a bad girl!*

Fortunately, a yawning Maxi distracted her. "What can I do, Angel?"

"Good morning, Maxi. You can check the coffee, please. I should have done that earlier."

Maxi went to the coffee pot. "It's almost full and should be enough for breakfast. I think I'll have some now though."

"I put on a fresh pot when I came in earlier." Justin appeared around the side of the wagon. "Good morning, Maxi."

"Good morning, Justin."

"I sure didn't hear you," Angel said in surprise. "You must be part Indian, sneaking around like you do."

"I have some secret talents too. You're not the only one that can surprise people with your many talents, you know."

"Well, I'd just like to see some of those talents," she challenged.

Maxi sipped her coffee, amused at the banter from the two, thinking they sounded like an old married couple.

An hour later, everyone was fed and out with the horses and cattle except for Angel and Justin. "They're moving the cattle out now, Angel. I'd like to help more with the herd today. When you catch up with them, stay on this side of the herd. Travis saw a few deer go into the willows up ahead, and I'm going to try and get fresh meat for tonight. Stay in sight of the herd, though, don't get too far behind and remember the signals. I've told everyone to watch for the red neckerchief."

"Okay. You go on now, and don't miss that deer. Venison steak sounds really good. I just have to fill my canteen. Then I'll be on my way."

"See you pretty soon. Hopefully, with a nice, fat buck. Oh, and, Angel?"

"Yes, what is it, Justin?"

"Be careful. Keep an eye out for trouble."

She was touched by his protectiveness. "I will, Justin."

She watched him ride away, then went to retrieve her canteen from under the wagon seat. She filled the canteen, then stood a moment at the edge of the stream. She listened to a bird's song, felt the warm sun on her face, and was grateful for her peaceful surroundings. She started to pray, *Oh, God, what a wonder…*

Suddenly, she was interrupted. One second, she was alone by the stream, the next, she was surrounded by Indians. One grabbed her arm and put his hand to her mouth signaling for her to be quiet. She froze with fear. He glared fiercely at her; she felt his breath on her face. He had a black stripe painted across his eyes like a mask. She couldn't pry her eyes away from the dark ones that glared at her. *Where did they come from? I didn't hear a sound. God, help me! Even if I scream, no one could hear me now. Please help me!*

He held her tightly as ten or more Indians on horseback came out of the trees. The one who seemed to be in charge slipped off his horse in one smooth movement. He looked older than the others. He wore leather leggings with a breechcloth, moccasins that came to his knees, and a leather vest with multicolored beads on tassels that hung down the front. His hair was long and loose in the back, and a braid fell down the front of each shoulder. Two eagle feathers hung off a knot of hair on the top of his head. She watched him warily as he stopped within a few feet of her.

The leader looked her over, starting at her feet and moving up to her white curls. He stared into her eyes. She stood her ground and stared back. *Don't show fear. Don't show fear!* Suddenly, as that thought came to mind, she felt a peace flow through her and knew it was from God.

The staring contest finally came to an end, and he turned to one of the men on horseback. The man got off his horse and came to stand next to the one in charge. She was shocked to discover he was a large, black man, dressed like the others, but he spoke to her in English.

"This is Chief Bear Claw. He says you come with us. I am Black Buffalo. You ride with me."

"I can't go with you now." Angel tried to sound firm, but her voice was shaky, scared. "My people are up ahead. I must go to them, or they'll come looking for me."

The black Indian was especially intimidating. "Lady, do not argue with the chief, or it will go hard on you and your people. He has enough braves with him to kill all your friends right now."

Oh, God, no! I can't let that happen. Help me, God. She summoned all her courage, looked at the chief, then back at the black man. "At least tell me why I must go with you now."

"The chief has heard of White Cloud and your great medicine. It is told you are a friend to all Indians. His only daughter is very sick. We must hurry. She will die if she does not get help soon. His young wife is grieving and sick in her heart."

"You should have told me that first. I'll go, but I need to tell my friends where I'm going."

"No! You come now! Do not argue."

"At least let me get my wicker…er, medicine box. And you be sure the chief knows I'm going because I care that his daughter gets well, not because he ordered me to go."

Black Buffalo said something to the chief who grunted and nodded. She hurried to the wagon and pulled her coat out from under the seat and put it on, then slid her arms into the straps of the wicker case.

Black Buffalo had mounted his horse and was waiting for her. He reached down and took her arm, easily hauling her onto the back of his horse. She hesitated to grab the man around the waist. But when he slapped his moccasin feet against the sides of the horse, she didn't hesitate to grab anything she could get a hold of. Eventually, she put her arm around the waist of the big, black Indian.

They soon slowed down to cross a stream, and she asked, "What if my friends come after me?"

"Chief told the dog soldiers, okay, White Foot, come."

Before she could ask what that meant, they were off again at a furious pace. *Dear God, please don't let anything happen to my friends. I couldn't live with myself if something happened to them because of me. I don't know what Justin will do when he finds I'm gone. Oh, and Maxi. What will she do? Don't let her come charging after me. You know she would take on a whole tribe of Indians if she had to!* She smiled at the thought of Maxi's bravado but not for long. They began to climb a rough mountainside, and it took all her focus to hold on. *I hope this poor horse doesn't die from this climb. Black Buffalo is heavy enough, but carrying double is cruel.* She could feel the horse's strong muscles tighten and push off as he scrambled to reach the top.

Angel thought they would climb forever, but suddenly, they stopped on the ridge. She peered around the big man to see what had stopped them. Several Indians were standing guard on the ridge and seemed to be arguing with the ones who had captured her. They were pointing and gesturing to the tree line where she and her captors had just come. *What are they looking at? Oh, how I hope it's not Maxi or Justin.* One of the guards quickly put an arrow in his bow, pulling in one swift motion. Before he could release it, Angel looked back and saw his target. "No!" she screamed. "No! Don't shoot!"

Justin studied the ground. *It was along here that Travis saw those deer, but I don't see any tracks. I'll go a little ways…ah, there they are.* He followed the tracks to a creek that was heavy with brush on the opposite side. *Think I'll move uphill a ways. Maybe I can spot them from higher ground.*

He tied Butch to a willow and pulled his rifle from the scabbard. As quietly as possible, he slipped uphill through the brush. *Wish I'd brought my moccasins. I'll be lucky to see any game with all the noise I'm making.* He found a good hiding place behind some rocks, knelt down, and scanned the creek and brush ahead. *There they are. Just as I figured, they're spooked. I'll be lucky to get even one shot.* He quickly put the rifle to his shoulder and sighted in a small buck, then pulled the trigger. The shot wasn't clean, and he was angry with himself. *Oh, man! Now I gotta track the thing.*

He went back to get his horse, then backtracked to where the deer had been. *At least I hit him. There's blood right there.* He got off his horse and followed the trail of blood for a short ways until he spied his prize. Justin was quick at dressing out the two-point buck. He loaded it on the back of his horse, then headed toward the herd. Clearing the willows along the creek, he scanned the back of the herd searching for the wagon. It was nowhere to be seen. A feeling of dread gripped him. *Where's the wagon? Something's not right…Angel should be up here by now.* He dismounted and untied the deer, letting it fall to the ground. Back in the saddle, he kicked his horse until he was in an all-out run.

Travis saw Justin race by. He yelled to Marty, "Keep watch! I've got to go see what's wrong." Marty waved for Travis to go on.

Reaching the wagon, Justin felt a moment of panic. "Angel!" he called several times, looking in every direction. He spotted her canteen by the stream and went to retrieve it. As he bent to pick it up, there was no way he could miss the small shoe indents that were surrounded by moccasin prints. "Indians! Oh, God, no!" Justin panicked. He frantically searched the area for more tracks hoping to figure out what had happened, which way they went.

Just then, Travis came riding up. "What's going on here, Justin?"

"It's my fault. I should not have left her until she was with the herd. They took her, Travis. They took Angel."

Startled, Travis demanded, "Who took her?"

"Indians. They grabbed her at the stream, about five on foot. Ten unshod horses came from that direction, then crossed and headed up the mountain. "I've got to go get her, Travis. It was my fault. I shouldn't have left her by herself. I've got to go!"

"Justin, look at me!" Anguish in the younger man's eyes didn't go unnoticed. "Don't let emotions rule you right now. Think calmly. You're going to need all your wits about you. I know you have to go, but let's talk about it first. Who do you want to go with you?"

"No one. I don't want anyone to go with me, Travis. I'll go alone." Justin's thought process was becoming clearer. "This is Cheyenne country, and if it was Cheyenne who took her, I might have a chance. They're friends with the Arapaho, and I know some of the Cheyenne warriors. We met some of them on the prairie a couple of years ago when Black Feather and I went hunting. We spent a few days together. If I'm lucky, maybe one of them will recognize me before the dog soldiers put an arrow in me. Makes no sense for anyone else to be put in that kind of danger."

"Are you sure, Justin?"

"Yes, I'm sure. I want to leave right away, but I do have one thing to ask."

"What is it? Just ask."

"Keep Maxi from following me. I don't need to worry about her too. And I'm sorry, but I'm afraid you're going to have a battle on your hands."

"Don't worry about her. She's tough, but I'm tougher."

"Thanks, Travis."

"I'll wait as long as I can."

"I know. Above all else don't come after me. If at all possible, I'll come to you."

"You just make sure you come back and bring that girl with you. You're not the only one who's getting attached to her. Now go on, before the trail gets cold."

CHAPTER 16

EVERY INDIAN ON that ridge turned to stare at Angel. "No, don't shoot. He's my friend." She slid off the back of the horse and ran to the brave with the bow and arrow. "Black Buffalo, tell him not to shoot. He's my friend." She stood gripping the arm of the brave. He didn't like her interfering but looked to the chief for instructions. Black Buffalo spoke to the chief. The chief said something to his warrior with the bow, who relaxed, and dropped the bow to his side. Only then did Angel let go of his arm. She turned toward the trees and walked out to meet her knight in furry armor. A short distance from her captors, she knelt and held out her arms. Sir Ugly walked into her embrace and licked her face in greeting. She could hear the low rumble in his throat as he kept watch on the Indians. "It's okay, Sir Ugly. You have to be good. Stay here, or I'm afraid they'll shoot you. I don't know if they eat dogs or not, but you have to stay here and be good. I bet you're the one I heard out in the grass last night. Why did you follow me, you sweet old thing?" She patted and scratched behind his ears and received another wet kiss for her efforts. "I have to go now. Stay here." She stood and put her hand, palm out, toward the dog. "Stay, please stay."

She walked back to Black Buffalo, hearing the Indians mumbling to one another. "They won't hurt him, will they?"

"Well, that depends on what he does, but probably not. They seem to think you have big medicine. They have not seen an animal like that before. They think he is a spirit you use in your medicine."

He pulled her back up behind him. She felt frustrated. "He's not a spirit, just a lonesome, old dog."

"Don't tell them that."

"How much further is it, Black Buffalo?"

"We are here."

"Where?"

"Right down there." He pointed down the opposite side of the mountain. The other Indians had already started down a trail off the ridge. Only when Black Buffalo's horse started the descent did she see it.

Nestled in the small valley, numerous tepees dotted the valley floor. Large pine trees with scattered patches of aspens framed the village in greenery. Multicolored artwork on the tepees added their own beauty to the natural setting. As they moved closer, Angel could see hunting scenes with shapes and symbols painted on the sides of the dwellings. She noticed a small lake at the head of the valley and followed it with her eyes to a stream that flowed from it to the lower end. A large herd of horses was grazing at that end. Lost for a moment in the wonder of it all, she forgot she was a captive. "It's beautiful!"

"You're surely right about that."

As they neared the end of the trail, she could hear voices of people spreading the word of their arrival. Children stopped playing. Women stood beside their various tasks of the day, solemnly watching their chief ride to the center of the village. *They're so serious. Or is it sad? Dear God, please don't let that little girl be dead. I want very much to help her. I don't know what's wrong with her, so please help me know what to do.* They had reached a very large, brightly colored tepee.

Black Buffalo held his arm out, and Angel grabbed it and slid to the ground. Young boys ran up to lead the horses away as the party dismounted. Angel was led to a small tepee that was to the side of the large one. A flap was pulled back, and the chief went in first, lowering his head to go through the doorway. "Follow the chief in, White Cloud, I'm right behind you."

A wall of heat smacked Angel in the face; a fetid odor assaulted her nostrils. Before her eyes could adjust to the dim light, she heard a whimper and tried to locate the little one. A small fire flickered in the middle of the floor sending its smoke through the hole at the top of the tepee. A very old Indian who seemed oblivious to everything around him sat to one side of the fire. He held a rattle in one hand and a fan of feathers in the other. His eyes were closed as he rocked back and forth, chanting unintelligible words that sent shivers up and down her spine. His continuous fanning directed smoke to the other side of the fire where she finally located the little girl.

Angel desperately wanted to hold her nose and run out of the tepee for fresh air. But another whimper sent her quickly to the side of the sick child. She focused intently on her patient, remembering how old Granny Anderson had taught her to talk through the process of examination. That way, she could tell if Angel was on the right track to finding the cause of sickness. Touching the girl's forehead, she began her observations. "She's burning with fever. Black Buffalo, has she complained of any pain?"

He interpreted the question to a young woman sitting by the girl's side, then relayed the answer. "At first, she complained of her throat, then her neck. Now she is too weak to answer."

Angel looked at the young woman. "Is this her sister?"

"No, it's the baby's mother."

Angel was surprised at how young the mother appeared to be but said nothing. She gently lowered the buffalo robe that covered the girl. "There's nothing on her feet or legs that would cause fever. There are no spots anywhere on her body, like measles or chicken pox." She slid her hand under the naked child and turned her slightly. The little body was limp and damp, seemingly lifeless. Nothing was found on her back. Angel gently felt the tiny neck, eliciting a faint moan from her patient.

"That's part of the problem. Her neck is swollen. It's not mumps, though, since the swelling is in the wrong place. Black Buffalo, I want to move her outside to the shade of a tree. I'll need the buffalo robes and cool water." Angel didn't wait for permission but went outside to the closest tree. She took off her case and coat, laying them on the ground, then waited.

A little disagreement went on inside the tepee, then came to an abrupt halt. The chief emerged, followed by Black Buffalo. The mother and an older woman came out next carrying the girl and a buffalo robe. Angel rushed to help them. "Put them right over here," she said, gesturing. The woman obeyed but with a suspicious look in her eyes. A wooden bowl of water was brought and placed by the robes on the ground.

Angel carefully removed her violin from the case and took out a large piece of flannel. After tearing off a strip to use as a rag, she laid the larger piece over the girl. She wet the rag, wrung out the excess water, and handed it to the mother. Knowing the mother didn't trust her, Angel moved slowly, showing and demonstrating how to bathe the girl with the cool water yet not let her get chilled. Taking a small packet from her case, she dissolved a quarter of the powder it contained in a little water. She explained that the powder was the inner bark of the willow. It would take the pain away, and they would then be able to get her to swallow a healing tea they would make.

When they finally got the girl to swallow the pain medicine, Angel saw Chief Bear Claw standing close. Angel spoke to him,

"Your daughter is a brave girl. The medicine I gave her is very bitter and hard to swallow. It will help her body fight the sickness. I will do my best to help her and pray to God, the one who made all men and created all things. It is up to him now. I will pray that he heals her." She turned her attention back to his daughter, encouraging the mother to keep bathing the feverish little body with cool water.

While waiting for the medicine to take affect, she spotted her violin. *Maybe some music will be calming*, she thought and picked it up. Playing softly, with her eyes closed, she started to pray. Hot, salty tears pooled behind her eyelids as she thought of Justin and Maxi and the others. *God, please don't let any of them do anything rash and come in with guns blazing. I ask, Father, that you heal this little girl. I will give you all the glory. You are my great healer.*

Angel opened her eyes a short time later and was surprised to see a large crowd had gathered and was listening to her play. They had come so silently, she hadn't realized they were there. She kept playing, softly and sweetly, and a hush fell over the valley. A tender breeze cooled her face and played with her curls, and Angel felt God's presence.

Later, Angel was delighted to see the little girl watching her. "Well, now, the medicine seems to be working." She found Black Buffalo sitting in the shade. "What are their names?" she asked him.

"Well, now, let me see. I 'spose in your talk it would be Sweet Song. She is the baby's grandmother. The baby's mother is Star That Twinkles, and the little one is Laughs in the Rain."

"Thank you. I'll call the grandmother Sweet." Angel looked through several small cloth bags in her case. "Will you tell Sweet I need her to help me? I want her to boil some of this in a little bit of water. We need to get the girl to sip small amounts of this liquid during the day. Also, she needs to get as much water and clear broth down her as possible. I'll call the baby Happy and her mother will be Star."

While Black Buffalo talked with Sweet Song, Angel noticed a commotion down at another tepee. *I'll have to ask Black Buffalo what that's all about.*

But he came back from talking to Sweet Song and said they had a problem.

"She says she is not going to give her granddaughter anything that she does not know what it is."

"I understand. Do you know what yarrow is?"

"I do not know anything about such things."

"Okay, then let's do it this way." Angel opened the small bag and poured some of the dried leaves and flowers into the palm of her hand and let Sweet examine it. Sweet ran her finger through and smelled the contents in Angel's hand. She smiled and nodded and spoke to Black Buffalo.

"She knows this plant," he said. "They use it for much healing. She knows what to do."

Sweet took the mixture into the tepee to set it over the coals. Angel then had a chance to ask Black Buffalo about the commotion at the other tepee.

"I was told Crazy Toad's wife is having trouble birthing her baby. She has had three girls already, but this one does not want to come into the world."

"Do you think they would let me help? Granny Anderson and I delivered a lot of babies back home. I might have an idea."

He took her to the other tepee and asked if they wanted White Cloud to help with the delivery. After a bit of discussion, Angel was allowed to go in. A warm, pleasant smell of sage greeted her at the doorway. "Black Buffalo, will you come in too?"

"I ain't going in there," he huffed. "It is not a man's place."

"Okay, then stand by the door in case I need you to interpret."

"I will do that much, but I ain't going in."

Angel stepped in further and saw three pairs of wide eyes staring at her. One pair belonged to the mother who was having the baby. The other two were fixed on faces that looked to be as old as Methuselah. Angel smiled quickly and nodded.

The wrinkled, old women murmured to each other for a minute. But it was ultimately the mother who determined what was going to happen as another contraction gripped her body. She gritted her teeth and growled a string of words at them. Then the contraction was over, and Angel encouraged her to lie back. "Relax now. I want to feel your stomach." The younger woman seemed confused, and Angel spoke loudly to Black Buffalo. "Tell her I want to touch her stomach!"

"Lord have mercy! I am going to get teased over this, helping a baby into the world. It's just ain't fittin!"

Angel couldn't help but laugh at his predicament. "I'm sorry. Just tell her. If I'm right about this, it'll be over rather quickly."

The woman gave permission, and Angel carefully felt her swollen stomach. Another contraction came. When it was over, Angel showed her how to get on her hands and knees. The mother looked at Angel like she had lost her mind, then shook her head no. "It's okay. Come on, do it." Angel smiled encouragingly. Reluctantly, the woman did as Angel demonstrated. "Put your head down and rock back and forth. That's it. Just go slowly." While the woman rocked back and forth, Angel stood up. She tried to ignore the two ancient ones who were discussing the situation.

"They think you are crazy, White Cloud. You want to leave?"

"No, not yet. Tell them the baby was lying with his face toward the sky. When the mother rocks, the baby flips over. Then it will be easier to come out."

"Now how am I going to tell them all that?" Black Buffalo said, with no small amount of frustration.

"I don't know. Just do the best you can. They'll figure it out."

In no time, the mother rolled to her back. When another contraction gripped her, she squatted and grabbed the pole that was used to hold onto while bearing down. The mother spoke to the older women through her pain, and they moved quickly to catch the baby. Angel watched the baby's head come into view; then, the rest of the body slid out onto the soft skin that was waiting. In the flurry of excitement, the three women forgot Angel was there, so she slipped out of the tepee.

"Thanks, Black Buffalo. Baby and mother seem to be fine."

"What was it?"

"You'll have to ask the mother."

"You don't know if it was a girl child or a boy child?"

"Oh, I know, but it's not my place to say."

Black Buffalo pleaded a little. "Can't you give me a little hint so I can tell Crazy Toad?"

Angel shook her head. "Not even a little hint. I need to go check Happy. Will you go with me?"

They walked back to the tree and saw that Happy and Star were cuddled together, sound asleep. Sweet was sitting close by watching over them while she worked on a piece of leather. A little bit of a smile made an appearance as she nodded at Angel.

They'll probably sleep for a while. Wonder what I can do now. Maybe I'll walk around and check out the village. "Everything's all right here," she told Black Buffalo. "I probably won't need you for a while. But can I ask you a question?"

"Yes. Go ahead."

"How did you come to be with the Cheyenne?"

He smiled and rubbed his chin, thinking a moment. "I am just a runaway slave from Mississippi. With the help of some fine people, I managed to escape and headed west. About died a couple of times, but God had other plans. The Cheyenne found me while I was in bad shape. They took me in and made me one of them. They had never seen a black man. With my black, curly hair, they thought I looked like a buffalo. They are my people now. I am proud to be one of *the people*."

All of a sudden, a commotion started drawing people to the tepee where the baby had been born. Crazy Toad was in the middle of a crowd holding his new baby high so everyone could see he had a boy. The baby howled his disapproval for being taken from the warmth of his mother, but that seemed to delight the crowd even more. One of the ancient women, who had helped with the birth, pulled on Crazy Toad's arm until he handed over the baby. Then she escaped back into the tepee. The men slapped the new father on the back, congratulating him for finally having a male child.

Suddenly, Angel thought of her own mother and remembered what she always said when a baby was born. She hurried and got her violin and had Black Buffalo go with her to Crazy Toad's tepee. The crowd was still milling about, celebrating. They stood aside and watched Angel expectantly as she approached the new father.

"Crazy Toad, I had a very wise mother. One thing she taught me was there should be a celebration whenever a baby comes into the world. So in honor of my mother and your new baby boy, I will play and dance for you."

Black Buffalo interpreted, and the people began to murmur and nod approval. Angel gave a sweeping bow, then placed her violin under her chin. She played a snappy Irish tune. The second time she played it, she danced an Irish jig that her mother had taught her. Then she stopped and told them, "All of you must join me now and learn the dance. Children, come!" She pointed to the children who were watching. "Come," she said, gesturing. Most of them were shy and hung back, but a few were eager to learn.

Slowly, she played the tune again, moving her feet bit by bit so they could follow her steps. They learned quickly, which encouraged the others to join in when they saw it wasn't so hard. Even adults along the sidelines were trying the new dance. "Good! Very good. Now let's do it again, altogether." She played while they all did the steps in unison. Then she put the children in a line so they could be seen moving together. "Everyone, follow me!" Angel shouted. She played her tune and weaved in and out among tepees and fire pits as the line of children followed her.

She finally led them to the wide, open center of the village where a huge, communal fire pit filled the middle ground. She stopped there and looked for Black Buffalo.

"You will have to interpret for me, please. I want to issue a challenge to see who can keep up with me." Black Buffalo gave the challenge, and cheers went up from the crowd as the dancers got in line. They looked excitedly at Angel. As usual, she started slowly, making it easy to keep up with her. Each time she played through, she picked up the pace, going faster and faster. The children, especially, were enjoying the celebration dance. Before long, everyone had dropped out except for one young girl, about ten years old. She was very agile and quick on her feet. The crowd cheered her on, encouraging her to keep going. But soon, she too gave up. The last time through the tune, Angel played as fast as she could, leaping in the air, her feet moving sharp and quick with the intricate steps of the Irish jig.

CHAPTER 17

THEIR TRAIL WASN'T hard to follow. *It's almost like they want me to follow them. They're not trying to cover their tracks at all, and that's something to worry about.* Only a few times did Justin have to slow down to read the signs but was quickly back on track. Getting close to the top of a ridge, he had the feeling that he was being watched. *This may be it. I know their dog soldiers are out there somewhere. I can't see them, but I can sure feel their eyes on me.* He began to pray. *Well, God, it's been awhile since I've talked to you. I'm sorry about that, but right now, I need some help. Please don't let Angel be harmed, and help me to find her. I probably don't have the right to ask, but I'm asking anyway 'cause she's special.*

Justin topped out on the ridge. The tracks here were confusing. Angel's footprints seemed to head into the timber. *What in the world happened here? Did she try to escape? No, she came back by herself.* Trying to decipher the horse tracks, moccasin tracks, and Angel's shoeprints, Justin ended up at the trailhead that led down the other side of the mountain. *Nothing to do now but keep going.*

They let me get this far, so they're probably going to let me go on. At least for now.

As Justin turned the first corner in the trail, he brought Butch to a halt. There down below was the Indian village. "Wow! They know how to pick a spot," he said softly. "That's beautiful. Well, Butch, if they let me get this close, I'll probably live another day. Tomorrow may be a whole different proposition." He urged his horse on down the trail but let the big gelding find his way along the narrow path. About three quarters of the way down, he brought Butch to a halt again. "As I live and breathe, Butch, would you look at that!" He sat and watched in disbelief as the scene unfolded before his eyes. *She's got to be down there somewhere. Maxi said she played the violin.* Then he spotted her. *Ah, there she is.* As she played some lively tune, she led a line of children to the middle of the camp while a group of adults trailed behind. *Looks like they're having a party. I can hardly believe it. And Angel appears to be the ring leader. This story is going to be interesting. Here I was worried sick about her, and she's out partying.* He sighed and smiled at the sight, then watched until the crowd closed in around her. "Let's get down there, Butch. I need to find out what's going on."

He entered the camp, and a young boy waited for him to dismount before leading his horse away. He was a guest now and had to be careful to show the proper amount of respect. He made his way to the crowd and joined himself to the outer edges. As the people became aware of his presence, they moved aside, and soon he was pushed to the front of the group. He watched in sheer delight as Angel and a young girl danced, what he guessed was, an Irish jig. The girl had a lot of encouragement from the crowd and was doing a valiant job of trying to keep up with Angel. It was proving to be too much for her, and at last, she took her place along the sidelines. Then it was just Angel, mesmerizing her audience as she played and danced her way around the circle that had developed. With ease and grace, the quick movements of her feet made her appear to dance on air, leaping and landing, as if on a cloud.

Suddenly, her eye caught sight of Justin, and she immediately stopped playing, staring in wonder at the handsome cowboy in front of her. She was almost afraid to hope, not sure if he was real or just a dream. She dropped her violin to her side. The crowd quickly and quietly melted back to their village life, leaving this strange white couple to themselves.

Moments passed as Justin looked into her big, brown eyes. They began to pool, and tears trickled down her face. She bowed her head, and her chest rose and fell with each sob she fought to keep inside. He reached out for her and lifted her head to look into her face again. "Why the tears, Angel? Did anyone hurt you?"

"No, they didn't hurt me." Her chin quivered. "I wanted you to come for me. But I was afraid they might shoot you if you did! I didn't even know if you could find me. Oh, Justin, I want to hug you so bad I can't stand it."

He wasn't about to let that comment go unanswered. His heart sang as he smiled down at her. "I'll take that hug a little later, but right now, I need to find out what's going on. Do you know why they took you?"

"Yes." She wiped her eyes on her sleeves. "The chief's daughter is very sick, and they wanted me to take care of her. I don't know why, but they just came and got me and wouldn't let me tell anyone."

Justin looked up to see the chief coming toward them with a big, black man and a few braves. They stopped and formed a little group in front of Justin. He immediately found out the black man was the interpreter.

"Chief Bear Claw welcomes you," the man told him.

"Tell the chief I thank him for letting me come to his village. I have heard of Bear Claw and have hunted with his braves."

"One of the warriors remembered you. That is why they let you come here. The chief wishes to talk with you. If you will come with us, we will talk and smoke."

Justin looked at Angel. "I need to go talk with the chief. Maybe I can find out if they're going to let me take you back."

Alarmed, Angel said, "What do you mean, *if* they let you take me back? They won't try to keep me here, will they?" Before Justin could answer, she declared, "They *can't* keep me here!" Her chin came up defiantly.

"Don't worry, Angel. I'm sure if they didn't intend for me to take you back, they wouldn't have let me come here in the first place. Don't worry, it'll be okay."

She relaxed. "If you say so, I'll try not to worry."

He looked intently into her eyes. "Trust me, Angel."

A hint of a smile tugged at her lips. "I do trust you. I'll go check on the chief's daughter."

They went separate ways, but Justin turned to see what direction Angel took. He could feel a change coming over him, and he was pretty sure he knew what it was. *Angel Hawkins, you're a treasure, and so help me, I think I'm falling in love with you. How could this have happened so fast?*

Sometime later, Justin found Angel as she was trying to communicate with a young woman. *Must be the mother of the sick child.* "Hi, Angel. Are you having problems?"

"Oh, hello, Justin. I'm having a hard time getting Star to understand that it's starting to get cooler now. I don't want her daughter to get chilled in the evening air. Before they take her in for the evening, she needs more medicine. Her fever is returning, but it's not unusual for a child's temperature to rise at night when they're sick. When the medicine takes effect, we need to get more water and broth down her."

"Wait! Slow down."

Much to Angel's surprise, Justin started telling Star what she had said. He used words sparingly, mostly talking in hand signs. Star nodded often, showing she understood. "I think she gets it now, Angel. Is there anything else you need to tell her?"

"Yes. It's time to give her the pain medicine now. That makes it easier for her to swallow the other liquids. Sweet, her grandmother, knows how to mix the other medicine. Also, she needs to make more broth."

Star was soon nodding in understanding as Justin gave her the instructions.

"What did the chief tell you, Justin? Are they going to try and keep me here?" She was sitting on the ground, mixing the first batch of medicine.

He moved closer to her, kneeling on one knee with his arms folded across the other knee. "You want the truth or do you want me to sugarcoat it for you?"

"Of course, I want the truth!"

"Well, then, there are at least three braves who want you for a wife."

"You can't be serious, Justin. That's crazy."

"Crazy or not, it's the truth." He grinned that crooked, little grin of his.

"What did you tell them?" She studied his face and felt her eyes, of their own volition, rest on his delectable mouth.

"I told them they couldn't have you. Your father has already promised you to me." He waited for her reaction.

"Justin, you know my pa is dead." She went back to her mixing.

"Not your earthly father. I was talking about our Heavenly Father."

Angel turned away trying to hide her blush. "You're talking silly, Justin. Don't tease me like that."

"It's not silly, but we'll talk about that later. Anyway, two of the braves said they would trade for you. One even offered me ten fine horses. The third one offered to fight me to the death for you."

"To the death?" she gasped.

"Well, no, not to the death," he admitted, that grin showing again. "Just to fight me, and the winner would take you for a wife."

"Justin Myers, I am not some old mule to be traded, bought, or fought for. You'll have to tell them that." She hoped she had sounded indignant.

"I don't think I'll have to. I told them that White Cloud, medicine woman, friend to all Indians, could make up her own mind. And I'm dying to hear the story of how you became White Cloud, medicine woman. I had no idea I was traveling with such a famous woman. Just another one of your surprises, I suppose?"

"Not anymore a surprise than you coming here and knowing how to talk to these Indians. How did you learn to do that? And I'm not famous."

"I can see we have a lot of things to talk about. But it looks like someone's coming, so it'll have to wait." He got to his feet.

Sweet came toward them carrying two wooden bowls. Black Buffalo was with her. "She said there is food prepared for you both. I will take you now, if you are ready."

"First, I have to give this pain medicine to Happy. I've just now mixed it." With Star holding the baby, Angel got a dose down her patient, with only a little whimper but a big grimace. "That should make you feel better." She smiled at the little girl. Looking at Black Buffalo, she asked, "What does Sweet have?"

"She says it is more of the healing medicine that she mixed earlier and some broth made from deer meat."

"Good, very good. Will you ask if they want me to stay here? Someone could bring me back something to eat."

"I don't need to ask her. I know she will want you to go eat. They have prepared a big feast for you. It would be an insult not to go."

"Okay. I haven't had anything to eat since this morning, so lead the way. I certainly don't want to insult anyone."

They followed Black Buffalo to the communal fire pit where a large crowd was gathering. Some older women were already seated on buffalo robes on one side of the pit. They motioned for Angel to sit by them. She recognized the two old women who were at the birth of the baby. They were all smiles now. One patted the place next to her, a signal for Angel to sit there.

Justin leaned down close to her. "I'll be over with the men. Don't think about what you're eating, just eat and enjoy it." He could tell that Angel was uncomfortable with all the attention.

But he was proud of the way she conducted herself, gracious and humble.

Black Buffalo overheard what Justin had said and added his own opinion, "Most likely, you'll enjoy all the food."

"Thank you for the advice. I'm so hungry I could eat that dog over there. Maybe even a horse." She saw the look on Justin's face. "They don't eat dog, do they?"

He laughed as he turned to leave with Black Buffalo, calling over his shoulder, "That's something else we'll talk about later."

All through the evening, Justin watched Angel as much as he could and still be polite to his eating companions. *She seems to be a natural with people. I think they're in love with her too. That lady is doing just fine.*

Angel was served first and tried everything they offered, which delighted every woman around her. Black Buffalo went to her when the meal was over to give her a message. "They want me to tell you that they are going to dance for you, now, so you will know how the people, the Cheyenne, dance."

She was enthusiastic. "How wonderful! I'm sure I'll enjoy it. Please thank them for me."

Darkness had fallen, and a huge fire was built in the middle pit. Flames were shooting high into the sky when the drums started. Justin leaned back with eyes half closed, feeling as though he had been taken from his world and transported to a magical one. The drumbeat throbbed in his veins and pounded in his heart, and all his pent up anxiety inexplicably melted away. He decided for this short time, he would relax and take pleasure in this surreal world and not worry about his friends. He would deal with the guilt later. He looked across the fire at the young woman with white curls and big, brown eyes, who was taking in everything with an expression of utter fascination. She affected him strongly. He felt emotions that he'd never experienced before. *If you only knew how much I want to take you in my arms and hold you forever, Angel Hawkins, it might scare you to death. Oh, God, how I want to love her and take care of her, more than anything else I know!*

His thoughts were suddenly interrupted. "Come, dance!" said a brave who was standing in front of him. He motioned to Justin.

"Huh?" Justin responded sluggishly.

Black Buffalo got his attention. "Come on, boy. They want you to dance with them. You need to show that little lady how an Arapaho dances."

"Uh, okay. Just let me take off my boots."

He rolled his pant legs up to his knees, then joined the circle of chanting braves. He moved in rhythm to the beat of the drums, acting out his own story of a thrilling hunt. With stabbing gestures, spins, and leaps, he bent and swayed as the dancers thrummed their way around the blazing fire. He was lost in the moment, dancing with abandon, uninhibited, and with purpose, like the others around him. He was…one of them.

Angel was breathless, caught up with the drums and the excitement of the dance. Her heart raced as she watched Justin. She couldn't take her eyes off him! *Justin Myers, you are one big surprise. I'd think you were an Indian yourself, with that dark, tanned face of yours. But your blond hair and white feet give you away… wait a minute—* She pinned two thoughts together. *White feet… that's what the chief meant, "Okay, White Foot, come." He was talking about you.*

Right at that moment, Justin threw his imaginary spear at his invisible prey and raised his fists in triumph. He screamed a cry of victory. This was supposed to end the dance. But Angel was unable to restrain herself as she clapped furiously and yelled, "Yippee!" at the top of her lungs. Her high-pitched shriek resonated through the darkness and hung on the air much longer than Justin's victory cry. Realizing her mistake, she felt the heat of embarrassment spread up her neck and over her face. For one awful moment, there was nothing but dead silence. Then all the women erupted into gales of laughter. To her surprise, and gratitude, the old woman sitting next to her started clapping and yelled, "Yippee!" In moments, all the other women were doing the same. Even the men took up the yell. The party broke up as everyone moved off in different directions to their homes. But the victory cry could still be heard, sporadically, and from every corner of the village.

Angel waited for Justin to pull his boots on. He stood next to her as yet another victory cry pierced the quiet of the night. He grinned down at her. "I just couldn't help it." She shrugged and smiled back at him.

"I'll walk you to your sleeping quarters. You've been invited to stay with Sweet and Star. I'm expected to sleep with the single warriors."

"Justin, would it be rude if I asked to sleep outside, somewhere close to the tepee? You could just tell them I'm used to sleeping out under the stars. I don't want to hurt their feelings, but it's so closed up and stuffy in that small tepee."

He looked at her tenderly. "Angel, I think they would let you do anything you wanted to."

Then she asked, "Did I embarrass you tonight?"

"Are you kidding? I loved it. Everyone loved it. They'll be talking about this night for years to come. They'll be telling stories about White Cloud and her cry of victory. They love you, Angel Hawkins." *And I love you, too.*

Angel got her wish. Buffalo robes were brought outside the tepee, and she was made comfortable.

On his way to the warrior's lodge, Justin would have been floating on air, except the nagging worry about Travis and the others. *Hang on, Travis. I'm coming. If all goes well, I'll see you tomorrow.*

By the next morning, Happy was obviously on the mend. Sweet had given her broth twice, with lots of water. She was still weak but definitely better. Angel gave a packet of her precious powder to Star and demonstrated how to measure it for the child. Soon, Sweet brought Angel some breakfast, something like cornmeal sweetened with honey that Angel found quite tasty. She finished eating and checked on the child once again. A commotion outside the tepee brought her out to see a crowd gathering. Black Buffalo and Chief Bear Claw were coming toward the tepee, along with Justin who was leading Butch. She stepped out to meet them and stumbled on something by the entrance. "What's this?" she asked, looking down at her feet.

The crowd was murmuring like the buzz of bees in an apple tree. She recognized one of the dog soldiers who had been on the ridge the day before. He was talking seriously to the chief.

Justin went to stand by Angel. He had a gleam in his eye. "You've done it again, Angel Hawkins. These people are in awe of your big medicine. Seems one of the warriors was guarding the camp and watched your spirit medicine bring you food." He looked confused. "Do you know what in tar-nation they're talking about?"

She looked down at the dead rabbit lying at her feet, then started to laugh as realization came to her. "Yes, I know what they're talking about. It's Sir Ugly."

Justin nodded. "You mean that dog?"

"Well, he followed me here." She quickly told him about the incident on the ridge the day before. "He's just a dog, Justin."

"I know, but to them, it's big medicine when an animal brings you food. It has to do with an ancient legend from the beginning of Cheyenne time. I don't really understand it all, but before there were weapons to kill their food, a Cheyenne woman stole a baby panther from its mother. She nursed and cared for the panther like her own baby. When it got older, it killed and brought her food. There's probably a lot more to the story, but that's all I could understand about it."

"What should I do?"

"I'm not sure, but I think you should make a big deal of it, somehow."

"I guess in a way, it is a big deal when a dog like Sir Ugly loves you enough to bring you food. Poor old thing. He's just lonely."

As if it was an everyday occurrence, Angel picked up the dead rabbit and held it high in the air. Someone, in the spirit of the occasion, started clapping and yelled, "Yippee!" Immediately, everyone started clapping and took up the victory cry. Angel was still embarrassed by the memory of the night before, but she composed herself and ceremoniously presented the rabbit to Sweet Song.

"Black Buffalo, tell Sweet Song that she is to take a large pot and cook the rabbit for tonight. All the people are to bring vegetables and anything else they want to put in the pot. They should share it tonight."

Black Buffalo interpreted her wishes, making a big production of all the instructions. When he finished, Sweet nodded her understanding, holding the rabbit like a treasured gift. He then turned to Angel. "White Cloud, that was a mighty fine thing you just did. Reminds me of the slave camps in my old days. We used to do that same thing to stretch the food when we didn't have much to eat. That was a good idea."

"I'm glad you think so. I wish I could be here to see how it turns out, but we need to go. Can we leave now, Black Buffalo?"

"Very soon. There is one more thing that needs to be done." He stepped aside, and Star came forward with a gift for Angel.

"Oh, this is beautiful!" She took the soft leather skirt and shirt, examining the meticulously decorated clothes. "Thank you so much." Angel beamed as she grabbed Star in a big hug. "I love it!"

The startled girl stepped back. There stood the old woman who had been at the birth of the new baby and whom Angel had sat by during the feast. The woman spoke, and Black Buffalo interpreted. "You have great wisdom for someone so young. I am glad our paths have crossed. To thank you for bringing by son's first male child into this world, we give you this gift." She held out a pair of calf-high moccasins that were decorated as beautifully as the clothing Star had given her. "May the great spirit, who created all things, bless your steps."

Angel's eyes misted as she hugged the old woman. "Thank you so very much." Then the woman surprised Angel by grabbing her and giving her a rib-cracking hug.

Justin whispered, "You deliver babies too?"

"Yes, I have helped deliver them," she quietly answered.

Chief Bear Claw approached next. He didn't say anything at first but reached out and took hold of one of Angel's curls, rubbing it between his fingers.

Then he said only one word.

Angel asked, "What did he say, Justin?"

"Soft," he quietly told her.

"Give me your knife, please."

"What…why? What are you going to do?"

"Trust me. Just give me your knife."

"I don't know why I'm doing this, but here it is."

She took the knife and cut off one of her curls and handed it to the chief. He said something, then turned and walked away.

"What did he say this time?"

"He said we can go now, so let's do it. Give me your gifts. I'll tie them on the front of my saddle. You'll ride behind me."

They moved as quickly as possible while still appearing to be polite to the remaining people. Angel put her coat on and slipped her arms through the straps of her case. He mounted, then pulled her up behind him. As Butch made his way up the mountain trail, an occasional "Yippee!" could be heard from below.

CHAPTER 18

THEY REACHED THE top of the ridge and stopped for a few moments to look one last time down at the valley. Justin felt like a new chapter had begun in his life. The wonderful girl behind him had her arms tightly around his waist, and he noticed she didn't let go when they stopped.

"You didn't have to fight to the death for me." There was merriment in her voice.

"No, they gave up when the chief told them they were foolish. He said even a fool could see our spirits had touched, and you would have no one but me. Something else we need to talk about," he said softly. Then he commanded, "Come on, Butch! Let's go find our friends!" The horse took off like he knew what was happening. And Angel hung on like she would never let go.

Sometime later, Justin pulled up. It was time to give Butch a rest and a drink from a creek they had come to. He helped Angel slide to the ground, then dismounted and led the horse to the creek edge. He took down his canteen and handed it to Angel. "Do you know how jealous I am of that old chief?"

"What are you talking about?" She took a drink from the canteen and wiped her chin. "Why would you be jealous of him?" She drank some more, then handed the canteen to Justin.

He took a drink and hung it back on the saddle horn. "Ever since I found you in that stable with hay in your hair and tear streaks on your face, I've wanted to feel your beautiful white curls and touch your lovely face."

She took his hand and brought it up to her hair. "It's always been that way. Seems like everyone wants to touch my hair." She felt the sensation of his fingers moving through her hair, and she shivered.

"It is soft," he murmured. His hand moved down to her soft cheek. She closed her eyes and leaned into the palm of his hand, savoring his touch on her face. He moved his hand away, and she looked at him with questioning eyes. "Tar-nation, Angel, if we don't hurry and leave, I'm going to kiss you."

"Then maybe I don't want to hurry."

"You better want to hurry. You're way too much temptation right now." He studied her face for a few moments. "I've got to know, Angel. How old are you? You look so young. You don't act young, but you sure do look young. I guess I'm hoping you're at least sixteen."

"Well, I'm old enough. I'm seventeen. What do you think of that?"

He grinned that crooked, little grin reserved just for her. "That's good. I think seventeen and twenty-two sound just about perfect. Now, let's go find those cows so Travis doesn't have to worry any longer."

She pulled his sleeve, and he looked down at her. "Before we go, there's something I have to know, Justin."

"Okay, what is it?"

"When you talked about our Heavenly Father, I took that to mean you're a believer. Are you a believer?"

"Yes, Angel, I am. I gave my life to Jesus Christ when I was eleven years old. I may not be the best believer, but I know I belong to him. My feelings for you are so strong and new. I need some time to be sure that I get it straight in my mind and heart, but I'm thinking you are the one God wants for me. I hope you're feeling the same."

She stared into his eyes for several moments. "Yes, I'm feeling the same."

Their desire was to linger in their newfound joy and in the mysterious magnetism that had drawn their hearts together. But knowing there were people who anxiously awaited them, they got on the horse and, without another word, rode off to find their friends.

CHAPTER 19

"WE CAN'T MOVE on, Travis. We've got to wait 'til they come back!" Maxi was beside herself, helpless, anxious, and irritable. It took a lot of self-control to keep her outward emotions in check. She'd done pretty good, but now, Travis was talking about moving on, without Angel and Justin. She could not accept this and stood glaring at Travis.

"We're not going to move very far, Maxi. We'll just let the cattle slowly graze north. They'll catch up to us in no time." Maxi wasn't the only one upset. This was the third time he'd tried to reason with Maxi since breakfast. "Don't think you're the only one having a hard time with this, young lady. I've been arguing with myself all night and all day about whether I should have gone with Justin."

Maxi nodded sadly and heaved a sigh of resignation. "Marty's waving at you, Travis. He must need you for something. I'll stay back here and watch for strays, if you want to go on ahead."

Travis watched Marty for a moment. "I don't think he's waving. He's pointing."

They both jerked their heads around to look behind them. Maxi squealed, "Oh, it's Justin and Angel! I hope she's all right."

"I hope so too. Looks like Justin's smiling and waving, so I doubt if there's anything wrong with Angel."

In moments, Butch stopped beside them in a cloud of dust. There were joyous greetings and wide grins. Travis reached up and lifted Angel from the horse. "It's about time you two showed up." He looked from one to the other and cautiously asked, "Is everyone okay?"

"Yes, we're both just fine," Justin quickly assured him.

"I'm sorry for all the trouble I've caused," Angel said.

"Well, little lady, I doubt you had much choice in the matter. But I'm sure glad you're back safe and sound."

Maxi stepped toward Angel. "Don't you *ever* do that again, Angel Hawkins! You had me worried to death. I've never prayed so hard in all my life. And it was awful to just wait and not be able to do anything." She looked accusingly at Travis. "Travis wouldn't let me help find you." Tears were on the verge of spilling over when she managed to bring them all to laughter. "He even threatened to tie me to the wagon if I even looked like I was going to go after you!"

Angel hugged her while they exchanged a few quiet words.

Travis was back to business. "I think these girls need some time together. Bill is hitching up the mules now. You okay to take over the wagon, Angel?"

She nodded. "Yes, I'm ready."

"Good. Maxi, you take care of the horses but stay with the wagon. Justin, send Bill out to the herd, and when the girls are moving, you come on out and help with the cattle. Find me first though. I want to know all about your little vacation." Travis mounted his horse, then looked down at the others. "The wagon stays in sight of the herd at all times now. Everyone understand?"

No one argued with that, and they all nodded. Soon they were on the move toward Fort Laramie.

Maxi rode alongside the wagon, close enough so she and Angel could talk. Angel told her about the Indians surprising her at the stream.

"Did you have your pistol with you?"

"No, it was in my coat pocket on the wagon, but I wouldn't have had time to use it anyway. It just happened so fast. I didn't hear them at all. Nothing. One minute I was alone, the next, I was surrounded by Indians. Maxi, the chief *knew* who we were. Anyway, he knew me as White Cloud."

"How could he have known that? Were they Ute?"

"No, they were Cheyenne. I have no idea how they knew about me."

"Well, why did they take you then?"

"I didn't know this at first, but Justin told me later that their old healer had died. The one who was learning medicine from him went to visit another tribe to learn from *their* healer. I guess they didn't have anyone else who knew medicine. The chief's daughter was very sick so they came and got me to take care of her. I wish I knew how they heard about me. Justin just said… they have their ways."

Angel continued telling the story of her capture. She didn't leave anything out except the personal parts about her and Justin.

"You yelled *yippee*?"

"Yes, I'm afraid I did." Angel's cheeks reddened just thinking about it. "I was so embarrassed when the women started laughing at me. Then the old woman I sat by started clapping and yelling yippee. Then the men started yelling it too."

Maxi was laughing hard by then. "I wish I could have been there. I would love to have seen that."

"I'm sorry you were so worried, Maxi. I was nearly frantic thinking you would come after me and shoot up the whole Cheyenne tribe. I think it worked out like it was supposed to though. And thanks for praying for me. Let's remember to thank God for answering your prayers."

"I hadn't thought about that, but you're right. I am thankful."

Angel's eyes drifted to a rider coming their way. She immediately recognized who it was. "Here comes Justin. He seems to be in a hurry. I hope nothing's wrong."

Justin came alongside the wagon and spoke quietly to Angel, "Don't slow down or stop, Angel. Keep the wagon moving along."

"Sure, Justin. Is something wrong?"

"There's a group of men, about seven I think, coming down out of the mountains. Maxi, pull your rifle and keep it ready. Angel, if you can get to your pistol put it on the seat next to you. Hopefully, there won't be any trouble, but it's better to be safe than sorry. I have a bad feeling about this bunch."

"I'll be ready." Maxi pulled her rifle out of the scabbard.

Justin watched the men approach. "They probably won't start anything, but if they do, don't hesitate, girls. Do what you have to do." They were tense as the group of men rode toward the wagon in a cloud of dust. Justin kept himself between the girls and the strangers. Angel kept the wagon moving, and Maxi kept to the side.

"Howdy!" one of the men called to Justin.

Justin nodded, but then their conversation was drowned out over the noise of the moving wagon. Maxi glanced back. "Angel, I've got to go back and help Justin. They were a mean looking bunch of ruffians. I can't leave him alone. You keep moving ahead."

"Be careful, Maxi. Thank goodness, here comes Travis and Paul."

Maxi rode a short distance behind Travis and Paul. She made sure they were not in the line of fire in case things turned ugly. One of the grungy looking men kept eyeing her. *Look while you can, mister. If anyone starts a fight, you're the first one I'll shoot.* She shifted her rifle while staring the man in the eyes. He must have read her mind because he quickly looked away. She couldn't hear all of the conversation but heard enough to know the men were trying to talk Justin into trading some of their horses.

"Sorry, but we're not interested." Justin kept his voice steady. "We need all the horses we have. It wouldn't be a fair trade anyway. Your horses look all used up."

The hard-looking man who was doing all the talking raised his voice. "You know, sonny, I could just shoot you and take what I want, including those two young gals you got." He leaned forward, stuffed full of self-confidence. "In case you hadn't notice… you're outnumbered."

The bunch of thugs chuckled and nodded at each other. Justin kept his cool, never taking his eyes off the leader. He played the man, waiting several moments before he answered. "Where'd you learn to count, mister? You better look around. I think it's you that's outnumbered."

He sneered. "You mean those two old codgers and that black-headed gal?" The man spat, then stared hard at Justin.

"Don't forget the Cheyenne warriors on the hill just back of you," Justin said calmly.

That got their attention. The men jostled around one another peering into the trees. "Where? I don't see no Injuns," The one in charge said. "You're just trying to trick us."

"No, he's telling you straight, boss. I'm pretty sure I seen movement up there. They're apt to kill us when we leave."

"They're friends of mine," Justin said. "If you leave now, I'll ask them not to bother you. I can't promise anything, but that's your best bet."

The gang of men looked at one another, then at their leader. "You win this time, boy. I'd think any good Christian would be willing to help another out and do a little trading. Let's get out of here, men." He growled a parting shot at Justin. "What kind of man would have Injuns for friends anyway?"

No one relaxed until the thugs were out of sight.

"Good job, Justin. That was quite a bluff you pulled about the Indians."

"It wasn't a bluff, Travis."

Travis looked surprised. "I didn't see any Indians."

"Wait a minute. You'll see them." Justin cupped his hands around his mouth, sending a series of hooting sounds up the hill. Immediately, a dozen or so braves materialized from the trees and came down toward Justin.

Paul chuckled. "Well, I'll be! How did you know they were there?"

"One of them signaled to me with a bird call. It's been so long since I've heard it, I almost missed it."

"Well, you give them my thanks," Travis said. "I'm going back to the herd now. You take care of things here."

"Do I need to stay, Justin?"

"No, it's okay, Paul. You and Maxi go on. You need to get her out of here anyway. One of the warriors has already asked about her when I was in their village. Hold her hand or something to show she's been spoken for. Oh, yeah, find out why they call her Princess Warrior."

Paul rode the short distance to where Maxi waited. She hadn't heard the whole conversation, and a puzzled look was on her face. "Did he say to hold my hand? Why would he say that?"

Paul flashed her an impish grin. "He's trying to save you from being an Indian squaw. Now give me your hand and smile like you're in love."

He held out his hand waiting for her to take it. But he was about to find out this cowgirl had a mind of her own.

"I don't intend to be an Indian squaw or hold hands with you! That's silly talk. Smile at you like I'm in love? Ha!" She tossed her head and looked in the other direction. To her surprise, he reached over and playfully tugged on her braid, then lightly hit the back brim of her hat, making it slip down over her face.

"Stop that!" She swatted at his arm as he tugged on her braid again, which enabled him to grab hold of her hand. She tried to pull it out of his, but he had a strong grip. Her eyes flashed. "Don't ever do that again!"

Paul was taken aback when he saw the hurt look on her face. "I'm sorry, Maxi. Did I hurt you? I didn't think I pulled hard enough to hurt."

She looked away for a moment. "No, you didn't hurt me, and I'm the one who should apologize. My brother, Michael, used to do that to me. When he teased me, he'd always pull on my braid, then knock my hat off. I guess I'm just missing my brother and my pa."

"I see." Paul studied the back of his horse's head. After a moment, he asked, "Do you hate him?"

"Hate him? No! I love my brother. I could never hate him."

"Good. Then there's hope for me. Maybe if I pull your braid and knock your hat off every once in a while, you'll find you love me too." In one quick motion, Paul reached over, knocking her hat in her face again. "Race you to the wagon," he dared and was off in a flash.

She couldn't let a challenge slip by and kicked Ginger's flanks. "Yah, Ginger! Go get him!"

Paul easily made it to the wagon first, but Maxi was right on his heels. "That wasn't a fair race. You got a head start."

"Someday, Miss Mayfield, we'll race again. Right now, I need to get back to work." He didn't wait for a response, just turned toward the herd, swatting Maxi's hat as he rode by. If he had looked back, he would have seen a little grin on her face, a sparkle in her eyes.

CHAPTER 20

ANGEL WAS RELIEVED when Justin joined her and Maxi at the wagon. "Maxi told me about those men wanting to trade horses. Is it true the Cheyenne were there to help?"

"Yes, they made a big difference."

"Are they still back there?"

"No, they left. They're hunting buffalo and didn't want to waste any more time visiting. By the way, Maxi, you and Paul were great."

"What do you mean?" Maxi looked warily at Justin.

"Your play acting helped convince Owl that you wouldn't make a very good wife. He's asked me twice now about you. He would have given many horses for you. I told him that you were too old. When you slapped at Paul, that proved my point. I told him he could see for himself that you don't obey, you're bossy, and hard to control. When a woman gets as old as you, it's hard to retrain them to be a good wife." Justin ducked his head to hide a snicker.

"I can't believe you said that. And I'm not old. I'm seventeen, and that's hardly old."

He glanced a knowing look at Angel. "I think seventeen is a perfect age. The young braves I've been around think the younger, the better. That way, they don't have to beat them as often."

"I think you're just telling stories, Justin Myers." Maxi tossed her head, trying to look indignant.

"Well, I've got to get out to the herd. But you think on it, Maxi. If you decide you want to be Owl's wife let me know, and I'll go find him." Justin turned serious. "Both of you really do need to be cautious. I don't think that bunch of men will come back, but you never know." He winked at Angel, then rode off.

Maxi watched him for a few moments. "Do you think he was serious?"

"About Owl wanting you for a wife? Yes, I think he was serious. If you could only see yourself, Maxi. You're a beautiful woman. When you're on your horse out there working the cattle, well, it's just quite a sight. You look like you were born to this kind of life. Any man, Indian or white, would be crazy not to want you."

"Well, thanks, but I don't know what to think about that."

The rest of the day moved along without incident. That evening, Justin told the girls they were making camp by a lake right up ahead. He told them he had already checked the area, and it was safe to pull the wagon on in by the lake.

Angel heard the concern in his voice. "Thanks, Justin, I know you're worried about us, but the last few days have made us more cautious." She waved her hand to send him back to work. "Go on now or Travis will think I'm holding you up."

"Ha! He's the one who told me not to let you two out of my sight."

Later that evening when everyone was settling in for the night, Maxi asked, "Angel, will you play for me tonight? It's so beautiful, and out here, your playing would finish the day off perfectly."

"I'd like that too," Justin said as he came around the corner of the wagon. "Play for us, please."

"You asked for it, so I don't want to hear any complaining."

A full moon reflected across the lake with hardly a breath of wind stirring. Justin and Bill stretched out on their backs close to the fire. Maxi spread her ground cloth by the wagon and lay on her side, head propped up by an elbow, watching Angel play.

Beautiful strains of the violin wafted toward Travis Buchannon as he rode slowly toward camp. Quietly, he dismounted and stood in the shadows, listening intently. Justin had heard him ride in and caught a glimpse of the man standing in the darkness. He thought he saw Travis wiping his eyes; then, he turned away. Justin hurried to catch up with him. "You okay, Travis?"

"Yeah, I'm okay. Memories came flooding in when I heard that fiddle." He waited a minute, struggling to get his emotions under control. "My Beth played the fiddle like that. She was good. Not as good as Angel but good. I loved hearing her play. Justin? When we get home would it bother you if I called on your mother? She might not want me around, but I think she's a wonderful woman. I'd like to know if she would consider having me in her life. Beth's been gone seven years now. I know she would want me to go on with my life. I didn't think I would ever love another woman, but I've been thinking of your mother for some time now. She's a special woman."

"Wow. I admit I'm a little surprised, Travis. I've never thought about my mother marrying again. I really think that should be up to her, of course. I'll tell you this, though, I know she's been lonely these last few years. In all honesty, I can't think of anyone I would rather be a part of our family than you. I think it's a compliment that you want to call on her."

"Thanks. Well, I better get back out there. Land's sake, that lady can play! If you let her get away, I'll be mighty disappointed in you."

"Oh, she won't get away if I can help it." Justin spoke with such confidence that Travis chuckled at him. "See you later."

Everyone had started to turn in when Justin went back to the campfire. As he slipped by the wagon, he heard a soft voice say, "Good night, Justin."

His heartbeat doubled, and he wanted to find the owner of that voice. He knew he didn't dare, though. He just sighed in resignation. "Good night, Angel. Sweet dreams."

The next two days were long and tiring, but no real problems cropped up. The landscape began to change, a slow opening up of earth and sky. The mountains gave way to long stretches of prairie grass in waves of rolling hills. Angel came to the top of a rise and stopped, set the brake, then stood up to get a good look at the sight before her. A short gust of wind sent the grasses swaying one way, then changing direction at the whim of the next gust. Shades of green and silver stretched out for miles in front of her. She shut her eyes, lifted her face to the sky, and stretched out her arms wide, looking as though she was ready to take flight.

That's how Justin found her.

She sensed his presence more than she heard his approach. "Oh, hi, Justin." Dropping her arms, she felt her face flush with embarrassment but smiled, glad to see him.

"Hi to you too. May I ask where you were going to fly off to?" His eyes danced with amusement.

"Sure, you can ask. I just had to stop and look. It's just like in my dream."

"And what dream would that be?"

"Remember when you found me in Mr. Spriggs's stable?"

"I sure do." The crooked, little grin made an appearance.

"When I fell asleep, I had a dream that helped me make up my mind about going with Maxi. I saw myself in a café in Denver where I had asked about a job. I was in a back room washing dishes. It was awful! I just kept getting smaller and smaller. It got harder to lift the dishes and reach the sink. I realized I was dying. I knew then I couldn't live in a city or I would just shrivel up and die. Then a wind came and lifted me high into the sky where I could see the mountains, lakes, trees, and all of God's creation. Then the wind changed, and I was flying lower. It took me across land just like this. It was the most glorious feeling of openness and freedom. This is how I want to live." She stopped and looked at Justin for a few moments. "You probably think I'm crazy. I don't usually pay any attention to dreams, but this one was so real."

He looked out at the land he loved, then looked back at the woman he loved. "No, I don't think you're crazy. It has the same affect on me." They silently studied each other for several moments. "Angel?"

"What is it, Justin?"

"Let's find some time to talk tonight, alone. I have some important things I want to talk to you about. We'll be in Fort Laramie before long, probably tomorrow, and I want to talk before then. Just keep it to yourself, okay?"

"Okay. We'll work it out some way."

"Now you need to get moving, Miss Hawkins, or the herd will be out of sight."

That evening after the campfire was started, the girls learned about peashooters. Marty came in with six pheasants that Bill had shot with a peashooter. They were impressed especially after finding out that it was another name for a sling shot, but the pheasant supper was a big hit.

When camp chores were done, Angel made her nightly visit to say good night to the mules. She walked into the open area where the mules were grazing. She scratched their ears and petted each one, then shooed them away. "Go on now, go on." When she heard someone approaching, she called out. "Justin, is that you?"

"Yes, it's me." When he got close, he held out his hand to her. "Let's walk over here." Taking her hand in his, he led her toward the spring where they had been getting water.

"Is something wrong, Justin?"

"No, there's nothing wrong. As a matter of fact it's just the opposite."

"What do you mean?"

"I'm not very experienced at sharing my feelings, but I want to tell you how I feel anyway." Justin had stopped so he could look down into Angel's face. "My insides have been in a turmoil ever since I first met you. I've sorted it out and know my heart now."

Moonlight shone on his face, and Angel could see his serious expression.

"Please tell me."

"Okay. For starters, I love you." He studied her face rejoicing at the smile he saw. "I just *know* that. When I'm away from you, I can't wait till I can be with you again. Just the thought of you leaving me drives me crazy. I don't know what to do, except ask if you would spend the rest of your life with me." He could barely see those adoring brown eyes as she looked up at him. "Do you think you could marry me? Spend the rest of your life with me, Angel Hawkins?"

She waited a brief moment before answering. "I thought maybe you knew already that my heart belongs to you, Justin. If you want to hear me say it, you shall. I would be blessed and honored to be your wife."

"Are you sure, Angel? If you need to think about it, I'll understand."

"I don't need to think about it. I know I love you with all my heart."

"Will you do something for me?"

"If I can. What is it?"

"Will you give me that hug you owe me?"

She didn't hesitate but took one small step forward and wrapped her arms around him. He returned her embrace, pulling her even closer, if that was possible. He whispered, "I don't ever want to let you go."

"I don't want you to either." They stood locked in each other's arms, savoring their special bond. "If we don't go before too long, someone will come looking for us."

"I know, but first, I want to tell you what I have on my mind, besides kissing you, I mean."

She pulled back just enough to look up at him. "Which are you going to do first? Tell me what's on your mind or kiss me?"

"If you keep looking at me that way, I'll kiss you, tell you what's on my mind, then kiss you again."

She didn't budge. Her eyes never strayed from his. Her heart was beating wildly. *Justin Myers, if you don't hurry and kiss me I may have to kiss you.* The thought barely crossed her mind when he lowered his head and touched his lips to hers, briefly, timidly. When it was over, she studied him for a few moments. "Is that the first time you've ever kissed someone, Justin?"

"Other than my mother's cheek, yes." He was suddenly embarrassed. "Was it that obvious? I'm sorry. I feel so stupid."

"Would it make you feel better if I told you that was my first kiss too?"

"Was it really?"

"Yes, it was. There's only one thing wrong with it though."

"What, Angel? Tell me."

"Well..." she began but hesitated.

"Go ahead, tell me."

"Okay. The only thing wrong was, it didn't last very long. Maybe you need to try again and make it last a little longer."

He smiled, relieved. "I think I can handle that."

When he bent and kissed her again, Angel found herself lost in the soft warmth of his lips on hers. "Much better," she sighed.

"I think I'm going to need a lot of practice to get it right."

"You can practice all you want after we're married."

"Speaking of marriage," he said, still holding her close, "I want to tell you what I've been thinking. When we get to Fort Laramie,

I'll make sure it's you and me who go into the fort for supplies. I want us to find a minister and get married."

"Oh, why so soon?"

"Well, when I get home there will be a million things I'll have to do, and it might be months, maybe even a year before we find a minister. Guess I'm being selfish, but I don't want to wait that long."

She was quick to agree. "No, I don't want to wait that long either. What about your mother? How will she feel about it?"

"My mother will understand. I'm so anxious for you two to meet. She'll love you, Angel. This next thing may be hard for you to understand, but I think it will be important for us to keep our marriage a secret. We won't be together as husband and wife until we get home. I really want Marty and Paul to be there with me when we get married, and I know you want Maxi with you, but we can't leave the herd alone. Someone would get left out. Travis is going to pick up the larger herd of cattle we bought at Fort Laramie. We'll have to take turns getting things done as it is. I've thought about every angle and can't come up with any other way. Seems to be the best way all around for just the two of us to be there rather than leave someone out. Maybe you can think of another way."

Angel was quiet for a while. "Maxi will be hurt, but I think she'll understand when I explain it to her. If you think that's the best way to handle things, then it's okay with me. I don't see any other solution either. I love you, Justin."

"I love you too." He pulled her close into another embrace. "We both need to go. I didn't realize it would be so hard to be apart." Justin gave Angel another quick kiss, turned her toward camp, and gave her a gentle push. "Go on now before I change my mind."

Angel didn't look back, for she knew if she did, she would run right back into his arms. *God, can this really be happening to me? Thank you so much for sending Justin into my life. I love him so. Protect him and all the men out there who are working tonight.*

She slipped into camp being careful not to disturb the others. As she sat on her bedding pulling off her shoes, Maxi whispered, "Did he kiss you?"

"I'll never tell."

"You just did. You really love him, don't you?"

"Yes."

"I think he loves you too."

"He does. He told me so tonight."

"I'm happy for you, Angel. Justin is a fine man."

"Yes. Yes, he is."

A silence fell over them as they both drifted into a deep sleep.

CHAPTER 21

JUSTIN WAS RIGHT. They did reach Fort Laramie early the next afternoon. The fort sat on a bluff above the Platt River. Camp was set up under some old cottonwood trees along the river. "What do you think of this spot, Samson?" The big, black mule responded to his name with a noise between the whinny of a horse and the braying of a donkey. Angel remembered her ma telling her a mule sounded like someone strangling an opera tenor. "You're right. I think it's downright pretty too."

Maxi came riding up as Angel was climbing down from the wagon. "Do you think we can unhitch the mules by ourselves, Angel?"

"I don't know why not. I've helped Justin enough now that I should be able to do it by myself. It's just easier with two people though."

"Okay, I'll help unhitch them. Then we can take them and the horses down river to water."

While they were letting the horses and mules drink from the river, Marty came riding up. "How are things going?"

Maxi answered, "Going good, Marty. Where are you off to?"

"I'm going to find a place to fish after I get some of those strong willow branches to make a couple of poles."

"I love to fish. I'll go with you," Maxi offered.

"Sure, I'd love the company. When I get the poles ready, I'll come get you."

"Before you go, Marty, I have a question."

"Ask away, I'll answer if I can."

"I was just wondering if we're going to cross this river? It's so wide."

"Yeah, we'll cross it. There's a place not too far up where we can cross without much trouble. Don't worry, we'll get you across." He smiled reassuringly, then rode off toward the willows.

Angel studied her friend's worried face. "What's really bothering you, Maxi? I know you're not afraid to cross the river. It's something else, isn't it?"

"Oh, I don't know. It's just…I'm not sure what I should do now."

"What do you mean?"

"I've been thinking that I should try to find someone who's going right to the Wind River area and will take us with them. I don't know where Marty's ranch is and how I'll get from there to find Michael. I hate the thought of trying to find someone else to travel with, but I don't want to be an inconvenience to Travis and the rest of them anymore. They've been so good to us."

"Why don't you talk to Marty when you two go fishing? He can help you decide what to do."

"I was thinking that maybe I should talk to Travis."

"It wouldn't hurt to talk to Travis too, but when we get to the ranches, it'll be Marty's pa who calls the shots. Travis works for him. I think Travis would give you wise counsel. Why don't you talk to both of them?"

"You're right. That's probably what I should do."

Dear, God, how am I going to tell her? If she doesn't go on with Travis and this bunch, I'll have to tell her I'm going on with Justin. Please, please, help Maxi know what to do. I'll trust you to work it out for us.

Marty and Maxi went fishing after the mules and horses were hobbled in some grass. Angel watched them ride off together. *It'll be interesting to see what happens with those two. They seem so comfortable with each other. I think there's an attraction between Paul and Maxi too. Poor girl, she doesn't have any idea what she's doing to those two cowboys. Poor cowboys, I should say.* She smiled inwardly at the thought of Maxi turning the heads of the young men who crossed her path and not even realizing how beautiful and tempting she is. *That's part of her beauty. She isn't conceited and doesn't wield her natural beauty to get her way. You're a special lady, Maxine Mayfield. I can't bear the thought of us going separate ways, but my life and heart belong to Justin now.*

She didn't want to dwell further on Maxi's decision, so she made herself busy with preparations for the evening supper. "Coffee, that's the first thing I need to do. She built a fire and made a full pot of coffee, then stood at the back of the wagon trying to organize a meal. *What will go with fish?* She sorted through the supplies, then made up her mind. *I better get at it if I'm going to get it all done. This will be fun.*

Angel was bending over the fire, cooking her surprise when Bill Gray came into camp. "Goodness, girl, what are you cooking? You're smelling up the whole countryside." He grinned and patted his stomach.

"It's a surprise. But if you want, you can get a cup of coffee and sample one. I need to know if they're fit to eat."

"If they taste anything like they smell, they'll be fit." He poured his coffee, anxiously waiting to taste Angel's surprise. "Apple!" he said, inhaling deeply. "I'd say it has apple in it."

"You'd be right." Angel picked up a sample. "Here, taste this. It's cooled down."

He took a big bite and closed his eyes while he chewed, and a look of pure delight spread across his face. "Yes, ma'am! They are definitely fit to eat." He bit off another piece, chewed and washed it down with coffee. "Shucks, I haven't had a fried apple pie in years. Brings back some memories." He licked his fingers thoroughly, longingly.

"They would taste a lot better with fresh butter and cinnamon, but I had to make do with what we had."

"You did right fine, little miss. But I think I need to sample one more just to make sure." He chuckled as he helped himself to another little apple pie.

Just as Bill popped the last bite in his mouth, Maxi came riding in. "What smells so good, Angel?"

"It's a surprise. Where's Marty?"

"We found a spot that we can bathe in. There's a little private alcove in those willows close to where we've been fishing. I can't wait to wash my hair. Marty's down there now, so when he comes out, we can go take our turn."

"That sounds great. Did you catch any fish?"

"Just a couple. They're not biting much right now, but Marty thinks they will be later on."

"Leave that pole here, Maxi, and I'll see if I can catch a few. I ain't too bad at fishing," Bill offered.

Throughout the afternoon, each one took a turn bathing while someone else took a turn fishing. Supper was a big mess of fish with cornbread, fried potatoes, and Angel's surprise of fried apple pies. The pies were a huge hit.

Travis was the last to come in to eat. "Where's the coffee and food? Land's sakes, it smells good around here. I hope you saved plenty for me. I could eat a whole cow right now. I'm so hungry."

"Well, it's not a cow, but there's plenty of fish. I saved back some of the other things we had. Help yourself."

"I hear you made a surprise. No one would tell me what it is, but I'm ready. Bring it on!"

As Travis ate, Angel chatted with him, "How did it go today, Travis? Did you find out about the other cattle?"

"Yeah, it turned out pretty good. The new herd is just a ways on the other side of the fort. They'll bring them over in the morning. I hired a couple of men to help get them home too."

"That's great."

"I hope so. I don't know the men of course, only met one of them. He seemed a bit rough, so you and Maxi watch yourselves. I trust our boys but these two bear watching."

"Okay, I'll tell Maxi. Are we going to the post for supplies in the morning?"

"Yes, I suppose you and Justin should go. I'll need all the others to help with the cattle. I'll be going in too. I need to find out if there's been any Indian trouble in the direction we're going, but it shouldn't take long. Actually, it shouldn't take too long to get the supplies either. The sutler at the post knows our ranches pretty good by now. He knows what we usually need and holds the supplies for us. Justin took a list in for him when we came through on our way to Denver."

Travis stuffed the last bite of pie in his mouth. "By the way, where's Maxi?"

"She went out to help with the cattle. She saw you coming in and thought you might want to take a bath. We all took turns with the fishing and bathing."

"I think I'll do that. There's just enough light to get it done if I hurry, but when I get back, I'll need some more coffee. And if there's any more of those apple things save me a couple. They're mighty good. You can fix those any time you like, young lady."

"Thanks, Travis. Glad you liked them."

CHAPTER 22

ANGEL DIDN'T GET to see Justin that night except for the brief time he came in to eat. And he was asleep by the fire when she awoke to start breakfast. The first thing she noticed was his clean shaven face. *He must have shaved when he went to the river to bathe. I wonder what it'll be like to kiss him without the scratchy beard.* A rush of emotion flooded her. *Today is my wedding day. I'm not even sure what day it is. June 5 or 6, I think. I've got to find out. What if we can't find anyone to marry us? What should I wear?* Her stomach started to knot. She closed her eyes for a moment to pray. *Father, help me through this day. I give it to you. Help Justin and me do the right thing. Help us find a minister to marry us.* When she opened her eyes, she was staring into Justin's smiling face. He was watching her.

He said silently, "I love you. Don't worry, it'll all be fine."

Her smile told him she trusted him, and she silently said back, "I love you too."

There was no meat for the morning meal. Maxi suggested a big batch of finger cakes and pitched in to help make them. They soon had a plate piled high and a pot of fresh coffee ready. When Justin finished eating, he hitched the mules to the wagon. Angel noticed the clean shirt he had on, and the smile that she'd seen that morning had never left his face. When they happened to have a private moment together, she told him, "If you don't wipe that grin off your face, someone is going to figure out what we're up to."

"Angel, the only thing that will wipe this grin off my face today is you saying you've changed your mind."

"Not on your life, cowboy. You're stuck with me now."

"I guess I'll just have to endure it then."

"Yeah, and I'm really going to make you suffer. I need to be sure there's enough coffee for the men while we're gone."

"Okay, the wagon's ready. When you get that done, we'll head out."

They had gone a short distance from camp when Maxi and Travis rode up. "Maxi is going in with you two," Travis told them. "We've been talking with Marty and decided she needs to leave a notice at the trading post for her brother. She's going on to the ranches with us. If her brother or any of his friends come here, they'll know where she is and come to her. If there's no response after a period of time, we'll talk to Mr. Swanson about some of us taking her to find him."

"That sounds reasonable," Justin agreed. "Sooner or later, everyone around these parts has to come here for supplies."

"I'm so glad you decided what to do, Maxi," Angel said.

Travis continued, "You'll need to help her put on the notice how to find the Double S. I'm going to hurry on to the army headquarters to find out if there's been any trouble in the direction we're going. Then I'll head back to the herd." He rode away after telling Justin, "Take good care of our ladies."

"I will. See you later."

Angel waited until Maxi was out of hearing range, then quietly asked, "What are we going to do now?"

Justin shrugged. "We don't have much choice, Angel. You'll have to tell her what we're doing and hope she understands. I want to find a minister the first thing, so while I'm making arrangements, you can talk to her. We'll go from there." He put his arm around her and gave her a gentle squeeze. "That okay with you?"

"Yes, I guess so. I can't imagine what her reaction is going to be, but somehow, it'll work out okay."

The road leading up the hill to Fort Laramie was a relatively easy climb. Buildings were scattered wide apart, and people were going in all directions, either walking, riding, or driving wagons. A small village of tepees was clustered on one side of the fort and a large wagon train filled another section of the grounds. Old Glory was flying above the main military compound, and noises of the troop's exercises could be heard on the parade ground.

"Goodness, it's a busy place, isn't it?"

"Yes, and it seems to get busier every time I come here. I'm going to go talk to that group of men by the gate and see what I can find out."

Justin brought the wagon to a halt and set the brake. He climbed down and headed toward the cluster of men who were standing around talking.

Angel dreaded what was coming next. She took a deep breath and waited. Sure enough, Maxi came up to the wagon. "What's Justin doing, Angel? I saw the trading post back over that way."

"He's trying to get information about a minister."

"Why? What does he need a minister for?"

Angel looked Maxi full in the face, her eyes pleading for understanding. She hesitated but not for long. This was the moment of truth, and she knew she had to tell her friend. As calmly as possible, she said, "Justin and I are going to get married, Maxi."

"You are?" Maxi stared at her, and slowly, it all came together. Now? You're going to get married *now*?"

"Yes, if we can find a minister."

"I can't believe it," Maxi exclaimed, staring hard at Angel. "Why didn't you say something? You could have told me." A dark thunder cloud of anger gathered over her head.

"I wanted to, Maxi, really I did. But we decided to keep it between us because we couldn't include everyone. We didn't want to hurt anyone's feelings, so we decided to go ahead with just the two of us. We were trying to think of everyone and not cause any trouble. Maxi, I would love to have you stand up with me. Please be happy for me."

The thunder cloud grew darker. "Angel, you can't do this. It's not right. You should wait."

"Why should we wait? Justin and I love each other. We want to spend the rest of our lives together. If we wait until we get to his home, it will be months, maybe a year, before we can be married by a minister. We both want a minister to marry us. This will be our best opportunity."

"You're going through with this no matter what?"

"Yes, no matter what. If we find a minister who is willing, Justin and I will get married today."

"Then I won't be a part of it." She quickly turned her horse and rode off, leaving Angel watching after her with tears pooling in her eyes.

Justin climbed on the wagon just then, looking very happy, but his happiness vanished when he saw Angel's teary eyes. "I'm sorry, Angel." Justin put his arm around her, giving her a gentle squeeze. "Maxi left, didn't she?"

"Yes, she did." Angel laid her head on his shoulder and wiped her eyes with the back of her hand. "She said she didn't want to be a part of it if we got married now."

He reached over and wiped away another tear that had slipped down Angel's cheek." Are you still wanting to go through with this, Angel?"

"More than anything in this world."

Maxi slowed her horse to a walk. She was fuming and puzzled. *I can't believe she would do this to me. I don't know how to stop her. What should I do? Think! Wait, I know. I've got to find Travis. He'll talk some sense into those two. I bet he'll put a stop to their silly notions right now. Where did he say he was going? Oh, yes, army headquarters.* She stopped a man in uniform and asked him for directions. She gave Ginger a gentle kick. *What luck. Travis is just now coming out the door. I can't wait to tell him.* She pulled up in front of the building and practically jumped off her horse right in front of Travis.

"Maxi, what are you doing here? You're supposed to be with Justin and Angel."

"I've come to get you. You've got to stop them, Travis."

"Stop who? What are you talking about?"

"They're going to get married. You have to stop them."

Travis stared at Maxi for a moment; then, finally understood what she was saying. "Why, that son of a gun! You mean they're going to get married now? Right now?"

"Yes! I couldn't stop Angel. I'm hoping you can talk some sense into Justin."

He studied her for another minute. "I'm not sure I understand, Maxi. Why would I want to stop them?"

She fidgeted. "Well…it's just not right. They should wait."

"Wait for what?"

She hesitated. "I don't know." She threw her hands up in exasperation. "Wait a proper time, I guess."

Travis looked long and hard at Maxi. With the sternness of a father, he finally asked, "What is it, really, you object to? Are you jealous of them getting married? Or possibly afraid you're losing a friend? Just what is it, Maxi?"

The words struck her a paralyzing blow. She stood frozen, staring at Travis, uncomprehending his rebuke. *Why is he being so mean to me?* Slowly, an understanding began to thaw her heart and clear her mind. The thunder cloud burst. Tears of shame and remorse stung her eyes, and she buried her face in her hands and sobbed. "I'm so embarrassed and ashamed. You're right. I am jealous, and I felt like I was losing my friend. Mostly, I was just plain jealous. Now, what am I going to do?"

He put his arm around her shoulders. "It'll be all right."

"I've got to find her," she said, wiping her eyes. "Angel deserves the best, and Justin is a wonderful man. I need to go stand up for her…if she'll have me."

"Now that's the right way to think. Why don't we both go find them and be part of their special day." He turned to mount his horse.

"I don't know where they went," Maxi said, getting on Ginger.

"They can't be too hard to find. Where did you last see them?"

"By the main gate into the military compound. Justin was talking to a bunch of men there."

"Let's go see if any of them are still around."

Quickly, they rode off, and Maxi took him to where she had left Angel and Justin. "They were right here," Maxi said, pulling up.

"Do you think you could recognize any of the men that Justin talked to?"

"I don't know," she said looking around frantically. "I…there! Over there. I think he was one of them."

"You stay here. I'll go talk to him." Travis made his way over to the young man who was leaning against a post smoking a cigarette. The man made gestures and pointed away from the fort. Maxi was encouraged. *He must know something. God, please let me find Angel.*

As soon as Travis was close enough, Maxi asked, "What did he say? Does he know where they are?"

"Cheer up, I know where they went. There was a young Methodist preacher in that group of men. He was inviting everyone to a service tonight at one of the wagon trains. The man agreed to marry Justin and Angel, said he would go get his Bible and his wife and meet them at the maple trees by their wagon train." Travis swung up on his horse.

"Let's hurry, Travis, I've got to get there."

"Okay, let's go. Just don't run over anyone."

Finding the place wasn't hard. There were only five maple trees in the neighborhood of the wagon train and they had cooperated very nicely by growing all bunched together. "There's Justin. I'll go talk to him. You find Angel."

Maxi spotted a young woman standing at the back of a wagon. She hurried over to her. "I'm looking for a friend. Her name is Angel. The preacher is going to marry her and Justin. Do you—"

A voice from inside the wagon called out, "Maxi, is that you?"

"Yes, it's me. Angel, I'm so sorry. Will you forgive me? I found Travis thinking I could get him to change your minds, but he made me see I was just jealous and afraid I would lose you as a friend. We both are here and want to stand up for you and Justin, if you'll have us."

"Of course, you're forgiven. And coming back to be with me means more than you'll ever know. I'd invite you in, but there's not room. I'll be out in a minute. I'm almost ready."

"There's a man coming over," said the other woman, who happened to be the preacher's wife.

"Who is it?" Angel called out.

"It's Travis." Maxi answered.

"Okay, I'm ready." Angel parted the heavy canvas curtains on the wagon.

Maxi gasped, "Angel! You're beautiful."

"Amen to that," Travis agreed as he joined them.

"That must be the doeskin clothes the Cheyenne gave you. They're lovely."

"They are, aren't they? My shoes were coming apart, so I decided to wear the moccasins. Then I thought, might as well wear the skirt and shirt too. Rebecca, here, put the flowers in my hair. Do I really look okay, Maxi?"

"Angel, I've never seen a more beautiful bride. Justin is a lucky man."

Travis spoke up then, "Speaking of Justin, he's one anxious cowboy waiting for his bride. Since you don't have your father here, I would love to walk you to that lucky man and give you away—that is, if you want me to."

"Oh, Travis, thank you! That would be wonderful."

The preacher's wife gave them some instructions. "Maxi, go stand beside the preacher. Then Travis can walk Angel over and hand her to Justin. He can take his place on the other side of the preacher." She looked at Angel. "You ready now?"

"Yes," Angel inhaled deeply. "I'm ready."

Maxi took her place by the preacher, watching joyously as Travis made his way to them with Angel on his arm. White daisies circled Angel's head, looking as if she wore a halo. She was radiant with happiness. Travis took Angel's small hand and placed it in Justin's. "Take good care of her, Justin, she's special."

Justin choked up. "I will, Travis." His eyes never left Angel's face.

Maxi didn't even try to hide her tears. She just swiped them away as fast as they rolled down her cheeks. *I can't believe I almost missed this. I really am jealous of the special love these two have for each other. God, I pray someday I'll find a love like theirs. I am so happy for Angel. Help me be the friend to her that I should be.*

Angel and Justin said their vows looking deeply into each other's eyes. The preacher asked for the ring, and Justin put his hand in his pocket and brought out a ring. When she looked at him in surprise, he nodded toward Travis. She glanced at him and said silently, "Thank you."

Travis nodded an acknowledgement as he blinked back his tears.

"Do you give this ring as a symbol of your love for Angel?"

"I do," Justin said solemnly.

"Will you receive this ring and wear it as a symbol of your love for Justin?"

"I will," she softly answered.

"You can place the ring on her finger," instructed the preacher.

When he slipped the ring on her finger, she noticed that Justin's hand was shaking. She looked into his hazel eyes and smiled.

"Then, before we all start crying, I pronounce you, Justin and Angel, husband and wife. You may kiss your bride, young man."

Justin did just that. Without hesitation, he put his hands on her shoulders, bent down, and kissed her soundly.

The preacher wrote out a certificate of marriage and had Maxi, Travis, and his wife sign it as witnesses. "Put the date next to your names," he reminded them.

"What day is this, Justin?"

"It's our day, Friday, June 6, the day you became Mrs. Justin Myers."

"That has a beautiful sound to it, Mr. Myers."

Travis broke into their conversation, "Sorry to interrupt you two, but Maxi and I are going to go on. I'll take her to the trading post and help with the notice for her brother. You two take your time and come back to camp when you're ready."

"Thanks, Travis. Can I talk to you and Maxi before you leave?" Maxi came over and stood by them. "Angel and I have decided not to be together as husband and wife until we get home. I figured it would be better all the way around. We'd rather you didn't say anything to the others. I want to tell my mother first before anyone else knows."

"It may be the longest week of your life!" Travis slapped Justin on the back. "But it's probably the best thing to do. We won't say anything, right, Maxi?"

"Your secret is safe with me."

"Let's get to the trading post, Maxi. We've got work to do."

As they rode off, Travis got Maxi's attention. "Maxi?"

"What, Travis?"

"I'm proud of you. You handled that like a real lady. Your turn will come someday. I hope you realize you haven't lost a friend, you've just gained a whole family. And I hope you'll consider me part of it."

"Thank you, Travis. I will."

"Looks like the rest of our herd is being delivered." Justin and Angel were sitting on the wagon seat on the edge of the bluff where Fort Laramie stood. They could see the Platte River and the prairie beyond. Mostly, they were enjoying being together.

"That more than doubles the herd you brought up from Denver, doesn't it?"

"Yeah, but it's still not a large one. We're having to build our herds slowly. The Double S is larger than my family spread. They'll be taking about two-thirds of this new bunch. But I don't want to talk about business things right now. I just want to spend the day looking at my beautiful wife. I wish you could have kept your doeskin outfit on. You took my breath away when you stepped out from behind that wagon. I figure I'm just about the luckiest man in the west."

"I'm certainly glad you think so since you just promised to spend the rest of your life with me."

"I hope it's a long one too." Looking down at Angel, he noticed she was gazing to the south, her eyes searching. He was pretty sure he knew what she was looking for but dreaded what he had to tell her. "What are you looking for? You're supposed to be looking at me."

"I'm sorry, it's nothing." She quickly brought her attention back to Justin.

"Angel, everything about you is important to me. I want you to always tell me if something is bothering you. That's how I think it should be between a husband and wife. We need to be honest with each other, sharing everything."

"I like that, Justin. I feel the same way."

They sat in silence, searching each other's face until his gaze fell on her lips. He leaned down to kiss his wife. "I sure like this practicing. Do you think I'll ever get it right?"

She giggled. "I promise to let you know when you can stop practicing. And I was looking for Sir Ugly."

"That's what I thought. I wish I could protect you from things like this, but the truth is, your dog is dead, Angel."

"Oh, I knew something was wrong. I've been looking for him for several days now. I never could get him to come into camp. When there were supper scraps, I left them out at night, and they were always gone the next morning…until the last few days. Do you know what happened to him?"

"Yes, Owl told me. That's how they found those seven men who came out of the mountains the other day. They heard gunshots, and when they checked it out, they found the men making sport of Sir Ugly. They eventually killed him. I'm sorry I didn't tell you sooner."

"That's okay. Thanks for telling me now."

"I don't want you to be sad, especially today."

"I'm fine. I know it's part of life to face these things. Besides, if animals go to heaven, that poor old dog won't be lonely anymore. Do you think animals go to heaven, Justin?"

He rolled his eyes and looked at the clouds. "Is this how it's going to be? You're going to expect me to answer all those hard questions?" He feigned exasperation.

"Of course. I thought husbands had all the answers."

"Well, this one doesn't. I do know the Bible talks about animals in heaven. It also says Jesus will come back on a white horse. Will that do for now, Mrs. Myers? These mules are getting impatient to be on their way."

"Yes, that will do for now, Mr. Myers."

CHAPTER 23

"IT'S A RELIEF to have that crossing over with. I was worried about Justin getting the wagon across the river," Angel confessed, then asked Maxi, "What do you think of that new stallion of Paul's?"

"He's one beautiful animal. Bill was telling me that Paul bought him from an officer at the fort. Because of health problems, he has to go back east and couldn't take the horse. Bill said the light-gray coat with the tiny black spots is called flea-bitten. The black mane and tail are really pretty with his coat. By the way, his name is Diablo."

"I heard Paul telling you and the others to watch yourselves around him until he gets to know the horse better. I'm not sure Paul would like you getting close enough to feed him apples."

"You saw me, huh?" Maxi had a mischievous grin on her face. As she rode away to check out some rocks that were ahead of the wagon, she called back to Angel, "If you don't tell him, he'll never know."

Time moved slowly the rest of the day as the men moved the cattle along. Bill Gray had trouble with Diablo misbehaving and trying to take a bite out of his leg, which brought Travis to the wagon in the afternoon. "Maxi, Paul and I were wondering if you can handle that stallion of his. He's causing all kinds of problems with Bill and the other horses. Bill noticed he seemed to favor you this morning. We'll tie him securely to the back of the wagon. Just watch him, and I'll keep Paul close on this side of the herd in case you need help. What do you think?"

"I'm willing to try it, Travis. I don't think Diablo would hurt me on purpose. Are you sure Paul is okay with it?"

"I'm not sure he likes it, mostly because he doesn't want you to get hurt."

After a long day Angel complimented Maxi. "You did good with Diablo today. I don't think it's the apples that make him behave, I think he just likes you."

"I hope so, 'cause I like him too."

The next morning, all of the men were out with the herd except one of the new hired hands who had lingered over his coffee. Angel was bending over the fire scraping out a pan when she felt a couple of pats on her backside. Whirling around, she glared at Tip, the new man. He stepped back feigning innocence.

"What do you think you're doing? Don't ever touch me like that again!" she warned.

Maxi had seen the whole incident from the back of the wagon where she was putting supplies away. Grabbing her rifle, she added her own threat, "If you don't get back to work right now, I'll shoot you where you stand!"

He turned and saw the rifle pointed at him. "Wait a minute, girls. You misunderstand me. There were a couple of burning cinders that landed on the back of her shirt. I was just trying to brush them off before she caught fire. You can put that rifle away. I didn't mean any harm."

"I'll put my rifle away when you get on your horse and ride out of here."

He put his hands up in surrender. "Okay, okay, I'm going. I don't think you should treat a man that way when he's just trying to help."

Maxi didn't lower her rifle until the man rode off toward the herd. "I haven't liked that man since the first time I saw him."

"I know what you mean. He's been leering at us all morning. The other man, I think his name is Mack, seems really nice and polite. He even offered to get more water for me."

"Yeah, he does seem a lot different. But let's not trust either one of them for now."

"Maxi?"

"What?"

"Should we tell anyone what happened? Do you think I had some live cinders on my back?"

"No, I don't think you did," Maxi said without hesitation. "But I don't know if we should say anything or not. I hate to cause trouble. Maybe we scared him enough that he won't do anything else."

"I hope so."

"We better get these mules hitched to the wagon, or that herd will be out of sight."

A short time later, Maxi saw Paul leading Diablo toward them. Angel halted the wagon. As Paul tied the horse to the back, he asked, "You sure you're okay with this, Maxi?"

"I'll do my best to take good care of him."

"It's not the horse I'm worried about. I don't want you to get hurt. Please don't take any chances 'cause he's been ornery this morning. They had trouble with him at the fort. He wouldn't let anyone but the major ride him."

"Okay, I'll be real careful."

Paul watched as Diablo walked to the end of his rope, getting as close to Maxi as he could. Maxi let Ginger close the distance between her and Diablo. She talked to him as the horses greeted each other whinnying and sniffing. "Good morning, Diablo.

Looks like we get to spend the day with each other." She patted his neck. "Are you going to be a good boy?"

Paul shook his head as Diablo gently nuzzled her leg and arm. "Well, I can see he likes you a lot more than he likes me or Bill. But be careful anyway. He still might try to bite or kick you."

"I don't think he'll hurt me on purpose, Paul, but I'll be careful."

"Good. I've got to get back out there. You know I'll be on this side of the herd in case you need me."

"Yeah, Travis told me."

"Okay then, see you later."

Paul was a good distance away when Maxi pulled out part of an apple from her pocket and fed it to Diablo. Angel commented, "It's a good thing we have apples."

"Don't tell me you haven't given those mules a treat of apples when you go out to say good night to them."

Laughing and quite unashamed, Angel confessed, "Guilty as charged."

The weather was sunny with clear skies. The wind would gust at times threatening to blow the hat from your head, but it was only a small nuisance. Maxi was scouting ahead, telling Angel which direction to go to miss large rocks and holes. Early afternoon, she came riding back to the wagon. "Angel, there's a shallow draw up ahead. The edge is slow and smooth. You should be fine, but I'm going to take Diablo on over to the other side. I'll wait for you there. Be careful."

Angel let the mules rest while she waited for Maxi to make her way down the draw and up the other side. Then she started the wagon forward. "Hup, Samson! Take it easy now. We've gone over steeper than this. Delilah, Mary, Martha, you too, easy does it. We'll be fine." The descent was a little tricky, but the mules made it to the bottom without incident. They leaned into their harnesses and, in no time, had the wagon at the top.

"That seemed fairly smooth. I see another dip up ahead a ways. I'll keep Diablo with me till we get over there and can—" Maxi quit talking, trying to bring her horse under control. "Ginger, whoa, easy girl! What's wrong with you?" Ginger wouldn't settle down, and Diablo lunged to the end of the rope that Maxi was holding him on. "Whoa, Diablo!" The big stallion stopped for only a moment. He faced forward, head high, nostrils flaring. His ears flicked and pointed forward. All of a sudden, he lunged, almost pulling Maxi from her saddle. He danced, pressing forward. "Put the flag up, Angel! I can't hold him much longer! What is it, Diablo? Easy, boy." Diablo would not settle down. A scream came from deep in his throat, challenging, threatening. The horse reared and pawed the air. As his feet came crashing down, he hit the rope and pulled it from Maxi's hand. Then, he was gone. *Oh, Paul! I'm sorry!* Maxi wasn't one to give up without a fight. She made a split-second decision. Kicking Ginger hard in the sides, she ordered, "Yah, Ginger, let's catch him!"

Paul's heart nearly thudded out of his chest. He couldn't believe his eyes. Diablo was running for all he was worth with Maxi right behind him, riding low and fast. She held the reins in one hand and a rope in the other. "What…! In a flash of realization, he knew what was going to happen. *She's going to try and rope him. She'll be pulled off her horse and—* Paul kicked his horse. Moving quickly he pulled his rope off his saddle and was off in an all-out race to intercept Diablo. Just as the stallion raced by, Paul moved in behind him. Bringing his rope up, he whirled it above his head. At the right exact moment, he let it fly, looping it over Diablo's head while keeping pace with the horse. From the corner of his eye, he saw another rope sailing towards the stallion. It was a perfect throw and rested right on top of his own rope. *Maxi!* They very slowly let their ropes grow taut working as weight to slow the stallion down.

Finally, Diablo went over a rise and came to a halt. Immediately, a formidable scream rose up from Diablo. From a herd of wild mustangs down in the draw came an answering challenge in the form of a white mustang stallion. He ran toward Diablo, slowed, and paced back and forth, pawing the earth. Diablo was ready to fight. He strained forward, pawing the ground. Maxi winced as Paul pulled his rifle.

"Hold him!" he shouted to Maxi. "If you have to let go, do it!"

The stallion dashed toward Diablo just as Paul raised his rifle and fired a shot into the ground in front of the mustang. The horse whirled around but came back with another run at Diablo. Paul shot again. The stallion was convinced to get his herd away. He turned, calling to the mares who had been nervously milling around. As he raced ahead, about fifty wild horses followed the white mustang over the next rise. *What a sight! I'm glad Paul didn't have to shoot the stallion.*

Paul's attention was on Diablo now. He started talking to him in a soothing voice. "Okay, boy, it's all over. Easy, boy." Diablo began to settle down, still looking in the direction of the herd that had disappeared in the foothills. Paul dismounted. The well-trained horses held the tension on the ropes that were on Diablo. Paul ran his gloved hand up the rope, still talking calmly. "Easy, now. I'm just going to take these ropes off." When he was close enough, he stroked Diablo's neck. "Easy, now. They're all gone. It's okay, now." Diablo shook his head and stomped the ground. But he allowed Paul to remove Maxi's rope. Getting hold of the lead rope, he lifted his own rope off next. "Got a little excited, didn't you, boy? Settle down. It's all over."

Maxi dismounted and started to coil her rope. "I'm sorry, Paul."

Diablo turned his head toward the sound of Maxi's voice, then walked calmly over to her. Paul watched curiously as the horse started butting her arm with his nose. "Oh, all right. You're making me give away my secret." She reached into her pocket and pulled out a piece of apple and fed it to Diablo.

"So that's why he likes you so much. You're spoiling my stallion, Maxi."

"I just wanted to make friends with him."

"Well, it seems you've done that. I hope we have plenty of apples."

"You're not mad at me then?"

"Yes, I'm mad at you!" He went to stand right in front of her.

She looked up into his stormy, dark eyes. "You are? Why?"

"Because you scared me half to death that's why. Do you realize there are a hundred different ways you could have been killed or badly hurt racing after him like that? What if your horse had stepped in a hole? Or that stallion had—I don't even want to think about what could have happened." Paul reached out, taking hold of Maxi's shoulder. "You are one wonderful, crazy, little girl!" He shocked her then by pulling her close and planting a kiss on her lips that left her stunned and speechless. He pulled away, and their eyes met and held for a moment. From the corner of his eye, Paul saw movement and peeled his gaze away from Maxi's face. There was Travis, sitting on his horse about thirty yards away wearing a big grin. "Uh-oh! The boss is watching. Gotta go."

Paul got on his horse and led Diablo away while Maxi followed him with her eyes. Her hand went to her lips, and she mumbled to herself, "I didn't know. I didn't know a kiss would be like that."

Travis rode over to her. "You okay?"

"Do you know what he did?"

"Well, I saw him kiss you."

"He called me wonderful, crazy. Then he called me a little girl. I *hate* it when someone calls me a little girl."

Travis had a hard time holding back laughter. "Don't be too hard on the poor cowboy. He's probably as confused right now as he's ever been. If it's any consolation, I'm sure he's aware you're not a little girl. I think maybe he likes you, Maxi."

"Likes me? He has a funny way of showing it. He hardly talks to me, and when he does, it's just teasing."

"Put yourself in Paul's place. Marty has already made it known he's going to court you. Those two have been competing since they were young boys. Paul usually just backs off and lets Marty have his way. Marty will inherit a nice ranch one of these days and be able to provide nicely for a wife. Paul probably thinks of himself as only a hired hand. In a way, Marty is his boss. Paul has more going for him than he realizes though. He has a nice start at a horse ranch on that high meadow of his. Get him to tell you about it sometime." Travis paused, trying to figure out what Maxi was thinking, then decided to leave it alone. "Shall we get back now?"

Maxi mumbled as she headed to her horse, "Men! Why do they have to be so complicated?"

Travis choked back a laugh, covering it with a cough.

Maxi mounted and noticed right away that Ginger was limping. "Wait, something's wrong with Ginger." Getting off again, she led her horse a few steps forward. "Looks like it's her left front foot." She ran her hand down the leg, then checked the hooves. "I don't see any rocks or anything in her shoe."

"We'll have Bill check it. Come on over and climb up behind me. We'll walk her over and see what Bill says." When Maxi was settled, he asked her, "How'd you learn to throw a rope?"

"At the ranches where Pa worked, the cowboys were always challenging me to shoot, race, rope, and ride. I loved to beat them. At first, I think they let me win. But I got to where I could give them a good run for their money."

"I don't think I'll ever forget the sight of you racing after that stallion, with your hair and hat flying behind you. Then, when you slipped that rope right over his head on the first try, I was downright flabbergasted. I think your pa would be mighty proud of his girl." Travis chuckled. "He might have turned you over his knee and gave you a good spanking for scaring him to death."

"Is that your way of telling me that I scared you?"

"You might say that."

"Well, I really am sorry. I just had to try and get him back."

"It worked out okay, and no one was hurt. Except, maybe, that horse of yours. There's Bill. We'll find out what he thinks."

They stopped in front of Bill. "Howdy. Looks like that horse has a limp."

"Yeah, that's why we came over. Will you look at her and see what you think?"

"Be glad to." Bill took his time examining Ginger's legs and hooves. Then he walked her around. "I don't see anything serious. Probably pulled a muscle or tendon. Let's get this saddle off her. You can ride one of these other horses for the rest of the day. When we get to camp later, I'll let her stand in the cold creek for a while, then put some liniment on her leg. You'll see, she'll be just fine. Don't look so worried."

"Thanks, Bill. I appreciate it. I'll saddle Sweet Raven and ride her for the rest of the day."

CHAPTER 24

MAXI GOT RAVEN saddled and skirted the back of the herd. She soon ran into Marty. "Hi, how's it going?"

"I'm doing good. I hear you had a little excitement."

"The exciting part was seeing the wild mustangs. They were quite a sight. The white stallion leading them was beautiful in a wild sort of way. His coat was dirty and mangy looking. Even from a distance, I could see scars from the fights he's been in, made him look dangerous. But I'm still glad Paul didn't have to shoot him."

"I don't think Paul would shoot any horse unless it was a matter of life or death."

"I'm glad it didn't come to that. Well, I need to get back. I'll see you later, Marty." Maxi rode toward the wagon, feeling Marty's eyes on her. *What am I going to do? I really like Marty. He's been so kind and friendly to me and so much fun! I love being around him.* Then Maxi's thoughts turned to Paul and her hand involuntarily went to her mouth. *My first kiss! And it happened so fast, and unexpectedly, I didn't get a chance to know if I liked it or not. Drat it, Paul! Why didn't you make it last a little longer?* Maxi laughed at herself. *I don't even know why I'm thinking about it. I probably won't be around either one for very long. I'll be going to Michael's ranch pretty soon. I'll just have to be friends with both of them.* Satisfied that she had reached the right decision, Maxi hurried to the wagon. She was surprised to see Diablo tied to the back. "Hi, Angel."

"Are you all right?"

"Yes, I'm fine. Ginger hurt her leg, but Bill is taking care of her. He doesn't think it's serious though. Other than that, I'm doing good." She waved to Justin, signaling that she was back so he could return to the herd. The fact that Paul brought Diablo back to the wagon was on her mind. *Paul must trust me if he brought Diablo back.* She remembered the conversation about thanking God for everything, so she prayed. *God, don't let Paul think badly of me. Thank you for keeping us all safe. The wild horses were wonderful.*

The day wore on without further incident, but there was a change in the air. "It's getting cooler, don't you think, Angel?"

"Yes, I think it is. I put my coat on a little while ago. There's no sign of storm clouds, but the breeze is definitely colder."

"A nice fire and hot cup of coffee sounds good right now. Better stop the wagon. Justin's coming."

Angel brought the wagon to a halt, waiting for her handsome cowboy.

Justin noticed that Angel had put her coat on. "I see you two have felt the weather getting colder too. Bill has been complaining all day that his bones ache. He said we're going to have a humdinger of a rainstorm. Since he's usually right, Travis wants to get across the river up ahead before we make camp. Even if it rains heavily in the mountains, but not down here, we could still have a flash flood. Let's switch, Angel. You ride Butch, and I'll take the wagon."

"I don't see any signs of rain." She climbed down from the wagon.

"Not yet, but it's coming." He pointed at the distant mountains. "If you look way out over the mountain, it looks like a buildup of storm clouds."

"Yeah, but that's a long ways off."

"Well, it can blow on in here in no time. We can get some mighty fierce winds out here on the prairie. If there's thunder and lightning with the storm, this will be the best place to hold up. Across the river, there's a draw that can shelter the horses and cattle. It'll be a whole lot easier to hold them in the draw than out on the flat land."

Justin drove the wagon across the shallow river without any trouble. He made sure the girls got over safely and helped them set up their campsite.

"I need to go on back and help get the cattle settled down. The men will let them water before they drive them into the draw to bed down. That'll take all of us. Is there anything you two need before I leave?"

Angel answered, "I think we're all set. But I want to talk to you when you come back in to eat."

"Anything that needs my attention right now?"

"No. It can wait until you finish with the herd."

Maxi watched him until he was out of sight. "You going to tell him what Tip did this morning?"

"Yes, I've decided I should tell him. I'll make sure he knows we don't think Tip will bother us again. I'll have to admit that I don't look forward to that man coming in for supper."

"Neither do I. Let's give him the cold shoulder and don't even look at him."

"I was doing that before he decided to touch me like he did. I looked on the back of my shirt and didn't see any kind of evidence of a cinder." Angel shuddered. "I'll stay out of his reach from now on."

In a few moments, Travis came in. "How are you ladies doing?"

"We're doing fine. We'll have the food ready pretty quick," Angel answered.

He went to the fire and held his hands over the flames to warm them. "Can't believe it got cold so fast. Man, that coffee smells good." He poured some in a cup and took a sip.

"Do you really think it'll rain, Travis?" Maxi asked.

"I've learned not to argue with Bill's bones. He's right most of the time. It might be a good idea if you girls would move things around in the wagon so you can sleep in there out of the rain and wind."

Angel looked into the back of the wagon. "It'll be tight, but maybe we can make enough room for us to sleep in there."

"Another thing you could do is gather up as much dry wood as you can and put the small tarp over it. We'll rig up a lean-to off the wagon with the large tarp so we can sit under it. Some of us may have to sleep under the wagon—that is, if we get a chance to sleep. Depends on the storm I guess, but we could be stuck here for a couple days if it rains very much."

Travis finished the cup of coffee. "I'm going to start sending them in two at a time now, if you're ready."

"Go ahead. We'll be ready by the time they get here."

Paul and Tip came in first. Tip tried to draw Paul into conversation like they had been buddies for a long time. But Paul remained rather quiet, covertly watching the girls, who were more withdrawn than usual. Finally, Tip left. Paul lingered a little longer, drinking the last of his coffee. He waited until Angel had left to get water. "Is there something going on that I need to know about? Not only were you two awfully quiet, but you seemed tense about something."

"I think we can handle it, Paul."

"I'd like to know what it is you're going to handle. Does it have anything to do with the new man?"

"We don't want to make a big deal of it, but he got rather friendly with Angel this morning."

"How friendly are you talking about?"

"Well, he…Angel will be embarrassed if we make a big thing of it."

"Tell me, Maxi." She knew by the intense emotion in his voice that she had better tell Paul what had happened.

"All right. Angel had her back to him and was bent over the fire. He walked up and patted her…" She stopped, having a hard time finding the proper word. "Her…backside," she finally blurted out.

Paul's jaw clenched, and anger flashed across his face. "Why didn't you want to tell me about it, Maxi?"

"Well, we felt like we made it clear to him that he was out of line. Angel told him to not ever touch her like that again. I saw it all and had my rifle pointed at him, told him to leave camp. He tried to make excuses and said he was just trying to get some burning cinders off the back of her shirt. But we don't believe him one bit. I think we made our point clear. And besides, Angel has decided to tell Justin about it tonight."

"I'll go talk to him and Travis now. You need to tell one of us about things like that from now on. Travis may send him packing anyway."

"That's why we didn't want to make a big issue of it. Travis had a hard time finding men to make the trip. We didn't want to make him shorthanded again."

Angel came back into camp as Paul put his foot in the stirrup and pulled himself into his saddle. "You tell Angel what I said."

"Okay, I'll tell her."

"Tell me what?"

"He figured out that something was wrong between us and that new man. I didn't have much choice but to tell him what happened this morning. I tried to tell him we handled it, but I think he was pretty upset. He's going to talk to Travis and Justin now."

"I'm glad the men will know. I just hope it doesn't cause any trouble."

As the others came in, the girls stayed busy. They forgot about the problem with the new man.

CHAPTER 25

"MAXI, I'M GOING to check on Samson and the girls. Be back in a few minutes."

"Okay, tell Justin hi."

Angel smiled. *I guess I haven't fooled her one bit. She seems to have caught on that Justin and I meet when I go say good night to the mules.*

The night was dark, just a bit of moon. Angel slowly made her way toward the mules and horses. She stopped at the mules and gave them a treat of apple pieces, then talked to them as they crowded for more apple and attention. *Justin must have been held up, or he would have been here by now. Guess I'll go on back.* She felt disappointed as she started back toward the wagon. *I shouldn't be surprised. He said it would take all of them to get the cattle settled down.* A slight breeze began to stir the willows along the waterway. A dark cloud glided across the dim sliver of a moon. Angel heard someone approaching from behind. A little thump of her heart brought a smile to her lips. *Good! He must have gotten off after all.* She turned and waited, straining to get a glimpse of Justin. The footsteps came nearer. "Is that you, Justin?" she said quietly. There was no response. She tried again as her heart accelerated. "Justin?"

Something was wrong. Her senses went on alert telling her to run, but she was a split second too late. Just as she turned to escape, she felt a vice-like grip on her arm that stopped her. "What's your hurry? I just got here."

Just as she feared, she turned to face Tip, the new man. "Please let go of my arm! You're hurting me!" She tried to jerk away, but his grip was strong and held her in place.

"Not until I've had my say. Seems you can't keep your mouth shut. Because of your uppity ways and big mouth, the boss man has sent me packing. Well, I'm going to leave all right, but not until I've shown you a thing or two."

"What do you mean? What are you going to do?"

"You'll find out soon enough." He turned, jerking Angel off her feet, and began dragging her toward the heavy brush.

Panic seized her. "Stop it! You're hurting me! Stop!" She tried to cry for help but couldn't get enough air in her lungs to make much of a sound.

"Might as well quit your pitiful whining. No one will hear you anyway." He pulled her to her feet while still holding firmly to her arm.

Then all of a sudden, a voice came out of the darkness, "Angel?"

Tip froze. He pulled Angel close and whispered, "You cry out, and I'll shoot your boyfriend before he knows what's happened."

Angel heard Justin calling again, "Angel?"

"Justin, is that you?" It was Maxi's voice this time.

"Yes, it's me. Have you seen Angel?"

"She left camp awhile ago. I got worried and decided to come looking for her. She's been gone too long."

The stench of Tip's breath assaulted Angel as he threatened her again. Whispering hoarsely, he spewed, "I can shoot two just as easy as one. Stay quiet."

God, what can I do? I don't want to get Justin or Maxi shot. I need help. What do I do? Suddenly, she felt the weight of the pistol in her pocket, the very one that Maxi had insisted she carry. She slid her hand into her pocket and gripped the butt of the pistol. *Can I really shoot someone? I don't even know if I can pull the hammer back with one hand.* Thoughts were scurrying through her mind. *I've got to try.* Angel placed her thumb on the hammer of the pistol and pulled it back until it clicked.

Hearing the click, Tip stiffened. Angel tried to pull the pistol out of her pocket. "What are you doing?" he growled. Everything happened at once. He stepped back, pulling her arm enough to make her thumb slip off the hammer. She pulled the trigger, discharging the pistol, but the bullet took a downward course.

Tip shoved her violently to the ground. A scream of pain rose from the hired hand, "You shot me! I can't believe it, you stupid, little girl. You shot me."

Angel pulled the pistol all the way out of her pocket. She pointed it at Tip. Her voice contained more confidence than she felt. "I'll shoot you again if you don't get out of here and leave us all alone."

They heard Justin and Maxi come crashing through the brush. Tip limped away into the darkness.

"Angel? Where are you?"

"Angel!"

She quickly answered, "I'm over here, Justin. I'm here."

In no time, he was on his knees at Angel's side. "Angel, did you get shot? Did I hear Tip with you? Are you okay? What happened, Angel!"

"Yes, it was Tip, but I'm okay."

"Did he hurt you?"

She was glad she couldn't see Justin's face clearly. His voice told her he was worried and angry enough to fight or worse. "Justin, calm down. Tip grabbed my arm and was dragging me away when you called me. He said he would shoot you and Maxi if I didn't keep quiet. I was so afraid. I tried to pull the pistol out of my pocket, and it went off."

"Did it hit you?" He was trying to see where she'd been shot.

"No, it didn't hit me. I think I shot Tip in the foot or the leg. I'm not sure."

"Good for you." Maxi was standing over Justin trying to see Angel.

"Help me up, please, will you, Justin?"

He helped her stand, then held her fiercely to himself. She could hear the beat of his heart as he pressed her head to his chest. "I don't think I've ever been so scared in my life. I was so afraid he'd hurt you. You should have told me sooner."

"I know, and I'm sorry. But really, I'm okay. You and Maxi came just in time."

"I want to get you two back to the wagon and check the area. Can you walk?"

"Yes, I can walk. I'm still shaking, but I can walk. Here, Maxi, will you take the pistol until I quit shaking."

"No, I want you to put it back in your pocket. When we get to the wagon you need to make sure it's fully loaded again. Tip may still be out there."

"She's right, Angel. Hang onto it."

Justin was checking the area around the camp when Travis came riding in. "Did I hear a gunshot? Is everyone okay?"

"Yes, the girls are okay. They're fixing beds in the wagon right now. That Tip won't be okay if I ever lay eyes on him again. He tried to drag Angel off into the bushes."

Angel shuddered as she heard Justin tell Travis what happened. "She thinks she shot him in the foot or leg. It was so dark out there I couldn't see any blood. I couldn't track him either."

"When its light, we'll see if we can figure out if he left or not. I better get on back and warn the boys. I'll need to have a heart to heart talk with that other new man, Mack McCallister. If Angel did shoot Tip, he'll be hurting pretty bad. I doubt he'll be able to cause much trouble tonight."

"If he values his life, he'll ride hard and fast. I won't give him another chance to hurt Angel or Maxi."

"Neither will I. If he wasn't hurt bad, he could still be a threat. I'll be back as soon as I can, Justin."

The wind was blowing in hard, cold gusts as Angel and Maxi settled for the night. "Can I come out and be with you for a while, Justin?" Angel had poked her head out of the covering at the back of the wagon.

Justin walked over to her with a cup of coffee in one hand and his rifle in the other. The light from the fire danced on her face. "If you come out here, I'll be distracted, and I don't want that right now. I'll feel a lot better with you tucked safe inside. Besides, it's really getting nasty out here. It'll probably start raining any time now."

"Okay. But I don't know if I can sleep. I'm still kind of wound up."

"I want you to try. If you can't sleep, then just rest. Think about all the nice things you want to do when we get home."

"Home. That sounds so wonderful. Sometimes it feels like I'll never be settled again."

"It won't be that much longer, sweet dreams," he told her as he fixed the flap across the back of the wagon.

"Good night, Justin."

About two hours later, the storm hit full force. Wind shook the wagon, rattling the tarp that was covering the girls. Rain fell so hard it was impossible to hear what was going on outside the wagon, or inside for that matter.

"You asleep, Angel?"

"Are you kidding? Who can sleep in weather like this?" For a moment, the wagon lit up as a lightning bolt flashed across the sky.

"I hate lightning. Have you ever heard of anyone being hit by lightning?"

"Sure, I've heard of it. But I never knew anyone personally that was hit. Have you?"

Maxi waited for the boom of thunder to die away. "Yes. I didn't see it happen, but a cowboy I knew was hit by lightning. Pa saw it happen. He wouldn't talk about it, must have been awful." The girls were quiet as another streak of lightning flared and waited for the rumble of thunder that was soon to follow.

"Those poor men out there. We may not be able to sleep, but at least we're staying dry."

"I wish there was some way to help. I guess the best thing we can do is stay put. We don't want to cause them any more trouble than they already have tonight. Are you scared, Angel?"

"What do you mean? Scared of the thunder and lightning or the hired man?"

"I was thinking of Tip, the hired man."

Angel thought a moment before she answered. "I suppose I am, a little. Not just for myself either. I worry about the others too. I just hope he left."

"Me too. We need to stay together and not go off alone anymore."

"I agree, anyway, for a while. Till we know what happened with Tip."

The girls quieted down as they heard movement outside the wagon. Men were talking in hushed tones. "Sounds like some of the men have come in for coffee and sleep," Maxi commented.

"I think Justin has managed to keep the fire going. I can see it flicker on the canvas cover."

"I hope so. Hot coffee will mean a lot to them right now. Let's try and sleep, Angel. We need to be able to help as much as we can tomorrow. The men will be worn out."

"Okay, I'll try."

It took awhile, but sleep finally came to both girls. As the storm made its way east, the rain settled into a steady rhythm.

Angel came awake with a start. "Maxi! What's that noise?"

CHAPTER 26

MAXI HAD BEEN sound asleep; the rain, making a steady pattering on the tarp roof, was soothing, lulling. Suddenly, being roused by Angel who had been spooked about some noise, she lay still, listening. "*Sh*, it's one of the men snoring. They must be sleeping under the wagon."

"What an awful sound," Angel whispered. "The whole wagon is vibrating. I've never heard anyone snore that loud."

"Me neither."

About that time, another long snort erupted as the sleeping man took in a deep breath, then let it out noisily. Angel grabbed her blanket and held it to her mouth, muffling her giggles.

"You're going to wake them up, Angel," Maxi scolded.

"Someone needs to wake him up." Suddenly, Angel dropped the blanket from her mouth. "Oh, my, I hope it's not Justin. I'll never get any sleep if he snores like that!"

It was Maxi's turn to cover her mouth as she grabbed a blanket. "Stop it, Angel. Don't get me tickled. We probably should get up anyway. It's turning light out."

"Okay, let's do it one at a time. There's not enough room in here for two of us to move around at the same time. I'll go first."

"Don't dilly-dally, Angel. Remember we have to stay together."

"All right. I'll wait just outside the wagon."

Moments later, they were standing together by the fire. "The fire had almost gone out, but I think I've got it going again. We should have a nice blaze by the time we get back."

"Good. A cup of hot coffee is going to taste mighty good this morning. It's so cold and wet. Let's go. Do you have the pistol?"

"Yes, I've got it. Remember the first time you asked me to carry it in my pocket? You knew I didn't like the idea. Now, I'll have to admit it makes me feel a little safer. Never thought I'd say that."

"I didn't either. What are we going to cook for breakfast?"

"I thought I'd fry up a lot of bacon and enough batter for finger cakes. I'll cook them fresh for the men as they come in."

"Good. I was going to suggest you make your finger cakes."

The day dragged on drearily, with intermittent drizzling but no heavy rain. The girls spent all their time in camp, cooking when it wasn't raining. Angel made a double batch of biscuits and fried apple pies. She also had a pot of beans simmering for most of the morning. "I think I've cooked up enough food, so if it rains hard again, we won't have to worry about cooking in the rain."

"The men could probably live off your fried apple pies."

Just then, Travis came into camp. "Do I smell them apple things you made before?" He went to the fire and looked around.

"Yes, Angel made some. They're over in that big tin at the back of the wagon. Be sure to put the lid back on tight so they don't get any moisture."

"I've got to get a cup of coffee first. How are you girls doing today?"

"We're doing good. I hate the mud, but guess that can't be helped." Maxi talked comfortably with Travis asking about Mack, the other new hand he picked up at Fort Laramie. She asked if he had talked to him about Tip.

"Yes, I talked to him right after we had that trouble with Tip. He's going to stay on with us. I don't know his whole story but seems he's been wanting to get away from Tip and the bunch he hooked up with a short time ago. I think he's a good man. As long as he behaves himself and does his work, he can stay. If he gets out of line, even once, I want to know right away. Do you two understand?"

"Yes, we understand. I don't think Mack will give us any trouble. He's very different from Tip. Angel and I both like him. He's polite and appreciative of anything we do. Makes you wonder why he would get mixed up with someone like Tip."

"Sometimes you don't really know a person until you ride with him for a few days. Well, ladies, when I finish this pie and coffee, I'm going to crawl under that wagon and see if I can get a couple hours sleep. Not getting any last night has finally caught up with me. Things are pretty calm now, so I'm going to take advantage of it."

"Travis, has anyone seen anything of Tip?" Angel wondered.

"No. Justin checked the area where you were last night. It has rained so hard he couldn't tell much of anything. The rain wiped out any sign of tracks. We're all on alert though. If he has any smarts, he'll head back to Fort Laramie and his other buddies. Don't worry too much about him."

"We're staying together as much as we can now, at least for a few days."

"Good. Now I'm going to try and get some sleep."

Late that afternoon, a break in the weather came. The sun played hide and seek behind clouds that drifted by. "Isn't it beautiful, Maxi? Everything is so fresh and clean. It just smells wonderful."

"Yes, it's nice, but I'll be glad when the mud dries up." Maxi grumbled. "I need to go for a walk and check on Ginger. Will you go with me?"

"Sure. Let's take the buckets. We can get fresh water on the way back."

They left the buckets on the bank where they had been getting water and walked to where the horses and mules were grazing. The animals seemed content to receive attention and a treat of apple slices. "I wonder where Diablo is," Maxi asked, looking around. Then she spotted him hobbled by a tree a short distance away. "I'm going to walk over there. Do you want to come with me?"

"No, go ahead. I'll stay here and wait for you. We'll still be in sight of each other."

As Maxi approached Diablo, his head shot up, and his ears turned toward her. "Hello, you beautiful creature."

"Are you talking to me or my horse?" a voice answered, making her jump.

"Oh, hi, Paul. What are you doing here, besides startling people?"

"I came to see Diablo and check Ginger's leg. I was hoping I'd have a chance to talk to you."

"Angel is waiting for me by the mules. I don't want her to walk back to the wagon by herself."

"We can both walk her back to the wagon."

A short time later, they returned to the horses. Maxi's curiosity finally got the best of her. "We've just been making small talk till now, Paul. What do you really want to talk to me about?"

"Well, I wanted to apologize for the other day."

"Oh? Apologize for what? What part of the other day?"

"Well…when I kissed you."

"And when you called me a...stupid, little girl?"

"Yes. I want to apologize for calling you a stupid, little girl. I'm not going to apologize for the kiss. But maybe for the way I kissed you. I felt bad about it." Maxi looked puzzled, so he continued, "I was so relieved that you weren't hurt, I just lost my head. If Travis hadn't been watching, I might have given you a proper kiss."

Unexpectedly, Marty appeared and walked up behind them. "What are you two doing out here alone?"

"We're just talking, Marty," Maxi explained. "Does Angel need me?"

"No, I just came to help you carry the water buckets. Angel said she forgot to get them." He gave Paul a warning look that Maxi didn't miss. "I don't think it's a good idea for you to be out here, Paul. Maybe you better get back to where you should be."

"I am where I should be, Marty. There's no need to get bossy."

Marty's jealousy clouded his thinking. He shoved Paul. "I told you to stay away from her, Paul."

"I don't want to fight you, Marty. You know I can whip you, so don't shove me again."

"If you keep trying to get close to Maxi, I'll do worse than shove you." He reached out and shoved Paul again.

Paul shoved him back. "Marty, don't touch me again, or you'll regret it. There's no need to make a scene over me talking to Maxi."

Maxi was stunned at their behavior. It looked like things were quickly getting out of control. *I've got to stop this before they start swinging at each other.* Maxi stepped forward to get between the two men, at the same moment that Marty swung his fist at Paul's face. His fist caught Maxi in the side of her head and sent her flying into Paul's arms. With a thud, Paul was knocked down on his backside, still holding onto Maxi.

Marty stared for a few seconds before realizing what had just happened. "Oh, no! What kind of fool am I! Paul, is she okay?"

"I don't know. Go and get Angel."

Marty ran and quickly came back dragging Angel with him. Paul hadn't moved. He was still sitting on the ground holding an unconscious Maxi. "What happened Paul?" She knelt down beside them.

"She got hit in the head."

Angel gasped. "How in the world did she get hit in the head?"

Marty answered with honesty, but despair was in his voice. "It was me, Angel. I took a swing at Paul, and she stepped between us. I'll never forgive myself. I can't believe I was so stupid."

"I don't think it's real serious, but I need to get her back to the wagon. Can you carry her, Paul?"

"That shouldn't be a problem." He easily got up and carried Maxi toward the camp.

"Let's be quiet when we get there," Angel warned. Travis is still asleep under the wagon, and I'd hate to wake him. He was so tired."

Marty groaned pitifully. "Oh, Travis will kill me!"

"If Maxi's not hurt bad, maybe he won't have to know," Paul offered.

"Thanks, Paul, but you know I'll own up to it."

Maxi moaned softly and put her arms around Paul's neck. "I think she's coming out of it."

In a soft voice, Maxi mumbled, "You smell good."

Amused and glad to hear her talking, Paul replied, "You like the smell of sweat and horses, huh?"

"Uh-huh."

"Well, I like the way you smell too. If I'm not mistaken, it's the scent of roses in your hair."

"Sit down over there away from the wagon, Paul." Angel pointed to a log that the men had been using for a seat.

"Hearing Paul's name, Maxi's eyes flew open, then quickly shut again. With a grimace of pain, she put her hand up to her head and moaned. "My head hurts, Angel. What happened?"

"Just be still. I need to check you out. Paul, keep hold of her in case she passes out again." She examined the side of Maxi's head, then told the guys, "I don't think there's a lot of damage. I found a small cut just inside her hairline, but I don't think it needs to be stitched. I'll clean it and put something on it though. Marty, bring that rag and bucket over there."

Marty brought the requested items and handed them to Angel. Pleading, he said, "Please tell me she's going to be all right."

"I'm sure of it, Marty."

"Maxi, can you ever forgive me?"

"You're forgiven, Marty. I remember what happened now. I stepped in between you and Paul, didn't I?"

"Yes, I'm so sorry."

"It's okay, Marty. It was stupid of me to step between the two of you. I just hated to see you fighting over me. We have to stay friends, all of us." She began to cry softly. "We'll talk about it later, Marty, okay?"

"Okay. I'll check on you later then." He turned and left to go back to the herd.

Paul stayed and held Maxi until Angel had finished cleaning the cut and putting salve on it. "Will you put her in the back of the wagon, Paul, and stay with her till I get fresh water. It won't take but a minute or two. Maxi, I want you to stay still and quiet this evening."

Paul carried Maxi to the back of the wagon and sat her down but still held her carefully. Looking into her eyes, he softly told her, "Marty and I have grown up together. I usually ignore him or just let him have his way. I won't do that where you're concerned, Maxi. I won't back off unless you tell me to." He was quiet for a moment, then continued, "When I was little, my mama would always kiss my hurts better." Paul took her face in both of his hands and, with the softest touch, kissed Maxi's head where she had been hit. Then he moved down to her mouth and ever so gently kissed her lips. "Now, does that make it feel better, mi maravillosa flor?"

"Yes," she whispered.

"Angel is back now, so I'm going to leave. I'll check on you later. Take care of yourself. And by the way, Ginger is fine."

She watched him walk off in the direction of the horses. Angel came up quietly and asked, "How do you feel now?"

Maxi looked a little embarrassed, ducking her head. "Wonderful."

"Climb on in there, and rest awhile. You may not feel so wonderful after that kiss wears off. Let me know when you need something for pain."

CHAPTER 27

"HERE'S THE PLAN, girls." Travis was finishing his breakfast. "That little rainstorm that came through last night is going to keep us here another day. It's just too muddy to move the wagon this morning. I plan on getting an early start tomorrow though. The next day or so, we'll be going through what is usually a dry basin. There won't be any fresh water, just pools of muddy water here and there, but nothing we can use or drink. You need to fill all the containers that you can find with fresh water. There won't be any firewood either. Collect as much dry wood as you can, and we'll wrap it in a tarp and tie it to the side of the wagon. Also, see if you can cook extra food today. That will save us from needing a lot of firewood later. We may have to eat cold food, but that's part of the fun. You've spoiled us as it is, feeding us with all that good cooking. I don't suppose you have any of those apple things left?"

"No, sorry, Travis. The men cleaned them out when they came in for their coffee last night," Angel told him.

When Travis started to leave, he thanked them for the breakfast but then stopped and stared at Maxi. "What's wrong with your face? Looks like you might be getting a black eye."

"I just had one of my dumb moments. Wasn't watching what I was doing, ran into something."

"Watch where you're going, little lady. You've got too pretty a face to be walking into things."

The girls talked while they carried out the chores that Travis asked them to do. Angel complained, "I'm already tired of this mud."

"Well, Angel. I think that's the first time I've ever heard you complain."

"You forgot I complained about the man snoring under the wagon."

"That's right. Did you ever figure out who it was?"

"Bill and Marty were the ones under there. I heard Marty say he sure hoped he didn't have to sleep that close to Bill again. So it must have been Bill. Are you going to talk to Marty today? I've never seen anyone feel so bad. Did you notice he didn't come in to eat last night? He asked me how you were this morning, ate real quick, then left before you came back from checking the horses."

"Yes, I noticed. I want to find the right time to talk to him, but I'm not sure what to say. I'm kind of mixed up about it. I like them both. But I sure don't want them to fight over me. I figure I won't be around very long since I'm going to go find Michael. I think I should just be friends with both of them. I guess that's what I'll tell him."

"That kiss Paul gave you didn't look like he wanted to just be friends. Was that your first kiss?"

"No, my second. Paul kissed me after we caught Diablo the other day. Was Justin the first one to kiss you?"

"Yes, he was."

"What did you think the first time?"

"I told him he needed to make it last a little longer. It was so quick I wasn't sure what to think. Just being that close to him made it hard to catch my breath."

"Well, did he?"

"Did he what?"

"Kiss you again and make it last longer."

"That's personal, Maxi."

"Oh, come on and tell me."

"Okay…yes, he did, and it was wonderful. I never dreamed a kiss could be that way. I just wanted to stay in his arms forever!"

"My experience was about the same as yours. The first time Paul kissed me, I wasn't expecting it. It was over before I had a chance to even think about it. I was even mad at him for a while, but last night made up for it. He was so tender and sweet to me. A kiss can be a powerful thing, can't it?"

"I can't argue with that. Shall we go gather the wood now?"

It was a productive day for the girls; they steadily worked at their tasks. By mid-afternoon, they had done all they could for the next day's journey across the basin.

"I guess I'm going to have to go find Marty. He hasn't been in all day. I want to talk to him before we leave in the morning. But I don't want to leave you here by yourself, Angel."

"I can solve that problem. Let's get Ginger and Sweet Raven, and I'll ride out with you.

"Okay, let's do it."

Angel made one final check on everything in camp, making sure it was okay to leave for a short time. They were soon riding toward the herd. "There's Justin," Angel pointed out.

"Okay, but I don't see Marty. Maybe Justin will know where he is."

Justin greeted them with a welcoming smile. "Howdy! What a nice surprise to get a visit from two of the prettiest girls around."

Maxi laughed. "That's not saying much. We're the only two women around for miles. Do you know where Marty is?"

"I saw him a few minutes ago. There he is just coming over that hill." He pointed it out for her. "Are you going to visit him?"

"Yes, I need to talk to him."

"Good. Maybe you can cheer him up. He's been so glum today you can hardly get him to talk. Travis asked me if I knew what was wrong with him. Neither of us can figure it out. Maybe your pretty face will drive the gloom away."

He studied her for a moment. "Speaking of faces, it looks like you're getting a black eye."

The girls laughed. "What's going on here? I have a feeling I've missed something."

"Angel can tell you all about it. I'm going to talk to Marty."

Maxi made her way around the herd, stopping to chat with Bill for a minute. Marty seemed uncomfortable but greeted her. "Hi, what are you up to?"

"I came to see you, Marty."

She came closer. He took one look at her face and turned away. "I don't know why you'd ever want to talk to me again." His voice, full of distress, made Maxi want to cry.

"Marty, look at me." He didn't, he just kept his face turned away. "I mean it, Marty Swanson, look at me!" His eyes were full of misery when he finally turned and looked at her. "Marty, I don't want you to feel bad about what happened yesterday. It was my fault as much as it was yours. I can't stand for you to stay away from me. You'll always be special. I want you and Paul to be my friends forever. Maybe when I find my brother, we'll still be able to see each other. I can't say for sure because I don't really know where he is." She paused, trying to find the words to make Marty feel better. "This bruise on my face? It'll be gone in no time. And I don't even have a headache. Guess I'm a tough Texan 'cause it'll take more than a little old punch in the face to hurt me."

A bit of a smile appeared on his face. "You're sweet to come and say all that to me. You can't imagine how sorry I am that it ever happened. I should not have swung at Paul. It wasn't any of my business that the two of you were talking." He paused, looking every bit repentant. "I guess I was hoping that we could be more than friends. I wanted to court you when we got home. I don't suppose there's any chance of that now."

"Let me be honest with you, Marty. Right now, I'm not sure of my feelings. I lost my pa, and I'm trying to find my brother. That's what I need to concentrate on. I'm mixed up right now because I think I love both of you. Maybe in different ways, I don't know. I think we all need to take one day at a time and get these cattle home. Will you give me time to sort out my feelings? Can we be best friends for now?"

"I'd like that, Maxi. Thanks for talking to me. I'll apologize to Paul the first chance I get."

"Good. Can I just hang around here for a while? You can tell me about your family and ranch."

Camp life was back to normal that evening. Marty came in with Paul to eat supper. Just as they were finishing, Travis came in. "Are you girls ready to head out in the morning? I've been scouting the land ahead, and it looks like the mud is drying up."

"We're as ready as we'll ever be," Maxi informed him.

"Good. You may have to stop every so often and clean mud off the wheels. Just take it easy on the mules. Justin lucked out when he ran into the people who were selling them. We need to get them home in good shape."

With a deep sigh, Marty murmured, "Home, that just sounds plum good."

Paul swallowed the last of his coffee. "We're heading back out, Travis. Do you want me to send Justin and Mack in to eat? I'll be going right by them."

"Sure, if you don't mind. We'll let them eat, then sleep first. It's a quiet night, and the cattle are pretty well settled."

"What about Bill? Has he eaten yet?"

"Oh, yeah, I almost forgot Bill! Tell him to come in too."

"Okay, as long as I don't have to sleep anywhere near him. He snored so loud the other night it vibrated the ground. You'd think there was an earthquake. Never been in one, but I bet it would be like sleeping near Bill."

They all had a good laugh when Angel told them, "The floor on the wagon lifted a few inches every time he exhaled."

The night sky was starry, the weather calm. Even so, the girls were not able to rest completely. Sounds of the night were intrusive. Cattle lowing or bawling, crickets chirping nonstop, the distant cry of coyotes, all mingled with the snoring of a tired cowhand. And always, right on the edge of their consciousness, they knew there was a slight chance that Tip would try to get even with Angel.

An hour into the morning, the basin came into full view. "Wow, there's not much out there," Maxi exclaimed when she came riding up to the wagon. "You won't need me to tell you which way to go. There's a few patches of grass here and there, but you can see the land for miles. It's hot enough the ground is drying up fast. I don't think we'll have any problems at all with mud."

"That's what I was hoping for. This may be the hottest day we've had yet."

Justin came up to the wagon. "How's it going? Doesn't look like you're going to have any trouble with mud."

Angel gave him a sweet smile. "That's what we were just saying. I think we'll be fine."

"Justin, I'd like to ride out with the men for a little while. Would you mind staying with Angel? Or is that asking too much?" Maxi grinned impishly.

"I can probably be persuaded to do that. The cattle are fairly calm now, so go ahead."

When they were alone, Angel commented, "You know, Justin, I've been thinking about our home, and now that I have one I want to know what's it like."

"It's really hard to describe and do it justice. It's beautiful in several different ways. When we climb out of the basin, the land begins to change into grasslands. They stretch as far as you can see. We'll slowly climb in elevation, and the ranches are in the foothills of the mountains. On a bench in those foothills, my father built the ranch. It looks out over the grasslands. Behind the ranch is a small pond. Beyond that are forests with all kinds of pine trees and aspens.

"There are two rivers in our area. One separates Marty's ranch from ours. The forests are filled with wildlife. It's a wonderful place to live and raise a family. I know there are dangers when living so secluded, but there are dangers everywhere. We started out in a small log cabin. Then my father built a bigger, nicer house for my mother. It took a long time but was worth it. Except he never got to enjoy it. He took sick one winter and died just before we were going to move in."

"I'm sorry about your pa, Justin. I've noticed you call your ma and pa, mother and father. What should I call your mother?"

Justin thought a moment. "I hadn't really thought about that. When we were young, Mrs. Swanson and my mother taught us boys. They both had good schooling back east, especially Calli Swanson. They insisted on respect, and we had to say mister or missus and mother and father. But when only family is there, we're not that formal. I've noticed Paul calls his mother, mama and used to call his father, papa. I just say mom. I think you should call her mom like I do. Around others…I don't know. We'll have to talk to her about it."

"I'm anxious to meet your mother. I hope she likes me."

"I don't even have to guess about that one. You two will love each other for sure. I can't wait for us to be a real family." Justin looked into Angel's dark-brown eyes. "I love you, Angel."

"I love you too, Justin."

"What do you think about Maxi? Is she all right?"

"Oh, I don't know. She's been quiet since Marty and Paul had their fight. It's for sure she has a lot to think about. The thing that's kept her going is finding her brother. She really thinks a lot of Marty and Paul. She keeps telling me she wants to be friends with both of them for now. I think it's Paul that confuses her the most. There might be possibilities for something there, but who knows. There's something else I want to talk to you about."

"What is it, sweetheart?"

"Maxi's been so good to me. I had nothing except my wicker case when we ran into each other. She's taken care of me and told me I will always have a home with her. Now I have a home, and she doesn't. If she can't find her brother or something has happened to him, I want her to know she has a place with me. Maybe I'm asking a lot of you and your mother, but I can't just leave her with no one."

"Of course you can't. I wouldn't want you to do that either. As far as Maxi is concerned, my mother would welcome her and love her like a daughter. My mom would have had a dozen kids if she could have. I don't think you'll have to worry about Maxi though. I have a feeling she'll be making her own family soon enough."

"I hope you're right, Mr. Myers."

"Of course, I'm right, Mrs. Myers, and don't you forget it."

The rest of the day was long, hot, and tiring. But that evening, when everyone had eaten and cleanup was done, the girls had a little extra time to themselves. The air was still plenty warm. They spread a ground cloth out and sat together looking up into the sky. "I've never seen so many stars, Maxi. Looks like you could reach out and gather a basketful."

"It is beautiful. Makes me homesick for Texas...and my pa. Seems so long ago and so far away. I felt kind of lost today when Travis said they were almost home. I wonder where my home will be."

"Don't be sad, Maxi. I don't know what will happen with your brother, but I do know that you'll always have a home with me. Justin and I talked about it today. He told me that both he and his mother would welcome you as family. You can rest in your heart knowing you will always have a home with us. I don't think it will be long before you'll have your own home, but even if it doesn't happen, we are sisters *forever*. We'll watch out for each other."

"Thanks, Angel. That means a lot to me."

"Did you get a chance to talk with Paul today?"

"Yes, I've talked to all of them sometime during the day. Travis keeps looking at me like he knows I didn't tell him everything about my black eye. But he hasn't pushed me, which I'm very grateful for."

Justin and Bill came riding into camp. "We get first sleep tonight," Justin told them as he selected a spot for his bedroll. "Angel, I surely would like to hear you play your violin tonight. Think you might play for us?"

Bill encouraged her too. "I love hearing you play, little lady. When I'm out there with the cattle, it makes me feel, well, closer to God. Somehow, I don't feel so alone. Those cows like to hear you play too. I know 'cause they told me so."

Angel laughed. "Thanks, Bill, you're sweet. Since you talk to the cows, tell them I'm glad they like my music. If my music can draw people close to God, it's worth all the hours my ma made me practice."

Bill got all enthusiastic. "When we get home, we'll have us a big party, won't we, Justin? We'll get all our musicians together and have a big shindig."

"Sure, we will. We do it two or three times a year, and it's about time to have our Fourth of July party."

"That sounds like so much fun!" Angel exclaimed. "We did things like that back home. I'll be looking forward to it."

Soon, she was playing her violin. Justin and Bill were stretched out on their beds, and Maxi leaned against a wagon wheel. Sweet music floated out on the basin, where unknown to anyone at camp, the hymns that Angel played were touching, breaking, and challenging the heart of the man, Mack McCallister.

Lord, speak to me, that I may speak
In living echoes of thy tone;
As thou has sought, so let me speak
Thy erring children lost and lone.
Oh, teach me, Lord, that I may teach
The precious things thou doest impart;
And wing my words, that they may reach
The hidden depths of many a heart.
Oh, fill me with thy fullness, Lord
Until my very heart o'er-flow
In kindling thought and glowing word,
Thy love to tell, thy praise to show.

CHAPTER 28

EARLY THE NEXT morning, Justin watched as they neared a large pool of standing water at the bottom of the basin. He heard Travis giving orders as he made his way around the herd. "Justin, try to keep the cattle on the east side of the water. Go tell Angel and Maxi to keep high on the east side of the herd. There's a large flow of drainage water from the mountains to the west. Must have rained heavy in the mountains last night. The sooner we get out of the bottom of this basin, the better I'll like it."

"You got it, Travis."

Justin approached the wagon minutes later, and Angel called out to him, "Hi, cowboy, need a ride?"

He grinned. "Wish I could ride with you, but I've got to get back." He relayed Travis's instructions to Angel. "It's a slow climb from here to home. You'll hardly notice but the mules will. I'm going to send Maxi over to stay with you till we get past this muddy water."

"She's already coming so you can go on back. We'll signal if we need any help."

"All right. See you in a while. Be careful." *Tar-nation something's not right. I feel like we're being watched.* Justin thought of his Arapaho blood brother, Black Feather, telling him to trust his instincts. His eyes scanned the area, especially around the wagon. After chasing a cow back to the herd, he circled around to the east side of the herd and rode close to Paul. "Hey, Paul, how's it going?"

"Fine as can be. These critters get kind of stubborn if they don't get to go where they want to. Right now, they'd like some of that water."

"You're right, but look over there. Travis and Marty are rescuing two that are stuck in the mud."

"Should we go help?"

"Nah, they'll have them pulled out by the time we get halfway there. Besides, I want to be close to the wagon. I have a feeling we're being watched. I know that sounds stupid, but that's how I feel."

Paul looked surprised. "You too? I've been uneasy myself but can't figure it out. Been too busy to think about it much."

"I'm going to go tell Mack to help Marty and Travis. Let's stay on this side and keep an eye out for trouble."

Paul looked up in time to see Mack McCallister coming their way. "You're in luck. He's coming over here."

"Yeah, and he's coming fast, like there's something wrong!" Justin tensed as Mack came riding up to them.

"Paul! Justin! There're Indians riding toward the wagon."

They jerked their heads around, taking in the scene. Paul spoke first, "You call it, Justin."

Justin appraised the situation quickly. "Okay, we all three ride to the wagon, easy like, as if we're going to talk. Don't ride fast like we're going to fight." They started out at an easy trot with Justin still talking, "I'm pretty sure it's a Sioux war party, so watch yourselves. Looks like they've already been in a fight and have some wounded with them." When he said the word wounded, realization struck him. *They're wanting Angel to take care of their wounded.* The thought no more than crossed his mind when he saw Angel get down off the wagon and walk toward the Indians. Maxi was on the wagon, standing tall and straight in front of the wagon seat. Her rifle was to her shoulder aimed at the leader. Justin's heart pounded! *Easy does it, Maxi. Don't panic.*

Justin arrived the same time the Indians did. He slid off his horse and stood by Angel. Both gave a sign of greeting. Most of the Indians weren't paying him any attention. They all had their eyes on Maxi. He glanced back at her. *Now I know how you got the name, Princess Warrior. Because that's just what you look like. These braves would love to carry the beautiful Princess Warrior away to their tepees!* Then he glanced at Paul and knew none of this escaped him either. Paul was positioned close to Maxi with the look of a man willing to die to protect his own. Justin knew he needed to get all the attention away from her. He spoke and signed, "We welcome you as friends."

The warrior in charge looked him in the eyes, then looked back at Maxi. He wore full war attire and had a painted body. He used hand signs and spoke while never taking his eyes off Maxi.

"Maxi, as near as I can tell, he's saying, 'Tell Princess Warrior, the one who protects White Cloud, medicine woman, we will not hurt White Cloud or her people.'" Justin calmly told Maxi to slowly put her rifle down but stay alert.

Angel didn't wait to be told what to do. She had seen at least two wounded men, one carried on a travois. The other was held on his horse by a fellow brave. Justin followed Angel to the travois, mesmerized by her actions. She quietly stroked the face of the young man, talking to him in soothing tones. "Hello, my name is Angel. I'm going to look at your wounds and see if I can help you. You're having a hard time breathing, aren't you? I'm going to remove this bandage around your chest and see what's there." Gently, she removed a blood-soaked bandage and discovered an ugly hole. It had been stuffed with some kind of dried plant. "Justin, will you ask if the bullet came out? I don't want to turn him over if I don't have to."

He communicated Angel's question. "He says the bullet is still inside, and Crooked Leg can't move."

Someone handed Angel a canteen when she asked for water. She used the red bandana she carried in her pocket and cleaned the blood that ran from the warrior's mouth to his neck. Her eyes were filled with sadness when she turned to Justin. "I'm guessing, but I think a bullet has gone through his lungs. It probably damaged his spine. He must be slowly bleeding to death inside. There's nothing I can do for him. I hate it, but I can't help him."

"I want you to tell that to the leader. Tell him the truth. They will respect that. I would tell him, but it will be best coming from you."

She nodded that she understood, then walked to the Indian leader. "I wish I could help your friend, but there is nothing I can do for him. He is in God's hands now. I can pray and ask God to heal your friend, but I think he will die soon."

After the leader spoke to Justin, he told Angel, "He asks if you will play your magic."

She was puzzled for a moment. "Do you think he means my violin?" Without waiting for an answer, she firmly said, "You have to tell them my music is not magic. Believe me, my ma made me practice for hours on end, and it isn't magic."

"Okay, I'll interpret that. But I think you're music is magic too."

"You don't mean that, Justin."

"Yes, I do. It amazes me the wonderful sounds and emotions your music stirs in me. I don't mean magic like a spell, but there is something spiritual about it."

They were both surprised when Mack McCallister spoke up, "I'll have to agree with him on that, Angel. I'll tell you sometime how much your music has spoken to me. I think it would be nice if you played your violin. Just let God do what he wants with the music."

She gave Mack a questioning look. "Okay, Mack, I can do that. But while I get my violin, have them bring the travois around to the shade of the wagon." She turned to Maxi. "You and Paul bring a bucket of water with a dipper. We need to offer these men some water. I want the wounded man on the horse over by the wagon wheel. From the looks of him, I'll have to stitch up his head."

Paul stayed close to Maxi, carrying a bucket of water, while Maxi offered each one a drink. Most of the Indian party had gotten off their horses. Some were standing while others sat on the ground.

Angel began to play. She sat close to the wounded warrior. Cowboys, Sioux Indians in their war paint, sitting or standing, were listening to Angel play her music. It was quite a scene. It looked peaceful enough, but there was a war going on in someone's heart, which no one else knew about. By the end of the first hymn, God had won the battle of the heart. And now, it was time to declare it.

Angel felt a tap on her shoulder. When she looked up, Mack McCallister was standing over her. "I would like to speak to the young man. Do the best you can to interpret for me, Justin."

Angel moved out of the way, and Mack knelt by the boy. "I speak for the one true God." His voice was clear and strong, loud enough for everyone to hear. "The God I speak for is the God White Cloud prays to. He is the creator of earth and all things on it. He created all men, Indian and white. He is sorrowful that all men do evil. Because men are evil, they cannot go to him. He is a holy God, who will have no evil where he is. God's only son was willing to come to earth and be a sacrifice for men. Even though he did no wrong, he shed his blood to pay the penalty of all men's evil ways so they can go to God when they die. If you want to go to the God of all men when you die, you need to tell him. Tell him you are sorry you have done evil and you accept his son's gift of shedding his blood. Tell him you want to give yourself to him when you leave this earth."

The warrior tried to speak but only choked on the frothy blood coming from his throat. "You can speak from your heart," Mack told him. "This great God hears your heart and knows what it says. Tell him with your heart."

The young Indian closed his eyes. Justin thought he might have already died, but he opened them again and tried to smile at Mack. His gaze shifted to the open sky, and he managed to speak a few words.

The Indians who heard and understood his native tongue looked in the direction the young warrior seemed to be looking. Angel grabbed Justin's arm. "What is he saying? What are they looking at?"

"He sees someone no one else can see, Angel. I could guess who that is, but I think you know."

Mack McCallister stood to his feet, blinking back tears. "He's gone."

The leader of the war party looked at his warrior and nodded, as if satisfied. He spoke to Mack, "Crooked Leg die brave with peace on face. Good."

Angel had already moved to the other warrior and started cleaning the gash on his head. "Do we have any whiskey with us, Justin?"

"That tool box under the wagon seat has a bottle of whiskey in it. Bill keeps it there, but don't tell him I told you. I'll get it."

Angel went to work cleaning the wound with water, then the whiskey. The man only stiffened a little but made no sound. When the wound was stitched, she put salve on the wound and wrapped a piece of her precious white cloth around his head to protect it. "There, that does it. Justin, tell them he has lost a lot of blood, and he needs to drink as much water as he can. Let's give him some water now. They may not have much with them." Someone handed her the bucket, and the man drank thirstily.

The war party mounted their horses, then waited for their leader who went to one of the ponies and pulled a buffalo hide off the back. He dropped it at Angel's feet. He spoke to Justin, took the pony to Maxi, and handed her the reins. She hesitantly took the reins and nodded. Giving her one last appraising look, he jumped on his horse, and the war party rode away taking their dead warrior with them.

Paul was the first to speak, "Justin, what just happened?"

"Something you can tell around the campfire for years to come, although I doubt very many would believe it. They came across some buffalo earlier. There's meat wrapped inside the hide. Angel can tan the hide for a robe. It's a gift to her for treating their wounds."

"What about the Indian pony, and what did he say to Maxi?" Paul wanted to know.

"He gave her about the highest compliment you'll ever get from a Sioux warrior. He said, 'Princess Warrior brave like Sioux warrior. She needs Sioux war pony to ride.' He gave her the pony to honor her. Then he said she would be a good woman to have at a brave man's side."

"Are you serious? He said all that?"

"Yes, all that and a few other things. I'll have to tell you later."

Mack was helping Angel and Maxi get the wagon ready to move again when Travis came riding up. "What in the world is going on over here? I've got cattle straying all over the place. Then I find you all over here having a party!"

Justin laughed. "Sorry, Travis. We had to take care of some unexpected business."

"Well, if you're through with your business, let's get back to work. Mack, you come with me. I want a full accounting of what just happened here. I'm sure I saw a Sioux war party just leave, and there has to be a story behind that."

"Sure, boss. You might not believe it, but I'll tell you."

Paul and Justin talked before they left the basin and decided they didn't like it one bit the way the Sioux braves were watching Maxi and Angel. It didn't escape either one of the men that they were eyeing Diablo too.

Paul decided it was time to ride Diablo but first he had to show the stallion who was boss. With very little resistance Diablo conceded to his master. "I think it would be safer now if you rode close to me, Maxi. That way Justin can stay close to Angel. Is that okay with everyone?"

The last two men coming in to eat roasted buffalo steak that evening was Marty and Mack. Angel noticed Mack discreetly bow his head to pray before he ate. This prompted her to engage him in conversation.

"Mack, you were amazing with that Indian boy today. Tell us about your life. I think there's more to Mack McCallister than we know."

Maxi encouraged him also. "I'd like to know how you got mixed up with a man like Tip."

Mack stopped eating but kept his eyes downcast. Finally, he looked up. "I'm ashamed to tell what I've done."

"I'm sorry, Mack, I didn't mean to get so personal," Angel apologized.

"No, it's okay. You folks have been good to me. I should tell you about myself." He took a few minutes to collect his thoughts. "I've been running from God for about a year now. I felt God was calling me to preach the Gospel to the lost when I was just a young man. After finishing my schooling, I was sure God wanted me to come out west and start a church. My wife and I were with a wagon train headed to Oregon when a runaway wagon ran over my wife, killing her instantly." He paused, trying to work the knot from his throat. After composing himself, he continued.

"She was a precious wife, and the loss of her was more than I could bear. I guess part of me blamed God. But mostly, I just couldn't get the picture out of my mind of that wagon running her down. I would close my eyes and see it happening again and again. I tried to get to her but, of course, couldn't make it in time. I seemed to be running in slow motion. I couldn't eat or sleep for the longest time. I finally sold the wagon and everything we had. Then just took off to nowhere in particular.

"I got mixed up with a bunch of no-accounts and tried to forget with liquor. I for one can tell you that doesn't work." He shook his head sorrowfully. "When our gang heard you were looking for hands to go up north, Tip told me he'd heard of where some gold was hidden in a cave up in the mountains. I didn't really believe his story but thought if he was right, and I could get some of that gold, I could break away from him and head to California. We joined the drive to get up to the mountains where you're going." Looking into the darkness, he told the group around the fire, "I'm not proud of what I've done."

"I'm sure we've all done things we'd rather just forget," Marty confessed. "I know I have."

Mack ducked his head a moment, then looked at Angel. "It was your violin music, the other night, that helped soften my heart and made me listen to God. I know he has forgiven me. I still don't understand why my lovely wife had to die, but I've finally put that in God's hands, where it should have been all along. Now I'm praying that he will show me what to do with my life. When I saw that Indian boy dying right before my eyes, something happened inside of me. I'm not sure what it means yet, but I'll know in God's time. I should have known I couldn't run from him."

CHAPTER 29

THE NEXT DAY was long, hot, and tiring. Angel sighed, "I hope there's a place in this river where we can take a bath. I need one in the worst way."

"Oh, so that's *you* I've been smelling." Maxi snickered. "I'll tell Justin to stay upwind of you tonight. Actually, between the two of us, we'd put a working man to shame. My hair smells like a muskrat." They erupted into a fit of giggling. "Have you noticed that when we're tired, we get silly and start giggling?"

Wiping tears from her eyes, Angel replied, "Yes, but that's okay. The Bible says a little laughter is like medicine. It's good for the heart."

Late in the afternoon, Justin approached the wagon. "Angel, when you catch up with the herd go on around them and find the big cottonwood trees up river. There's a good beach and waterhole for bathing and swimming."

"You smelled her too, huh?" Maxi mumbled.

"Maxi, hush!" Angel scolded.

Justin looked puzzled. "What'd you say?"

"Oh, nothing," Maxi replied innocently. The look on her face, though, made Angel start giggling again. The mood was contagious, and neither could stop laughing.

"Okay, you two, pull yourselves together. It's going to get dark soon, and the rest of us want to take a bath before we come in to eat. Bill shot a deer for supper. He'll be bringing it over in a bit. Oh, watch for rattlesnakes over there. I checked it out and didn't see any. But I still want you to be careful. I'll take care of the mules," Justin called back to Angel. "Just go take your bath."

"See? He did smell you."

"Maxi, if you don't hush, I'm going to throw you in that river."

"What makes you think you could throw me…you little wisp of a girl. Oh, sorry, wisp of a *woman.*"

"Just because I'm small doesn't mean I'm weak."

The girl's laughter and banter drifted all the way to the river. Justin rode up to Travis, looking amused.

"What got into those two?" Travis wanted to know.

"I'm not sure, but it's a nice sound," Justin replied with a huge grin on his face.

"Yeah, it's good to hear their laughter. I don't suppose they've had a lot to laugh about lately."

The crew was extra tired that evening, but their spirits were revived after baths and a fresh deer steak meal. Paul and Justin were the last to come in to eat. After Paul finished his supper, he turned to Maxi. "Will you walk a ways with me? I want to show you something, and we need to be away from the firelight."

Curious, Maxi agreed. "Sure. What is it?"

"You'll just have to wait and see."

Angel watched until they were no longer visible. "I wonder what he wants to show her."

"Probably the lights of home," Justin answered.

"You mean you can see them from here?"

"Sometimes, if the conditions are right. Calli Swanson has this thing about lighting a fire to guide her men home. There's a big fire pit out front of their house, and when they think we're close, they build a big fire. We're usually spotted by one of the ranch hands who is out on the range. It's a lot further than it looks, but we should be home tomorrow afternoon if we get an early start." Justin studied Angel for a moment. "How is Maxi doing?"

"It's hard to tell. She tries to act like she's got everything under control, but inside, I think she's having a rough time. So much has happened to us in the last few weeks. Losing her pa was really hard on her…they were so close. Plus, she's anxious about finding her brother. Paul and Marty both show an interest in her, and that has been confusing. I don't know what will happen there. She likes them both, but I think she looks at Marty as more of a brother. I'm guessing, but I wonder if she's falling for Paul." Angel shrugged. "Only time will tell."

"I hadn't thought about all that," Justin said thoughtfully. "If you think it'll help, tell her when we get home we'll get the men together and decide what can be done about finding her brother. Be sure she knows that in the meantime we expect her to stay with us. She'll probably be invited to stay at the Double S Ranch too, but make her understand that her home is with us when she wants it."

Angel looked lovingly at Justin. "You are so sweet and thoughtful, Mr. Myers."

"Then be a good, obedient wife and come sit by me, Mrs. Myers."

"What a delightful invitation. I'm so tired I won't argue."

"Watch it, there's a hole right here, don't stumble." Paul had hold of Maxi's hand.

"It's so dark out here. I can't imagine what you think I'm going to be able to see."

"The darkness is what makes it possible. Come on over here." He guided her until she was standing in front of him. Placing his hands on her shoulders, he turned her straight north. "I want you to look straight down my arm, way off in the distance. Every once in a while you can see a tiny spot of light." He waited a moment. "Do you see it?"

"No, not yet. Where, Paul?"

"Keep looking. There! Did you see it that time?"

"I think so…yes! There it is again. Is that your home?"

"Couldn't be anything else. It's a lot farther than it looks though. Out here, things seem closer than they really are."

"How exciting. I'm sure you're glad to be so close to home."

Paul didn't answer immediately. He leaned forward and slid his arms around her waist pulling her back to lean against him. She didn't resist but relaxed in his arms. They stood that way for a while, watching that tiny speck of light. Finally, he whispered, "What I would like to do is stay here with you, *mi maravillosa flor*, but I've got to go back to work." Reluctantly, he released his hold, took her hand, and led her back to camp.

Maxi slipped her hand out of Paul's. "Thanks for the walk. I really enjoyed it."

"I enjoy being with you—what in the world is Justin up to?"

"What do you mean?"

"Well, look at him. All snuggled up, hanging onto Angel like they were married or something."

Sure enough, there they sat on a blanket, leaning against a tree with Angel in Justin's arms. They were both obviously asleep. Maxi turned her back and stifled a giggle.

"I'm glad you think it's funny. I better go wake him up before Travis comes in."

"No, wait. It's okay, Paul. I'll wake Angel in a minute."

"What's going on, Maxi?"

"Well…I promised not to tell. You'll know soon enough though. Be assured, it's okay. And don't say anything about it, please."

Maxi sensed his hesitation, but finally, he nodded. "Okay, if you say so. I've got to go. See you in the morning. Good night, Maxi."

"Good night, Paul."

She stood watching the sleeping couple. *I hate to wake those two. They're sleeping so soundly all snuggled together. They look so sweet.* A twinge of jealously niggled at her but not for long. *Angel, I really am happy for you. I just hope someday I can find what you and Justin have.* She went over and gave Angel a gentle shake. "Angel, wake up. You need to go to your bed now."

The prospect of being almost home energized everyone. "Angel, over to the northwest, there's a road of sorts. It's easy to find and easier to travel on. You should be able to see the herd and keep pace with us. We're going to have to get the herd away from the river, but we'll be right behind you."

"Okay, Justin, see you in a little while."

A couple of hours later, Angel stopped. "Let's give the animals a rest while the herd catches up. We can sit in the shade and wait."

"Okay, sounds good to me," Maxi agreed.

They sat comfortably in the shade of the wagon eating dried beef and watching clouds float by. Angel couldn't hold her feelings in any longer. She blurted out, "I'm so nervous I can't stand it! The closer we get to the ranches, the more my stomach churns."

"I know. I'm nervous too. Do you think they'll send us on to the ranch by ourselves?" Maxi was thoughtful then added, "That would be downright awkward."

"We're both going to be sick if we don't stop this. We act like we've never met people before." Angel moaned, "But I haven't met my mother-in-law before."

"I see what you mean, but if she's half as nice as Justin, you're a lucky woman. And if she doesn't like you...she's crazy."

Angel laughed. "You do have a way with words."

"Maybe we won't have to wait long to learn the plan. Here comes Travis."

He reached the wagon and got right down to business. "This is what we're going to do. Paul and Bill are coming now with the horses. They'll escort you to the ranch. The household items will be unloaded first, so pull the wagon right up to the front porch. Maxi, help with the horses if they need you." With a wave, he was gone.

"Okay, Samson, Delilah, up this road is home. Mary, Martha, help them out! Hup, now."

Close to two hours later, Angel drove the wagon onto the drive that curved in front of the ranch house. She set the brake and tied the reins, unaware of the commotion going on inside the house.

"Calli! Come here quick! Who's that bringing in the wagon?"

Calli peeked over her friend's shoulder. "I don't know, Judith." Suddenly, she sucked in a short breath. "As I live and breathe, it's a girl!"

"Oh my, look at all those beautiful white curls, Calli. Where do you suppose they found her?"

"I have no idea. There goes Bill and Paul with the horses. Who's that with them? The one in the black hat?"

"I can't tell, too much dust. Probably someone they hired to help with the herd. I better go tell Carmen her son is home."

"Did I hear my name?" A woman came in from the kitchen.

"I was coming to tell you that Paul and Bill just now came in with the horses. And it looks like we have a guest out front. We'd better get out there and welcome her, or she'll think we're rude. I guess we are rude, just staring out the window at her."

"I don't think she's seen us yet, Calli," Judith commented.

"She?" Curious, Carmen pulled back the curtain. "A young lady?"

Judith smiled. "Yes, a young lady. We haven't had a girl around here for…goodness, we've never had a girl around here. Just our rowdy boys."

"Well, let's get out there." Calli led the way out the front door.

Angel turned to see three smiling women looking at her like they had just spotted a pot of gold at the end of a rainbow.

"Hello, and welcome. I'm Calli Swanson. These are my friends, Judith Myers and Carmen Miles." The women nodded in greeting. Calli continued, "Tell us your—" She never got to finish her sentence.

Maxi rushed around the corner of the house. "Angel, Paul said for us to come help with the —" She stopped at the end of the porch staring at the women. They stared back.

A few awkward moments passed, then Judith exclaimed, "I can't believe it! There are two of them." Laughter erupted from all three women as the girls waited, not sure how to respond.

Angel was dumbstruck. She couldn't take her eyes off the woman named Judith Myers who was an attractive, full-figured woman, her hair and eyes the same color as Justin's.

Finally, Judith got her breath long enough to explain their laughter. "Please forgive us, but we were in shock to find one young lady in the front yard. Two just seems like a dream."

Maxi managed a smile and stepped up onto the porch. "I'm Maxine Mayfield. Pleased to meet you."

It was the day for interruptions. A ranch hand hurried around the same corner delivering a message on the run. "Paul said for you to hurry. I'm going to unload the wagon and take it out back. Oh, hi, Mrs. Swanson. You want to show me where to put things?"

"Carmen will help you with that, Peter." Disappointment edged her voice when she spoke to the girls. "I was hoping to visit with you now, but I guess that will have to wait. You two go on and help Paul. We'll have a long visit later."

Maxi gave her a quick smile. "We'll be looking forward to it."

By late afternoon, the flurry of activity began to wind down. Bill came to the barn door and announced, "Mrs. Swanson said to wash up. It's time to eat."

As the others made their way out of the barn, Angel hung back. "Justin, wait."

One look, and he became alarmed. He could clearly see she was on the verge of tears. "Sweetheart, what's wrong? Did something happen?"

She hung her head, mumbling so softly he could barely hear her. "I'm so embarrassed. Look at me. I'm so dirty and look a mess. I can't go to supper like this."

"Angel, look at me." Obediently, she looked up into his hazel eyes. "It's taking all the willpower I have, not to take you in my arms and hold you until you believe everything will be all right but we don't have time. Listen, this is a ranch and we've been on a long cattle drive. Everyone knows that. It won't matter one little bit to anyone what we look like." Gently, he squeezed her shoulders, winked, and smiled. "You okay now?"

She nodded slowly. "I suppose you're right. I just feel out of place is all."

"You're never out of place when you're with me. This is your home now. Ready to eat? I'm starved."

She felt a little foolish but let Justin take her hand and lead her out of the barn.

"Come on, they're waiting for us," Marty urged everyone. He led the group to the back of the house. As Maxi rounded the corner, she stopped in her tracks.

"Marty, this yard is just beautiful!"

"Thank you. We all worked hard on this place. Paul's father did the planning and we built it in a Spanish-style." The house was built in a U shape, a lush lawn between the wings of the building. "There's usually a tiled courtyard but mother wanted a park-like setting. She did all the planting and decorating."

Mr. Swanson called them to a large table placed in the middle of the lawn. Delicious smells enticed them to hurry and find a place to sit. Justin made sure he was sitting next to Angel, with Maxi on her other side. Mr. Swanson sat at the head of the table with Mrs. Swanson on his right and Marty on his left. Everyone quieted down and looked expectantly at their host.

"We are blessed this evening to have all our family and friends home safe and sound. We are also blessed to have several guests. I've met Mack McCallister, but I haven't met these two young ladies." He nodded toward the girls.

Justin stood quickly. "I'd like to introduce them, Mr. Swanson."

"Sure, Justin. Go right ahead."

"Our mothers haven't met Mack. I'd like to introduce him first. Mother, Mrs. Swanson, and Mrs. Miles, the man down by Bill is Mack McCallister. Travis hired him at Fort Laramie to help bring the cattle home. He has been a good hand, and I'd like you all to know that he'll be coming to the Paradise to help us on our ranch for a while." Murmurings of welcome and approval were heard as Mack nodded in acknowledgement.

Justin then turned to Maxi. "Mr. Swanson this is Maxine Mayfield. We all know her by Maxi." He looked down at Angel and said softly, "Angel, stand by me."

She stood, pressing close to him. "Mother, I apologize for telling you this way, but I can't wait any longer. I want to introduce to all of you, my wife, Angel Myers."

For several seconds, there was nothing but silence as this announcement soaked in. Judith suddenly stood to her feet. "Justin, what are you saying?"

"Angel and I were married in Fort Laramie by a minister there. She is my wife, Mother."

Judith could only stare at him, words failing her. She then stared at Angel, who grabbed Justin's hand and hung on for dear life. Tears brimmed Judith's eyes. Finally, Justin asked, "Are you okay, Mother?"

"Okay?" she shouted, hurrying around the end of the table. "You ask me if I'm okay?" She grabbed Justin's face and pulled it down to hers, planting a big kiss on his cheek. "You have just made me the happiest mother in this whole country." She grabbed Angel in a hug that almost crushed the breath out of her new daughter-in-law. Everyone clapped and congratulated the newlyweds. Still hugging Angel, Judith whispered in her ear, "I've prayed for you for a long time, my dear."

Mr. Swanson got everyone's attention again. "Now that introductions have been made let's pray and eat." Mr. Swanson prayed, asking God to bless the food and bless Justin and Angel's new life together. A unanimous voice rose from the group, and all said, "Amen!"

The food was wonderful, and conversations all around the table were warm and satisfying. When everyone had finished eating, the women began clearing the table while the men grouped at a corner of the yard to discuss men things. Justin pulled his mother aside. "Mom, Angel and I would like some time alone—"

"Say no more, son." Laughter and joy danced in Judith's eyes. "You two go on with my blessing. I'm sure Calli will be glad to put me up for the night."

"Thanks, Mom. I have so much to tell you, but it's a long story. Will you please take care of Maxi? She and Angel are very close. When you come home, be sure and invite her to come with you."

"Of course I will. I'll be home sometime tomorrow afternoon. Then I want to hear the whole story, and I mean the whole story."

"Okay, Mom. I love you, and thank you. Tell Angel I've gone to saddle our horses."

A mixture of emotions flowed through Judith as she watched her son stride confidently toward the barn. She made her way over to Angel and Maxi who were by the roses. "Angel, Justin said to tell you he's gone to saddle your horses. He's taking you home tonight."

Angel felt herself blush. "Aren't you coming, Mrs. Myers?"

"No, dear. I know how it is to be young and in love. You two need a little time to yourselves. I'll be home sometime tomorrow. And I won't have any of this Mrs. Myers stuff either. It's Judith or Mom. I can't tell you how happy I am to welcome you into our family." She hugged Angel, then grabbed Maxi with one arm and included her in the hug. "We are all going to be family." She looked at Angel. "I'll take good care of Maxi for you. Now, I'll go help with cleanup." Mrs. Myers left the two girls alone.

"She's wonderful, Angel. I'm so happy for you."

Angel's eyes grew large. "I'm scared to death, Maxi. What am I supposed to do?"

"Justin loves you. He'll take good care of you. Trust yourself to him."

Angel heaved a big sigh. "Thanks, you're right. How did you get so smart?"

"I was born that way, didn't you know? There's Justin now. Good night, Angel."

Maxi walked to the corner of the house with Angel, then watched as Justin gave her a boost into the saddle. As the newlyweds rode off, Maxi slipped further around the house and stood by a tree. She watched them until they were out of sight, still holding hands. A tear slid down her face followed by another. She couldn't seem to stop them and soon gave up trying. She leaned into the tree for support and sobbed. Moments passed; then, she felt hands on her shoulders turning her around, wrapping her in an embrace. She went gladly and clung to Paul, crying until her tears were spent. The two stood for a long time holding each other.

"You okay now?"

"Yes, thank you, Paul."

"You're welcome." He took a handkerchief from his pocket. "Here, take this." He waited for her to dry her eyes and blow her nose. "I want to give you a little advice."

"What's that?"

"This is a wonderful place. These are wonderful people. I know you'll miss Angel, but try to enjoy yourself while you're here. The women are going to love having you around. I've asked my mama to watch out for you. If you need anything, talk to her. I'll look forward to spending time with you, whenever I get a chance."

"Thanks, I'll take your advice. And I'm fine now. I don't know what got into me. I'm not usually a crybaby."

"I know, *mi marabillosa flor*." He brushed her forehead with a kiss.

CHAPTER 30

MAXI LINGERED AT the tree until she felt composed, then returned to the back lawn. She was grateful to see Mrs. Miles waiting for her. "Maxi, let me show you where you'll be sleeping tonight. You can freshen up before going into the front room where we're having coffee and dessert."

"Thank you, Mrs. Miles. I do need a few minutes."

She led Maxi to a door off the courtyard. They stepped into a room that was lit with candles, warm and inviting. On one side was a bed covered by a richly colored quilt. A dressing table, with mirror and bench sat against the other wall. Freshly cut flowers accounted for the sweet fragrance filling the room. And by the door, a table held a ceramic water pitcher with matching bowl. On a peg above the table hung a clean towel. "I hope you'll be comfortable here. Do you need anything else, Maxine?"

"I can't think of…oh, wait. I do need my saddle bags and slicker. My nightgown is in the saddlebags. I'll go get them."

"I don't think it is going to rain tonight, and there is a gown in the dressing table. First thing in the morning, I'll ask Paul to get your things and bring them right away. Will that be all right?"

Maxi didn't want to make a big deal of it, so she replied, "I suppose so. I guess I'm just a little nervous."

"That's only natural, but you don't need to be. I think you'll feel better after you visit with everyone tonight. They're very nice people and are happy to have you here. Personally, I'm looking forward to getting to know you since my Paul could not keep his eyes off you at dinner."

Surprised, Maxi felt herself blushing. But she couldn't deny what she herself had been aware of. *I wonder if she noticed that Marty couldn't keep his eyes off me either.* Realizing that Mrs. Miles was teasing her, she began to relax. She smiled at this woman who had the same beautiful smile that Paul had, a smile he only flashed in rare moments. "I can't tell you how much I'm looking forward to getting to know you too, Mrs. Miles."

"We'll be great friends, Maxi. Now freshen up and come on through that door over there. It'll take you to the kitchen, and you'll be able to find the front room from there." She stood at the door looking at Maxi for a few seconds, then turned and left the room.

Mrs. Miles had been right. Maxi enjoyed the evening even though she was plied with questions. She told them of her father's accident and how Angel had come along at just the right time. The hour was late when Travis finally spoke up. "I need to get some sleep. If you all will excuse me, I'll turn in." He looked at Judith. "When you get ready to leave tomorrow have someone come for me. I'll be taking you home…if that's okay."

"That's really not necessary, Travis…but…if you'd like to escort me home, then I'd be happy to have the company."

"I would like very much to see you home. Good night everyone."

Questioning looks covered a few faces as Travis left the room. Finally, Calli looked at her friend. "Since when do you need someone to take you home, Judith? You've been making that trip by yourself for years now."

"Well, I guess since Travis decided he wants to take me."

Maxi didn't miss the pleased look on Judith's face.

When Maxi started toward her bedroom, Judith put her arm around her. "I hope you don't mind me sharing a bed with you tonight, Maxi."

"Not at all. It'll keep me from missing Angel."

"Sounds like you two have become quite close in the last few weeks. Going through hard times together can do that."

"I can't imagine what it would have been like without her. She's wonderful, Mrs. Myers. You're going to love her."

"I think I already do."

Mrs. Myers and Maxi quietly got ready for bed. When Maxi was in her gown, she sat on the bed. "Mrs. Swanson and Mrs. Miles are so nice," she commented.

"Yes, indeed they are. I guess I feel about them like you do about Angel. We're more like sisters than friends."

Judith sat down on the other side of the bed. "You ready for me to blow out this candle?"

"Yes, that's fine."

"Maxine, would you mind if I prayed before we go to sleep?"

"I would love that. Angel and I have been reading a chapter from our Bibles each night and saying a prayer together. She told me how to give my life to Jesus."

"That's wonderful, Maxine."

As the room grew quiet, Judith prayed a prayer that warmed and comforted Maxi's heart. "There's so many things I want to know. But you need your sleep, so we'll talk more tomorrow. Good night, Maxine."

"Good night, Mrs. Myers."

The next morning when Judith and Maxi showed up in the kitchen, Calli and Carmen were waiting for them. "We wanted to have breakfast with you two, so we waited." Calli beamed at them. "Carmen has fixed a wonderful breakfast for us. Are you two ready for coffee?"

The women sat around the kitchen table, eating, sipping coffee, and talking up a storm. After awhile, Calli ventured a new subject. "Judith, it's my turn to have the Independence Day celebration this year. I want it to be a wedding party too for Justin and Angel. I'll bake a big wedding cake, and we'll make a grand day of it. What do you think?"

"You're right, Calli. You have the Fourth of July this year, and I have Thanksgiving. It's a wonderful idea to have a wedding party for Justin and Angel. Thank you for thinking of it."

"Angel will love it," Maxi put in.

They spent the rest of the morning making plans, talking, laughing, and enjoying their time together. Finally, Judith announced her need to get home. "Maxi, are you going home with me today or later?"

How sweet. She wants me to feel like my home is with her. Thank you, God, for leading me here to these wonderful people.

Before she could respond, Calli jumped in, "Oh no, don't leave, Maxi. I would love to have you stay here for a few days. You can help me some more with the party plans. Anyway, it's not fair for Judith to have all the fun. It will be pure joy to have you here, won't it, Carmen?"

"Yes, I would love to have you too, Maxi."

She couldn't say no to the two women who stood watching her, anxiously awaiting her answer. She nodded her acceptance. "Okay, if you're sure I won't be in the way."

"Then it's settled," Calli said triumphantly. Her eyes twinkled mischievously as she looked at Judith. "I guess you'll just have to make do with Travis on the ride home."

Travis saddled their horses, then went to the house to get Judith. "Our horses are saddled. We can go whenever you're ready."

"I'm ready, Travis. Good-bye, everyone. I'll see you in a few days. Maxi, do you have a message for Angel?"

"Tell her I'm doing fine. I'll see her soon."

The couple started out in uncomfortable silence. Finally, Judith broke the ice. "It's nice of you to take me home, Travis. But why do I feel you have something on your mind?"

"Probably, because I do. As a matter of fact, I have several things on my mind."

She smiled. "I'm listening."

"First, I want to tell you how proud I am of Justin. He's a fine young man. He handled himself on this trip with good common sense and maturity. It was a pleasure to make the trip with him."

"That's nice to hear. I think this trip did mature him a lot."

"I'm sure it did. Angel is one special lady as you'll find out. She's so cute, strong, talented, sweet, and caring. I can't think of enough words to describe her. I hope you're not upset that I didn't discourage them from getting married at Fort Laramie. They were so in love they were going to do it, no matter what."

"I'm not upset. I would like to have been there, but I understand. It just made good sense to have a minister marry them while they were there. I'm glad you were there for Justin. He probably needed a father that day. Thank you."

"It was my pleasure. There's one other thing that happened on the trip." He paused as if trying to figure out how to proceed. "I decided to give myself the freedom to go on with my life. One night, I got to thinking about my Beth. I realized that's what she would want me to do, go on with my life. I also realized that I've been clinging to the past. I've thought of you many times in the last couple of years, Judith, but I felt I was being unfaithful to Beth. Now, I know how silly that was. I've asked Justin if he would mind if I called on you. He gave me his permission and blessing. Now I need to ask you. Would you consider letting me call on you? Maybe consider me being a part of your life?" Her smile was hard for him to figure out. "You think that's funny?" he asked, pulling his horse to a stop.

"No, please don't misunderstand." She stopped alongside him. "It just struck me as funny that you would ask my son if you could see me. Honestly, that was a sweet thing to do."

"Well, he is the man of the house. I didn't want it to be a problem for him. Having an older man come into the picture might be difficult."

"Of course, you're right. I'm glad you did it that way. It was a wise way to handle it."

She was quiet for a while. They were still stopped, and Travis was getting fidgety. "Is it that hard of a question, Judith?"

"No, I'm just trying to decide how to voice what I feel. Would you mind if I'm honest with you?"

He prepared himself for rejection. "I prefer you just say what you think. I'll understand if you don't want anything to do with me. I don't have much to offer a woman but love and companionship. So just go ahead and say it."

Judith turned in order to face him. "I've been waiting a long time for you to come to me. I've thought of you many times but knew you weren't ready. I was beginning to think you never would be. We're not young kids anymore, and I don't want to play silly kid games with you. I would love for you to call on me. I can tell you I care a great deal for you already. I think we'll know in a short time if we can find love with each other."

Relief was evident on his face. "I agree, let's not play games. If either one of us feels like we should quit seeing each other, we need to be honest and say so. But I can tell you right now"—he reached for her hand and held it gently before bringing it to his lips—"I'm looking forward to spending time with you." He released her hand and looked fully into her lovely face.

Her cheeks warmed under his gaze. "Thank you, Travis. I'll enjoy spending time with you too."

They continued on to the ranch, talking comfortably with each other. As they neared the front of the house, Judith stopped. "Listen." They could hear laughter. "This house hasn't had laughter in a long time, Travis." Another bout of laughter was heard. "We'd better make ourselves known or we'll all be embarrassed. When we get to the porch stomp your feet real loud."

Travis grinned and nodded.

Their stomping caused the house to go quiet. Judith opened the door, entering like there was nothing unusual going on. Standing in the middle of the room was Justin, bare feet, no shirt, just his pants were on. An embarrassed Angel hid behind him.

"Hi, Justin, Angel. Travis and I are going to the kitchen, and I'm going to fix us something to eat. Would you two like something?"

"Sure, Mom. We'll go get ready and be down pretty quick."

A muffled voice came from behind Justin, "I'll come help as soon as I can, Mrs. Myers."

"Don't worry about it, Angel. I can handle lunch. Come on down when you get ready." She headed into the kitchen with Travis right behind her. "This house is finally going to see some joy and laughter." Judith said to Travis.

"Joy and laughter," he repeated. "That's a good thing."

The four had a pleasant time visiting and eating. "Justin, can I get you to take care of my horse when you finish eating? I won't be going anywhere for the rest of the day."

"Sure, be glad to, Mom. I went out early this morning and helped with chores. Bill is going to work with Mack today and show him how the ranch works. He said the two of them could handle the day without me."

"That's nice. You just enjoy your day with Angel."

"Okay, I'll get back to work tomorrow. My wife and I are going for a walk in a little while." He winked at Angel.

"You two go on then. I'll clean up."

Travis stood and pushed in his chair. "I need to get back to work, Judith. Thanks for the meal."

"Let me hang my apron up and walk out with you." Stepping out onto the front porch, Travis suddenly seemed nervous. "What is it, Travis? You have something on your mind?"

"Yes, I want to kiss you good-bye. Is it too soon?"

Judith's cheeks flushed. "Do you know my heart is beating like a silly school girl's? If you don't come over here and kiss me good-bye, I'll have to come over there and kiss you."

"Well, since I'm old-fashioned and feel the man should take the lead, I'll come over there." He closed the gap between them and took her in his arms, giving her a kiss that wasn't just a peck on the cheek.

Opening her eyes, Judith looked up into his blue-gray ones. She whispered, "That wasn't a good-bye kiss, Travis. That was an 'I'll be coming back soon' kiss."

He smiled down at her. "I'm glad you got my meaning." Still beaming, he walked down the steps, mounted his horse, and rode toward the Double S Ranch.

"Well now, don't you look deep in thought." Carmen found Maxi at the kitchen table drinking another cup of coffee. She had been at the Double S Ranch for two days.

"I guess I'm just missing Angel," she confessed. "I've enjoyed being here with you and Mrs. Swanson, but I want to visit Angel. If I knew the way, I'd go by myself."

Marty came into the kitchen just then. "You wanting to go somewhere, Maxi?"

"I was just saying that I would like to visit Angel."

"I've got a little time on my hands…if you can be ready pretty quick."

"That would be great. I don't know whether to take all my things or just visit and come back."

Carmen advised her, "Why don't you visit just for today. That way you can see how you feel about staying longer next time. You are undoubtedly welcome at the Paradise, but Calli and I would love for you to make this your home until you find your brother. Then you can visit Angel whenever you like."

"That's a good idea, Mrs. Miles, thanks. Okay, Marty, I'll be out in a few minutes."

She went to change while he went to saddle their horses. Several minutes later, he called in through the front door, "Hey, Maxi, I'm out front with the horses."

"I'm coming." She stepped into the front room, and he smiled, showing his dimples and bright, brown eyes. "Let's go."

They mounted and rode off toward the river. "Do you know how good it is to have you here with my family?"

"They're wonderful. You're a very lucky man. I appreciate you taking me to see Angel. How far is it anyway?"

"I'd guess four or five miles. Just a nice little ride."

In a short time, they reached the river. "This is great. You all built a bridge across this river."

"Yeah, we pull wagons back and forth between the ranches. It's washed out a few times, but we keep rebuilding it. Mother and Mrs. Myers appreciate it more than anyone else."

They started across the bridge, but Marty suddenly stopped his horse. He sat still, listening. "Did you hear anything, Maxi?"

She drew Ginger to a stop beside him, listening intently. "I hear something but…sounds like someone calling out."

"Yeah, I heard it too. Seems to be coming from up river in those trees. I better check it out. You stay here."

"Not on your life, mister, I'm going with you."

"Okay, but stay behind me, be ready for anything."

"Go, hurry! Someone's in some kind of trouble!"

CHAPTER 31

WHEN MARTY AND Maxi broke through the brush along the river, they came to an abrupt halt on the edge of a sandy area. In front of them was an Indian girl, knife in hand, bravely holding a man at bay. The man had his back to them, but the girl spotted Marty over the man's shoulder, and a look of surprise crossed her face. The man took advantage of the moment, lunging for her knife. He grabbed her wrist and twisted until the knife fell from her hand. With the fury of a cornered wild cat, she lit into the man, raking her fingernails across his face, and kicking wildly. Enraged, the man slugged her in the face, dropping her hard to the ground.

Marty jumped off his horse, and the two men faced each other, half crouching. The man threw the first punch at Marty's face. Marty ducked, then connected with a blow to the man's face and a hard jab to the gut. Air swooshed out of his lungs. Another swing from Marty, and the man was on his back, gasping for air. He held his hands up, signaling he'd had enough.

"What are you doing attacking a girl like that?" Marty yelled.

The man sneered. "It's none of your business. She's just an Injun, so why do you care? A man ought to have a little fun with a squaw now and then without anyone interrupting him. Just get on out of here and leave us alone."

"Anything that happens around here is my business." Marty stared hard at the man. "I know you!"

Maxi sucked in her breath with surprise and recognition. "It's Tip! The man who helped with the cattle drive. He's the one who tried to take Angel."

Marty pulled his pistol. "Get up, you lousy excuse for a man." Tip stood, swiping at the blood oozing from his nose. "Throw your pistol on the ground, and move real slow. I don't like you and it wouldn't take much for me to shoot you where you stand." Tip slowly pulled his pistol and dropped it in the sand. Marty kicked it out of the way. "Get the rifle off his horse, Maxi."

Maxi ran to Tip's horse and quickly pulled the rifle from its scabbard, hardly taking her eyes off the man. "Got it."

"I'm going to say this once, mister. Get on your horse, and get as far away from this country as you can. I'm going to spread the word that if you're ever seen anywhere around here you won't be shown any mercy. You won't be given another chance to cause trouble or hurt anyone. You better head west and not turn around. I'm not sure I should even give you this chance."

"You can't send me out into this country without a gun," Tip argued.

"I'm tempted to do just that, but I'll give you one. Maxi, empty all the shells out of his rifle. Make sure they're all out."

She laid her own rifle down, then took a good look at the one in her hands. Instantly, she stopped cold. Her heart leaped in her throat as she stared at the rifle.

Marty glanced at her. "What's wrong?"

She looked hard at Tip, enraged. "Where did you get this rifle?"

"I found it!" He spat on the ground.

"Where did you find it?" she demanded.

"Well, if you have to know, I found it on a dead man."

"Did you kill that man?" she said through tight lips.

No, I didn't kill him, not that it's any of your business. He was already dead and couldn't use it no more, so I took it." He spat again, and bile rose in Maxi's throat.

"What is it, Maxi?" Marty was alarmed at the look on her face.

"This is my brother's rifle. Pa gave it to him on his sixteenth birthday, a year before he left home."

"Are you sure? How can you tell?" Marty asked, never taking his eyes off Tip.

"Yes, I'm sure. Pa had Michael's initials engraved on it. MM for Michael Mayfield."

Tip became agitated. "Listen, lady, I never killed your brother. My friends and I stumbled on a ranch up north last fall. We were just looking for grub. The place had been raided. Didn't look like Injun's doings either. Far as we could tell, it was rustlers."

"Did you…bury him?" Maxi's voice cracked.

"I might have done some bad things in my life, but I'm not that bad," Tip sputtered. "Yes, we buried both of them. They was two young cowboys. Wasn't much left of the place. Only reason the raiders didn't take the rifle was 'cause he was laying on it."

A cold rage gripped Maxi. "Shoot him, Marty!" A second later, she yelled, "Never mind, I will!" She lifted the rifle to her shoulder, and the man started begging for his life.

"Wait, don't shoot me like this. I tell you. I didn't kill him!"

"Maxi, hold up. Listen to me a minute," Marty said.

"What!" The rifle was still aimed at the man.

"I don't blame you for wanting to shoot him, but let's get the others to help us decide what to do. Get the rope off my saddle. We'll take him with us."

A long, shaky moment passed; then, Maxi relaxed her stance and lowered the rifle. "All right, Marty. I trust your judgment." A moan came from the girl lying on the ground. She tried to sit up. "I better check on the girl. I hope she's okay."

"Go on, then. I'll get this weasel tied on his horse."

"Much obliged," Tip muttered.

"Don't thank me," Marty snapped. "I have no idea what will become of you. As far as I know, everyone will vote for Maxi to shoot you after all. Keep your hands up, and if you try anything, I'll shoot you myself."

Maxi knelt on the ground beside the girl but saw she was really a beautiful young woman with long raven hair. Her smooth, dark, flawless skin was marred at the corner of her mouth where it was split and swollen. A trickle of blood ran down her chin. "You poor thing," Maxi muttered. "Can you hear me?" She gently shook the girl's shoulder.

The girl blinked several times trying to keep her eyes open. She murmured a few words, but Maxi could only make out the word Marty. She faded into darkness again.

"Marty, she said your name. Do you know her?"

"I don't think so. I'll be there in a minute. Almost got him taken care of."

Maxi pulled off her scarf and went to the water's edge to get it wet. She washed the girls face hoping it would revive her. "I think she might be coming out of it again."

Marty quickly tied Tip's horse to a tree. "Don't do anything stupid, Tip, and you might live awhile longer." He hurried to where Maxi was kneeling beside the girl. "Do you think she's all right?" he asked.

The girl responded to Marty's voice and opened her eyes. "Marty, you…came…" A tear formed and ran down her face. She tried to push herself off the ground, but it was too much for her.

"Easy now, move slowly," Marty cautioned. He slipped his arm under her neck and gently lifted her to a sitting position, cradling her in his arms. Maxi was touched by the tenderness that he showed the girl. "You know my name, but I don't know yours," he said.

The girl opened her eyes, which were a deep, dark brown. Marty stared into them and couldn't seem to pull away. "You know my name as well as I know yours, Marty Swanson," she managed to say around the pain in her jaw and lips.

"I do?" He was completely flabbergasted.

The girl's English was remarkable, and Maxi felt a twinge of jealousy as she watched the play of emotions on Marty's face. They seemed to go from confusion, to recognition, to disbelief.

"Spotted Fawn?"

"Yes, it's me, Black Feather's little sister. I used to tag along and torment you boys when you played. Do you remember me now?"

Maxi was surprised. *I think this girl has strong feelings for him. I wonder if he even knows it.*

"Yes, I remember you now but you're … wow … all … grown up," Marty stammered.

"Help me up, Marty."

As Maxi reached down to help, the Indian girl looked confused. "Who is this?"

"This is Maxi. She's a friend. Maxi, this is Fawn."

They brought Fawn to her feet while Marty steadied her. "My head swims like the swirls in the river." She leaned into Marty. "I feel foolish being so helpless."

"You don't need to feel that way. He hit you pretty hard. You're lucky you fell on sand instead of rocks. What should we do, Maxi?"

"We need to take her to Angel. She'll know what to do. Can you get her on your horse? She could ride in front of you, and you can hold her in case she passes out. I'll keep my rifle on Tip and make sure he doesn't get away."

"Okay, let's try it." Marty guided Fawn to his horse, gently lifted her up, then got on behind her.

Maxi noticed how he wrapped his arms around the beautiful Fawn. She also noticed that neither one seemed to mind the close contact when Marty told her to lean into him for support. *Did I just see a smile on that beguiling face?*

She went to Tip's horse and untied the reins from the tree. His hands were tied to the pommel of the saddle. Looking up at the man, she told him, "I'll shoot you if you try to get away."

He looked at her with more hate and disgust than Maxi had ever seen. "How can I get away all tied up like this?"

Ignoring his remark, Maxi put Michael's rifle in her scabbard. Then mounted her horse, holding her own rifle trained on Tip. "You go first. I'll be right behind you."

"Just make sure you don't shoot me in the back."

By the middle of the morning, three horses trotted into the yard of the Paradise Ranch. Justin came out of the barn to greet them and stopped short when he saw Tip tied to his horse. "What's going on, Marty?"

"I was bringing Maxi over to visit Angel when we ran into a little trouble. I'm sure you remember Tip. We found him trying to attack Fawn."

Justin glared at Tip, then looked at the girl riding in front of Marty. "This is Spotted Fawn?" He smiled up at the girl.

"Yes, Black Feather's little sister."

"I'd say she's grown up. Is she hurt bad?"

"I don't think so, but we need Angel to look at her and make sure. Tip slugged her pretty hard."

"My mother and Angel were working out in the garden earlier." Justin looked across the yard. "Here they come now. Let's get her in the house. Can she stand?"

"Yes, but she's dizzy. How do you feel, Fawn? Think you can stand?"

"I'm not sure. I do want to try. I don't want to be a big baby."

"You're not a big baby, Fawn, not at all. Just move slowly. Justin will hold onto you so you don't fall."

Fawn slid off the horse, but as soon as her feet hit the ground, she swayed toward Justin. "My head still swirls, my stomach doesn't feel so good."

Marty was on the ground then and swooped Fawn up into his arms. "I'll carry her in, Justin. We need to get Tip in the house where we can watch him."

Angel's face registered alarm when she ran up to greet Maxi. She immediately recognized Tip. "What's he doing here?"

"I'll tell you in a bit, sweetheart," Justin said. First, we need you to take care of a friend of ours. Marty is carrying her into the house. Tip tried to attack her and slugged her pretty hard."

Angel turned all business at that news. "Of course, come on, let's get her checked out. See you in a few minutes, Maxi."

Justin turned to Maxi who was holding Tip at gunpoint. "Let me have your rifle, Maxi. I'll take Tip in, if you'll bring the horses up to the house."

When Tip was on the ground, Justin shoved him toward the house. "Get going, and don't do anything stupid. It would give me great pleasure to make coyote bait out of you."

Maxi followed with the horses. She noticed that Tip was limping. *Good! Looks like Angel did do some damage to the man's leg. Too bad she didn't shoot it off.* Her thoughts turned to Michael. *Oh, Michael, did this man kill you? God, help me to figure it out and know what to do. If Michael's dead, I have no one. How can I know for sure?* Tangled thoughts raced through her head. She just couldn't bring herself to accept what Tip had said. Too much was going on at the moment to deal with the new and unexpected information.

Justin halted Tip at the porch and tied him securely to one of the posts. Then Marty came out, and he and Justin talked in low tones about what to do with the man.

Inside the house, Angel was finding out what had happened to Fawn. "My name is Angel. I was told that you were slugged in the face. Is that the only place that man hurt you?"

Fawn lay very still on the sofa with a pillow under her head. Slowly, she opened her eyes and stared up at Angel. "Are you… White Cloud that the Cheyenne sing of?"

Smiling at this beautiful girl, Angel responded, "I suppose I am."

"I am honored to meet you. I am too much trouble for you to bother with. I will be okay. My name is Spotted Fawn of the Arapaho people. My father is Black Crow, chief of our tribe."

"I'm pleased to meet you, Spotted Fawn. You're not any trouble at all, and I'd like to take care of you for a little while. I need to make sure you're okay. I don't think your jaw is broken, but it will be sore for a few days. You're going to have a good bruise too. Were any of your teeth broken when he hit you?"

Fawn ran her tongue over her teeth to be sure. "No, they're okay. It hurts to talk. My head spins when I move, but even that is better."

"Good. That will pass if you lay quietly for a while. We'll get some cold rags to bathe your face. Do you hurt anywhere else, Fawn?"

"Only my arm. He grabbed and twisted it to get my knife."

"Let me look at it. Can you move your wrist and fingers?"

"Yes."

"I'm sure it's bruised." Angel leaned close to Fawn. "You need to be truthful and tell me if he hurt you in any other way."

Fawn looked a little confused, but slowly, comprehension showed on her face. "I always tell the truth. No, he did not force me to lie with him." Her words were heated, dark eyes flashing. "I would have split his belly and let his insides fall to the ground if he had done that to me."

"No one would blame you for that. Now, lay still and relax. We're going to put a cold rag on your face." Angel spoke to Mrs. Myers, "I need to get the coldest water possible and some rags. It'll help the swelling on her jaw and face."

"I'll take care of it. Water from the mouth of the spring will be the coldest. I'll send someone to get it." Judith hurried from the room.

Maxi had been sitting close to the front window staring out at the men on the porch. There was something different about her that Angel couldn't quite put her finger on. She studied her for several minutes. Finally, she asked, "Maxi, are you all right?"

"I suppose so," was the quiet answer.

"Lay still, Fawn. I'm going to go talk to my friend." Angel walked quickly over to Maxi. "Maxine Mayfield, there is something wrong, and you had better tell me what it is right now!"

At that moment, the front door opened, and Justin stood in the doorway with Marty right behind him. "Angel, we're taking Tip back to the Double S. We want Mr. Swanson and Travis to decide what to do with him. Most people would just hang him and be done with it." He looked at Maxi. "Sorry about your brother, Maxi."

Angel looked surprised. "What about your brother? Is that what's bothering you? Did you hear something about him?"

Justin quickly stepped over to Angel putting his arm around her shoulders. "I guess she hasn't told you yet."

"We haven't had time to talk. Tell me, Justin."

"Well, when they rescued Fawn, Maxi discovered that Tip had her brother's rifle. He said he found it on a…dead man," he finished almost in a whisper.

A voice interrupted their conversation. "Where do you want this bucket of water, Angel?" Everyone's attention was drawn to the kitchen doorway, where Mack McCallister was standing holding the bucket.

"There!" yelled Tip from the front porch. He was craning his neck to see into the room and had obviously recognized Mack's familiar voice. "There's my proof. He was with us. He can tell you I didn't kill her brother."

Mack was taken aback. "Tip? What are you doing here?"

Marty explained quickly, "We found him attacking our friend down by the bridge. Maxi found her brother's rifle in his possession. He said he found it under a dead man. Is it true, Mack? Were you with his bunch when he found the rifle?"

"You remember, don't cha, Mack?" Tip yelled through the doorway. "When we was looking for some grub and found that little ranch that had been raided? Remember, we found them two dead cowboys? It was last fall, remember?"

"Yeah, I remember. Looked like the work of rustlers." Mack suddenly realized the significance of the two dead men. He put the bucket down and walked over to Maxi. "That was your brother, Maxi? I am so sorry."

"I don't know what to think, Mack. All I know is, Tip had my brother's rifle." She looked steadily at Mack. "What did the man look like? Can you tell me?"

Mack's face twisted like he might be sick. "Don't think about this too much, Maxi. They had probably been there for several days. There's no way to describe what he looked like, only that he was probably young, with black hair."

"Yeah!" Tip volunteered. "The other one had more light-colored hair. Tell her we buried him real nice, Mack."

Angrily, he turned on Tip. "*We*, Tip? There was no *we*. You and your friends left me there by myself to bury them, then catch up with you." He shook his head sadly and stared hard at the floor. "I should have gone in the opposite direction."

"Is there anything else we need to know, Mack?" Marty asked.

"I don't guess there is. I can tell you we did not raid the place or kill those two men. And Tip did find the rifle under the man's body."

Maxi tensed, "Are you sure, Mack?"

"Yes, I'm sure, Maxi. I'm sorry but I was standing right there."

Maxi sighed in resignation as Angel wrapped her in a hug.

"Thanks, Mack," Marty said. "We're taking Tip back to the Double S and let Travis and my father help us decide what to do with him."

"Hey!" Tip protested. "You have to let me go! I told ya I didn't kill nobody, and the rifle was up for grabs. You have to let me go."

Three men stared menacingly at Tip, making him shrink back.

"We don't have to do anything," Marty said evenly.

"You. Be. Quiet!" Justin yelled at the man.

"Do you want me to go with you? I'd be glad to tell the rest what happened."

"No, but thanks," Justin answered. "I'd rather you stay here at the ranch. Bill is checking on some cows out east of here. He thought there might be calves with them so he'll be bringing them in for branding."

"Sure, I'll stay around here till you get back. You want me to work on that door you were fixing?"

"That's a good idea. Let's go, Marty. I want to get this over with." He handed Maxi's rifle back to her.

"I guess I should go back with them," Maxi said, looking at Angel.

"Maxi, don't go." Judith seemed truly anxious for Maxi to stay. "Why don't you stay here for a while. I think you need to be here with Angel. Travis is coming to supper tonight. He can take you back with him afterward."

"Please, Maxi," Angel pleaded. "Please?"

"Okay, I'll stay for supper and go back with Travis. Will you tell your mother and Mrs. Miles, Marty?"

"Sure, it's probably a good idea for you stay here for a while. I'll see you tonight."

The girls watched out the window as the men rode away. Angel shuddered. "I'm glad that awful man is gone."

Maxi put her arm around Angel's shoulders. "I am too."

Judith sat on the edge of the sofa putting cold rags on Fawn's face. "Angel, dear, why don't you and Maxi fix us something to eat. I'm going to stay right here and take care of Fawn."

"Be glad to. Come on, Maxi."

"Okay, I don't feel very hungry, but I'll go help."

"You may not be hungry, but I bet you won't turn down a cup of coffee."

"You know me too well."

Once in the kitchen, Maxi looked fully into Angel's face and smiled. "You look fantastic, Angel. Are you happy?"

"I can't tell you how happy I am. Justin is wonderful. And his mother? She's everything I could have hoped for in a mother-in-law. God has been very good to me."

"It shows. I couldn't be more happy for you. Now, what can I do to help?"

"Not a thing. You just sit right there, and I'll serve you a cup of coffee." Angel got a cup from the cupboard, poured the coffee, and handed it to Maxi. "I'm so sorry about your brother. Do you believe what Tip said?"

Maxi took a sip of the coffee and thought about that. "I don't believe Tip, but I do believe Mack. It doesn't seem real. I feel like I should cry or something, but I can't. I'm just numb. Is something wrong with me?"

Angel went over and gave her a hug. "No, there's nothing wrong with you. Everyone grieves differently. There are no set rules, so let it come naturally. Your mind and heart will work it out in their own time."

"How did you get so smart?"

"I was born that way, hadn't you noticed?"

They talked about their days apart until Angel was through with the meal preparations. She went to the doorway of the living room. "How's it going in here? Do you want me to bring you a bowl of this stew?"

"I don't think so. Fawn wants to try and get up now. She says she doesn't feel dizzy anymore. Do you think that's all right?"

"I don't see why not, if she wants to try." Angel went to the sofa. "I'll help you. Just move slowly." She helped her into a sitting position. Stay that way for a minute or two and see how your head feels."

"My head no longer swirls. I can stand now," she said with certainty.

"Okay, let's walk to the kitchen, and you can sit at the table with us. Do you want to try and eat some stew?"

"I think my stomach would be mad if I didn't. It smells so good."

Judith went to get a couple of cups from the cupboard. "If there's hot water on the stove, I'll fix a pot of peppermint tea. Fawn and I always enjoy a cup of tea when she comes to visit."

"There's plenty of hot water ready. I'll join you in a cup of tea," Angel said. My ma and I always had tea parties. I guess that's how I learned to love a cup of hot tea."

The four women seated in the kitchen slowly began to warm up to one another as they got better acquainted. Maxi asked Fawn, "How did you learn to speak English so well?"

"I had a wonderful teacher." She smiled and nodded at Judith.

"Fawn was one of my first students," Judith explained. "Her father, Black Crow, wanted all the village children to learn the white man's language. He said they must learn to live with the white man, and learning the talk would be important."

Fawn added, "He said his great-grandfather had a vision about many white men moving into the land of the Arapaho. The vision told that there were more than could be counted. His great grandfather said we must learn their ways and live in peace or be no more on the land. That's why he will not make war on the white man. He welcomes them as friends as long as they do no harm to our people."

"So Fawn and another girl from her tribe, Willow is her name, came to be my first students. In the summers, they would bring some children and stay for a few days. We would have school here. Then Fawn and Willow would take lessons back and teach the younger ones at their village. They did as much as I did, maybe more."

"That's wonderful," Angel said.

"I agree." Maxi realized she really liked this beautiful, young Indian girl. "I hope we can be friends, Fawn." Then a look of confusion crossed her face. "That is, as long as I'm around. I don't know what I'm going to do now."

Judith heard sadness in her voice and quickly took charge. "Don't talk like that, dear. You're going to make this your home for as long as you want. Forever, if need be. Angel says you're like a sister to her, and that's good enough for me. We are family now. We'll look after one another. That includes you too, Fawn."

The girls looked at Judith Myers with gratitude and admiration. Angel moved first. She went around the table and hugged her surprised mother-in-law. "Thank you, Mom. I love you."

Maxi and Fawn followed. By then, Judith had tears in her eyes. "I love all three of you," she managed to say. "You all three are my girls now."

CHAPTER 32

THE NEXT MORNING at the Double S Ranch, Maxi walked into the kitchen and was immediately enveloped in the arms of Carmen Miles. "I am so sorry about your brother. Marty told us all about what happened yesterday. I feel so sad for you."

"Thank you, Mrs. Miles. Do you know what they decided to do with Tip? Travis told me at supper last night they hadn't decided for sure."

"You'll need to ask Mr. Swanson or Marty. Justin and Travis gave their opinions before they left. They said they would trust Mr. Swanson to make the final decision." She placed a cup of coffee in front of Maxi. "At breakfast, Mr. Swanson said he was calling all available men to the bunkhouse for final instructions. We'll have to wait until one of the men come in. It probably won't be very long now. Did you have a good time with Angel?"

"Yes, considering everything that happened on the way to the Paradise. Mrs. Myers is so sweet and treated me like family. It was good to be with Angel again. I needed to be with her after I heard my brother was dead." She sighed deeply. "I've known her for less than a month, and she knows more about me than anyone else in the world." Tears welled in her eyes and spilled down her cheeks. "She's the only one in the world I have now."

"You are wrong, Maxi." Carmen's voice was very gentle. "You've found a place in the hearts of everyone around here. And here comes one of them now." Maxi looked at the kitchen door as Marty walked in.

"Morning, Maxi. It's nice to have you back here where you belong."

"Good morning, Marty. I'm not sure where I belong anymore, but it's nice of everyone to make me feel at home."

"And you are," he said, winking at her. "Mrs. Miles, would you pack a small lunch for me and father. We'll be leaving shortly. I'll be happy with anything but dried beef."

"I'd be glad to, Marty."

"Can I ask where you're going?" Maxi questioned.

"Sure, you can ask. You need to know what we decided anyway. No one really has the heart to hang or shoot Tip. We all know that's probably what he deserves. In most places, they would just hang him. What my father finally decided is for us to take him most of the way to the Sweet Water River. He made every one of our men take a good look at Tip and told them if they ever see him on our range, they are to shoot him.

"He told Tip that he didn't deserve another chance, but he was going to get one. He preached a sermon to him about changing his ways. I've been on the receiving end of some of my father's sermons, and they can be downright convincing. If the man has any sense at all, he'll leave the country and decide to mend his ways." Marty stopped and gazed at Maxi. "I hope you agree with our decision, Maxi."

"I'll just be glad when that man is gone."

"Me too. And that's why I need to hurry and get ready. Dad will be coming for me in a minute. He hates to wait on anyone."

"Do you need any company on the trip?"

"No, but thanks. Dad wants just the two of us to go. I think he wants to talk with me about some ranch things, and we're going to check on the cattle in the west canyon. Maybe next time though."

The kitchen became quiet after Marty left. Maxi watched Carmen stir something in a bowl. "What can I do to help?"

"You can take your pick of things to do today. Calli is out working in her flowers and will be working in the garden later. We plant a big garden each year. I'm going to be baking most of the morning. You can certainly help me in here. You might just relax or explore the ranch. Calli and I will be quilting and sewing tomorrow. Do you like to sew?"

"I don't really know how," Maxi admitted. "I can mend a little or sew on a button, but that's about all. My ma died when I was young, so I didn't get very far on learning those kinds of things. I'd like to learn though."

"That's good. Calli and I will teach you."

"There's a lot more I need to learn than just sewing, Mrs. Miles. You may decide the job of teaching me is more than you want."

"I doubt that. I've always wanted a daughter. I think it will bring me great joy to teach you whatever you want to learn."

Maxi was content to help Carmen in the kitchen for a while, then enjoyed working in the garden with Mrs. Swanson later that morning.

After the dishes were done that evening, Maxi hung up her dish towel and wondered what she could find to do. Marty and his father hadn't returned yet, and Paul had hurried out to do one last chore. She felt a presence behind her; then, a soft voice whispered, "Out past the garden, there is a trail that eventually ends up at the river. I think there might be someone waiting for you there. It's a nice evening for a walk, don't you think?"

Maxi turned to see Carmen with a twinkle in her eyes. "That does sound like a good idea. I think that's just what I'll do. Thank you, Mrs. Miles."

Trying not to appear too anxious, Maxi walked out into the backyard, heading toward the garden. She was startled by a sudden fluttering in the pit of her stomach. The anticipation of being with Paul affected her like nothing she had experienced before. *What's this I'm feeling? Excitement 'cause I'm going to meet Paul? He makes me feel so many things when I'm around him. I wonder if this is what it's like to be in love.* She slowed her pace. *I wish I could talk to Angel.*

Up the trail, she spotted Paul. She waved and picked up her pace again. He didn't return the wave, but with the setting sun full on his face, she could see that dazzling smile she loved. He stood casually waiting for her, cowboy hat tipped back on his head, thumbs hooked in his pockets, and his eyes locked on her.

"Are you following me, Miss Mayfield?" The smile didn't fade as he tried to sound serious.

"Of course not, Mr. Miles. A lady doesn't follow a man around. That wouldn't be proper behavior."

"If it's not proper for a lady to follow a man, you had better walk beside me then."

She feigned deep contemplation. "Well…I suppose it would be proper for a lady to be escorted on a walk with a handsome cowboy such as yourself."

He didn't answer, just held out his hand to her. Without hesitation, she put her hand in his, and they walked toward the river. A comfortable silence followed them for quite a while. Then he spoke softly, "Marty told me about your brother. I want you to know how sorry I am it turned out the way it did."

"Thank you, Paul."

"How are you feeling now that you've had time to think about it? Do you believe what Tip said?" He stopped and faced her, putting his hands on her shoulders. "I mean, do you feel you need to check out the story? I'll help you in anyway I can. I have responsibilities here, but as soon as I'm able, we could make a plan."

She was touched by his earnest concern. "I've thought about it a lot. To me, it just doesn't make sense to run around trying to find out if Tip's story is true. I don't trust him at all, but I do trust Mack. His story was the same as Tip's. I just know that Michael would never have given up that rifle if he was alive."

Paul nodded, then took her hand again. He led her to a log lying on a sandy area by the river. She sat on the sand, leaned back against the log, drawing up her knees and wrapping her arms around them. He dropped down beside her. "I feel so strange and empty when I think about Michael. After praying last night, I decided to give it to God. Unless he leads me otherwise, I'll leave it with him." She looked up and searched Paul's face. "What are you thinking? Does that make sense?"

"I think it makes perfect sense. If you ever change your mind or need to talk about it some more, I'm always here for you."

"Thank you. My biggest problem is, what do I do now? I really have nowhere else to go. Angel says my home is with her now, but it seems awkward to think of living with Justin and Angel. They are wonderful, and I know I would be welcome. Mrs. Myers is such a precious and generous person. She said I'm one of her girls now." Maxi rested her chin on her knees. "I don't know, Paul." Her voice was edged with frustration. "Just pray that I'll know what to do."

"I will, and I'll ask Mama to pray with us too. I don't know how far my prayers will go, but Mama's prayers will definitely reach heaven." A peaceful silence fell between them as they sat sharing each other's company. Finally, he realized the sun would soon be gone. He took Maxi's hand in his and kissed the back of her fingers. "I hate to leave, but we probably need to head back. Before we go, I have an invitation for you."

Curious, Maxi looked up at him. "Invitation? What kind of invitation?"

"I want to invite you to go with me and Mama up to the high meadows this next Sunday. We'll pack a big lunch and spend the whole day there. I'm anxious to show it to you. What do you say? You want to go?"

"Oh, Paul, I can't think of anything else I would rather do. What a wonderful idea. Is there anything I can do to get ready?"

"You can ask mama, but I'm sure she'll say no. She was so excited about the three of us going up there together. It'll be a lot of fun."

Paul pulled Maxi to her feet. "Let's get you back to the house."

It was a brisk walk back, but Maxi was in a bubbly mood and chattered most of the way. "I'm so excited, Paul. A few more days till we'll have the Independence Day celebration. Your mother said she would help me make the wedding cake for Angel and Justin. And then, I get to go see your high meadows the next day. I can hardly wait!"

"I'm looking forward to it too."

They reached the edge of the garden, and Paul reluctantly let go of Maxi's hand. "I have to go check on a new foal before I go to the house, so I'll see you later."

"A new foal? Can I go see it?"

"Sure, tomorrow morning would be a good time."

"Well, okay then. I enjoyed the walk. See you tomorrow."

She was disappointed but knew he was probably thinking how it would look for the two of them to be out in the barn together after dark. *He's protecting me, again. What a special man you are, Paul Miles.*

Both ranches worked hard to get ready for the big party on Saturday. Maxi was involved with everything, from cooking, to sewing, and decorating. Friday evening, she sat staring critically at her reflection in the mirror. *I need more than a face washing for the party. What can I do with my hair?* Never one to care about fancy clothes, makeup, or social graces, Maxi didn't understand her discontentment. *With two split riding skirts and three blouses, it shouldn't be too hard to decide what to wear. Fiddlesticks! Why should I care? Might as well wear a rain slicker. It wouldn't make any differ-*

ence anyway. For the first time in her life, Maxi began to realize, she *did* care. *I want to look pretty for…who do I want to look pretty for?* Her heart whispered the answer. *Paul, I want to look pretty for Paul.* A sudden knock on the bedroom door startled her.

"Come in."

"Sorry to disturb you, dear." Carmen opened the door. "I brought a clean towel for your room. Is there anything else you need tonight?"

"Thank you, Mrs. Miles, I can't think of anything right now. You know, you don't have to wait on me," she said, trying to smile.

"I know, but I enjoy it. It's my job to take care of these things. A woman has to do her share to pay her way. I'm treated like family enough around here." She studied Maxi for a few moments. "When I came in, you had such a sad face. Is something wrong?"

"Did I really have a sad face? I didn't realize it. I must have been deep in thought."

"What could you be thinking about that would make you look so sad?"

"Nothing at all serious. I was just wishing I had a pretty dress to wear tomorrow."

"Oh, you don't have a dress to wear?" A big smile broke out on Carmen's face. "I will be glad to make you look like a princess."

CHAPTER 33

"ARE YOU SURE we have everything, Mom?" Justin surveyed the back of the wagon.

"Let me go over my list one more time. We have the pies, both hams, bread, pickles, peach jam, apple butter, and potato salad. Well, I guess that's it. Are the chores all done?"

"Everything is under control. Mack said he had a couple more things to do. Then he would go on over. When he comes back, Bill will go over."

"Did you cover all the food in the wagon, like I told you to, Justin?"

"Don't I always do exactly what you tell me to?"

"Do you really want to discuss that?"

"No, as a matter of fact, I don't. Have I told you how pretty you look, Mom?"

"Smart of you to change the subject. Speaking of pretty, why don't you call your wife down. Then you can see what pretty really is."

"Okay, I'll run up and get her."

"Wait, let her come down the stairs by herself. She needs to show off for her husband. She's worked hard to look beautiful for you."

"Now, that's a show I'm anxious to see!" He hurried to the house. Inside, he called up the stairs, "Sweetheart, are you ready? We need to be going." He peered up the stairs waiting for Angel to appear. Suddenly, there she was, at the top landing, smiling sweetly. About halfway down, she paused, for effect.

"Well?" She had on her Sunday dress, the pink one, with a splash of small flowers. Her hair was piled on top of her head, tied with the pink ribbon Maxi had bought for her.

"Angel Myers, you are the most beautiful woman I have ever laid eyes on."

"Do you like my hair? Your ma…I mean mother fixed it for me."

"I love everything about you. Now come down here, and give me a hug before we go."

"No hugs. You might mess up my hair."

"Don't you know it's a husband's privilege to mess up his wife's hair?"

"You would have to catch me first, and we both know you are too old and slow to do that."

"Is that a challenge?" His eyes gleamed.

"No. I'm coming, but you be good now."

"I'm always good."

He didn't let her step off the last step. He slipped his arms around her waist and gave her a crushing hug as he lifted her off her feet, then set her on the floor. He nuzzled her neck, whispering, "You smell so good, I could—"

"You're hopeless," she murmured, half-heartedly pushing away. "I thought we were in a hurry, and if you don't let me go, you'll wrinkle my dress."

"Okay, okay. But don't think you can look that pretty and I can keep my hands to myself. I'll do my best, but it'll be hard. Now, let's go before I change my mind and mess up your hair."

The ride to the Double S Ranch was pleasant. Angel drove the wagon with Mrs. Myers sitting beside her. Justin rode along on Butch. They were warmly greeted as soon as they arrived at the ranch house. The women gathered on the front porch telling each other how pretty they looked.

"You look beautiful, Maxi. Did Mrs. Miles do your hair?"

"Yes. She gave me this blouse and skirt too. But look at you. I love your hair up like that."

"It wasn't easy, but Mother Myers managed to get it pinned up."

The ladies lingered on the front porch while Marty and Justin carried in the food. When the last dish was set down in the kitchen, Marty grabbed Justin's arm. "Let's hurry and get out of here. The men are out back in the courtyard."

"I won't argue with that. Let's go."

On the front porch, the women settled on chairs, benches, and blankets to visit. Carmen and Maxi went in to get beverages for the ladies. "Maxi, why don't you take this tray of drinks out to the ladies, and I'll fix a tray for the men out back." Maxi carried the tray out the front door just as Paul came in the back door to the kitchen.

"Who was that?"

Carmen looked up at her son. He was staring at the front door with a puzzled expression. "Are you serious?"

"Yes, I couldn't see her face, but I don't think I've ever seen her before. Is there someone new at the Paradise?"

Carmen realized that he was indeed serious. She had to laugh. "She'll be right back, so I guess you'll have to wait and see for yourself. If you'll open the back door for me, I'll take this tray of drinks out to the men."

Paul held the back door open for his mother, just as Maxi came back in the front door. She set the tray on the counter. "Hi, Paul. You look nice. That must be the new black shirt your mother just finished. It really looks good on you." He had the strangest look on his face. "What's wrong? You look like you've just had a shock."

"As I live and breathe, Maxine Mayfield, you'll be the death of me!"

"What are you talking about? I wouldn't do anything to hurt you."

"Well, you just have. I'm going to have to fight every man around here just to get one dance with you. If they even try to get out of line, you let me know. I'll black their eyes."

"Don't be silly. You can have all the dances you want."

"Then you can't dance with anyone but me 'cause I want them all." He couldn't tear his eyes away from her. "You look so beautiful. I didn't even recognize you. Turn around and let me get a good look."

Maxi twirled around a couple of times. "Do I really look that different?"

His voice was thick with emotion. "You would look beautiful no matter what you did. But I think with your hair up like that, you look, maybe…older and…I can't think of the right word. I can tell you this, though, if my mama wasn't coming in the door right now, I would take you in my arms and kiss you."

Maxi flashed a coy little smile, batting her eyes in a way that comes naturally to all women. "If it was like the last kiss you gave me, I wouldn't mind at all. I might even want two." With that, she slipped out the door.

Carmen came in to see her son looking like a love-starved puppy staring after the lovely Maxi. She grinned at him. "Very nice, don't you think?"

"Huh? What did you say?" He stood like a statue, still staring.

"Never mind. Go back out with the men. And take that plate of cookies with you."

A short time later, the rest of the guests were seen making their way toward the house. "Here comes our Arapaho friends," Calli announced. "Look, Judith, is that the chief, Black Crow?"

"Oh my, it sure is. What a special day. We finally got him to come."

"Carmen, go get the men. They need to be out front to greet the chief."

The Arapaho neighbors were approaching in ceremonial procession. Chief Black Crow led, sitting on a magnificent horse, wearing a full headdress, with the finest, intricately decorated buckskin shirt and pants. He alone was a splendid sight.

"Angel, there's Fawn. She looks regal sitting on her pony, doesn't she? I wonder who the young man is beside the chief?"

"That's Black Feather," Judith answered. "He's the chief's son and one of Justin's best friends. And that pretty, little woman behind him is Sky Flower, his wife."

The men came around the side of the house with Mr. Swanson in the lead. He formally greeted the chief while Justin interpreted. There was a lot of gesturing and nodding; then, the men and older boys made their way back to the courtyard. Peter and another ranch hand took the horses to the corral.

Calli stepped off the porch to greet the women telling the others to follow her. Children of different ages milled around. Sky Flower had the youngest one on her back in a cradleboard.

Maxi and Angel headed for Fawn. "How nice to see you again. You look absolutely beautiful," Maxi complimented.

"Thank you. You both also look beautiful. We have brought food for the celebration. Where should we put it?"

"I'll show you. Tell the ladies who have food to come with me," Maxi answered.

Fawn said something to the women, and a few followed after Maxi. Then she turned to Angel. "The young woman who is supporting Grandmother is Willow. She needs a place for Grandmother to sit down. Grandmother refused to stay at the village. She came to see the healer, White Cloud. She wishes to be with you."

"I am honored, Fawn. I'll take care of her. You go ahead and visit."

"Thank you, Angel."

When the women found places to sit, there was a time of guarded conversations. Most of the children spoke a little English, at least enough to interpret for some of the older women who had not learned to speak English. Maxi made her way over to Angel and sat on the corner of the blanket she shared with the aged Grandmother and another woman.

"Maxi, this is Grandmother of the Arapaho tribe. And this is Willow. Willow is the one Mother Myers told us about. She was one of her first pupils."

"Yes, I remember. It's so nice to meet you, Willow. Is this your grandmother?"

"She is everyone's grandmother. It is a name we use to show great respect. We all call her Grandmother."

Maxi gently took the small, wrinkled hand of Grandmother's in hers. "It is very nice to meet you, Grandmother. I am glad you could come today."

Willow and Grandmother spoke quietly; then, Grandmother looked at Maxi, and a broad, almost toothless grin spread across her face. "She wants to know if you are Princess Warrior, the one who protects White Cloud?"

"Yes, that's the Indian name that was given to me by Red Fox, chief of the Ute tribe."

"Grandmother thinks you are weak for a warrior. You have no strength in your hands. She will give you herbs to make you stronger so you can defend the great White Cloud."

Angel ducked her head and grabbed her mouth to stifle a giggle, covering it with a cough. Maxi could hardly hold back her own. "I was afraid I would hurt Grandmother, so I was being gentle."

Angel assured the old woman, "I promise you, she is very strong and has done a good job of protecting me."

Willow told this to Grandmother, and they too joined in the laughter. "Grandmother says it makes her heart glad to hear that. She also says she is strong and will not break so easily."

After a few moments, Angel and Maxi excused themselves to go help with dinner preparations. They headed to the house to find Carmen. "Is that a birthmark on Willow's face?" Maxi asked.

"Yes, Mother Myers told me about it. That's why she has never married. The men in the tribe think it's some kind of curse, and they'll be cursed with bad medicine if they marry her. Her mother died right after she was born, which didn't help any. Grandmother took her and raised her."

"How sad. She's so pretty, except for that mark on the side of her cheek. Is there nothing that can be done?"

"Not that I know of. She can't be a whole lot older than us. I hope we can make friends with her."

"I don't know why we couldn't. She doesn't seem to be shy. Maybe, just quiet."

Calli met the girls in the front room. "Will you two get Fawn to help move everyone to the backyard? We're going to set the food out now. Take the chairs and blankets."

"Sure, Mrs. Swanson. Then we'll help carry the food out."

Two long tables were laden with food of all kinds, including the two hams and a side of beef that had been cooked on a spit. The Arapaho brought wild turkey and venison and other kinds of dishes. Mr. Swanson said a blessing; then, he and Black Crow went first to fill their plates. The other men went next, then the women and children. Soon, people began to relax and enjoy the meal. Murmured conversations hummed all over the courtyard, interspersed with laughter and friendly banter.

Toward the end of dinner, Bill Gray approached Angel. "Miss Angel, are you the one that made that apple pie?"

She flashed a big smile. "Yes, I'm guilty. Do you like it?"

"I do declare, young lady, I didn't think anything could beat your fried apple pies. I just got to tell you that apple pie over there is the best thing I ever threw my lip over. Why, between me and that chief, I think we almost ate the whole thing. You can make me one of those pies any time you want to."

"I'm glad you enjoyed it, Bill. I'll remember that." She flushed with the high praise.

Justin was in charge of the games. He waited for everyone to finish eating and let their food settle, then got their attention. "Okay, everyone, let's move our chairs and blankets to the front of the house. That's where we'll be playing the games."

The younger people whooped in excitement and grabbed up their chairs, making a beeline to the front yard. The older people took their time gathering up blankets and chairs, groaning at the weight in their stomachs but grinning good-naturedly.

Justin found Angel and pulled her toward the house. "I need to talk to you real quick, sweetheart."

"What is it?"

"Just come in the house."

Once inside, Justin explained, "I need you to get your violin. I just found out the reason Black Crow came today was so you could play and dance for his new grandson and the other children, like you did at the Cheyenne village."

"Goodness, I don't know how they found out all these things."

"Probably when they're hunting. They meet and share stories. The Cheyenne and Arapaho are friends. That's how I met some of the Cheyenne dog soldiers. I was hunting with Black Feather, and we ran into some of them. We spent three days hunting together. It was a good time and probably what kept me alive back at the Cheyenne village. Anyway, we need to put on a bit of a show for the chief. Think you can do that?"

"Of course, I can. I'd do about anything for you." Her smile was proof enough. "You'll need to get my wicker case from under the seat of the wagon."

"I'm so proud of you I could bust. I'll get your violin and wait out front for you. I love you, sweetheart."

Angel caught Mrs. Miles as she came through the room. "Mrs. Miles, could you help me with something?"

"I would be happy to help, if I can. What is it you need?"

"I need to raise the hem of my dress…just enough so everyone can see my feet."

Mrs. Miles looked confused and stared at Angel. "You want me to hem your dress? Right now?"

"No, not really hem it. Just pin it up in a few places. I'm going to dance and people need to see my feet."

"You are going to dance?" Carmen repeated, still not sure if Angel was serious or teasing.

"Well, yes. It's kind of hard to explain, but if you'll help me, you'll soon understand. Will you help?"

"I will be glad to help. I'll get my sewing basket." Carmen was back in a minute. She had Angel stand on a stool, then went to work tacking up her hem. She confessed, "This is one dance I would not miss for the world. Am I doing this right?"

Angel looked at the tacked up hem that made scallops all around the skirt.

"Oh, that's perfect. I'm glad I wore my old shoes and not my new boots. It'll be easier to dance in these."

"Good. I'll tie this knot, and it's done. There! How's that?"

"Wonderful. Let's go on out now. Justin is waiting for me. You go first, Mrs. Miles. I'll follow you."

Angel stepped out on the front porch, and Justin handed her the wicker case. He turned and whistled loudly to get everyone's attention. They all gathered in front of the porch.

"Before we start the games, I have a special treat for you. Angel is going to play her violin, and I know you are going to enjoy this."

After a warm-up song, Angel played something snappy to get into the spirit of the Irish tune she would dance to. Then she made her way to Chief Black Crow, who was seated on the ground. "Justin, will you have Sky Flower bring her baby over." Black Feather brought his wife and their baby over and stood on either side of the chief. Angel then spoke directly to the chief.

"My mother was a very wise woman. She told me that there should always be a celebration when a new baby comes into the family. Chief Black Crow, in honor of your new grandson and all the children here, I will play and dance for you."

She began the Irish tune and played it all the way through. Then she danced the jig in unhurried paces. "Justin, bring the children around, and let's teach them the steps."

The children were shy at first but slowly got into the spirit of the dance as they caught on to the steps. Soon, everyone was invited to join in. Riotous laughter erupted as Black Crow and Mr. Swanson attempted the steps. Even the baby was in on the excitement. Sky Flower had the cradleboard on her back and was learning the dance steps along with everyone else. The baby flapped his arms, squealing with delight over the bouncing rhythm of the music. Almost everyone had caught on when Angel began playing a little faster. Each time through the song, she picked up the pace. Finally, all the dancers dropped to the sidelines and watched in amazement as Angel jumped and flew around the yard. At last, and out of breath, she finally collapsed on the front steps of the porch. The crowd cheered and applauded wildly.

Then, quite unexpectedly, Black Feather and Black Crow, cried out, "Yippee!" The whole group of Arapaho joined in the White Cloud victory cry, "Yippee! Yippee!"

Angel turned several shades of red, stood, and bowed to the crowd, then rushed into the house. Justin took over then. “Let’s get the games started.”

The young men were fierce in competition, but a spirit of friendship prevailed throughout the afternoon. They competed in knife and hatchet throwing, bows and arrows, and rifle contests. Leg wrestling and arm wrestling was a favorite of most of the men, but the one thing they all looked forward to was the horse racing.

The men began lining up at the starting line, Marty beside Justin. “I don’t know if Butch will be able to win this year,” said Marty. “Paul has been working with Diablo, and he sure looks fast.”

“Well, Butch and I will give him a run for it anyway. I’m kind of anxious to see what that new stallion can do.”

“As the last of the men were getting ready, Maxi sidled up to Paul. “Would it be okay if I race too?”

“I know you’re good on a horse, Maxi, but we get kind of rough out there. I don’t think our friends would hurt you on purpose, but I’d feel better if you didn’t race with the men. Why don’t you get the young women to race? Fawn would probably do it. But I warn you, she’s a good rider. They ride bareback on their ponies. Hey, maybe you could ride that Sioux war pony. That would make it an even race.”

“Well, I haven’t ridden bareback in a long time, but it sounds like fun. I think I could do it.”

“It’s up to you.”

Maxi didn’t miss the concern in his voice. “I’ll see if I can talk some of them into a race.” Then she scolded, “Don’t look so worried! I’ll be fine.”

Marty was right. No one could catch Diablo. Justin stayed close, until the last quarter mile when Paul let Diablo have his head and run all out, winning the race. Black Feather rode his father’s big horse and almost overtook Justin.

"One day, I will beat you, my friend," Black Feather told him.

"You almost did today, Black Feather."

The ladies' race was a lot of fun. Maxi, Fawn, Sky Flower, and a girl of about thirteen raced on the Indian ponies. Maxi almost slid off twice during the first leg of the race but soon caught up with the others. When they rounded the halfway tree, it was hard to tell who was in the lead. But to everyone's surprise, the thirteen-year-old moved ahead and won. The yard exploded in cheers.

Maxi thanked each girl for racing with her. "It was so much fun. We'll have to do it again sometime."

Immediately, dark thoughts crowded her brain. *Now, why did I say that? I may not be here much longer.* Her heart flopped heavily in her chest. *But I can't think of that right now.* She shook off the mood, refusing to ruin the day with decisions she would have to face in the very near future.

CHAPTER 34

PEOPLE WANDERED IN different directions after the ladies' race. The young men went to the river to swim. Mr. Swanson, Travis, and Bill taught Chief Black Crow how to play horseshoes. The women went to the cool of the back courtyard. Some with children rested on blankets. Grandmother napped in a rocking chair that had been brought out just for her. Calli and Judith found time to visit with each other for a short while under a shade tree.

"I'm so proud of our girls," Judith bragged. "They are so gracious to everyone and are always right there to help."

"I noticed you said *our girls.* I've come to think of them that way too. Isn't it amazing what the presence of those girls have done around here? And Angel, did you know she could play the violin like that?"

"No, I didn't. I was just as surprised as everyone else. I got to thinking about it and realized Justin and I have kept her so busy she hasn't had time to play her violin. Now that I know, I can tell you she'll be playing a lot more. I don't think I could ever tire of hearing her play."

"I couldn't agree more. You'll have to share her with us once in a while."

"Where are all the girls, anyway?"

"Maxi took all of them to the front room so they could visit without disturbing those that are sleeping. I'm glad most of the younger ones can speak English. You've done a wonderful job with them, Judith."

"I can't take all the credit, you know. It was Fawn and Willow who brought them down for lessons and continued with them once they went back to their village."

"They have both turned out to be beautiful women, especially Fawn. I wonder why she's never married. Most Indian girls marry quite young, don't they?"

"Yes, they do. Fawn is a very special girl. Many braves have asked for her, but she refuses them all. She says her heart already belongs to someone, and she will not give it to another."

The women sat in silence for several moments; then, Calli mused, "I wonder who that could be."

Judith breathed a silent prayer for her friend. *God, help Calli. I'm sure she will soon be finding out who it is that Fawn is saving herself for. Calli is a wonderful Christian, but she may need your help on this.*

Just then, Carmen Miles came out the back door and approached her two friends. "Calli, do you think it's time to put the food out again? The girls are in Maxi's room freshening up. She wanted to change out of her riding skirt and fix her hair. It's all fallen down since the race. I'm going to help her with that. Then I thought it might be time to feed everyone again."

"I'm sure you're right, Carmen. Why don't we all go see what the girls are up to and freshen up ourselves. Then we can put the food out together."

The three made their way to Maxi's room but stopped short of going in. They stood outside the door and listened to the girls' chatter for a few moments, smiling at each other and nodding in agreement that it was a happy sound. Carmen knocked and opened the door. "May we come in?"

"Sure, come in," Maxi invited. "We can squeeze in a few more."

It was a squeeze too. Angel and a few of the girls sat on the side of the bed while Willow sat on the floor, and Maxi sat on the bench in front of the mirror.

Carmen reworked the braids on Maxi's hair and put them on top of her head, securing little white flowers in place. "Anyone else want their hair fixed?"

Fawn surprised everyone when she spoke up, "I would love to do something different with my hair, but I'm not sure what. I always wear braids. I would just like something different."

"Well, let's see what we can do." Carmen looked carefully at Fawn. "Why don't we brush it out. I have two beautiful combs that can hold it back on the sides. What do you think?"

"I would like that very much, I think."

"Good. I'll go get the combs, and you start taking out your braids. Will someone help her?"

"I will," Judith volunteered, "but first, Fawn, why don't you put on the dress we made for you?"

"Do you think I should?"

"Only if you want to." She had never seen Fawn look unsure of herself. "It does look beautiful on you."

The room got quiet as all eyes watched Fawn make up her mind. "I will wear it," she finally declared, "since you and Angel made it for me, Mother Myers."

"Good, I laid it out in the other room so it wouldn't get wrinkled. Come with me. We'll find a place for you to change. I brought a petticoat that you'll need to wear with it. Then we can come back here and get your hair done."

Carmen came back with the combs. "Anyone else want their hair fixed while I'm waiting for Fawn?"

Sky Flower and the other Indian girls pointed to the one who had won the horse race. "Bright Eyes wants Hunter to notice her. Can you make such a skinny one beautiful?" Sky Flower teased.

Carmen came to the rescue of the flustered girl. "I think she is already beautiful, but I'll gladly fix your hair, Bright Eyes. How would you like it fixed?"

Bright Eyes pointed at Maxi. "I'm sure Hunter would look at me if I could be beautiful like her."

"I'm sure he will. Now, come on over here, and we'll get started."

Mr. Swanson got the attention of those who had gathered for the evening meal. "Before we start eating, we have a presentation to make. Justin, will you and Angel come up here with me?" A questioning look passed between them, but they made their way to where Mr. Swanson was standing. "We didn't get to be part of your wedding day, so we want to be part of the celebration of your life together."

Right on cue, Carmen and Maxi came out the back door with two beautiful cakes, a white cake and a chocolate one. "I made this one all by myself," Maxi said quietly to Angel as she proudly held the white cake. Then glancing at Carmen, she added, "Well, *almost* by myself."

"Thank you, Maxi. I'll eat some of it first."

Mr. Swanson said, "We also have some wedding gifts for you."

Carmen gave them two beautiful, intricately crocheted doilies. Judith gave them a quilt she had made. Calli's gift was a tablecloth with elaborately embroidered edges. Black Feather and Sky Flower presented them with a gift that made Angel blush several shades of red. An exquisitely decorated cradleboard.

Justin put his arm around Angel's shoulders and hugged her. He hesitated a bit before he spoke, "Angel and I are overwhelmed by your generosity. We thank you from the bottom of our hearts." He cleared his throat, twice, then said, "Now, let's eat. I can hardly wait to taste that chocolate cake!"

As the evening meal was winding down, several musicians gathered at the edge of the lawn and began tuning and warming up their instruments. Calli held her accordion, and one of the cowboys brought out his mouth harp. A couple of men were tuning their fiddles when Paul appeared with a guitar and joined the group. Maxi could be heard exclaiming, "Paul! You play the guitar? That's wonderful!" He smiled at her, then focused on the tuning.

Everyone loved the music. Each musician played his own solo piece, and Travis called a few square dances. Judith found herself, again, sitting with Calli while they watched all that was going on.

"I think this is the best party we've had yet, Calli."

"It really has been a lot of fun. I think our Arapaho neighbors are catching onto the way we dance. They learn fast. Look, even the children are trying."

Judith watched the children a few moments, then noticed that Travis was coming her way. He stopped at her chair. "I've talked them into a waltz. Will you dance with me, Judith?"

"I would love to, Travis."

The music started. Calli was claimed by her husband for the waltz. Judith noticed that Calli paused and stared at Marty as he took Fawn in his arms and danced away with her.

When the waltz ended, Judith and Calli went to their seats again. Judith sat quietly waiting for what she knew was coming.

"You knew, didn't you?" Calli finally said.

"I've known for years, Calli."

"Why didn't you say something?"

"I thought about it but decided it wasn't for me to say. Besides, I didn't know Fawn would keep her resolve. She's loved him for a long time. He just never seemed to notice her, except as Black Feather's little sister."

Calli sighed deeply. "Anyone with eyes can see that he's noticed her now. Not that I blame him. She is gorgeous. That yellow dress you and Angel made for her is perfect for her complexion. And Carmen did a beautiful job on her hair."

"There's so much more to her than good looks, Calli. She's a hard worker, smart, and you know she's a believer and has given her life to Christ."

"Yes, I remember you telling me. Thanks to you most of the children profess a belief in Christ."

"I wish Black Crow could understand, but he doesn't want to leave the old ways." Suddenly, her voice took on a tone of excitement. "Would you look at that!"

"What is it, Judith?"

"Over by the pine tree. Mack McCallister is talking with Willow. Now wouldn't that be something?"

"Goodness, Judith. There's so much going on in this yard I can't keep up with it all."

Across the yard Maxi and Sky Flower were visiting, when a husky voice sounded behind Maxi. "I believe this dance is mine." She turned to see Paul with his hand out to her. "You did say I could have all the dances I wanted. I'm just claiming your promise."

"I'm a woman of my word." She placed her hand in his, and he led her to the dance area. The music started, and a woman began singing in Spanish. Maxi glanced over and saw that it was Carmen. "Your mother plays the guitar and sings too? What a pretty voice. What's she singing about, Paul?"

"It's a song about a beautiful Mexican girl who has a very wealthy family. There is a poor young man who works for her father herding his sheep. He has fallen hopelessly in love with the girl. He cannot declare his love since he is poor and has nothing to offer this beautiful, young girl he loves. What the young man doesn't know is the girl is in love with him too. She thinks the young man cares nothing for her, and she cries at night looking out to the hills where the young man watches the sheep."

"That's the saddest song I've ever heard. Would you do that, Paul? If you really loved a girl would you tell her?"

"If I loved a girl, I would not be afraid to tell her. Actually, the song ends when they both decide to go tell the other one of their love. They meet in the garden, and in the moonlight, they declare their love for each other, embrace, kiss, and live happily ever after."

"Maybe I like that song after all." She looked deeply into Paul's dark eyes. "Are we still going to the High Meadow? I'm really looking forward to it."

"Yes, we'll still go. We need to leave as early as possible so we can have a nice, relaxing day. Mama and I are looking forward to it too. It's been a long time since she's been up there. Since Papa died, I've not been up there a lot either."

As the song ended, so ended the party. Black Crow was seen thanking Mr. Swanson, and the Arapaho people were gathering their belongings.

Paul and Maxi went over to Marty. "Where's Fawn, Marty?"

"She went in to change her dress. She wants to leave it here for when she visits again."

"Oh? She's going to visit again?"

Marty shuffled his feet a little, then looked at Maxi. "If she doesn't…I'll go get her."

Maxi smiled. "I hope she knows that."

"She knows."

Justin brought the wagon around to the front of the house and loaded the things that would go back to the Paradise. He made sure Butch was tied securely to the back of the wagon. They said good-bye to everyone, and the wagon left the Double S Ranch.

Down the road a ways, Angel said dreamily, "What a wonderful day. Did you enjoy it, Justin?"

"Yes, I did. It was probably the best Independence Day celebration we've had yet. Chief Black Crow doesn't really understand the meaning of it, but I'm glad he came. I was so proud of you, Angel. I'll have to admit the best part of the day was when I got to dance with my wife."

"You're sweet. I was very surprised when they brought out the cakes. That was so nice. It was probably the first cake Maxi has ever made."

Justin looked over Angel's head at his mother. "You're awfully quiet, Mother. What are you thinking about?"

"Just about the day. I had a good time, and I'm really tired. Travis is coming over tomorrow and wants to spend some time with me. I'm looking forward to that." Then, as an afterthought, she said, "I think I'll get him to walk up to that clearing I like so much. I go up there when I need time to be alone and think. Maybe, I'll pack a lunch to take with us."

"That sounds like fun," Angel said around a yawn. She laid her head on Justin's shoulder and declared, "I'm not tired… I'm *exhausted!*"

CHAPTER 35

MAXI WOKE TO tapping on her bedroom door. Startled, she sat up in bed as Carmen stuck her head in. "Paul and I are having breakfast. Are you still going with us?"

"Don't you dare leave without me! I'll hurry, and be ready in a few minutes." She threw the covers aside, mumbling, "I can't believe I slept this late."

"That's okay, Maxi. You were just extra tired from all the excitement of yesterday. Don't hurry. I'll set your breakfast on the back of the stove."

"Thanks, Mrs. Miles. I'll be out soon."

A short time later, Paul greeted her as she walked into the kitchen. "Good morning sleepyhead."

"Good morning, Paul. I'm embarrassed I slept in so late."

"Well, don't be. We don't have a time schedule. I'm just looking forward to being with you and Mama today. Come on out to the barn when you finish eating. I'll be getting the horses saddled."

She tried not to gulp her food and found it hard to tamp down her excitement. *A whole day with Paul! Hope the weather stays nice. I just love every minute that I'm with him. He makes me feel so safe and…special…maybe… loved.* Her heart danced as the word "loved" popped into her mind. *Love. How do you know if it's love?* She shook her head, took the last bite of bread and jam, and swallowed the last of her coffee. *I don't have time to think about it now.* Jumping up, she quickly washed her dishes and darted out the door.

Mrs. Miles was mounted and had a lunch basket tied behind her saddle. Paul couldn't help but tease Maxi when she came running toward the barn. "Come on, slow poke, we're ready to go." When she went to her horse, she checked to see that everything was in order. After making sure the cinch was tight, she pulled herself into the saddle. "Didn't trust me, huh?"

Maxi looked puzzled. "What do you mean?"

"Didn't trust me to saddle your horse right." Paul tried to look offended.

"Oh, I didn't even think about it. I guess it's just a habit."

"Well, it's a good habit. I'll take the lead, if that's okay with you two. Maxi, you come next, then Mama." Paul walked his horse past Maxi, tugged playfully on her braid, then hit the back brim of her hat, knocking it in her face.

"Is it going to be that kind of day?" Maxi asked, following Diablo.

"It's going to be whatever kind of day you want it to be."

"Is that a promise?"

"That's a promise."

The narrow trail zigzagged up the mountainside. Paul would stop now and then pointing out different features and points of interest. "There's a road of sorts over that bluff. That's how we bring supplies up to the meadows."

"How far is it, Paul?"

"About two or three miles up this trail, but by the wagon road, it's probably around five miles."

"I love it. It's beautiful up here. You can see the whole countryside."

"Wait till we get to the meadows. The view isn't as open since it's surrounded by timber, but it has its own beauty. Won't be long now. We're almost to the first meadow where our house is. We call it the big meadow."

In just a short time, they passed through a stand of trees; then, the trail opened up. He stopped and waited for Maxi and his mother to come alongside him; then, they sat in silent wonderment, taking in the beauty before them.

Aspen, white birch, and evergreens bordered the meadow of tall, lush summer grass. Smatterings of vibrant wildflowers adorned the meadow like a colorful patchwork quilt. At the back of the meadow, a log house nestled in beside a barn and several outbuildings, all in different stages of construction. A third of the meadow was fenced, a stream flowing diagonally through the middle.

Maxi inhaled deeply, slowly letting her breath escape in a whisper. "I've tried to picture what this would be like. Never could I have imagined anything as glorious as this. No wonder you claimed this spot. It's surely what heaven must be like."

Paul nodded in agreement; then nudging his horse, he started down the road that led to the house. They reached the barn first.

"Is it hard for you to come here, Mrs. Miles?"

"A little, I think." She looked toward the house. "This is the first time I've been back since my husband died. Paul wouldn't come for a long time, but then this spring, he started coming up to work on the fence using those lodge pole pines he and his father worked so hard to cut and haul." She looked around, wistfully. "We had a lot of good times up here."

"What would you like to do, Mama?"

"Let's show Maxi the back meadows, then have our picnic at the lake. Later on, we can come back to see the house."

"Sounds like a good plan. You take the lead this time, Mama."

He dropped back to ride alongside Maxi; then, they followed his mother to a stand of trees, out behind the house.

"You didn't tell me there was a lake up here," Maxi said.

"I wanted you to see it for yourself."

They rode the edges of the back meadows, then circled around to the lake. Carmen chose a shady spot for their lunch, and they dismounted. "Are you two hungry yet?" she asked, spreading out a couple of blankets.

Paul untied the picnic basket. "I'm starting to get that way. How about you, Maxi, you hungry?"

"Yeah, a little. I'd like to wade in the lake and cool off first, then eat."

"Okay, you go wade and I'll take care of the horses." He grinned mischievously as she headed toward the lake. He took the horses a short distance away, loosened their cinches, pulled his rifle off his saddle, and then went back to where his mother was sitting on a blanket. "This should be funny," he said quietly.

"You should warn her, Paul," she scolded.

"Not on your life. She can take it. That's one of the things I love about her. She's tough but not hard, all woman but not spoiled."

Carmen looked at her son. He was watching Maxi with love in his eyes. "Sounds like you have fallen for this tough, unspoiled woman."

"Yes, I've fallen hard. I can't bear the thought of her leaving this place, and I won't—"

At that exact moment, a loud squeal came from the lake. Paul threw his head back and laughed as Maxi came running out of the water. Carmen ducked her head trying to hide her laughter.

"It's like ice! Why didn't you tell me?" Walking up to him with boots in her hands, she got right in his face. "You did that on purpose, Paul Miles."

"Who, me? Never."

"Yes, you." Maxi was having a hard time not laughing at his antics. "Is it always that cold?"

"Oh, yes, sometimes colder. If you're cooled off now, may we eat?"

They enjoyed a pleasant meal together, talking and laughing. Paul finally asked, "Would you like to wade in the water again?"

"Ha, ha. Not in this lifetime. But I would like to explore."

"Since this is your day, we shall explore. Would you like to come along, Mama?"

"No, I'm going to stay right here and take a nap. You two go and explore all you want."

Paul got his mother's rifle from her horse and took it to her. "Here's your rifle. We won't go very far."

"Thanks, I'll be fine."

Paul smiled and held out his hand to the woman he had fallen in love with. She put her hand in his, and they walked down the path that circled the lake. Eventually, he pointed to an outcropping of rocks. "Let's go up there and sit awhile so we can talk."

They climbed to the top of the rocks and found a place to sit. Maxi looked around from their perch. "How pretty it is up here. Look, there's ducks in those reeds over there. Do you ever fish in the lake, Paul?"

"Oh, yeah. When we came up here before Papa died, we'd fish for our supper. There's some good-sized fish in that lake."

He scooted closer, put his arm around her, and she leaned into his embrace. Her mind and heart felt completely at peace. *This feels so right. I love this man so much. I'm sure it's love, now, but I don't want to get ahead of you, God. Help me know what to do.*

"Maxi, do you know I love you?" Paul whispered.

Startled, Maxi's peaceful heart started to beat faster. She took a few moments before answering, "I think you care for me, Paul, but you've never told me you love me. I guess, I hoped you did."

"When we danced last night, I told you I wouldn't be afraid to tell a girl that I loved her. Well, I'm telling you now. I love you, Maxi. I want to spend my life showing you just how much I love you. Do you think you could love me and spend the rest of your life with me up here on this ranch? It's not much right now, but I hope it will be some day. It'll be a lot of work, but I think it'll be worth it." He paused. "I feel if you were with me, I could do about anything."

She willed her heart to slow down, then looked up into his face. "I need a little time to think about it, Paul."

Disappointment showed in his eyes, and he looked away. "Okay. If you need time, I understand."

A few moments passed. "Okay, I'm ready."

"You're ready to explore some more?" he asked without much enthusiasm.

"No, I'm ready to tell you, I love you too, and I want to marry you. It'll make me the happiest women in the world to spend my life up here helping you build your ranch." She threw her arms around his neck, hugging him fiercely. "Yes, Paul, yes!" Then she jumped to her feet leaving him momentarily stunned. "I want to tell the world!" She turned and shouted, "Yes! I will marry you, Paul Miles." After the rush of emotion, she looked sheepish. "Does your mother know? Have you told her?"

He stood and pulled her back into his arms. "Since you told the fish in the lake, the ducks, and that little rabbit in the bushes, I'm sure she heard it too. You've made me a very happy man, Maxine Mayfield." He kissed her tenderly, then passionately, and they held each other for a while, whispering their love. "I love you, *mi marabillosa flor*."

"What does that mean, Paul? It sounds so romantic."

"Someday, maybe, I'll tell you. Right now, though, let's go find the canoe, and I'll take you for a ride around the lake."

"You have a canoe! That sounds like so much fun. Maybe your mother will go with us."

"Why don't you ask her? Maybe she'll go if you ask."

"Okay, I'll do that."

They walked hand in hand back to the picnic site and found Carmen sitting up watching them approach.

"Did you get a nap, Mrs. Miles?"

"I did try, but it was so noisy it was hard to sleep. Someone was yelling about marrying someone. I think the name I heard echo across the lake was Paul. Does this mean I am to have a new daughter in the family?"

Maxi dropped to her knees in front of Mrs. Miles. "Yes, isn't it wonderful! We're going to be a family. I do hope you approve."

"I am delighted, Maxi. I don't think Paul could have found anyone better to be his wife. I am very proud to have you for a daughter. From now on, call me Mama or Carmen."

"I would love to call you Mama, like Paul does." Maxi hugged her, then excitedly gave her an invitation. "We're going for a ride in the canoe. Please come with us."

"That does sound like fun. It's been awhile since I've been in that old canoe." She gave Paul a warning look. "You better not dump me in the lake this time."

Maxi sucked in her breath, glaring at Paul. "You wouldn't dare!"

"Oh, yes, he would," Carmen assured her. "That's one of the boys' favorite things to do, dump someone into the cold lake."

He held his hands up in surrender. "Okay, okay, I promise I will not turn the canoe over."

Paul pushed the old, hollowed-out log canoe onto the edge of the lake, and they all climbed in. Along with Marty and Justin and with the help of their Indian friends, they had made the canoe years ago. Now he glided it silently through the water, touching one side of the lake, then another as they leisurely whiled away the afternoon.

Maxi sighed contentedly. "It's so peaceful. I wish I had a fishing pole."

"It won't be peaceful very long. Look at that sky to the west, Paul," Carmen warned.

"Glad you saw that, Mama. Looks like we have a thunderstorm coming our way. Better head to the house and wait it out." He began to paddle faster as they headed back to their picnic spot. "It'd be a lot easier to paddle if you two hadn't eaten so much of that cake." That comment got him in big trouble. He was quite wet by the time they finished splashing him with cold water.

The wind from the storm hit just as they reached the back of the house. Paul found a stout piece of wood to pry off the three boards that had been nailed across the back door to secure it. "You two go on in. I'll take the horses to the barn."

They hurried through the doorway. "This is the kitchen we're standing in," Carmen explained as they let their eyes adjust to the dim light. "Someday, we'll have a nice screened-in back porch. There aren't any shelves or cupboards yet, but we brought a cook stove and work bench to use while we worked up here." Pointing to one side of the room, she continued, "That door goes to a large storage room, and this other door goes down to a cellar. It's kind of rough down there now, but it'll be nice when it's finished." She fanned her face. "It's stuffy in here. Let's go to the front room and open that door so fresh air can circulate."

They stepped into the front room. "Oh, my! I'm surprised this room is so big. It doesn't look this big from the front of the house."

"I love this room." Carmen's voice was full of pride. "My men did a good job on it. When the wind dies down, I'll go out and tie the shutters back so we can look out on the meadow. You wouldn't believe what it took to get all those small pieces of glass up here for those two big windows." She opened the front door to let in some light, propping it open with the only chair in the room. Then she swept the room with her eyes. "Don't you love the open ceiling? There's a loft on one end that's useable. This door leads to a nice-sized bedroom, and on the other end is a smaller bedroom. Ah, and the fireplace. My favorite thing of all. Not only does it heat the house, but it's designed to cook on. With the small stove in the kitchen and this fireplace, it will be perfect… for the two of you."

Immediately, Maxi turned to look at her. "You mean the three of us," she said evenly.

Carmen smiled tightly. "I think I should stay in the little house at the Swanson Ranch. You and Paul don't need me hanging around."

"Oh, but I do need you. I can't tell you how important it is to have you here with me and Paul. I've missed out on so much not having my ma all these years, and there's so much to learn. Please, Mama, I not only need you, I want with all my heart for the three of us to live here in this house and be a family." She rushed on, not realizing that Paul had come in and was standing in the doorway. "I'm a little grumpy in the mornings before I have my coffee, but I'll do my best to not be hard to live with."

"You are a wonderful girl, Maxi. I don't think you would be hard to live with. It's just that I don't want to intrude on your and Paul's life." She looked over at Paul in the doorway and gave him a look that pleaded for help.

"Don't look at me, Mama. You know that's the way I'd want it too. This is all Maxi's idea. We haven't talked about it at all. This is her own decision."

Carmen looked from Maxi's sincere face to Paul's smiling one. "How could I possibly say no? If you both are sure…nothing would make me happier."

Sighing with relief, Maxi put her arms around Carmen. Paul noisily cleared his throat. "Now that we have that settled, we need to make some plans." Both women looked at him intently. "Is tomorrow too soon to get married?"

A stunned silence took over. They turned and stared at each other until Paul chuckled, and they realized he was teasing. Maxi stood in the middle of the room with a blank expression on her face. She was aware that Paul and Carmen were waiting for her to say something. She blurted out, "I don't know what to say. What do I need to do to have a wedding?"

They both laughed; then, Carmen offered, "I would like very much to make your wedding dress. I could have it done in a few weeks."

Wind rattled the shutters as plans were made for the coming wedding. No one paid attention to the rain shower that bathed the meadow and washed the wild flowers as they danced on a soft breeze following the storm.

"Oh, look, it's stopped raining, and the sun is out. I want to look at everything from the front porch." Maxi hurried out with Paul and Carmen close behind. She stopped at the edge of the porch breathing in deeply. Paul came up behind her, slid his arms around her waist, and rested his head lightly on hers. "It smells so good and clean." She lingered contentedly taking in the picturesque scene from the front of the house that was soon to be her new home.

Moments passed. Paul felt her body tense and begin to tremble. Alarmed, he turned her around. "What is it, Maxi? What's wrong?" He pulled her close to himself, holding her tight. She began to cry in earnest as she clung to him and sobbed. "Are you hurting? Are you sick?"

She shook her head. "No, I've never been so happy in my life."

Relieved, he began to relax. "Do you always cry this hard when you're happy, *mi marabillosa flor*?"

"No, I don't ever cry. I don't know what's wrong with me. I…I just wish Pa and Michael were here." A great deal of effort went into that confession, which started a new wave of sobs as she soaked the front of Paul's shirt.

A knowing look came to Carmen's face, and she gently touched Paul's arm. "She needs to grieve for her papa and brother. Let her cry it out." Quietly, Carmen slipped around the side of the house and disappeared.

Her tears finally subsided, and she blew her nose on the handkerchief Paul handed her. "I'm sorry, Paul. Seems I'm always getting the front of your shirt wet with my silly tears."

"It's okay. You can cry on my shirt any time you need to." He kissed the top of her head, his voice comforting. She managed a weak smile as she looked up into his face.

"Thank you. I need to sit down. Can we sit on the side of the porch?"

"Sure. Remember, this is your day. We'll do whatever you want."

They got comfortable; sitting side by side, she leaned against him. "Paul, are you a believer?"

He chuckled. "Now where did that question come from?"

"Well, Angel told me that a believer should not marry a nonbeliever. She called it, I think, being unequally yoked. I feel like you probably are, but I want to ask to be sure. Do you mind talking about it?"

"Don't mind at all. I hope we can always talk about anything. I haven't thought about that day for a long time, but I gave my life to Jesus Christ some years back. A small wagon train going through our area had some trouble. We helped them out, and they invited us to their Sunday services that next day. They had a preacher on that train who preached a sermon so powerful it shook me up bad. I had been rebellious, giving my papa a bad time. I sat on that grass hating myself for the way I treated him, and mama too. I knew I needed to change, so I just then and there prayed with that preacher and asked God to forgive me. Then I gave my life to him. As a matter of fact, Justin and Marty made the same decision. That preacher took us right down to the river and baptized all three of us."

After some moments in thought, Maxi said, "Thank you for telling me about it, Paul. I gave my life to Christ when Angel and I were in Colorado Springs, but I've never been baptized. How will I ever be baptized?"

Carmen came around the corner of the house and heard Maxi's question. "I didn't mean to eavesdrop, but I have an idea about that. Judith is going to ask Mack McCallister if he'll have a worship service for us on Sundays. Maybe you could ask him to baptize you."

"That's a great idea. What do you think, Paul?"

"Don't know why not. When we ask him to marry us, we can ask him at the same time if he'll baptize you." He glanced sideways at her. "The lake would probably be the best place."

"Not on your life! I've bathed in the river, and it's not nearly as cold as that lake." She brightened considerably as they laughed and bantered with each other.

"It's getting hot on this porch," Carmen said. "We'll need to put a roof on it, Paul."

"That's just one of the many things I'll have to do before we can move in next summer."

Maxi stared in disbelief. "*Next summer*? Why do we have to wait until next summer?"

"Well, there's a lot to do to get it all finished."

"Like what?" she pressed the issue.

"Like Mama just said, the roof on this porch, the back porch, the barn doors, shelves in the kitchen, and dozens of other things."

"We don't need all of that to live in the house. It'll be easier to work on those things if we're living here. I think the only thing that needs to be done, right away, is shelves in the kitchen. Oh, and furniture. What will we do about the furniture?"

Carmen solved the problem. "Everything in the little house at the Double S belongs to me. We'll have enough to furnish the house. I think Maxi may be right, Paul. Shelves in the kitchen, and we can live here."

"But—" he started to protest.

Carmen kept going, "If we spend a couple of days up here, you can build the shelves, and Maxi and I can fix up the house."

"But—" he tried again.

"If we work hard and steady, we could have the house ready to move into by the time you get married, say, around three to four weeks."

"Oh, how marvelous that would be!" Maxi's excitement was contagious.

"While I sew your wedding dress, you can make curtains for the windows, Maxi."

"If you'll help me, I would like to try."

Paul listened patiently as the two women excitedly talked about how they were going to fix up the house. Finally, he cleared his throat rather noisily to get their attention. Maxi looked at him with innocent eyes. "Did you say something, Paul?"

"No, but I would like to."

"Oh, okay. We're listening."

He rolled his eyes. "Is this how it's going to be? The two of you ganging up on me all the time?"

"Not at all, Paul. Seriously, don't you think we can do it? Don't you want to move in this summer?"

"Of course I want to. But do you realize everything that will have to be done to live up here this winter? We'll have to have enough firewood to last for months. Preparations for the animals will take some doing, and what about food? We will want to eat you know."

"I'm sure Calli will give me a share of all the food we put up from the garden."

"I can buy a cow from the Swanson's and a pig from the Myers," Maxi volunteered. "Maybe some chickens. And we can hunt for wild game."

They looked at her in puzzlement. Defending her statement, she told them, "I do have a little money. I want to be part of making this our home." She turned her pleading eyes to Paul. "Don't you think with the three of us working together we can do what needs to be done? If not, then I'll understand."

He looked from his mother to his future wife, then threw his hands up in surrender. "When you look at me that way, there isn't anything I wouldn't try to do for you. But don't think it'll work all the time," he said with a sly grin. "I'll talk to Mr. Swanson and work it out."

Maxi threw herself at Paul, wrapping her arms around his neck. "Oh, I have so much to tell Angel. Thank you, Paul. I'll work hard, you'll see."

"I know you will. We'll all have to work hard, but we can do it." He held his future bride in his arms looking over her shoulder to his mother. "Is there any food left from the picnic? I'd like to eat and get back down to the ranch. Gotta get my evening chores done."

CHAPTER 36

"THANKS FOR FEEDING me again." Travis scooted his chair back from the table, stretching out his long legs. "I'm glad you saved that apple pie, Angel. If it had been at the party yesterday, old Bill and Black Crow would have eaten it too. I've never seen anyone eat as much pie as those two did. You're a good cook, young lady."

"Thank you, Travis. I'm glad you like my pie." She turned to Judith. "Mother, why don't you two go ahead and take that walk you were wanting. Justin and I will do the cleanup. Then I'm going to take a nap."

"I'll help you clean up if you let me take a nap with you." Justin's mischievous suggestion made Angel blush. She hurriedly started clearing the plates.

Laughing lightly, Judith got up from the table. "Let's get out of here, Travis, before they change their minds." She grabbed her hat from the peg by the door. "I don't know when we'll be back but don't suppose it'll be too long."

The day was perfect for walking—sunny, with a gentle breeze. They walked unhurriedly as she took him to the place she called the flat. It wasn't very steep but did have a slight incline. "Here it is, Travis. Have you ever been up here?"

"Maybe a long time ago, I'm not sure. It's a nice spot though. Enough trees for shade but open enough to see the country."

Judith took a deep breath of the clean air and exhaled slowly. "This is one of my favorite spots. When I need to be alone and just think or pray this is where I come. Let's sit on the log over there. We can talk awhile."

"You're the boss today. I'll have to say, though, I like your plans for relaxing." He sat on the log beside Judith. "It's been kind of hectic around the ranch. I can't seem to find time to be alone with you."

"You're right," she said, scooting closer to him. "But I'm afraid it isn't going to get any better. The gardens are about ready to harvest, and you know what that means. We'll be canning and drying foods for the winter. There's going to be a lot of apples this year. My trees are doing good. Calli's peach trees are not producing as much as last year, but we'll have enough for jam and pies."

They were quiet for a while, enjoying their surroundings and appreciating their time together. "Did you enjoy the party yesterday, Travis?"

"Yes, I did. I think it was the best time we've had since I've been up here." He glanced sideways at her. "The best part was dancing with you. I haven't danced like that in a long time."

She smiled. "I haven't either. Seems like everyone had a good time. I was pretty tired by the time we got home though. What's nice is this…a day to rest."

Travis lowered himself to the grass and leaned back against the log. Then he cleared a spot next to him. "There now, you can sit right here by me."

She sat down on the cleared spot and took off her hat to enjoy the breeze that was playing with the brim. "You know, I've always thought this would be a good place to build a house. Actually, we thought about this spot when we first came here, but I was eventually outvoted. And rightly so. It just isn't big enough for all the barns, corrals, and outbuildings we were going to need."

Travis put his arm around Judith and leaned his head against the top of hers. He sighed deeply. "We don't always get what we want, do we?"

"No, we don't. Seems like things work out, though, if it's given time."

They sat in silence again. For a while, Judith thought that maybe Travis had fallen asleep. Finally, he said, "You know, Judith, it's not too late for you to have that house here. Is there water up here?"

"Yes, over where all those bushes are there's a spring. It runs off into the little pond behind our house. What are you thinking?"

"I'm thinking we could build a small house up here, for us. I've saved enough money to build one. We wouldn't need a lot of outbuildings. Maybe we could work out a deal with Justin to buy this little piece of land."

Laughing at his sudden enthusiasm, she teased him a little. "Aren't you getting ahead of yourself, Travis Buchannon? You have a house built up here with you and me living in it, and you haven't even asked me to marry you."

"If I asked you right now would you say yes?"

"You'll just have to take your chances and ask."

He turned to look at her, slowly taking in her beauty—not a young beauty but beautiful just the same. He saw a woman of strength, with kind eyes, and a quick smile. "I don't want to rush you, Judith, but I really want to know. Will you marry me, love me, grow old with me?"

She didn't look away, kept her eyes right on his. "Yes, to all three questions. I will marry you, I will love you, and I will grow old with you. Spending the rest of my life alone has been one thing I haven't allowed myself to dwell on." Touching his cheek, she kissed him. "I will surely enjoy every moment we have growing old together."

"I'll do my very best to be a good husband to you." A strange, little quirk of a smile grew on his face. "I feel like a kid on Christmas morning. I'm so excited!" A second later, he asked seriously, "How long do you want to wait, Judith?"

"Well, we don't have to wait at all. I've asked Mack McCallister if he would conduct church services for us next Sunday. I was going to have you tell everyone at the Double S when you go back. If he will, we'll ask him to marry us right at the end of the service. We don't need to tell anyone before then. I really don't want a lot of fuss. We'll just surprise everyone."

"You know, I like that idea. Let's do it." He was silent for a moment, studying her. "Are you sure, Judith?"

"Yes, I'm very sure."

For the rest of the afternoon, they checked out the spring and talked about their future house and a number of other things. "This is a perfect place for us to be," he said. "It's not too close to the main house but close enough to walk back and forth. The grandkids can come and see us whenever they want. We'll probably have grandkids before too long. Just think, Judith, *grandchildren*."

"What about your own children, Travis?"

"I don't have any children, you know that."

"I know, but what if you did have children. I'm not an old woman, only forty-one. It's really not out of the question. Does that bother you?"

He stood still and stared at Judith. Then a grin suddenly spread across his face. "I hadn't even thought about such a thing. I'd given up on having my own children. I'll have to get used to the idea, but nothing would make me happier."

"Good. We'll work out a deal with Justin. Since the ranch is at least part mine, I'll just claim this flat for us. We'll draw up a paper and put it in our name. Let's just put the rest in God's hands. What do you think?"

A gust of wind tore Judith's hat out of her hand, making Travis chase it down. "Looks like there's a thunderstorm coming in pretty quick. We better get back before we get drenched." Taking her hand, they started down the path. "I'm going to have a hard time acting normal this next week. I'll try to come over a couple of times before next Sunday. That way if I need to do anything, you can let me know. Do you want me to talk to Mack about marrying us?"

"Yes, that would be nice. I'll leave that to you. Let me know if there's any problems, and be sure to tell him to keep it a secret."

Surprise everyone they did. The next Sunday, everyone who was able to attend Sunday services at the Paradise Ranch came and filled up the living room. Chairs were brought in and put in a semicircle around the fireplace. Angel played her violin for a time of singing. Mack chose to stand in front of the fireplace and preached a good sermon on forgiveness. He testified to his own need for repentance, God's forgiveness, and the need to forgive those who have wronged us. A prayer ended the sermon. Then he asked everyone to stay seated.

"We have a surprise this morning. Travis, will you get your bride and bring her up here? You all are going to witness the marriage of Travis Buchannon and Judith Myers."

Justin just could not keep himself from blurting out, "And you called me a sneaky cowboy!"

The room erupted into good-natured laughter. Travis took Judith's hand, and together, they went and stood in front of Mack McCallister.

"If I can have everyone's attention, we'll get these two married. Travis and Judith, will you join hands and face each other, please?" The couple did so, and Mack continued, "We are gathered here today in front of God and these witnesses to join these two in holy matrimony. This is not going to be a long service, but that doesn't mean it's not serious. I think these two know how serious it is and are not entering into this lightly. While they say their vows to each other, let's all think of what it means to say vows before God."

The sweetness and importance of what was taking place affected each one in a personal way. Justin reached over and held Angel's hand. Calli Swanson found her handkerchief and wiped her eyes. Marty smiled when he saw Paul and Maxi give each other knowing looks. "There is no ring to give at this time, but I would like to ask the two of you when there is a giving of a ring, will you, Travis, give it as a token of your love for Judith? And, Judith, will you wear it as a symbol of your love for Travis?"

At the same time they answered, "We will."

"Then, I am very privileged to pronounce you man and wife. Travis, you may kiss your bride."

"Travis kissed Judith and hugged her, whispering in her ear, "You are a beautiful bride, Mrs. Buchannon."

Mack had a hard time getting everyone's attention again, but when they settled down, he told them he had another surprise to announce. "I've been told we are having a meal now. As soon as we finish with the meal, we are going to the river. I've been asked to do something that brings me great pleasure. You are going to witness Maxi's baptism."

"How wonderful!" Angel exclaimed, running to Maxi. "I hadn't even thought about you being baptized." The girls hugged, and all the women headed to the kitchen to prepare the meal.

Spirits were high when they left for the river. Someone voiced what they all felt when Mack brought Maxi up out of the water. "What a wonderful day."

But the surprises were not over yet, for from the other side of the river, they heard someone shout, "Wait!"

On the opposite bank stood Spotted Fawn and Willow. Judith called over to them, "Hello, Fawn. Hello, Willow. What are you doing here?"

"We came to tell you the berries up the canyon are ready to pick. I brought you some." She held out a basket. "Is this what you have told me about, the thing called baptism?"

"Yes, Fawn. The preacher just baptized Maxi. She is a new believer."

"Is this for all believers?" Fawn asked.

"Yes, it's for all believers."

Everyone watched as Fawn and Willow waded out into the current. They could hear Fawn's words as she spoke to Mack, "I would like this baptism."

Mack took only a moment to get over the unexpected request. "Baptism is for those who have accepted Jesus Christ as their Savior, Fawn. Have you done this? Do you understand what I am talking about?"

"I understand. Mrs. Myers has explained all about how Jesus, God's son, died for me. I asked him in here," Fawn said, patting her chest over her heart. "He made me clean inside and has come to be with me always. That is what I know."

Looking up at Judith and seeing her smile in agreement, Mack nodded. "Spotted Fawn, it will be my pleasure to baptize you. Come, stand here in front of me. Because Spotted Fawn has confessed Jesus Christ as her Savior and wishes to show to all of you that she is a believer…I baptize you, Fawn, in the name of the Father, Son, and Holy Ghost." He brought her up out of the water, and many amen's were heard from the bank.

Fawn smiled brilliantly. "Thank you, Mr. Preacher. Willow will be next." She reached for the basket of berries that Willow was holding and stood by waiting for her friend to be baptized.

Mack grinned so big it almost split his face. He declared in a loud voice, "This day just gets better and better! Willow, come stand here, by me." He spoke quietly to her for a few moments, then to their friends watching as he said, "Willow assures me she has confessed her sins and has asked Jesus to be her Savior. So I baptize you, Willow, in the name of the Father, Son, and Holy Spirit." When he brought her up out of the water, she looked at him with a shy smile. "Thank you. I am very happy."

After everyone had left, Justin, Angel, Travis, and Judith found themselves in the kitchen looking like they weren't sure what to do next. Judith laughed. "Well, let's sit down and talk. I hope you aren't too upset with us, Justin. This just seemed to be the best way for us to get married."

"How could I be upset after what Angel and I did? Really, I couldn't be happier for the two of you."

"Thank you," she said gratefully. "Travis and I are going up to the flat and spend our first night together up there."

"Up to the flat? Did I hear you correctly?"

"What's the flat?" Angel asked. "Where is it?"

"It's a flat piece of land up the hill a short ways," Justin explained.

"Yes, Travis has a tent set up for us," Judith went on. "We have it all fixed up. I'll tell you all about it later, but it's what we want to do. We're going to leave right away and may stay for a while in the morning. Don't worry about us, okay?"

"If that's what you want to do, then you should do it." Justin stood and went to Travis, giving him a big, manly hug. "Welcome to the family, Travis."

"Thanks, I'll take good care of your mother."

"I know you will."

The young Myers couple stood at the back door watching the newlyweds walk hand in hand up the hill. "What a day! Let's go out to the front porch. We need to relax and smooch on the porch swing, Mrs. Myers. I think chores can wait a few more minutes."

"What a splendid invitation, Mr. Myers. I accept."

CHAPTER 37

THE NEXT FEW weeks were full of work and more work. Everyone was busy with the necessary activities needed to survive living on a frontier ranch. All the women spent a day of work and fun on the High Meadows Ranch, scrubbing and cleaning the house from top to bottom. Then, Maxi and Carmen devoted all their spare time to preparing for the wedding and the move into the house. A week before the wedding, they rode up to the meadow. They were doing last-minute preparations while waiting for Justin and Angel, who were bringing a wagonload of household items. Paul was coming with them to clear the wagon road if it was needed. Carmen paused in her work and looked out the front window. "I hope they don't have any trouble getting the wagon up that old road. It hasn't been used in a long time, but it's the only way to get a wagon up here."

"That's why Paul is coming with them," Maxi reminded her. "To clear the road if it's blocked or help if they have trouble. He hasn't had the time to check it out before now."

"You're right. I know they'll be okay. A mother just has to worry about something, it seems."

Maxi stood in the middle of the room and slowly surveyed all their work. "It's really starting to look like a home, isn't it?"

"Yes, and the curtains are beautiful. They add a special, homey touch. You did a good job on them."

"Thanks. I couldn't have done it without you and Mrs. Swanson helping me."

"We didn't do that much. When the wagon gets here—" she stopped in mid-sentence looking intently out the window.

"What is it?" Maxi came to stand beside her.

"I'm not sure. It looked like a man crawled into that tall grass out there. What on earth!" Even as she spoke, she was reaching for the door.

"What are you going to do?"

"I'm going out there and see what's going on," Carmen said as if that was the most reasonable thing in the world to do. "I'll call to him and let him know we saw him. I don't like the idea of a man hiding out there. If I call out, maybe he'll show himself."

Maxi grabbed Carmen's arm. "Wait! I don't like this. If you're going out, then I'm going with you, but we're taking the rifles."

Paul had put a gun rack by the front door, insisting that the women always have their rifles handy. Reaching up, Maxi took two rifles down and handed Carmen's to her. They stepped out on the porch.

"Wait here." Carmen stepped down off the porch. "I'll walk out a ways and call to him. You watch and see if you can spot anything."

"Be careful, Mama," Maxi pleaded. Carmen slowly began walking into the meadow. "Don't go too far."

"I'll be all right," Carmen called back over her shoulder. She walked out a lot further than Maxi liked.

What could possibly be out there? Whether man or beast, Mama saw something, and I've got to be ready. Her senses were alert, and her keen eyesight swept the meadow. Suddenly, she detected movement at the far edge, just outside the tree line. Training her eyes on the spot, she tried to make out what it was, while calling out, "Mama! Something's at the edge of the meadow!"

Carmen didn't understand at first. She turned toward the porch, looking at Maxi, her back to the tree line.

Then Maxi could see what it was. Her heart dropped with a thud. *Bear!* She had never seen a grizzly bear but had heard enough stories about the huge beast to know that this had to be one. A nightmare come true began unfolding right before her eyes. Adrenaline pumped through her veins, she screamed and pointed, "Over there!" Carmen turned to look as the bear charged her. In a split second, Maxi was off the porch and fired a shot. She worked the lever on her rifle and shot again. Carmen seemed to be frozen in place. The bear closed in. It was too close to Carmen for another shot, but Maxi knew she had to try, though it was risky, or Carmen would have no chance at all. She started to squeeze the trigger when all of a sudden a man leaped out of the tall grass and lunged at Carmen. He tackled her to the ground and landed on top of her. The grizzly swung its huge paw at the man, knocking him a few feet away. Maxi shot again. The beast roared, stood on his hind legs clawing the air. In a flash, he was on all fours charging Maxi. Automatically, she worked the lever on her rifle and fired again. The bear just kept coming. Maxi put another bullet in the monster that was almost on top of her now. *Die, you stupid thing!* She fired again. Then, it was over. The mountain of a bear dropped at her feet.

Almost to the meadows, Justin and Angel were bringing the loaded wagon, following Paul on Diablo. At the sound of the gunshots, Paul stopped to listen, counting them in quick succession. "Something's wrong!" he yelled to Justin. "I've got to go!" He kicked Diablo's flanks, and they raced ahead toward the meadows. Coming out onto the big meadow, his stomach lurched in fear as he took in the scene. His mother was picking herself up off the ground just a few feet from a man with blood all over his back. The man was valiantly trying to stand but kept falling back to the ground. Paul looked toward the house and saw Maxi standing by the porch, rifle in hand. She was staring at the largest bear Paul had ever seen. He shouted to his mother, "Mama, are you all right?"

"I'm okay, Paul. Go to Maxi! I'll see to this man."

Diablo was skittish, refusing to go. "He smells the bear," Paul said aloud. He bailed off the horse and started running, closing the gap between him and Maxi. She was still standing over the bear with a strange look on her face. "Maxi, are you hurt? Are you okay?" She didn't answer, just stood looking down at the bear. He gently pried the rifle from her hand and laid it on the porch. Then he took her by her shoulders, giving her a little shake. "Maxi, look at me. Are you okay?"

"He just kept coming, Paul…he just kept coming."

"I know, baby, I know." He wrapped his arms around her. "He won't go anywhere now. He's good and dead."

"I just shot and shot, and he…just kept coming…I feel funny…"

Paul felt her knees buckle and gently lowered her to the ground.

Just then Carmen came running up. "Is she okay?"

"I don't see any blood or injuries anywhere. I think she just fainted. She was talking to me and just collapsed. Who's the man?" he asked, without taking his eyes off Maxi.

"I don't know, but he's badly hurt. I told him to hold on, that we'd be back to help him."

Looking up, Paul saw the wagon coming. "Angel's almost here. She can help us."

Carmen waved and signaled for Justin to bring the wagon up to the front of the house. Just as soon as the wagon stopped,

Angel jumped off the seat and ran to Maxi's side. She eyed the bear warily. "What happened, Paul? Is she hurt?"

"I can't find any sign of her being hurt. Do you suppose she just fainted?"

"It's hard for me to imagine Maxi fainting. Wait…she's coming around."

Maxi opened her eyes and looked up at Paul, then at Angel. "What happened? Why am I on the ground?"

"I think you might have fainted," Angel told her.

"That's silly. I've never fainted in my life. Please help me up, Paul."

Paul lifted her to her feet, keeping his arm around her. "My head feels a little funny," she began. Then her eyes landed on the bear. "Now, I remember. Are you sure it's dead? Mama, are you all right?"

"I'm fine," Carmen answered.

Justin had been checking out the bear. "He's dead, Maxi. You don't have to worry about him hurting anyone now."

Without a second thought, Maxi gave the grizzly a kick. "You horrid beast! What took you so long to die?"

"Well, she's back to her normal self," Angel said, laughing. "I'd say she's going to be just fine." She looked at Paul. "Who's that man over there?"

"I don't know. Mama, who is he? Did you get hurt?"

"I got the breath knocked out of me when he shoved me to the ground and landed on top of me. He probably saved my life. Looks like the bear got to him though. I do not have a clue who he is or why he's here, but we need to go help him now!"

Angel was already on her way to the man. She bent down beside him and surveyed his clawed up legs. "Sir, can you hear me? Our men are going to move you to the house. Do you feel you have any broken bones?"

"Don't think anything's broken, ma'am." He had a soft voice and talked through clenched teeth.

"Okay, then, we're going to help you get up. Go slow, if you can't make it, tell us. We'll figure something else out. Are you ready?"

He nodded weakly.

Angel stepped back and let Paul and Justin help the man to his feet. He was tall and wiry, in excruciating pain, and grimaced with every movement. He could barely stand, much less walk, but even so, apologized, speaking softly, "I'm sure sorry I brought this on you all. I should have run the other way."

"If you'd run the other way, you might be dead now," Justin told the man. Seeing that he couldn't walk, Paul and Justin grasped him around his waist and wrapped his arms around each of their shoulders, then slowly, haltingly, carried him toward the house.

"That wretched animal…has been chasing me for two days now. Thought I was a dead man several times." He paused after every other word, but the need to explain himself was apparent. "That young lady with the rifle surely saved my life and the life of that beautiful woman I knocked down."

They had reached the porch by this time. Angel encouraged the man to focus on the steps ahead of him. He couldn't lift his legs at all, so Paul and Justin lifted and pulled him up the steps as gently as they could. He moaned and balled his hands into fists each time his feet hit the steps. Angel followed behind trying to figure out how to help, but it was hard to know where to touch the man. His left pant leg was shredded, and most of the material had stuck to his leg with drying blood. They paused in front of the door, unsure of how to proceed. Three men abreast couldn't go through at the same time. Sensing their predicament, the man braced his arms on the door frame long enough for the others to slip in the house.

"I think I'm going to pass out or be sick," he murmured miserably.

"We're almost there. Try to hang on," Justin encourage. "What's your name?"

"Scott Trinity," came the strained answer.

Carmen already had the couch covered to protect it and motioned for the men to lay him there. Angel took control in her firm but gentle way. "Lay him on his stomach, Justin. I need to stop the bleeding on his back. Mrs. Miles, I'm going to need any supplies you have and some hot water. Also, towels, rags, sewing kit, and anything that will work for bandages."

Angel and Carmen worked silently over the man, stripping his torn and bloody shirt away from his back. They cleaned the wound the best they could, but it was still oozing blood. Carmen kept sponging his back until the bleeding slowed. Angel looked around for Maxi, who had gone to secure Diablo, and was just coming in the front door.

"Maxi, I may need some help cutting away this pant leg. Are you up to helping? It's okay if you're not."

"Sure, I can help." Quickly, she knelt by Angel's side.

"I need to see what condition this leg is in. Let's peel away this bloody fabric from the wound."

Scott Trinity gritted his teeth and moaned. He had such a tight grip on the frame of the couch that his knuckles were white.

"Mr. Trinity, how did you meet up with such a mean bear?" Maxi asked. "It might help take your mind off the pain if you tell us how this happened."

"I'll try. Started a few days ago. He caught me by surprise when I was checking out a creek up north of here." Mr. Trinity shuddered. "Didn't have my rifle close, was still on my horse. Stupid thing to do! Stupid, stupid, stupid!" He buried his face in the couch for a few moments. "He killed my horse first or I wouldn't be here today. Best horse I ever had too. Then...I ran for my life." He paused, breathing deeply a few times.

"Guess he stayed with the horse awhile 'cause I got ahead of him. We played cat and mouse the next day. I fired every bullet I had in my pistol, but it didn't faze him. He caught up with me last night." Scott squeezed his eyes shut and remained quiet, but his grip on the couch frame intensified. After awhile, he continued,

"The only thing I could do was climb up a tree. He caught my leg before I could get out of his reach. Sure thought I was going to be his supper. I managed to smash him in the face with the heel of my boot, and he let me go long enough for me to get out of reach. I was in that tree all night, the longest night of my life. When day broke, I didn't see him anywhere, so I climbed down. I was getting too weak to run, so I just kept going as fast as I could… and here I am."

"You are a brave man, Mr. Scott Trinity," Carmen said.

"You sure are." Maxi was in total agreement.

Angel had figured out what needed to be done by the time he finished his story. "Mr. Trinity, what I have to do now isn't going to be any fun, but it *has* to be done. There's already infection in some of the deeper claw marks on your leg. I need to clean it really good. We'll have to watch it closely for a while or you could loose your leg. Amputation is something I can't do, so we'll just have to make sure that doesn't happen. I need to put some stitches in the deeper cuts across your back. I'll do my best to cause you as little pain as possible." Angel looked in sympathy at the mangled body on the couch. "Is there anything we can do for you before I start?"

"Can't think of a thing, young lady. I'd just like to be out of this pain. Maybe someone could say a prayer for me."

"I will be glad to pray for you," Carmen answered.

Angel turned all business again. "Justin, I need something to disinfect his wounds. Do you suppose the box under the seat of the wagon still has that bottle of whiskey in it?"

"I'm sure the box is still there. I'll go see if the whiskey is."

"I'm not a drinking man, but if there's enough of that whiskey, I might, just for today, turn into one."

Justin was back in moments with an almost full bottle of whiskey. Angel looked relieved. "Good, there's enough for your wounds and some for you to drink. Carmen, will you give him a couple of drinks, then hand the bottle to me."

As usual, Angel started talking her way through the procedures. "I'll stitch up those gashes on your back first." Carmen slid off the couch and knelt beside Mr. Trinity. She took his hand in hers and started to pray, softly, in Spanish. Her gentle and quiet voice had a soothing affect on the patient and everyone else in the room.

Soon, Angel stood and moved down to the man's legs. "Maxi, will you get some fresh, hot water? This is going to be extremely painful, try not to thrash around, Mr. Trinity. I know it'll be hard but do the best you can." She looked at Paul and motioned for him to sit on the edge of the couch. "Be ready to hold his legs if necessary." Then, she got down on her knees and went to work.

Scott Trinity never complained. He sucked in his breath through clenched teeth, gritting them as his body steeled for the pain. He once apologized to Carmen for squeezing her hand so tight. He relaxed his grip, now and then, but never entirely let go. Her hand seemed to be his lifeline.

At long last, Angel stood. "That's the best I can do. Carmen, will you get those strips of clean cloth to wrap around his back and chest? I'll come back first thing in the morning and bring some herbs that will help with the healing."

"Sweetheart," Justin said to Angel, "if you don't need us anymore, Paul and I will unload the wagon. We need to go before too long. I don't want to take the wagon back down that road after dark."

"Go ahead, Justin. We're okay in here. I'll come help as soon as I can."

"Don't worry about that. We can handle it." He gave his special lady an affectionate smile. "You did good." He turned and left with Paul.

Maxi decided to help with the unloading while Angel started cleaning up the mess she'd made. Carmen was still holding Mr. Trinity's hand. Rather, he held her hand. "Mr. Trinity, if you could let go of my hand, I will go put on a pot of coffee and fix you something to eat."

He looked embarrassed as he eyed this beautiful woman. "Well now, that's asking an awful lot. I've gotten attached to this hand in the last hour. Guess Mr. Miles wouldn't like it much if I kept holding onto it. So for a cup of coffee, I'll let it go."

"Mr. Miles died a couple of years ago, Mr. Trinity." She stood and stomped her feet lightly to work out the kinks from being on the floor so long. "You may call me Carmen." She turned and walked into the kitchen, leaving Scott Trinity with a smile on his face—a *pained* smile but a smile nevertheless.

After the wagon was unloaded, Paul and Justin used the mules to drag the bear away from the house. They hung it from a tree and skinned it as quickly as they could. Maxi watched for a short time, then went back in the house.

"There are ten holes in this hide, Paul. Maxi sure is good with that rifle. Of course, Mr. Trinity may have put in some of those holes."

"Yeah, she's good all right. Her father did an excellent job of teaching her to handle a rifle. I just hope she doesn't have any problems with this. She acts tough, but this bear is enough to give an old mountain man nightmares. I'm afraid it's bothering her more than she's letting on."

"Could be. Just help her through it. She'll be okay."

"Talk about good. That wife of yours seems to know her business when it comes to doctoring." He paused a few moments in reflection. "I'm sure glad you and Marty took a chance in Denver and brought them along. How are you and Angel doing? You like being a married man?"

Justin grinned. They had started walking back to the house when he answered, "Not sure I have enough words to tell you. I didn't think I could love her any more than when we got married, but my love just grows more and more each day. I've heard people say that very thing but never really understood it. She brings so much joy into my life. I can't imagine how it would be if she wasn't with me now. And if you knew how close Travis came to sending those two girls back to Denver, you'd be thanking the good Lord every day that he didn't." Justin slapped Paul on the back. "You just wait and see. In a few days, you'll begin to understand."

Paul grinned at Justin without further comment.

They reached the house as Angel poked her head out the door. "I'm ready to go."

The women hugged and said good-bye; then, the Myers couple climbed on the wagon and headed back to the Paradise. Carmen wouldn't leave Scott alone for the night, and Paul wouldn't leave Carmen there alone with Scott. So spending the night on the high meadows was what they decided to do. They stayed busy the rest of the evening, making beds and cooking something to eat. Carmen took care of Scott Trinity who managed to halfway sit up so he could eat and drink.

As they were preparing to retire, Scott turned to Paul. "I truly hate to bring this up, but I need to make a trip outside. Young man, do you think you could assist me?"

He started to answer, but Carmen spoke first, "Mr. Trinity, you are not going to make any trip outside. The only trip you're going to make is to that bedroom." She nodded in the direction of the small bedroom. "There is a chamber pot in there you can use. Paul will help you. When he gets you settled, I'll come in and see if you need anything."

Scott was attempting to stand when Paul moved over to steady him. "Ma'am," he began, "I couldn't take someone's bed. I'll just mosey on outside, then sleep on the couch."

"Mr. Trinity, you are a guest in our house. The polite thing is for you to do what we ask. This is going to be a home that takes good care of its guests. Now, Paul, help him get settled in the bedroom."

Scott and Carmen did a little eye sparring; then, Scott shrugged. "Whatever you say, ma'am."

"Carmen," she corrected him.

"Carmen," he repeated.

Scott slowly and painfully shuffled his way through the bedroom door while leaning on Paul. Paul closed the door behind them. "You're a smart man, Mr. Trinity. When she gets that look in her eye, well...you might as well do as you're told."

"She can be a little spitfire at times, eh?"

"That's one word you might choose."

Scott eased himself down on the side of the bed. He looked up at Paul and admitted, "She was right about one thing. I couldn't have made that trip outside and back even if I'd wanted to. But I'd rather you didn't tell her that."

"Your secret is safe with me."

"Thanks, Paul. Us men have to stick together. Now, I could use a little privacy. Tell your mother to give me a few minutes before she comes in."

"You got it."

The women had finished making a fresh bed on the couch. Paul dejectedly looked at the couch, then at his mother, then at Maxi. "I suppose I get the couch, and you two get the other bed." It wasn't really a question but a stated fact.

Carmen went over to her son and patted his cheek. "My poor Paul," she said, sweetly. "Only a few more days, and you can have the bed in that room. It will go by fast, you'll see."

He looked at Maxi with longing in his eyes. "Not fast enough for me."

No one got much sleep that night. Carmen slept lightly, in case she was needed. Scott couldn't find a position to lay in that didn't hurt. Paul's mind was busy trying to figure out how he could have saved his family from the bear attack. Maxi lay awake with her eyes wide open, staring at the ceiling. *I can't stand this any longer*, she thought. She slipped out of bed as quietly as she could, tiptoeing through the front room into the kitchen. She stood there barefooted and wrapped in a blanket. She heard someone at the kitchen door and knew right away who it was. "Sorry I disturbed you, Paul," she whispered.

"I couldn't sleep, anyway. You okay?"

"Yeah, I'm okay. I suppose I'll eventually get over it, but when I close my eyes, all I see is that bear coming right at me. I can even smell his awful breath."

Paul took the few steps necessary to wrap her in his arms. "I'm sorry, baby. Wish I could have been here and protected you from having to go through that. I'm very proud of how you handled yourself. You know you saved Mama's life, don't you?"

"I guess so, but it happened so fast I don't know how I did it."

Paul laid his head on the top of Maxi's. "Things like that become reflex. I bet your pa made you practice using your rifle like that."

"Yes, he did. He was a good pa."

"Arc you still okay about living up here with me and Mama?"

Maxi looked up into his face trying to make out his features in the dark room. "Paul Miles, you listen to me. Nothing will keep me from your side and from living up here in our home. If you think a little, old bear is going to scare me away from you and our place here on this meadow, you don't know me very well."

Paul hugged Maxi a little tighter. "I love you, Maxine Mayfield, and can't wait to make it Maxine Miles." Then he kissed her to prove it.

CHAPTER 38

CARMEN WAS RIGHT; their wedding day was upon them before they knew it. Maxi had picked a spot close to the house, where the ground would be level enough for benches and chairs. They would face a large bush of wild roses that still had red-orange blossoms with yellow centers. Their friends had arrived and were seated and waiting. On the porch, Marty and Justin were waiting to be escort for Angel and Fawn. Inside the house were three very excited young women.

"Maxi, you look gorgeous! Carmen did a beautiful job on your dress." Her dress was pale yellow with ivory-colored lace at the neck and short sleeves. Calli had made a pair of slippers to match the dress. On her head was a piece of ivory Spanish lace. "And curls! How did you do that?" Angel asked, in amazement.

"Mama Miles showed me how to make rag curls. You take a piece of cloth, wind the hair around it, and tie it up. I love curls! They make me feel so pretty." The soft black waves cascaded loosely down her shoulders and back.

"You're beautiful, Maxi," Fawn said quietly. There was a sense of awe in her voice. "You look like a princess."

The girls smiled at her. "You'll have your day, sometime soon. You just wait and see."

Angel asked, "Has Marty told you how he feels about you?"

"Yes, we talked a little yesterday. He said we would talk more today. I love him so much and have waited so long for him. I don't know what I'll do if he doesn't want me."

"Doesn't want you! I've seen the way he looks at you. He watches you with love in his eyes. He can't keep his eyes off you," Maxi declared.

"I hope you are right."

"Mama Miles is playing my song. Let's go, girls. I love you both. Thank you for being with me today."

Carmen played and sang the same love song that Maxi and Paul had first waltzed to. As she sang, Marty escorted Fawn across the yard and to the front of the little group of wedding guests. Then, Justin escorted Angel. Next, came Maxi on Travis's arm. A gentle breeze rustled the leaves on the aspens. Somewhere in those trees, birds were singing. But Maxi and Paul didn't hear any of this. As they said their vows, all they heard was the love beat of their own hearts.

A celebration followed the ceremony with food and friendly conversation. Maxi slipped away to her bedroom looking for a handkerchief for Calli. She heard the bedroom door quietly close and turned to see Paul leaning against the door. He had a big smile spread across his face.

"What are you doing in here?" she flirted with him.

"Just watching the most beautiful woman in the world. I keep thinking if I watch her long enough, I'll convince myself that she's really mine."

"Paul, Mama will be going to the Swanson's tonight. Where will Scott Trinity be going?"

"Oh, he'll be gone too. We'll be all alone, just you and me."

"Did he get invited to the Swanson's?"

"Yes, Seth Swanson invited him to stay for a few days. They seem to have hit it off really well. He's been telling Mr. Swanson about his army days. He told him how he left the army with a friend who turned out to be a drunkard. They parted company, and he headed to the mountains to pan for gold and to trap. Seems he just wanted to spend time on his own. Then that bear caught him by surprise and killed his horse. He'll soon be heading back to see if he can salvage any of his things. I want to ask him to come back and help us here on the ranch for the rest of the summer and fall. I'd like to give him a place to stay for the winter. The trouble is, I can't pay him, just put him up and feed him. Are you comfortable with that?"

"I think that's a wonderful idea. He's such a gentleman. I really like him, don't you?"

"Yes, I like the man or I wouldn't ask him to stay here for the winter."

"Paul?" she said in a singsong way.

He looked up suspiciously. "When you say my name like that, it makes me wonder what you're up to."

"When two people get married, don't you think they should share everything with each other?"

"Yes, that's how I think it should be. What are you getting at?"

"Well, I need to tell you something. I have some money, but it's ours now, right?"

He hooked his thumbs in his pockets. "Go on, just spit it out."

She explained how her mother had inherited money from her parents when they died and how her father had sold the farm and all they owned. "Pa divided the money and hid it in different places. The bank notes are sewn in the hem of my rain slickers. The gold coins he hid in different places in our packs and among our other belongings. Some of it was supposed to go to Michael, but I guess it's all mine now. I mean, it's ours now. We can use it to pay Mr. Trinity. You can pay him what you think is fair. Please, use it for whatever we need." She stood watching him, waiting.

He was stunned for a minute. "Where is all this money now and how much are we talking about? One hundred, two hundred? Is it less than a hundred?"

Maxi stared at the floor. "More than a thousand," she said quietly. "Are you mad at me? Please don't be mad at me. Not today."

Paul went to her. He lifted her chin and looked into her eyes. "Mad? No. Amazed? Yes. I can't believe you and Angel carried all that money across the territories. We'll talk about this later, but you'll always have a say in what we do with any money we have. Okay?"

"Yes, thank you, Paul."

He kissed her forehead. "Now, we need to get back to our guests. Go on out to the front yard. I have a surprise wedding gift for you. I'll bring it out there."

"What is it?" she asked, excitement in her voice.

"It's a surprise. You'll just have to wait and see."

She started for the door, flashed a sweet smile at him, and said, "Hurry, I can't wait to see what it is."

In the front yard, Maxi made the rounds speaking to her guests. She was talking to Travis when Paul came around the corner of the house with her wedding gift. In his arms, he carried a small bundle of black fur. He walked up to her and placed the wiggling ball of fur into her arms.

Maxi squealed in delight. "Oh, Paul, he's adorable! How wonderful, thank you! He's a perfect gift." Maxi tried to give Paul a kiss, but the little puppy got between them and started licking her face.

"You're welcome," Paul said patiently. "First, you need to know that he is a she. And you must also promise me you will always give me more attention than the dog."

"Of course, I will!" She set the puppy on the ground, threw her arms around Paul's neck, and gave him a kiss.

The yard erupted into a gale of riotous laughter when the puppy promptly peed on Paul's freshly polished boot.

EPILOGUE

DOUBLE S RANCH

"BURR, IT'S COLD out there tonight!" Mr. Swanson had come in from his evening rounds, making sure all was as it should be.

"I can feel it in the house too. I'm afraid winter will soon be upon us," Calli Swanson commented, not looking up from her sewing. "Come on over here and sit by me. I'm about finished with the hem on this dress."

The two lounged comfortably near the warm fire, and soon Calli laid down her sewing. "There, that's all done." She scooted closer to her husband, and he put his arm around her as they snuggled quietly together, staring into the flames. "I can't believe how our lives have changed these last few months. I really miss Carmen and Paul. It just doesn't seem right around here without them."

"I know what you mean. We knew the day would come when they'd move on with their lives. I'm happy for Paul. He's a good man. I'm just glad Scott Trinity is working with him this winter. I sure do like that fellow."

"I have a feeling there's someone else up there who likes Mr. Trinity. By the way, did you see Marty and Fawn when you were out?"

"Yes, I visited them in the little house for a while. They said they would be in pretty quick. They were about done with what they were working on."

"I think it's a good idea for them to fix up the little house to live in after they're married. I didn't like the idea at first, but they've enjoyed fixing up their little love nest. I'm also glad Judith talked me into asking Fawn to stay and help with all the fall canning. It gave me a chance to get to know her better. You know I had reservations about them marrying, but she's a wonderful girl. She's so devoted to Marty. I can't find any fault with her. She's a hard worker and smart, not just intelligent but good old common sense smart. We've had some good conversations about how the world is changing. You know, like how their children might have problems with people outside our ranches. It breaks my heart to think of people calling my grandchildren *half-breeds*."

"Don't worry about that, honey. They'll be Swanson tough!"

"They'll have to be around all the settlers that are coming west. We talked some the other day about how her own people are going to have to change. I hadn't really thought about how hard it might be for the Indian people." Looking at Seth, she added with a smile, "What I'm really afraid of is that she's going to spoil Marty so badly no one will be able to stand him."

"Well, now, correct me if I'm wrong, but isn't that what a good wife is supposed to do? Like right now I could use a cup of hot coffee and some of that berry cobbler you made. If I had a good, loving wife, she would go get me some."

"First of all, Mr. Swanson, your future daughter-in-law made that cobbler. I love you, but you can go get your own coffee and cobbler. And while you're at it bring me a cup of coffee."

PARADISE RANCH

Sitting at a small desk in their bedroom, Angel was busy writing. Justin was curious as he came in from his early morning chores. "Hey, you're not dressed yet. What are you writing, sweetheart?"

"It's a letter. I'm almost finished with it. I want you to read it and tell me what you think. Why don't you go get us a cup of coffee. I should be done by then."

He came back in a few moments with two cups of coffee. She handed him the piece of paper. "Sit on the bed and read it. I'm anxious to see your reaction."

He sat on the bed with a look of apprehension on his face. "I don't know what you are up to, but it must be good." He began reading while she watched his face with anticipation. When he finished the letter, he didn't move, just sat for a few minutes, scanning the letter again. When he finally looked up, his hazel eyes spoke for him. He handed the letter back to her, opened his arms, and she rushed into them. They embraced for a few minutes. Justin whispered, "I love you so much! You're so special. That letter is a beautiful thing to do. I don't hardly know what to say."

"I want to know everything you have to say, but it'll have to wait. I want to put this on the kitchen table before Mom goes in to start breakfast. Come and go with me. We'll hide in the pantry so we can see her reaction."

In the pantry, a little celebration was going on. "You're happy aren't you, Justin?"

"I can't tell you how happy I am. I can't believe—"

"*Sh*...I think I hear her coming."

"No, I think that's Travis coming in. You're right. Mom's coming in the other door. They're going to hit the kitchen about the same time. This should be fun."

Travis came in the back door, hung his coat on the peg, and headed for the coffee pot just as Judith came in from the front room. "Honey, would you like for me to pour you a cup of coffee?"

"Yes, thank you, Travis. How about ham with your eggs this morning?"

"Sounds good to me. There's an envelope on the table with your name on it."

"Oh, what is it?"

"I don't know. It was there when I came in."

"Well, what in the world. It says to Judith from Marie Hawkins. Who's that? Wait a minute. That's Angel's mother's name."

"Open it up, and see what it says. I'm curious now."

Judith tore at the envelope. She sat down and read aloud to Travis.

> Dear Judith,
>
> I'm writing this letter to say thank you. If I could be there in person, I would give you a big hug. Thank you so much for loving my Angel. Thank you for raising such a wonderful young man. I know he's wonderful because he chose my girl for his wife. She was alone in this world, and you and your son have taken her into your hearts and home. I will forever be grateful. Life is strange at times, and we don't always understand why things happen the way they do, but I rest in heaven knowing she is loved and cared for. Travis, thank you for watching over Angel as she made her trip across the territories. I know you will be a good father to her. You all are going to make a wonderful family. God is so good.
>
> I send my love to all. Hug Angel and Justin for me.
>
> With love,
> Marie Hawkins

PS: When you rock the baby that Justin and Angel are going to have the first of May, please kiss and hug him for me…a lot.

The celebration moved from the pantry to the kitchen.

HIGH MEADOWS HORSE RANCH

"Paul, I'm going to walk outside before it gets too dark. Want to go with me?"

"Sure, I'd love to. It's cold out there, better get a jacket. I don't think your shawl will be warm enough."

Bundling up and heading out the door, Paul and Maxi walked toward the horse pasture. "I love this time of evening. The aspens are beautiful. When the evening sun hits those golden leaves, it's breathtaking. We have a wonderful home here in our High Meadows."

"I'm just glad we have a little time to enjoy it. If Scott hadn't come back and stayed, we would still be hauling firewood. It's good to have that done. Now my sweet wife can stay warm all winter."

"He's been a hard worker. Really, you both have worked hard the last few months. I'm so proud of you, Paul. We are about as ready as we can be for the winter."

"There's always something to do around a ranch. Scott and I have a few more things we need to get done before the snow falls, but for the most part, we have the hard stuff done."

"The other day when Scott and Mama came back from a walk, they were holding hands. I think they're getting serious. Does that bother you, Paul?"

"I'll have to admit, it did at first. It seems strange to think of her with someone other than Papa. But I've had a change of heart about it." Paul pulled Maxi a little closer and whispered in her ear.

"I got to thinking the other day about how you have filled my life. I love you more every day. I don't know what I would do without you, *mi maravillosa flor*, my beautiful flower. The loneliness would be more than I could bear." When he pulled away from his wife, he spoke with passion. "I don't want my mama to have that kind of loneliness for the rest of her life. Scott is a fine man, and I would be glad if she found happiness with him. Hey, you're shivering. We'd better get back in the house."

He put his arm around her, and they headed back toward the house. "Where's that dog of yours?"

"She's over by the shed, snooping around. I can't believe how big she's getting."

"Well, you named her right. Snoops fits her perfectly. You call her on in the house, and I'll bring in another load of wood."

"Okay, I'll be in by the fire waiting for you. Come, Snoops!" At the door, Maxine Miles paused and took one more look at the meadow before going in the house. *Thank you, God. I love my High Meadows home.*